14405 92

THE
COLD MOONS

THE
COLD MOONS

Aeron Clement

**Delacorte
Press**

Published by
Delacorte Press
Bantam Doubleday Dell Publishing Group, Inc.
666 Fifth Avenue
New York, New York 10103

This work was first published in Wales by Kindredson
Publishing.

Library of Congress Cataloging-in-Publication Data

Clement, Aeron.
The cold moons / Aeron Clement.
p.   cm.
ISBN: 0-385-29694-0
1. Badgers—Fiction.   I. Title.
PR6053.L475C65 1989
823'.914—dc19   88-28550
                                                              CIP

Manufactured in the United States of America

First U.S.A. printing

April 1989

Illustrations by Jill Clement

10 9 8 7 6 5 4 3 2 1

BG

Acknowledgements

My special thanks to Dr. Ernest Neal, the author of the standard British work on badgers, *The Badger* (Collins, London), and *Badgers* (Blanford, Poole). His expertise in communicating to the reader his unrivalled knowledge of the badger is so very much appreciated.

Thanks too are due to the officers and members of the badger protection groups of Great Britain whose magnificent efforts in helping to protect the badger leave us all greatly indebted to them.

My thanks are due to my friends for their encouragement and support, particularly Tom Harling and Bernard Kindred, and to Donald Martin and his colleagues at Dynevor Printing Company for their diligence and care.

I am also indebted to Tim Binding and Joanna Swinnerton, whose help and advice in editing the book has been so valuable, and to my new friends Susan Moldow and Tina Diaz of Dell Publishing for all their efforts on my behalf.

My special thanks to my agent and friend, Caroline Dawnay of A. D. Peters & Co., and her colleagues Anthony Jones, Anthony Gornall and Carol MacArthur. Further thanks are due to Lizzie Grossman of Sterling Lord Literistic, New York, for her endeavours and kindness.

Above all I owe my family much gratitude, to my wife, Jill, and my daughters, Allyson and Caroline, whose loyalty and support made the writing of the book so much more a joy than a task.

For permission to reproduce copyright material, grateful acknowledgement is made to Her Majesty's Stationery Office.

Perilous Dawn

Oh, nestling, nestling, are you being born
For your eyes to close and not see the morn?
Oh, nestling, nestling, what can you have done
To return to sleep and not see the sun?
Why do they come to slaughter and ravage?
What have you done to deserve such carnage?
Nowhere to walk or play, you dare not roam,
Yet you cannot stay in this place called home.
Oh, nestling, nestling, have faith to survive,
The morrow you'll find that you're still alive,
To seek a haven where man is not seen,
ELYSIA, free and lush, so verdant green.
Time is short, life may soon be extinguished,
ELYSIA you find, or you are finished.

Contents

Foreword

Badgers are among the more striking survivors of the original wild mammalian fauna of Great Britain. The animal enjoyed some protection in England and Wales under the Protection of Animals Act 1911. Specific protection for the badger was accorded through the Badgers Act of 1973, which, among other things, made the so-called sport of badger digging and the use of badger tongs illegal.

In 1970 a field-study by Ministry of Agriculture veterinarians was organised to inquire into the exceptionally high incidence of bovine tuberculosis in cattle in the south-west of England. Statistics showed that TB outbreaks in cattle herds in the south-west were four times that of the national average.

It so happened that just as the team was completing its work and reporting its findings, an observant Gloucestershire farmer, frustrated at repeated failures to trace the source in his cattle, got the idea that badgers with setts on his land might be a source of infection. In 1971 he took one that had died in the open to the Ministry of Agriculture's Animal Health Office in Gloucester, where a post-mortem revealed that the animal was riddled with tuberculosis lesions.

As a result of further evidence, which showed that on a number of farms in south-west England where outbreaks of TB in cattle had occurred badgers had been caught and proved to be infested with TB, badger-control legislation was introduced in 1975. This empowered the Ministry of Agriculture to issue licences for the killing of badgers by means of poison gas for the purpose of preventing the spread of the disease.

In consequence, several new badger-protection societies were organised and for the first time one began to hear talk of the extinction of the animal.

Some years after the first discovery of a badger suffering from tuberculosis, the disease became more widespread among cattle, and members of the farming industry put pressure on the Agriculture Minister to exert even tighter control. Although most of the national newspapers appeared to take an unbiased attitude to the problem, there were a few that tended to side with one view or the other. As outbreaks continued to be reported, the pressure on the government to take stronger action grew more intense, and when sporadic outbreaks of the disease occurred in humans, the *Daily News* and the *Morning Tribune* were quick to give headline coverage supporting the extermination league. The government, under mounting pressure, eventually conceded and passed a bill to set up a special department whose purpose would be to extingish badger life in the United Kingdom.

The *Daily Chronicle*, a newspaper in favour of conservation and wildlife protection, stated that although a clear connection could be made between the disease in badgers and newly infected cattle, it was probable that the badgers had initially contracted the disease from the cattle themselves. It also said that the badgers, due to their close confinement in their setts, could be vulnerable to being reinfected by cattle. It stressed that other species of wildlife, such as rats, voles, shrews, weasels, moles, foxes and birds, had also been found to have this particular tuberculosis strain, although far less significantly than badgers. Finally it emphasized that there had been breakdowns in tuberculosis control in cattle in areas where no infected badgers had been found or were known to exist in the neighbourhood.

The wildlife conservationists firmly upheld these views. When the anti-badger campaign started they were initially successful in gaining the sympathy of a large section of the public and therefore managed to restrict the badger extermination program to those areas where the infection had been found in both badgers and cattle.

However, as the deadly infection spread through the rural areas, public opinion steadily turned against the badgers, encouraged by the sensationalist attitude of the *News* and *Tribune*. The Ministry of Agriculture announced that the extermination program would be carried out by Major T. G. Robertson. A central investigation unit would be based in Gloucester and would control five regional badger extermination (RBE) units, covering Scotland, the north of England, the Midlands and all areas of Wales and the Border Counties. These RBE units would organise teams of exterminators who would embark on the progressive eradication of badgers using the method of force-pumping hydrogen cyanide gas into the setts. The public was urged to give every assistance possible to the authorities. The face of the badger stared down at everyone from notices placed at railway stations, bus terminals, schools, public buildings and billboards. The voices supporting the preservation of the life of the badger had now grown faint.

As agreed, the program would at first concentrate on those counties where bovine tuberculosis had been discovered in both cattle and badgers, and teams were transferred from regions that had a low incidence of the disease to regions where the outbreaks were numerous. After six months a survey of the results indicated that the Ministry was satisfied that badgers had been eradicated from the south-west, Dorset, Wiltshire and Hampshire. The Midland Counties unit had completed over 90 percent of its work, and those covering the south and south-east of England had achieved nearly 75 percent success. Other than in Wales, the Border Counties region, Scotland and the north, it was anticipated that by the end of the following six weeks, badgers would be eradicated. Then all efforts would be concentrated on the remaining areas in the hope that the animals would be totally eliminated by the end of the year.

After months of pressure from conservationist and badger protection leagues that supported controlled extermination, representatives were eventually allowed access to the data being monitored at the central investigation unit in Gloucester. After two days of intensive research, the conservationists were able to process the results into a computer. One particularly staggering fact emerged: Bovine tuberculosis was still occurring in areas where no badgers had been present for nearly six months, particularly in young stock born of disease-free parents. This information was passed to the *Chronicle*, which informed its readers the following day that the case against the badgers was very far from being proved and stressed that the campaign should be halted.

This argument was countered by both the *News* and the *Tribune*. They maintained that not enough time had elapsed for the tuberculosis strain to be extinguished and that the systematic eradication should continue.

The extent of the disease that could spread from these badgers was repeatedly emphasized in both newspapers. Graphic illustrations, charts and pictures of diseased humans and cattle were used to persuade the public to continue to give its support to the program of eradication. Of course many people were not aware that some of the pictures actually showed cattle suffering from diseases that had no connection with tuberculosis and that could not possibly be linked to badgers.

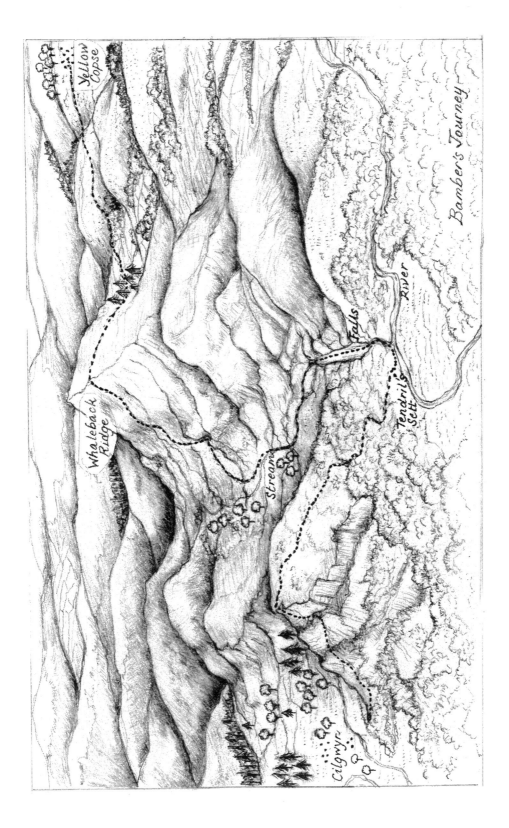

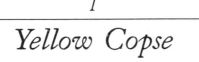

Yellow Copse

The evening air lay heavy with the drifting fragrances of new leaf incense, which sent shivers of expectant pleasure through the inhabitants of Yellow Copse. The creatures of the woodland glades sighed with gratitude that the time of the cold moons was over and rejoiced as they became aware once again that all things were possible and were just beginning.

A pair of badgers had emerged from their sett much earlier than was their customary time of the last few moments of twilight. The pale yellow sun still had some time left before its glow became lost behind the hill-fringed horizon. The day had been exceptionally warm for the time of the year and had given the impetus the countryside had needed to arouse itself from its cold time sleep. The badgers were soon under the influence of the bewitching enchantment of the earth's reawakening and sat back on their haunches, savouring the sheer joy of being alive.

The boar and the sow had strolled into a sheltered glade where the air was warm and still and where the buds on the trees and shrubs were swelling as if to burst, releasing a scent even sweeter than that of the sweet briar wind. The time would soon come when the waning paleness that filtered through the skeletons of the trees changed to a richer green light as the sun shone through translucent young leaves.

The badgers hardly said a word to each other as they moved out of the glade, through a thicket and on to one of their well-worn pathways, which criss-crossed the sloping meadow that stretched down to a slow babbling stream. They were amazed at the transformation that was taking place, yet they had seen the magical transition many times. Their attention was drawn to some hares disturbing the tranquillity of the evening. Two bucks were flexing their muscles as they prepared for combat. They circled around each other slowly, bristling with ferocity, seeking the chance to strike. Then, as the first jab was thrown, they attacked. Their limbs flailed wildly, each hoping to catch the other with a mighty blow from one of his powerful hind legs, strong and powerful enough to force his foe to submit and withdraw, leaving the unconcerned and bored doe, who was nibbling at some fresh young dandelion leaves, all to himself.

The two badgers moved along the pathways, leaving the insane hares behind them. They passed close to the stream and saw that the sallows growing there were already beguiling the moths with the sweet scent of their catkins and buds. As the pair travelled back up the slope, towards the hedgerows and trees, they marvelled at the number of shrubs and bushes that boasted their catkin tassels. Trembling yellow, white or green mouse-tails that quivered at the slightest puff of wind were sported by the birch, aspen, yew and hazel. A sudden lift in the evening breeze sent the yellow yew pollen flying through the air and, upon hearing the flutter of wings, the badgers turned and saw some willow-warblers hurtling through the birch, tilting at the catkins, sending clouds of yellow pollen floating and leaving the last of the warblers to emerge dressed in a coat of gold.

Wherever the badgers looked they saw new evidence of the loveliest time of the year. There was the yellow celandine, the buttercup and the primrose, whose beauty overcame the deadness of the russet-brown leaves of the copper beech that grew beside them. There were cuckoo flowers, blue and white periwinkles and violets and the yellow colt's-foot with its purple sprouts. Yet among so much splendour they were completely captivated by one flowering shrub in particular, the blackthorn bush. Yesterday it had been dark and austere, but that evening it was brushed with hundreds of snow-flossed plumes. Although there were no leaves yet, these would come soon and provide the brimstone and magpie moth with their main source of food. At present, however, the blackthorn was the jewel of the woodland glen. The badgers were enraptured by its beauty, which for a fleeting moment was enhanced as a swooping jay flew past, resplendent in its magnificent new plumage.

There were many feathered inhabitants in Yellow Copse. The birds would soon be returning to their hidden refuges for their night's sleep but until the sun had disappeared they would give voice to their happiness as they busied themselves with nest building. The wrens, robins, yellowhammers, linnets and chaffinches were to-ing and fro-ing, fetching twigs or leaves in their beaks as they put the final touches to their nests, for soon the females would lay their eggs as birth-time was about to begin in the animal world. The two badgers began foraging and it was not long before they had satisfied their appetites. They returned to their sett in total contentment, blissfully happy at the joy of living in a place that was nothing less than perfection.

For some eleven years the sett had been the sole property of Bamber and Dainty. They had discovered the soft brown earth below a ridge of beech trees when they were not quite yearlings, and when they had absent mindedly strayed from their birth setts and had got lost in play. They had not met again until the following year but they had forgotten neither the ridge nor each other.

The sett was apart from the others. They had shared it with no one but themselves and their nestlings in the years that they were born. Now was the time when Dainty became agitated, for the nestlings were due again. Unlike most other badger sows, Dainty did not merely tolerate Bamber at the first blush of life but needed his presence always, and Bamber thrived in the environment of paternal responsibility.

The sett had four entrances, and was completely hidden by some gorse bushes and a ridge of trees that had grown both in size and number over the years. The birth chamber had been cut into a side wall, some six feet or so inside one of the entrances to the sett, with bedding prepared ready for the birth of the cubs.

Dainty's agitation grew as she always felt her body tingle with excitement at this time and had always previously been comforted by Bamber's pride and strength. But this time she saw something else in his face. She noticed an odd interruption in his calmness which she could not understand as his snout periodically sniffed the air. Perhaps it was his realisation that this might be the last time she would be able to give birth to cubs as they were both gently ageing.

Bamber did his best to give an air of assurance to Dainty that all was well, but last night and especially today he had had a strong feeling of foreboding. He quivered with a hidden fear for he had been introduced to the scent of man. The community of which he and Dainty were a part was in a small copse, with broken hills and crags on either side. The land was a mixture of shale, soft earth, stone and scrub with brushwood and clumps of trees and thickets interspersed here and there. It was known as Yellow Copse, yellow after the burst of colour that came from the gorse each year.

When Bamber had gone out during the previous night after he and Dainty had returned from their evening stroll, he had wandered a little further than usual and had ventured into the domain of his brother, who was part of the communal sett where some twenty badgers lived. His brother, whose name was Oatear, so called after the white marking on one of the black stripes on his face, had explained that for the first time that he could remember he felt unsafe because the two-legged animal known as man had visited the copse. He couldn't explain why, but the upright ones had been digging near the entrances to the setts and had closed most of them up. The humans had first arrived there three days ago and had returned each day. Although the badgers had been left in peace at night to forage and feed, the men had returned at dawn and had stayed until the light of day had begun to disappear. What were the men searching for? They had left many worms and beetles on the surface of the disturbed earth, easy pickings for the first of the badger family to emerge. Bamber went to explore for himself and, when nearing a closed-up entrance, experienced man's scent for the first time. He could not reason why such a feeling of alarm and of menace should immediately take possession of him. He rushed back to his own sett, to Dainty, where the snugness and contentment of their partnership was so comforting, yet the discomfort, the fear, did not completely go away.

Though the earth outside was tinged white with an early-morning frost, Bamber felt more at ease as he gazed at his beloved Dainty. She had been resting on the deep lush bed of the birth chamber for some time and now the arrival of the nestlings was imminent. Bamber caressed Dainty, nuzzling the soft undercoat of fur on her flank. She looked so beautiful, covered by a mantle of thistledown, the guard hairs accentuating the beauty of her colouring, the black of such intensity, and the white a soft brilliance.

That evening, after the cubs were born and had started suckling from Dainty, Bamber made many trips out hunting for worms, and although he had eaten some, he brought most of his prey back for Dainty. He promised himself that he would return for more, well before twilight, as he felt so hungry, and he would also have to continue to feed Dainty as he did not want her to leave their cubs. When Bamber could not give Dainty a sensible reply to her query as to why he did not want her to go out, she put it down to him getting sillier as he got older.

Bamber's rest had been disturbed all day as he kept waking up believing he could hear whinnying sounds coming up the copse from the communal sett. He couldn't remember dreaming so much and so often before. He told himself it was because of the excitement of the previous night, and dozed back to sleep again with worship in his eyes as they closed upon the vision of his Dainty and their new family.

He awoke in the late afternoon to see Dainty gazing contentedly at her cubs, and then felt the hunger inside him. He remembered his promise to forage earlier than usual and went up to the entrance that opened at the foot of an old beech tree. The day's sun was saying its farewell by giving a touch of shimmering coral to a pale blue sky. Life was so wonderful, he felt that the glory of Asgard was around him.

Bamber decided to climb to the top of the ridge where a little thicket lay hidden by some large stones and where he knew he would find a plentiful supply of worms. Bamber and Dainty always kept the place a secret, for it provided a sure source of food at times of long drought.

As Bamber neared the top, a feeling of terror gripped him as strange sounds drifted up the hillside. Although Bamber was exceptionally large and weighed well over forty pounds, he cowered, not only at the unusual noises, but also at the scent that reached him. There was a mixture of smells in the air. One was new to him and seemed to catch in his throat, but he recognised the other. It was the smell of blood, blood of his own kind, the smell of death.

Bamber realised that he must shake himself free of this fear and eventually he forced himself to try to discover what was happening at the communal sett. As he made his way down, the air became thicker with the smell that seemed to grip tight in his throat and make his breathing laboured. He stumbled through some shrubs and collided with something warm and soft. It was Oatear lying on his side, hardly able to move. He was twisted in agony and in his death throes as he gasped to Bamber to run. With his final words he managed to explain that death had come to all in the communal sett, brought by the animal man.

Bamber for a moment was frozen, but his senses returned as he quickly thought of Dainty. He hurtled through bush and shrub, sometimes falling and rolling, down to the sett. He rushed to the entrance near the nest chamber, and though the choking air was ever increasing and the sounds of man were ever nearer, he arrived breathless at the sett entrance, ready to escape with Dainty. They would each take a cub and would start again. They would find a new paradise where they would always be inseparable.

Bamber knew Dainty would, without hesitation, protect the cubs, and he saw that she was covering the entrance with her body, her forepaws over her face, trying to make the colours of her coat blend into the background. Bamber nudged her with his snout and as he explained that they had to escape quickly, he moved her away from the entrance. The choking air rose up at him from the sett below. The cubs, where were the cubs? He tried to re-enter the sett, but the air was overpowering him. Then he realised that Dainty had not moved. He returned to her and discovered that she was colder and the suppleness of her body was fading.

He had to get her away from the sett so he gripped her with his teeth at the back of her neck and tugged and dragged her upwards to their thicket. There was clear air there and plenty of worms. The spring of fresh, clear water started to flow from there. It was their special thicket. Bamber's chest felt as if it would explode and it took every bit of strength he had, but he dragged his beloved Dainty into the safety of the thicket. He rushed to get her some thick, long worms, placing them by her tongue, which hung out of her mouth. He dashed to the spring and filled his cheek pouches with fresh cool water and pressed it into her mouth. The water just ran off her tongue onto the grass.

Bamber turned to stone, as if rooted. There was a deathly silence. Then, as the numbness of the shock began to wane, Bamber was overwhelmed with anguish. The eyes of his Dainty, his beloved Dainty, which had always burnt with splendour, which glowed with the radiance of life, had dimmed, unseeing forevermore.

Bamber lay by Dainty's side, wanting to join her on her journey to the hills of Asgard. Their own paradise world, their private Elysia had perished, a world their new-born cubs had been destined never to see. He lay by his adored Dainty for hours under the clear moonlit sky, his eyes blurred with tears. He raised himself and prepared her for the next life. He groomed her and washed her, his tongue cleaning every hair of her coat. He dug a hollow in the earth and pulled her body into it. He covered her with leaves, thickly and gently, nudging her face for the last time as the last few were laid. He fell to the ground and sobbed with wretched desolation.

Bamber eventually fell into a sleep of grief, waking as the dawn broke and for a moment searching for his Dainty. The night's memory returned with mournfulness. Then he remembered Oatear and realised that his brother had tried to warn him. Had he, Bamber, survived to warn others of the destruction to come? Bamber hid in the shrub of the thicket until nightfall, then moved in the direction of the hills of the falling sun. He turned once more and raised his snout to scent the thicket. The fragrance of fresh earth came to him, the scent of the solitary pine and of leaves already decaying. Bamber slowly moved over the hill, his senses of smell and hearing leading him on, his eyes blinded with tears.

2

A Chance to Live

It had been Bamber's intention to seek worms early the previous evening, but all thoughts of satisfying his hunger of the day had been forgotten. Bamber was single-minded in his endeavours to get away, to escape his grief, to find his kind. Yet he did not long for companionship, his anguish stabbing at him as he stumbled and staggered onwards.

He was now in strange territory although he understood some scents but, not stopping, he crashed through bracken, gorse and shrub, hoping to find his kind, always in the direction of the falling sun. Unyielding in his efforts, he had, after just a few hours, reached the floor of the next valley. Even then he did not rest but paused for a moment to scent some hummocks where moles had once cast soil. There was not even a lingering scent of his fellow beings. The fear that had gripped him drove him on and something very powerful was spurring him to find his goal. He now believed he was seeking Dainty. She was not just a vision of blessed memory but real and waiting for him in a new sett, a new home prepared by other badgers. But where was this badger hamlet? Onwards, ever onwards, rising up through a pine forest, now fearing none of the scents that crept through the perfume of pine. His paws crunched on the pine needles and, as he came out of the forest, his dim eyes noticed a veil of light rising over the hill behind him. His aching body felt weary, and as he struggled into a cluster of thorn bushes, hidden from the world, he murmured "Dainty," and his eyes closed.

The cry of an owl woke Bamber with a start and he crawled out of his resting place to find the area around him bathed in moonlight. He had slept long and deeply but the efforts of the previous night had left him with an aching stiffness. But his strength of purpose did not allow him to think with any sort of clarity. His hunger hurt and the dryness of his throat made him feel miserable but his depression would not let him pause in his drive as, shaking his heavy coat, onwards he toiled. The trees were fading behind him and now he was into heather and stone. He was soon in a loftiness of terrain that he had never before experienced. There was no longer any vegetation. He was on an escarpment of rock and shale, rocks that had been splintered by the many winters of frost and frozen snow of centuries past. His front claws that had been so powerful were cracking and his paws were cut and bleeding. There was no respite, however, although his fatigue was overpowering, for his thirst told him he had to get over the hill and down to a spring on the other side, or even to a stream in the next valley. Even though his mind was willing, the strain was starting to slow him down. His strength came from his obsession and somehow before the morning sun arrived, he clambered over the bare whaleback ridge. Now each step was agonisingly painful, his paws in shreds. He partly stumbled, rolled, tripped and fell on his downward path, until he could hear the sound of water trickling on the rocky ground. He drove headlong for the water source and, on finding it, gulped until his stomach was heavy. He noticed that under a crag there was a passage into the rocky surface, and upon reaching it, staggered inside and succumbed to absolute exhaustion.

Bamber awoke in the early afternoon. He was now unrecognisable as the badger he had been just three days earlier. He was already a pathetic sight, his once full and glossy coat ragged and dull, but worst of all were his paws. The pain from the torn flesh of his pads was searing. He felt so desolate and alone, not knowing if any other badgers were near or how much longer it would be before he found them.

He saw two click-beetles crawl under a large stone and slowly and painfully got up, nearly screaming with the excruciating pain that shot up his limbs from his paws. He needed real food. During an evening's foraging he would normally eat more than two or three hundred worms, some fifty or more beetles, a frog or two and quite often even more. He stretched one of his paws to turn the stone over, but he had no claws left, just painful stumps. Then he tried to push the stone with his pad but the pain was too much to bear and he fell backwards in agony.

Even though it was still daylight, Bamber's instinct made him move out of the cave, telling him that he must take every risk for his destiny to be fulfilled, and slowly and ponderously he moved down the hill. Above him there was a mackerel sky, yet it was long after the sun had fallen before he stopped to rest. Footsore and practically at the end of his endurance, he rested at the side of a narrow stream that fed the sylvan floor of the dale. After a few moments' rest he eased himself into the water to cool his paws of fire. The flow of the stream was carrying him along but he no longer cared where he was or what he was supposed to be doing. His body numb, he drifted along over the shallows of rippling waters, tumbling and tossing over some falls.

Fate showed its hand as Bamber was swept into a curve in the bank of the stream, only a short distance from where the tributary joined the river. He lay in just a few inches of water for some time before his inner mind roused him from semiconsciousness and forced him to crawl up onto the bank of lush, soft grass. Bamber, having passed the limit of endurance of any of Logos's creatures, slipped into insensibility as the mists closed over him.

It was some three days later when Bamber discovered that he had either passed from this earth or that he was dreaming, but in the drabness of his dank unfamiliar surrounding he was not sure of anything. Yet there was a scent he understood better than any other. Although his body was weak and spent, his spirits began to soar. His senses became more acute, and then he heard a shuffling sound in the corner of what now appeared to be an ancient sett. His natural instincts made him bark his greeting, the fur on his once-proud tail fluffed as best as it could and there was a meek response from the other creature. It was a soft whinny, but it was enough for Bamber to understand that his hidden companion was a female badger. Bamber, being too weak to move, encouraged the stranger to show herself. He stared intently into the gloom as the dim shape moved forward. As it came up to him he realised that he had never seen such a grotesque, crippled figure ever in his life as that which now confronted him. One of her rear legs was twisted underneath her body and instead of two eyes there was only one, while the other side of her face was just a scarred hollow. Her coat had many bare patches, just patterns of glossy skin. As fear engulfed him, she introduced herself by giving him her name, Tendril. Bamber passed once more into oblivion.

As he stirred out of his slumber, he was immediately aware of warmth at his right side. He attempted to rise to his feet, but the weakness was still with him and he slumped down. He noticed that the female badger was standing close to him. It was her body that had been giving him comfort. Had he dreamt that she had said she was Tendril?

He grunted at her and she responded with a whinny. She approached and tried to nuzzle him. Bamber withdrew his head and curled his lip at her. She did not retreat, for she realised he was no longer the majestic male he had once been, but an ailing figure. Bamber realised that his weakness left him to the tender mercies of his companion, but disfigured though she was, there was an air of saintliness about her that encouraged Bamber to ask her if she had told him that she was Tendril. She confirmed that she had. Although Bamber's paws were still very sore, he certainly felt better than he had when he had stumbled into that stream. He could not remember anything since that moment. How had he got to this sett? Why had his hunger pains subsided? Why did he feel so rested? These and other questions he fired at Tendril, only to be met with a clicking of her tongue and told to eat and rest. Eat? How could he eat when his strength forbade him to move more than a few inches? He noticed her pushing something across the floor of the sett towards him. The small mass was alive, a mound of food, black slugs, cockchafer grubs, large juicy worms, some dor beetles, two pigeon eggs and some very moist grass. He noticed that the black slugs had even been cleaned of their slime. Tendril had taken meticulous care of his food. He devoured it ravenously but even the efforts of masticating tired him and, licking his lips, he closed his eyes and drifted into sleep again.

Bamber stretched his limbs out on the ground. Tendril was no longer present but her scent was strong. He felt forlorn and dejected. He had been awake for only a moment or two, gathering his thoughts, when he heard Tendril's whinnying as she approached the sett entrance. Bamber was more aware of her lameness as she rolled from side to side. She noticed that Bamber was awake and came over to him. She emptied her full cheeks onto the floor, leaving a mound of worms and grubs. She nudged Bamber but he remained still. She went back out of the sett and returned as quickly as her deformity allowed, this time her cheek pouches filled with water. She put her mouth to his and let the water run onto his tongue, carrying out this task without rest, time and time again. When Bamber's thirst seemed quenched she sat by his side, grooming his coat, cleaning his paws, delicately pruning his facial guard hairs. Seeing that Bamber was comforted, she then began explaining her story and how Bamber had arrived in her sett.

She told of the days, some seven years ago, when the sett in which they lived had been ravaged by men with dogs. Some of the dogs had been sent down into the sett, and the family of badgers, when trying to escape, had found all but two of the sett's entrances blocked. The badgers, in total panic, had stampeded for the two shafts of daylight. As they emerged out of the sett the badgers were set upon by a number of larger dogs, whose efforts were encouraged by three or four men. Some of the badgers had been killed instantly while the others had tried to make a fight of it, but were outnumbered by the dogs and were ripped to pieces. Tendril had had her flanks torn by one dog, whilst another had gripped her about her head, his canine tooth piercing her eye. The excruciating pain had made her shriek in agony and to writhe with such force that she had torn herself free. Her only escape was to get back down the sett, but as she had turned, one of the dogs had gripped her stifle and broken it. She had buried herself as deeply as possible in the sett and awaited her doom. For three nights and days she had waited but nothing had happened. Her body was racked with pain, and anything being better than a prolonged and lingering death, she had managed to crawl out of the sett to try and find her family. When she got outside, she saw the result of the slaughter, which man and dog had left lying about the sett entrance. Eleven torn and mutilated bodies, mostly un-recognisable, lay strewn about, carrion for the fox and crow. Some were already covered in grubs as they lay exposed to the sun, being eaten by their own prey before they had their chance to journey to Asgard to meet with their ancestors, safe in the eternal protection of Logos. Tendril was the only survivor. Although her instincts had wanted her to carry her deceased family out of the glare into the darkness of a chamber in the sett, she had not had the strength to do it and the demand for her own survival took command. Because she had had to crawl about for her food and drink, the broken leg had set in a twisted position underneath her. Resting by day in the sett had pre-vented the flies from tormenting her. It had been early in the year when the devastation had occurred and it was at the time of falling leaves when her body was at last free of pain, but the damage was irreparable, as she had lost an eye and was carrying a shattered leg. She had cleared the surroundings of the re-mains of her family and had walled them up behind one of the blocked entrances. Her father, mother, brothers and sisters had all perished. Not knowing where to go and due to her disability, which prevented her from travelling any distance, she had re-mained in solitude until she had heard Bamber moaning in his consciousness and had found him lying in a shallow pool near to the sett. He was in such a state that it appeared that even Ahriman, the Master of Hades, the controller of Sheol, had spurned him. Bamber had, for just a moment, made Tendril believe that it was seven years ago and that her father had survived. It had taken practically all her strength to lift him back onto the bank from where he had fallen into the water and, because of his size, it had taken most of the night to drag him the seventy badger steps to the sett entrance. She had nursed him day and night, cooling his paws with chewed grasses and herbs which she had chilled with water, quenching his thirst and gathering his food. For the first two days Tendril did not expect Bamber to survive as death appeared to cast its shadow over him, but then the air about him seemed to be translucent and Tendril realised that Logos would not call him at this time. To have survived his ordeals there had to be a special and omnipotent reason and she understood as Bamber explained what had happened to him. She realised why he had been spared and she also understood his belief that he would meet his Dainty again. Her heart ached and her wistfulness was deep and peaceful as she closed her eyes and let her dreams help her to believe that she was Dainty.

The sun rose and fell many times before Bamber had sufficient strength to leave the sett, longer than the complete life of the new moon, and during all that time Tendril nursed him with loving care. Bamber recovered well although the strain of that journey left its mark, but his task was not complete and his journey had to continue. His feet had now healed and his claws had started to grow again, but he noticed that his front pads were twisted and realised that this would always be so. He foraged for food, building up his strength as fast as he could but he could not collect his food as quickly as he used to. He ate anything that he could find—mushrooms, yew berries and even carrion—as well as the usual worms that are the favourite food of all badgers. He would go a little further each night to estimate his fitness, leaving Tendril behind, and she whimpered to herself as the thought of Bamber's impending departure stabbed at her heart.

When it appeared to Bamber that he could comfortably forage for his food, even after travelling for half the night away from the sett, he decided it was time for his journey to continue. Tendril, although understanding the reason for his journey, desperately tried to persuade him to stay a little longer, as he was still far from being strong enough to complete his marathon.

She could not remember any other badger family living in the valley, even before the massacre, and that meant that he had the mountain to climb without any help which would require more than determination, more even than his desire to find Dainty.

Tendril had not accompanied Bamber on his nightly strolls other than during the first few nights after he had recovered sufficient strength to wander on his own. Her faltering gait had prevented her from keeping up with him but that evening she was determined to stay with him no matter how great the difficulty was. She bravely shuffled along behind him, pleading with him and begging him to stay at least until the warm time was over. She tried desperately to convince him that he stood a much better chance of completing his journey if he reached a higher level of fitness than he had at present. She told him that she would willingly help him to make a full recovery, nursing him and caring for his every need.

Tendril impressed upon Bamber how beneficial the area surrounding her home was, as even she, who had been as close to death as any creature could be, had recovered in the beautiful land of her home. She began extolling such beauty in detail, pointing out with her paw the richness and variety of the flora as they moved through the colourful florescent glades. The white field-rose and pink dog-rose tangling their way through the hedgerows; the comfrey drooping its pink flowers which would soon change to blue and foxgloves breaking into bell after bell under the birches. The yellow broom was scented and flowering, the bugle raising its blue spires by the tufty ruts on the edge of a thicket attracting a rare bee hawkmoth to hover at its blossoms. She interrupted her eloquence only with renewed pleas to stay, and although she realised that Bamber was not going to change his mind, she continued to describe the splendours that surrounded them. The two badgers passed through patches of blue speedwell, then avoided a dense bed of wild garlic that was exuding its rank odour in the evening air. Bamber now began to circle back to Tendril's sett, passing yellow pimpernel flickering their golden blossoms and the incandescent flowers of sweet woodruff. Tendril called to him to look at the abundance of strawberries that grew along a raised bank of earth. Though they were small and coloured green and yellow, they would soon be scarlet and full of delicious sweetness. Some heath butterflies, Meadow Browns, Large Whites and Orange Tips flittered past them as the two badgers moved across a small meadow leading down to the stream where Tendril had hopefully believed that her abject loneliness had at last come to its end. She trembled at the thought of the returning isolation and parted from Bamber, taking a more direct route back to her sett. She passed through some birch trees and, as the feelings of sadness became stronger with every step, the gentle badger skirted a nightingale's nest which lay hidden in the sturdy stems of some bluebells. Tendril saw the mother was sitting on her clutch whilst the father, afraid for the six olive-green eggs, hopped from bough to bough on a birch, uttering his cries of protest at Tendril's trespassing. Tendril shuffled down into her sett, preparing to accept once again a life of solitude. She knew that Bamber had made his mind up and would soon be moving on.

Forty suns had crossed the sky since Bamber had been found by Tendril, and the evening arrived when he rose knowing that when darkness came he would be continuing his travels. He realised that Tendril would be left in a world of total isolation, a loneliness that he certainly could not have endured. He understood his indebtedness to her but the compulsion in his heart forbade him to allow his gratitude to cloud his judgement. He would return for her as soon as he had found some other badgers and had passed the warning on.

As Bamber nuzzled Tendril's coat he noticed that she no longer looked hideous but was a badger whose beauty shone with love and tenderness. He slipped quietly away into the gloom of the dusk. Tendril knew that she would never see him again and a tear welled in the corner of her eye. It rolled down her cheek, followed by others, and she sobbed as the memory of her days with Bamber and the lost family of so many years ago tore at her heart.

Bamber was soon past the furthest point that he had foraged. This time, however, he did not plunder but stopped only briefly to consume some worms, rolling a small dead branch over to disclose a feast of grubs and larvae. Having fulfilled his present need, he pressed on. He felt his lack of fitness tugging at him much earlier than he expected and, much against his wishes, reasoned that he must slow his pace down. When dusk came he had reached the foot of the hills and he quenched his thirst from one of the many streams that poured its spray down the mountainside. He found some more worms and a few puffballs and, crawling into the long grass and wild barley that grew near some oaks, came across some partly chewed, half-developed acorns. He quickly swallowed them, drew the grasses over him and fell asleep.

His slumber was broken by the snarl of a large dog fox. Bamber broke his cover quickly, fluffed his fur up, curled his lip and growled back. The fox stood his ground and Bamber realised that the fox's earth must be near and that his scent had alarmed the fox as he had emerged on his nightly hunt for prey. Bamber slowly backed away, not wanting to waste his strength or time when he had so much to do. He had met foxes before and had always defeated them when they had dared to challenge him. He retreated out of sight of the fox, who continued to bark his warning signs, and turned and hurried away. When the fox scent had faded, he stopped and began his foraging. He came across a pond that rippled and gave voice to the song of frogs. Bamber enjoyed frogs, although there was some extra work to do before eating them. He seized a frog between his teeth, bit it hard and threw it out of his mouth as the frog urinated. He then scraped his claws rapidly on his prey and, finally, crunched it whole in his mouth. The scraping was done to reduce the amount of the nauseous secretion that frogs and especially toads produce from their skins. Then, having drunk from the pond, he moved away, but was unable to resist two long and fat worms that were in his path.

Bamber scolded himself for being too greedy and overfilling himself when he had the mountain to climb. He could not accept that his recent brush with death had strained him to the extent that his body had been permanently damaged.

He laboured upwards, first over grass and bracken, then onto the heather. He tired fast and had to find a place to rest and, before dawn, sleep was already beginning to snatch at him. The pads of his paws, although healed, were no longer in the hard, leathery condition that they once had been, and it was on the fifth night after leaving Tendril that he eventually crossed the summit of the mountain, footsore again and feeling increasingly weary. His climb down the mountain became more ponderous each hour, but his belief that he would find his kind in the verdant expanse below him drove him on, although he had developed repeated pains in his chest and an ever-increasing shortage of breath. He realised that he would not reach the safety of the woods that night and, exhausted, he settled into a cleft in the rock and let his body drift into sleep.

Bamber's efforts had now taken their toll and the darkness of the following evening had been about him for some hours before he awoke. His defiant will roused him to a final effort and, without taking further food or water, he ventured down the lower part of the hill. He reached a small plateau that was covered with bilberry and blackberry bushes, and winding through them, he struggled to the edge of the plateau. Looking a short distance down, he saw what he had been searching for— one, two, three and more entrances to a sett or even setts. The scent of badger was overpowering, but he could not go further; the pain in his chest was paralysing and his breath came in short infrequent gasps. Then he saw in the shaft of light that broke through the cloud from the dawning sun, his kind, badgers, returning from their night's search for sustenance. Bamber's strength was spent; he was not able to attract their attention, and before he could make a final effort to call to them, his eyes closed. As his mind ghosted into a netherland his last thoughts were whether they had seen him and if Dainty would catch his scent. He pleaded for Logos to wait just a short while longer.

3

Extermination

PAWS NEWS

THE BADGERS MIRACLE HELP

DAILY NEWS

South Wales,
Monday, 11th March

The success of the badger extermination programme continues. At a news conference, held today at the offices of the central investigation unit, it was confirmed that badgers have been exterminated from all regions of England and Scotland and that only in areas of South and Mid Wales do they still exist.

All nine extermination squads, each comprising five members, will now concentrate their efforts on eradicating the remaining badgers. Delays in the extermination in South Wales have occurred because of the difficulties that arose during the investigation of the industrial belt of the eastern part of this region, which mostly consists of expired coal workings, closed-down steel and tin manufacturing plants and other industrial wastelands.

Plans have been drawn up that encourage us to believe that the programme of extermination will reach a successful conclusion within the next six weeks.

THE MORNING TRIBUNE, SOUTH WALES

Thursday, 14th March

The badger extermination units arrived in force today in the area of dense forest in Mid Wales known as Yellow Copse. Under the command of Major T. G. Robertson, the teams carried out a full investigation of the area, noting which sett entrances were to be blocked up and those into which the poison gas could be pumped. Most of the setts are close together, but one with four entrances was discovered a little way off from the others, hidden under some beech trees and surrounded by gorse bushes. The director of operations informed us that preparatory work will be completed within three days, after which the gassing will take place.

The *Morning Tribune* believes that the nation owes a great debt of gratitude to the members of the extermination units, whose diligence and devotion to their task have brought them to the point of success.

DAILY CHRONICLE, SOUTH WALES

Tuesday, 19th March

The first efforts to eradicate all the badgers in Mid Wales have now taken place. The devastation is alarming. Some badgers crawled pitifully to the entrances of their setts in an attempt to escape, only to choke to death on the gas or be shot. One member of the team, on sighting a lone badger moving slowly up the hillside, went to investigate, marvelling that any animal was able to struggle so far with such a volume of lethal gas inside it. When he reached the badger it was motionless, and looking down at its face, he saw that its eyes were wide open in a swollen stare and its gaping mouth was full of cuckoo-spit froth. The dead animal had a distinguishing mark in the shape of a white ear of corn on one of the black stripes on the side of its face.

After reporting the results of the extermination at Yellow Copse to Major Robertson at the investigation base, the teams of exterminators were instructed to proceed in the direction of Cilgwyn. Little is known about badgers in this area, which is wild and thickly forested and some distance from human activity.

4

Cilgwyn Cadre

There had been badgers in the woods, now the forest, of Cilgwyn for well over a hundred generations. It was probably the most heavily populated badger area in the country and, as it was some considerable distance away from mankind and its environment, it had thrived into a place of well-ordered habitat. It provided the badgers with everything they could possibly require and, in addition, the community was organised into an ensemble of pattern behaviour controlled by a parliament of senior badgers. This was called the Cadre and a leader was appointed who would minister the Cadre until such time as his wisdom and leadership lacked the necessary power, when he would step down and a new leader would be elected.

There was a central sett system at Cilgwyn, surrounded by minor sett systems. The majority of the senior badgers lived in the central system, which not only had family apartments, storage rooms, funeral chambers and passageways, but also housed the Hall of the Cadre.

Some of the minor systems surrounding the Cadre sett had been enlarged over the past few years but none of the present badgers could remember the Cadre system being any different from the way it was now. It had over thirty entrances and its tunnels and chambers were in six layers under the grassland and woodland of Cilgwyn. It was the perfect type of soil and landscape for badgers, well-drained in lias sand with some limestone rubble at the highest part of the setts, which lay in a gently sloping valley.

The halls of the Cadre were situated in the centre of the sett, with no other chambers above or below them. They were as long and as wide as ten badgers head to tail and twice as high as the tallest badger. From the Cadre four tunnels led into a labyrinth of more than three hundred passageways, many of which were private and led to family apartments.

There were numerous rules and regulations laid down for the conduct of the badgers in the Cadre system. Certain entrances were to be used for the collection of bedding, while others were forbidden to cubs. There were entrances that led close to the dung-heaps, or pits, and there were some that were solely for the use of the councillors of the Cadre. It was the rule that any violation of the code of practice set by the council would bring various forms of punishment, such as extra bedding collection or extra cleaning. Should a repetition of a malpractice occur, then the punishment could be the withdrawal of foraging time or even imprisonment in a bare chamber devoid of bedding or any other possible sustenance, from which the culprit was taken to water under guard.

There were just forty minor sett systems surrounding the Cadre system. These were made up in a variety of sizes ranging from a simple two-chamber sett to the more elaborate seven-chamber sett. The smaller setts were usually inhabited by a pair of badgers having had a first generation of cubs, the largest setts usually housing three or sometimes four generations

There was also a well-worn path system in the woods of

Cilgwyn. These paths or routes led away from the entrances to established foraging ground, bedding areas, dung-pits, sleeping-out places and the scratching and playing trees. The entrances to the right of the Cadre sett led into Cilgwyn forest, which covered an area as large as a hundred meadow fields or more. To the left of the sett were small copses, an area that was covered by deciduous woodlands, grasslands and hedgerows made by man centuries ago and now covered by blackberry, nettle, wild raspberry and strawberry and herbs of many kinds. Running through the valley, bringing the fresh, crystal water down from the mountains, there were two streams approximately three to four hundred badger paces below the entrance of the lowest sett. The forest itself was primarily deciduous, although on the highest part there was a short range of conifers.

The Cadre leader at this time was known as Eldon. Whilst all the previous leaders of the Cadre had been elected by the council, who were themselves elected by all boar badgers over four years old, Eldon had been given the honour because Jason, his father, had ruled with such wisdom and love. The badgers had unanimously promised him that Eldon would succeed him, in appreciation of what Jason had done. It was usual for the leader to step down once age and infirmity took their first real grip, but Jason was held in such reverence that every badger wanted him to live forever. They had no doubt that Jason was indeed a descendant of Logos Himself. Eldon, the Cadre leader, lived in a chamber system next to the central halls with his wife, Scylla, but they had never had cubs of their own. The council had four senior members supporting the leader. These were Buckwheat, Chantar, Palos and Molyar, and the council had their workers who had no family ties. These were the Soothsayer, Honeyberry, the Matchmaker, Migola, the Healer, Rhea, and the Sage and Chronicler, Greyears. Further assistance was given, particularly in the cold nights of winter, by Harvey and

Topsin. These two, holding in their minds the treasure store of badger lore and fables, could always keep the young badgers in awe and could also guarantee to hold the elders spellbound when the badger legends were expounded in the Cadre halls with a blizzard raging above them.

Over the past few years the council had met less and less frequently. As far as Eldon was concerned there hadn't been adverse conditions to warrant much discussion. Buckwheat and Chantar had expressed a desire to hold such meetings more regularly, but Eldon had fobbed them off with his repeated explanation that there was no need to look for trouble where none existed. Eldon had been leader now for six years and had never carried out his duties with any relish. He just wanted everything to stay as it was, organised, efficient and peaceful, in order that he could enjoy his sleep and his food.

There was no need to call a council meeting to allocate a punishment as there was a standard laid down, which Greyears, the Chronicler, looked after. Rhea, the Healer, took care of the odd cold or stomach upset, so there were no illnesses to worry about. Eldon always thought that meeting to discuss a new partnership or family unit was ridiculous anyway. That's what the Matchmaker was for, and he had informed her two years ago that she must accept the responsibility of naming the new cubs. Although Eldon could never understand why his father had held meetings every new moon, there was one who did and that was Buckwheat, who had been a council member before Eldon had been appointed leader. He had once asked Jason why he was so rigid in his insistence at holding such regular meetings. Jason had explained that the Cilgwyn system had succeeded because the council set an example to all the other badgers; the councillors showed they were responsible and caring, and there was no one whose troubles could not be sorted out trivial or otherwise. Buckwheat, whilst appreciating what

Jason had said, did not fully understand the possible effects that could accrue should the council disregard their duties. As each season passed Buckwheat became more enlightened and now fully understood the reasoning behind Jason's thinking. His mind became increasingly troubled and he discussed with his friend Chantar how to find a remedy to cure the ills that were slowly spreading over Cilgwyn.

Buckwheat lived in his own five-chambered sett with his wife, Fern, their son, Beaufort, and their son's wife, Corntop, who was the daughter of Beaufort's friend Chantar and his wife, Nepra. Chantar lived in his own sett, too, only a few steps away from Buckwheat and, since Corntop had moved into Buckwheat's sett, had become a frequent visitor. The sett was always in immaculate condition; there was never any soiled or loose bedding in the passageways or stale bedding left from one winter to the next in the communal sleeping chamber, which was used during the cold winter nights. There was no discarded carrion and the internal dung chamber was used only during blizzard days and this, too, was cleaned as quickly as possible.

One night after foraging, Buckwheat and his family returned quite early to their sett, their appetites having been quickly satisfied, for there had been a drizzle the previous day and the worms were in abundance near the surface. Buckwheat, Beaufort and the others had gorged themselves in a feeding place that was exclusive to Buckwheat and his family. Only council members had this privilege as their sole reward for carrying out the responsibilities of government. Buckwheat had caught a slight whiff of badger scent in his feeding patch that was not of his own family and this bothered him. Beaufort told his father that it was a scent carried further than usual on a sudden gust or breeze because he did not want him to go into one of his long drawn-out lectures on discipline breaking down.

As Buckwheat was about to enter his sett, he saw that

Chantar, too, was returning home. Buckwheat invited him over for a chat, and when they were resting on a fresh bed of clean rye grass, he noticed that Chantar was troubled. Buckwheat told Fern to take the other females to another chamber as he had council business to discuss with Chantar. Fern looked quizzically at Buckwheat, as there had not been a council meeting for some four or five moons and she wasn't aware that one was to be held in the near future, but she did not query Buckwheat. Fern and Corntop absented themselves to the dandelion bedchamber that Fern kept for special guests.

Chantar knew that Buckwheat was aware he had something on his mind and he explained immediately that whilst he did not object to sharing his private feeding grounds with strangers in times of hardship, he most certainly did in times when food was abundant. He explained that a large patch of his feeding area had been cleared of worms before he had got there and the scent of two badgers not of his family had been noticed not only by him but by Nepra too. He had recognised the scent as that of the Palos family, yet he could not understand why they would want to encroach on his feeding area as they were privileged with their own. Chantar had set a warning for all other badger families by leaving heavy secretions of musk along the hedgerow bordering the area that had been poached and had also left feces there to underline the warning. Nepra, whilst accepting the musking, did not think that the matter warranted such unhygienic cub-like behaviour, but Chantar was adamant that it needed such treatment for the warning not to be taken lightly. Having listened to Chantar's revelations, Buckwheat was convinced that he had not been mistaken in his own suspicions that he had arrived only just in time at his own feeding grounds to prevent poaching. He made up his mind to take the matter up with Eldon the following evening. Eldon would be asleep by now and, with a full stomach and his usual air of

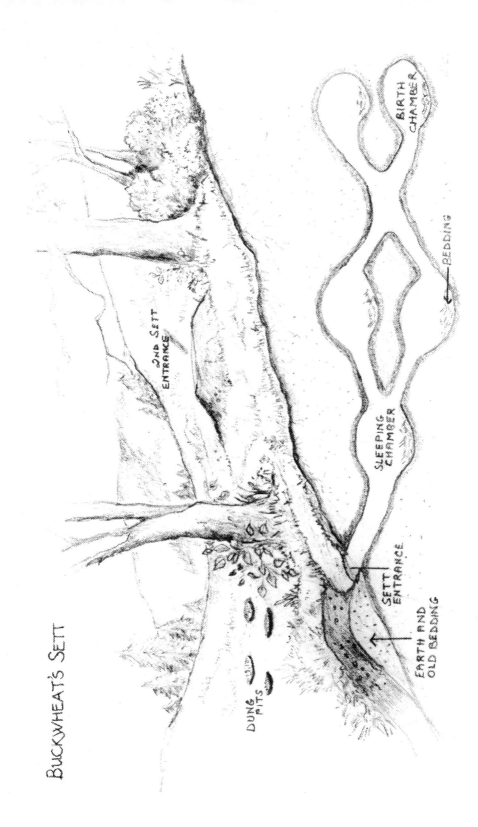

BUCKWHEAT'S SETT

2ND SETT ENTRANCE

BIRTH CHAMBER

SLEEPING CHAMBER

BEDDING

SETT ENTRANCE

DUNG PITS

EARTH AND OLD BEDDING

contentment, would certainly not appreciate Buckwheat calling and rousing him from his thoughts of easy living.

Buckwheat did not have a restful sleep, his tossing and turning making Fern restless too. She had been with him now for twelve years and had thought that his growing impatience and more frequent days of restlessness were signs that he was getting older. There were certainly alterations to his outward appearance. His coat no longer shone with the vigour she fondly remembered and his gait was not quite as sprightly as a year or so ago. He had for so long been a fine figure of a badger to look at, with the bearing of a leader, carrying himself amongst the badgers with such dignity. She had often noted the admiration of the other females for him. Now he was acknowledged with respect but the admiration was for Beaufort, who, if anything, was more handsome in appearance than his father.

Yet Beaufort appeared to lack ambition. He was less volatile than Buckwheat and always obedient to him, even though in size he now looked down upon his father. Beaufort sought peace and was quite prepared to fend and forage for his family without the privilege of private pasture, but he did not seek any added responsibility. He wanted to hear the sounds of gentle breezes, feel the warm sun on his back as he lay in an open sett, hear the soft tinkling of the mountain stream, scent the lush strawberries and honeysuckle flowers, and to gaze upon Corntop, nuzzling her softness. Why should any badger ask for more? Yet he, too, was now troubled by his father's misgivings at what first appeared to be trivial occurrences in other badgers' lives. But poaching? Palos's family? Beaufort could not bring himself to believe that Palos would even consider poaching or, for that matter, would carry out even the smallest misdemeanour, but he had always felt that there was a strange attitude surrounding Palos's son Kronos ever since they were cubs.

Kronos, now nearly five years old, had set his aim at the

eventual leadership of the Cadre and had collected a handful of accomplices around him. Although he had not taken a wife, a female companion shared his sett. She was known as Vespid and had to share his companionship with his cronies, all younger than him and all but one without wives. Kronos seemed to have a dominant influence on those near him. Vespid did not discourage his companions and would even tolerate them staying overday in their sett. But Kronos was never carefree, happy or kind and there was a distinct selfishness about him. His friends, however, admired him. Kronos knew that to achieve his aims he would need as much support as possible and flattered even his nearest friends to deceive. He didn't want the leadership for the protection and well-being of the badgers, he wanted that leadership to suit his way of life. From an early age he had shown courage but an ugly needless courage. He would show off to Gnos and Vulcan, or Zygos and Oatos, and even his younger brother Zoilos, demonstrating how to turn the largest stone over, how to kill young rabbits, how to dig quicker than anyone else, how to leap in the pool after the fish or frogs.

Beaufort had never really taken much notice of Kronos, not since they were yearlings when he had pinned Kronos down in a playful skirmish. He had always felt that whenever Kronos looked at him after that there was a chill of vengeance and hate in his stare, yet he had never allowed it to bother him. It could well be Kronos showing off to his cronies again, but poaching was a serious offence against the regulations of the Cilgwyn Cadre. Eventually, Beaufort relaxed and, with the soft coat of Corntop caressing his side, he felt a restful warmth spread over him and he dreamed the same sweet dream he had had so many times, the dream of living in a paradise, a dream that he awakened from each evening only to venture out and find reality.

That particular evening his slumber was shattered by the uplifted voices of Buckwheat and Chantar complaining that something had to be done. Chantar had been disturbed by sounds of digging outside one of his sett entrances. He had emerged to find that bedding in the soiled bedding dump had been pulled about the sett entrance and, as he heard the culprits rush away, one of the scents that he had noticed was the same as the previous evening, Palos's family.

Beaufort rose from his warm bed and ambled over to his father and Chantar. He realised that his father's patience was at the point of breaking, as staccato growling reaffirming his intention to alert Eldon to the recent events was the only sound emanating from him, his coat fluffing up and falling back continuously. Then Buckwheat spoke as if the whole badger community was listening. He announced that an emergency meeting of the Cadre should be called that very evening and that he would use his prerogative as a council member in insisting upon it. He grunted to Fern that he and Chantar were off at once to see Eldon, and the two badgers moved out of the sett with great haste. Beaufort decided it was time he and Corntop went in search of their food, but Fern decided to stay until Buckwheat's return.

Eldon had, for some time, made the effort to rise from his bedchamber only when his hunger pains were no longer bearable and when the excess weight became too much for his limbs to bear. This evening, however, his sleep was disturbed by the voice of a male badger apparently making firm demands, and the voice of his wife, Scylla, getting higher pitched and appearing close to panic. It was Buckwheat insisting that he must see Eldon immediately, and Scylla explaining that Eldon was busy and that Buckwheat would have to wait. Scylla was getting more and more frightened at the thought of Eldon being roused from his slumbers, something she dare not even think of for fear of being chastised for days and either being bitten or receiving a cuff from Eldon's heavy paws. Her worries disappeared as she heard Eldon coming up behind her. Being always polite to his wife in public, Eldon courteously asked Scylla to stand aside. He noticed Buckwheat and then Chantar close at his side. Eldon had no further time to ask them what they wanted. Buckwheat's feelings were still running high and he demanded that, as a council member, his rights as such be recognised and that a council meeting of the Cadre be held that evening. Eldon did not argue, not having seen such a sense of purpose in Buckwheat's face ever since Buckwheat had insisted some years ago that, as senior councillor and next only to the council leader, he had the first choice of private feeding grounds. Eldon, eager to appease Buckwheat, quickly confirmed that he would send for Palos and Molyar immediately and whilst the messengers were gone perhaps Buckwheat would explain why there was such an urgency to call a meeting. Buckwheat, with an air of authority, told Eldon that he would have to wait until the meeting was in session. Then, together with Chantar, he entered the central system and walked steadily down the long corridors to the Cadre Hall, calling at the chambers of Greyears, the Chronicler and Sage, to tell him to attend the meeting.

Buckwheat and Chantar squatted in their places to the right side of the leader's dais and were quickly joined by Greyears, who took his position up some ten badger paces further back in the Hall from Chantar. Within a few moments the sound of agitated voices could be heard coming down the corridor and then Eldon entered with Palos, Molyar and Kronos. Buckwheat rose immediately and asked why Kronos should be there. Palos replied that it would be good experience for Kronos to learn about the council before he became a council member. In a strong and powerful voice Buckwheat roared that it was not the leader's choice, nor the father's choice, nor even the choice of the council that enabled a badger to be elected a councillor. It was the choice of all mature badgers, and Kronos had no right whatsoever to be there. What was more, neither Eldon as leader nor Palos had the authority to invite him. Eldon, not wanting the meeting to go on any longer than he could help, confirmed that Buckwheat was correct and commanded Kronos to leave. Chantar looked at Kronos, whose eyes were fixed on Buckwheat with a look of such hate and malice that he shuddered with a terrible feeling of foreboding. As Kronos turned and went away, Chantar also noticed Palos's ill-contained fury.

Eldon called the meeting to order and stated that it had been summoned by Buckwheat, invoking his powers as a council member. Without waiting for further speeches Buckwheat requested that what he had to say be recorded by Greyears and noted by his council colleagues as an official complaint. He reeled off one transgression after another which at first appeared to be very minor and trivial. He listed careless collection and wasting of bedding, not keeping to pathways in the sett areas, lack of supervision of cubs by young mothers. He believed that, if allowed to continue, things would get worse until the pattern of living would break down and family life would be shattered. Instead of love and happiness there would be greed, theft, promiscuity and anarchy. He then told of his suspicions of the previous evening and related Chantar's experience in his feeding area. Eldon, whose eyes had begun to close halfway through Buckwheat's lengthy sermon, was now wide awake, not so much worried about the feeding areas of Buckwheat and Chantar being invaded, but that his might be next. Then Buckwheat explained what had happened earlier that very evening to the soiled bedding dump of Chantar. Even Eldon accepted that this was going too far and asked for suggestions to curb this malicious behaviour. Although he felt it was not being done by badgers intent on disregarding the council law, it was surely a game or prank being played by the younger element of the population. Chantar looked in admiration at Buckwheat, who, as far as he was concerned, should have been the leader after Jason. He realised that Buckwheat's warnings and demands would fall on deaf ears as far as Eldon and the two others were concerned, although Palos looked uneasy and kept very still.

Eldon rose and stated pompously that he would take the matter in hand and ask the Chronicler to issue warnings to all sett-owners that any more occurrences of this mischievous behaviour would result in a further meeting being called to discuss the matter more thoroughly. Buckwheat was dumbfounded. He had always known that Eldon was self-concerned, weak and spineless as far as resolute leadership was concerned, but this situation could not be treated in such a perfunctory manner. Buckwheat's knowledge of the laws was second only to Greyears's, and he asked Greyears to confirm that in the statutes laid down by their forefathers when the Cadre was originally formed there was a law clearly stating the procedures that had to be carried out when such misconduct occurred, and that the council had no alternative but to ensure that such procedures were carried out. The law could not be altered unless the changes were proposed in council and approved by the majority of the community. Eldon, who had been standing all this time, slumped back in his place, his grandiose bearing completely deflated. Why couldn't Buckwheat leave things as they were? Hadn't everyone been happy up until now?

Greyears stated that violation of the private feeding areas of the council members and purposeful intent to scatter another badger's soiled bedding were listed under the heading of secondary serious acts of misconduct and carried punishment of three days' extra digging, seven days' bedding collection, complete removal of soiled bedding from the dump of the offended badgers and four days without food. Buckwheat insisted that the community be assembled and told that such punishment would be meted out to the guilty badgers. To ensure this was done, two or three senior badgers would be appointed to investigate the matter and to apprehend the badger or badgers responsible. Before Eldon had a chance to put his seal of approval on the matter a major disturbance could be heard in the corridors outside the council hall.

5

The Stranger's Message

Eldon instructed Greyears to discover what the commotion was about, and before Eldon could continue he was interrupted by Greyears returning with two young boars escorted by some senior badgers. Greyears stated that the meeting had to be interrupted as the young badgers were the bearers of serious and important news. They were introduced as Gruff and Fircone. Buckwheat recognised them as friends of Beaufort. Eldon commanded Gruff to speak, and the young badger, shaking with excitement, explained that whilst out foraging together, he and Fircone had crossed the stream in the lower part of the valley and had decided to explore the little copse of elders in order that they might find a tree to scratch and clean their claws that had picked up mud from the wet earth at the sides of the stream. After leaving the sound of the splashing stream behind them and upon reaching halfway up the hill on the opposite side to the sett area, they had both heard strange whimpering sounds. At first they were not sure whether to return and inform their seniors, but after a few moments had decided that, as there was no alien scent about them, they would approach the

sounds with caution. They had stealthily crawled up the hill
with the slight breeze in their faces so as not to take their scent
towards the strange sounds. As they approached the rim of the
plateau on top of the hill, they had recognised the sounds of an
ailing badger in distress, but, whilst the scent was that of a
badger, it was not one they recognised as belonging to the
community. They had realised that the animal was not capable
of moving and eventually had summoned enough courage to
approach it with trepidation. It had not been frightened when it
noticed them, but had muttered just a few words and then
fallen back into unconsciousness or death. The listening badgers
urged Gruff to hurry up and tell them what the stranger had
said. Gruff, shaking with excitement, said that the stranger had
asked to speak to an elder of the badgers and then had said his
name—Bamber.

The meeting was forgotten, even by Buckwheat, as the badgers made their way hurriedly along the corridors and out of
the sett, moving quickly down the hillside and crossing the
stream. They were now being followed by a large number of
other badgers as the word had got around that a stranger bad-

ger had been seen that was not of the community. It had been many generations since strangers had been to Cilgwyn. Eldon stopped the onward march, as for a moment he wasn't sure whether it would be safe and, furthermore, he didn't really know what he should do. He suggested that they should discuss the matter and draw up a plan of approach to the stranger. Buckwheat stated that, as the stranger was obviously very weak and ill, no time should be lost and that he and Chantar and any other council member should go ahead and investigate whilst the other badgers stayed where they were until news was brought down. There were over two hundred badgers gathered in small groups, discussing the sensational happening. They waited by the small copse of elder trees as Buckwheat, Chantar, Palos and Eldon climbed the hill up to the stranger. Buckwheat noticed the huddled, still shape on the ground and realised that it was a male badger. He had never seen such an aged badger before. He looked as if he had survived a hundred winters or more. He had obviously been a large and strong badger, but now his coat was bedraggled, torn and dirty, his paws sore and bleeding, and his eyes, staring but not appearing to be seeing, were sunk deep in his head. But then Buckwheat saw a slight movement from the stranger and realised that this pitiable, tragic figure of a badger was indeed still alive. Buckwheat had no fear within him, only a sense of compassion as he tenderly approached the stranger's side. He wasn't sure if he could be heard as he gave his name and explained that he was an official elder. The stranger turned his head and looked at Buckwheat. There were embers in those dark, deep-sunk eyes that were not quite extinguished and seemed to flare up a little as he spoke again. He told Buckwheat that his name was Bamber, that he had journeyed for many moons over strange lands and hills, and but for the strength of Logos would have failed to warn them of the disaster to come. Buckwheat noticed the eyes of this aged badger dim as he slipped into unconsciousness once more. But he pressed closer and felt the life-beating rhythm remaining within the travel-worn body.

Buckwheat asked the others whether they understood that this stranger had given a warning of impending doom and that he had come with the power of Logos within him. In order that they could discover more they must give every help to this brave and heroic badger, this messenger from Asgard, or they would experience the wrath of Logos and their ancestors in Asgard falling upon them. Buckwheat sent Chantar down the hill to tell some of the other badgers to break off some of the elder tree branches and fetch them up the hill together with a large quantity of soft green bedding. Four or five branches, a little longer than a fully grown badger, were quickly supplied, twigs and ivy interwound the branches in no time and the whole was then covered by a very deep layer of grasses, clover, bracken and leaves. The other badgers worked industriously, climbing up and down the hillside until the stretcher was completed. Buckwheat, Chantar, Beaufort and Gruff lifted Bamber gently onto the stretcher. Buckwheat then told Beaufort, who had arrived earlier bringing an elder branch, to get two other friends of his and, with Gruff, carry Bamber to their sett. Eldon queried why it should be Buckwheat's sett, and seemed relieved when Buckwheat said he didn't think it right that the leader of the Cadre should have his life and sleep interrupted constantly by the continuous calling of visitors to see the stranger. The leader's councillors were there to assist the leader and relieve him of the trials and tribulations that this eventful arrival would bring. For the first time in his life Eldon thought of Buckwheat with a sense of gratitude. As the litter, carried by four young badgers, made its way down the hill, Eldon announced to all the other members of the Cilgwyn badger community that he had decided that the stranger from Logos, known as Bamber, would be housed in the home of Buckwheat and his family, where there would be plenty of room and more peace to help the ailing one to recover. There would be no visitors allowed until further notice, and two guards would stay within close proximity of Buckwheat's sett to see that this order was obeyed and act as messengers to carry any news that might transpire to Eldon himself. At Buckwheat's request Eldon agreed that Greyears would temporarily move to Buckwheat's sett in order that any conversations could be recorded and interpreted.

Buckwheat walked ahead of the litter and arrived back to find that one of the chambers in the sett had already been prepared by Fern. He saw that she and Corntop were lying on the bedding of dandelion leaves and fern to give some added warmth to the stranger. The litter was lowered outside the entrance and Beaufort seized it with his powerful jaws, pulling it with ease along the tunnel to the chamber entrance. Bamber was eased off the litter and gently rolled onto the bedding. Corntop and Fern pushed the warm fern and leaves about Bamber, although it appeared to them a forlorn task. Buckwheat stood outside as Rhea, the Healer, arrived with roots of the dandelion, foxglove blossoms and, wrapped in a leaf of colt's-foot, a masticated mixture of sweet cicely, bergamot and sassafras. She was followed by two young female badgers, Tassel and Groundsel, who carried water from the stream in their pouched mouths. Fern and Corntop moved quickly out of the chamber as Rhea placed her medicines close to Bamber. Her assistants in turn put their mouths close to Bamber's and allowed the water to trickle in, although there was no movement from Bamber's tongue. Buckwheat impressed on Rhea that she must do her utmost to help life return to the stranger. Rhea's reproachful glance at Buckwheat made him feel ashamed. As if Rhea, wonderful dear old Rhea who had saved so many lives, would do anything else.

Tassel and Groundsel lay on either side of Bamber to give him warmth as Rhea gently crushed the milk from the dandelion roots into Bamber's mouth, followed by minute doses of her ancient potions, made from recipes that had been passed down from healer to healer through the ages.

Except for his family, Rhea's group and Greyears, Buckwheat cleared all the badgers away from the sett and told them to go about their normal nightly business. As Beaufort followed his father back inside the sett he noticed that the two sentries had taken up their positions. They were Zoilos, Kronos's brother, and Vulcan, and there was little that would escape these two, thought Beaufort as he disappeared out of sight.

The warmth in the sett had grown substantially due to there being eleven badgers in and around the sick chamber. Rhea worked incessantly, cajoling and caressing Bamber. When Fern queried, quite some time later, whether there was any improvement, Rhea shook her head and with a crestfallen face explained that the stranger was now on the pathway to Logos and that his journey could not be halted. Whether it was the sound of voices so close to him, or the hand of Logos, Bamber stirred and feebly muttered his name once more, then Logos's, and then that there was no more time. Buckwheat edged nearer, gave his name and, encouraging Bamber to relax, told him he could talk as soon as he regained his strength.

For two days and nights Rhea nursed Bamber, amazed that he still lived. He drifted in and out of consciousness and then seemed to change. An incandescent light appeared around him, a glow of such intensity that it had a strange but comfortable and peaceful effect on his new friends. He called Buckwheat to him and told him of his home, the devastation of life, his lost Dainty and their cubs, his journey, the assistance of the merciful Tendril, and then gave his warning that Buckwheat and all the other badgers must move on in the direction of the falling sun until they found a new home, an Elysia. They would recognise it. It would be overflowing in its bounty, with food, soil, spring-water streams, glades of various trees and hedgerows carrying fruit, herbs, and flowers. Then they would be given signs of good omen. If no scent or sight of man had come, they could start life again with the blessings of Logos. Buckwheat gazed at Bamber with adoration and reverence. This was indeed a saint amongst badgers. He bent down and placed his face against Bamber's, clutching him tightly in his grasp, willing the old one to understand that his task was now completed and would not be in vain and that his brave unselfish deeds would remain a cherished part of badger lore throughout the ages. As Buck-wheat rose he could see that the glow had finally dimmed. He realised that Bamber had at last bowed to his yoke and would soon be taking fresh spring water with his Dainty again.

6

The Warning and the Prophecy

The arrival of the stranger, Bamber, at Cilgwyn was the sole matter of discussion among all the badgers. From the news that had been given them, very few believed that the stranger would survive the terrible ordeal he had agonisingly endured, and even those few badgers marvelled that he had lived two more days.

When the news of Bamber's death was first given to Eldon, his immediate thoughts were those of gratitude. He had not liked this disturbance to the community, as his life of ease could have been somewhat upset. He had already had two days of disturbed sleep, his relaxation being constantly interrupted by messages from Buckwheat. After the news arrived he immediately went to Buckwheat's sett. His main purpose was to play the whole episode down and to authorise a very quiet funeral for the visitor. On his short journey to Buckwheat he caught snatches of conversation from passing badgers and noticed many groups huddled closely together, deep in talk. Some mentioned "messenger of Asgard," "angel of Logos" and "warnings of doom." There was certainly an air of excitement over the whole community.

Eldon had always held Buckwheat to be a badger of inner strength, an exemplary councillor, but that evening when he met Buckwheat he noticed an aura of such impressiveness, such stately dignity and eminence, that his mission was soon forgotten and he found himself agreeing with practically everything that Buckwheat said. Beaufort, who was witness to the encounter, was full of admiration for the qualities of his father and told himself that his own nature was such that he could never fulfil his father's hopes and ambitions for him.

Eldon agreed that as soon as darkness fell the following evening Bamber would be buried in a grave dug for him on the spot where he had been discovered, so that it would look across at the Cilgwyn setts for eternity. It would serve as a memorial to a badger of heroism, whose martyrdom had been for the benefit of his own kind. Eldon, whilst agreeing with Buckwheat, found it difficult to understand from where this greatness arose, but he had the sense to leave well enough alone and certainly did not want to get involved in a lengthy argument that would keep him from some thick juicy worms. Eldon further agreed that after Bamber's interment there would be a meeting, in the open, on the gentle slope leading down to the stream, of all the badgers of mature age, males over two years and females of more than eighteen moons, to discuss Bamber's words of warning. As Eldon quickly took leave of Buckwheat he approved that Buckwheat would supervise the proceedings of the next evening, his only thought then being on his feeding grounds and his bedchamber.

Buckwheat spent most of that night calling on friends and acquaintances, delegating the many different tasks that had to be carried out for the funeral of a leader. It was the least Buckwheat could do as a gesture of his gratitude to Bamber.

Beaufort, with his friends Gruff and Fircone, had been dele-
gated the duty of digging the grave, and he accepted with a
pride that left him confused. Then, having explained to his
friends their part in the proceedings, he noticed that they, too,
gratefully accepted their share of labour. As the day broke
Beaufort's thoughts prevented him from enjoying sound sleep
when he nestled close to Corntop on their warm comfortable
bed. He could not understand why three badgers should so
willingly accept extra digging when this was normally given as a
form of punishment.

Eldon, returning to consciousness after his long day's sleep,
became irritable as his head filled yet again with sounds of
heated discussion coming from other chambers and passageways within the sett. His memory of the previous evening with
Buckwheat eluded him as he ventured out of his bed to discover
what all the noise was about. The first badger he saw was Palos,
then Molyar, then Kronos and a few others, all gesticulating
wildly and trying to make their voices heard. They were silenced by an ear-splitting high-pitched bark from Kronos,
which also made Eldon stagger backwards in momentary terror. As soon as he regained his composure, Eldon insisted that
Palos should explain such unwelcome behaviour. Palos soon
told Eldon of Buckwheat's plans and arrangements and asked
why the strange visitor whose presence at Cilgwyn was of only
two days' duration should be granted a leader's funeral. He had
not experienced any benefit or gift that this so-called angel of
Logos had bestowed on the community. Palos further ques-
tioned Buckwheat's authority in making such arrangements
and said that the meeting called for after the funeral should not
be about the confounded visitor but should discuss Buckwheat's
overstepping the mark in his application of his powers as senior
councillor and, if necessary, should vote to replace Buckwheat
with someone else. Palos's words exploded from him vehe-

mently, he had slept very little during the day, his mind filled with jealousy at the admiration for Buckwheat reflected in many badgers' eyes. His uneasiness had been encouraged by the repeated goading of Kronos, who kept telling his father that it would be Buckwheat who would persuade the badgers who their next leader should be.

Whilst listening to Palos's outburst, Eldon eventually gathered his wits about him and remembered his discussion with Buckwheat. Not being in Buckwheat's presence and away from the spellbinding atmosphere of Buckwheat's sett, Eldon realised that he should have dealt with the matter more fully. He would never admit his mistake to anyone and, after prolonged oratory, he persuaded those who confronted him that there was no motive of influencing power in the application of his rulings. Each badger would have the opportunity to address the community at the evening's meeting, after hearing the message from Bamber, the stranger, and Greyears's interpretation of it.

Buckwheat, with Chantar, called on Eldon and, seeing that Palos and Molyar were already in his sett, asked the councillors to escort the leader to the head of the cortege that was ready to leave Buckwheat's sett for the burial ground. Eldon emerged into the light of the full moon and saw a corridor of badgers lining a route from Buckwheat's sett down the hill to the stream and continuing after the stream, past the elder trees up to the flat-topped knoll where the remainder of the badger community had assembled. Beaufort, Gruff, Goliath and Whortle had been given the further task of pulling the bier carrying Bamber's body down to the stream. Thereafter they were joined by Fircone, Burpee, Whirligig and Growler in pulling the burial litter up to the grave.

Bamber had been laid onto a bed of freshly cut green reeds, his body secured by the leaves of wild iris, then covered with the heads of the flowers of dandelion, buttercup, celandine, oxlip, summer pheasant's eye and colt's-foot, all yellow and bright, to light his journey home to Logos. This duty had been lovingly undertaken by Fern, Corntop and Nepra, the collection of the flowers having been made by many young badgers who had never witnessed a funeral of importance and who looked forward to such a spectacle with delight and wonderment.

As the cortege passed through the corridor of badgers, those who were left behind fell in after the litter. As Eldon and his councillors waited at one side of the grave, Beaufort and his friends pulled the flower-covered litter to its edge. When Beaufort stood back he saw Kronos and his friends standing behind Buckwheat. When Buckwheat had suggested to Kronos that he might wish to be a litter-bearer, Kronos had firmly rejected the invitation, stating that he wanted no part in such a preposterous tribute to an old, ordinary badger. Beaufort had seen his father's look of disdain turn to pity as he watched Kronos walk away.

The four council badgers gently pulled the shrouded body into the grave and, as they stood back, Fern and Corntop gathered the flower heads that had fallen about the ground and covered Bamber's wrapped body once more. As they finished Buckwheat stepped forward and addressed his friends and neighbours.

Buckwheat related Bamber's journey as if he himself had witnessed each eventful day. At first his voice could not be heard by all that were gathered, as some chatted amongst themselves. It was not long, however, before everyone became spellbound, hanging on to Buckwheat's every word. After detailing the hazards and dangers of Bamber's journey, Buckwheat immortalised him in an exaltation of his loyalty to his kind, his allegiance to his unknown brothers, his illustriousness in giving his life to save his species, indeed a very worthy messenger from

Asgard, to where he had now returned. Bamber would now rest peacefully in Logos's bosom with Dainty once more at his side. He would forever be part of Cilgwyn legend, and being present at his requiem was an honour that should be cherished by all present for the rest of their earthbound time.

Palos then solemnly brought to their attention that, before they dispersed to their foraging and other labours, a meeting was to be held on the slopes with their great leader, Eldon, and other council badgers. The meeting would take place at the highest point, in order that they could be heard, to discuss the stranger's visit and his words of warning. The badgers quietly dispersed, although unable to shake off the sense of hallowedness that had enshrouded them.

Buckwheat remained for a few moments, gazing down at the newly sealed tomb. To touch greatness is something very few individuals of any species are fortunate enough to experience. It was the first time that Beaufort had seen his father weep, but he felt no shame, as he knew that he was the son of a badger who had such true compassion for all of his kind. He walked with quiet pride as he escorted his father to the most important meeting of his life.

7

The Touch of Man

It was only the third time that the eldest badger could remember a meeting of all the community being held, the first time being at the funeral of Jason, and the last occasion on the elevation of Eldon to leadership. Whilst there were some badgers who were apprehensive about Buckwheat's tale of Bamber and the warning, the majority, including Eldon, Palos, Molyar and Kronos, weren't at all sure why it was necessary to hold such a meeting. Even Beaufort wasn't aware of the significance of Bamber's warning.

Eldon wasn't at all sure what to say and thought it best that Buckwheat should open the proceedings by explaining why he felt it necessary that all the badgers should be gathered. Buckwheat first asked his audience why an absolute stranger should travel such a distance, which resulted in him sacrificing his life to give a warning of devastation to come unless the warning would be heeded. The great enemy, which Cilgwyn was only aware of from stories through the ages, their badger lore and from the records of generations past, had ended the lives of many badgers and destroyed their homes. The great animal man had killed with a strange power over the air that the badgers breathed, making them choke and their bodies distort into frozen grotesque shapes. The immortal badger, Bamber, had found them, not just to tell them of the carnage but to warn them to leave Cilgwyn before such a holocaust engulfed them. Plans should be made immediately to relocate the entire community in a new Elysia such as Bamber prophesied they would recognise. That meant many tasks such as planning the care of the sick and elderly, chaperoning the young ones, organising forward scouts to seek resting places. They must act quickly. There was no more time to discuss Bamber and the reasons for his sacrifice, other than to acknowledge the urgent need to escape from impending death.

Eldon was speechless with amazement. He had never thought there would be a badger advocating a move away from his precious Cilgwyn, his peaceful paradise where every badger he had known had found happiness. Buckwheat, whose behaviour had been rather strange of late, must have reached old age sooner than expected.

Before Eldon could voice his opinions Palos stepped forward to calm the excited crowd. The air of apprehension had now been overtaken by an atmosphere of fear and disbelief. Palos, with Kronos at his side, seized the opportunity to improve his chances of becoming the next leader by giving an impression of calm, assured authority. When he had finished speaking there was a noise of gaiety and laughter, as many badgers cheered and shouted his name. Palos had asked them if they had seen any proof of the stranger's travels. While admittedly he had been in a terrible condition, was he not perhaps feeble-minded? Why should the ranting of a sick badger influence the well-being and future of Cilgwyn? Had not the badgers of Cilgwyn been safe throughout the ages? When had they ever experienced the presence of man?

The badgers, now reassured, were keen to hear more from Palos and he did not let them down. The chance he had been waiting for had come, the humiliation of Buckwheat. He believed that Buckwheat had squandered Eldon's trust by giving such a funeral to a doddering old badger. Why had Buckwheat called a meeting of the community? Why had he wanted to create insecurity amongst them? Why should it be Buckwheat who interpreted that silly badger's story? Was Buckwheat misusing the trust placed in him by his fellow badgers, the trust conferred on him by his election to his honourable position of councillor? Had not Buckwheat committed treason?

The badgers' emotions were being roused and cries of approval broke out spasmodically from amongst the crowd. Kronos's friends were certainly doing their best to ensure that the badgers would accept Palos as the natural successor to Eldon. They were hanging on to every word that Palos said, and as he stepped back the cheering barking was thunderous. Palos now held nearly all of them as clay in his paws, and realising this, he demanded that Buckwheat and his family be exiled as the punishment for treason. Palos knew that with Buckwheat gone there was nothing to stop his ambitions being fulfilled.

Even Beaufort by then had misgivings and doubts, but, looking at Buckwheat, he remembered his father's face and eyes as he had come away from the grave. The same strong belief still shone from Buckwheat's eyes.

Eldon, not aware of Palos's ulterior motives and feeling annoyed with Buckwheat for letting him usurp his authority, was ready to call an end to the meeting and have the badgers disperse to their usual evening haunts when Buckwheat stepped forward again. His speech astonished everyone as he stated that his deeds and actions were nothing but honourable. The badgers had always known him to be fair and honest. He had never sought leadership or a position of responsibility. It had been placed upon him and he had accepted it as an honourable duty. He still could not understand why he should be the badger to warn and prepare the others, but he urged the assembly to wait and listen to another, the Chronicler and Sage, Greyears, who had also been at Bamber's side when the old one had spoken.

Greyears, now one of the oldest at Cilgwyn, shuffled to the forefront, as near to Buckwheat as it was possible. He had always had strange visions of evil when near to Kronos, but always felt comfortable and secure with Buckwheat.

He mustered all his strength to give power to his voice so that all could hear him. When he cried that everyone should heed Buckwheat's words, there were again outbursts, this time trying to shout Greyears down. But Kronos's friends failed to get the support they had believed would come and soon there was complete silence, allowing Greyears to continue. There were many badgers who respected him for the goodness that they knew was within him, the wise badger who presided at each one's birth and at the joining of paws when male and female became united as one. He had always prophesied long life and happiness to all of them who kept goodness and Logos in their hearts. Greyears never chatted idly and whenever he spoke it was profound, benevolent and sincere.

He continued to speak, referring first to the chronicle which stated that calamities like this had occurred in the distant past, then stating that they must heed every word that Buckwheat had said and that it was a warning for that very time, not a vision of moons to come. There was no time to waste. Bamber, the herald of hope, had placed his faith in Buckwheat until such time as a badger emerged who would lead them to a new home. The new leader would be found before the nights became longer than the days and before the first whispers of falling leaves came upon them. They should move in the direction that had been given to them, to the falling sun, for one day they would catch it and they would know that they had arrived in the promised land. There the pattern of Cilgwyn would be reinstated, and the security and happiness that had once been theirs would return, this time forever, for man need no longer be feared but could be trusted as a friend. There would be disbelievers who would attempt to shatter the pattern of life they knew and understood. This would lead to nothing but tyranny for those who followed badgers of such accursed minds. Everyone should return to their setts and talk over the future with their families while Eldon and the council prepared the plans for the journey. Before they allowed sleep to overcome them, and sleep they must to give them fresh strength, they should search within themselves for the resolve and determination to succeed. All should consult their pillows and there they would lose their fears and find the way to their dreams.

For a few moments a pall of silence hung over the gathering, and then the badgers' murmurs and whispers crescendoed into a deafening clamour. Eldon and Palos gesticulated wildly, but it was to little purpose. Greyears raised Buckwheat's paw, and the noise abated as he addressed them once more. He advised them to remain calm, but was again interrupted by Palos, who insisted it was Eldon's right as leader to advise them and not Buckwheat's. Buckwheat, out of respect for the appointed leader, stood aside and Eldon came forward, appearing very flustered—the least likely figure to command discipline and order in a situation close to panic.

Eldon felt he had been caught up in a nightmare and couldn't really believe what he was witnessing. Last night's worms must have eaten some mildewed leaf. In his daze he did manage to respect Buckwheat's plea for calm and declared that the Cadre would meet immediately after the meeting was over, when the matter could be discussed more fully and logically. His audience made no attempt to leave for their setts until Buckwheat advised them that it was in everyone's interest to do so and would allow the meeting of the Cadre to commence without further delay. Whatever transpired would be relayed to them at a gathering to take place the following evening.

As the badgers moved off Eldon turned to go back to his sett to think things out for himself first. He wouldn't allow himself to believe that he had to prepare to leave Cilgwyn. He was sure that Palos was right this time and that Buckwheat was mistaken in his understanding of that interfering old badger. Why had he allowed such an exalted burial? It was now well into the latter part of the night and he hadn't eaten anything, although normally he would have been bulging with food by this time. His thinking became more confused as he remembered Greyears emphasising the importance of the message from the stranger and its forewarning of danger.

Neither Buckwheat nor Palos allowed Eldon to rest. They were close behind him as he entered his sett and were soon joined by Molyar and Chantar. Eldon's calm intentions of going to his chamber changed to irritation as he realised they were behind him.

Soon after they had settled in the Cadre Hall they were joined by Greyears. Palos, not wanting to completely alienate himself from Buckwheat at this time, suggested that whilst it was possible to make initial plans, it would surely be better for the community to see some warning sign that the enemy would come to Cilgwyn. It would be far more logical to desert their homes at the first opportunity that availed itself after such confirmation of danger than to perhaps needlessly abandon their setts.

Buckwheat, with the support of Chantar, pleaded with Palos to accept the situation with urgency and to have faith in Greyears's prophecy, gleaned from the death-bed words of Bamber. Eldon listened to the arguments and counter-arguments, too tired to make any contribution himself. Buckwheat realised that he would not persuade Palos that night, and that it would be more worthwhile to make arrangements for their eventual escape. He finally compromised with Palos and his mute supporter, Molyar, and agreed that the decision of time of departure should be made by the community at the next evening's meeting, although he was dismayed at the delay. Buckwheat realised, too, that at the moment of need, very little dependence could be placed upon Eldon, as by this time snorts of slumber could be heard coming from him. Chantar nudged Eldon awake and the position of compromise was explained to him.

The direction they should take had already been given by Greyears. A plan for the community's exodus was prepared and the difficulties that were likely to arise from such a major upheaval were given close attention. Palos, knowing deep down that neither Buckwheat nor Greyears were liable to mislead the community, had become a little nervous at the thought that there really might be some truth in the matter. He did not want his power diminished should events prove that possibility to be reality, and he became very much involved in the plans for the future.

They agreed that cubs under four full moons old would be in the charge of their mothers. All other cubs would, at the start of each night's journey, form into a group and be shepherded by ten senior female badgers all under the supervision of Harvey. He was a badger who had never had cubs of his own, his partner, Linnet, having been crushed under a falling tree when she had been his mate for just a few short days. Harvey's love of cubs and their fondness for him, owing to his constantly telling them stories of long ago, made him the ideal badger for such a task and it would be a labour of love that would make him feel that his destiny was at last being fulfilled.

The biggest concern was for the sick and elderly. To move them would inevitably hasten their final parting, but they could not be left behind, as Palos suggested, to suffer such an agonising death. Buckwheat realised that the community's progress could not be slowed down to the extent that the welfare of a few would jeopardise the future of them all. He felt that the old ones should be assisted on the first night's journey until they came to a place where the ailing badgers could be hidden in the bushes and wild grasses, leaving a small party of three or four hale and hearty volunteers to protect them and help them until peace returned. Sett digging would not be allowed under any circumstances as this would betray their whereabouts, defeating the whole idea of the escape. Those that appeared to be in their final moon would be taken, too, even if it meant their journey to Logos being hastened. It was surely better to die with friends they knew than to suffer the bursting of their lungs from the treacherous fumes.

For the first few nights food would have to be eaten when they were on the move. The length of each night's journey would be determined by the tiredness of the young cubs and the suitability of the resting place to camouflage their presence.

It was agreed that the Cadre would meet to discuss progress after each night's journey, and then to plan the following evening's march when the badgers were gathered together.

Eldon, as leader, would head the march with the four council badgers spread amongst the others, encouraging them to maintain a steady pace. Their sons would also assist them in helping along those who were falling behind. Straying off and separating would not be allowed, as this could expose their existence to man.

Palos asked Buckwheat how long the journey might last, and was told that it could be many moons before they arrived at their new home. Bamber had said they would be given a sign that they would understand and that every badger would find a peace, an everlasting peace, when they reached that haven.

The four members turned to receive Eldon's approval. He nodded his consent, still believing the time of enactment of such plans lay in the dreams of alarmists and cranks. It would just be one or two more bothersome nights before he could slip back into his old lackadaisical ways. As the meeting closed he followed his friends to the entrance of the sett, intent on going to his feeding ground as he was now ravenous and, on an empty stomach, would not be able to enjoy his long-awaited rest. As he emerged he was astonished to find that day was breaking. He was further unsettled by a beating of wings and noticed a large black shape had perched on the smooth boulder that rested in a hollow in the earth, and he shuddered as he saw it was the raven, a bird of evil omen.

Buckwheat, hungry and exhausted, discovered on his arrival at his sett that Fern had left some cleaned black slugs just inside the entrance. He sighed gratefully as he snuggled into the thick bedding that she had prepared. It was the first time that Buckwheat had had to himself since Bamber's arrival. His limbs felt heavy and weary but he trembled a little at the thought that a number of his friends might not survive the journey to come. He fretted at the thought that his age was against him and that he, too, might not have the required fitness to survive. This worrying speculation prevented him, tired as he was, from falling asleep. Where would the leadership into the new life come from? Eldon's chances of survival were even less, as he had lost the determination to fend for himself. Palos and his friends would use the leadership for the benefit of themselves and no one else. His old and trusted friend Chantar would have all the right intentions but did not possess the strength needed to carry them out. What of the other senior badgers Nomus, Dramble, Snailer or Bramley? None of them had shown any desire for responsibility. They had no experience, and although they were good and solid citizens of the community, one could not depend on them for anything more. His anxiety became more acute as he thought of a leaderless group of badgers journeying to nowhere in complete disarray, to live a life of permanent roaming, never finding peace. Why couldn't Beaufort show more consideration for his kind or more interest in fostering the faith of past generations of Cilgwyn, essential for the protection of the continued well-being of future generations? Why hadn't Beaufort pledged his troth to show his acceptance of being custodian of Cilgwyn badgers as Buckwheat had done? Buckwheat's mind was distressed but his exhaustion finally persuaded his tired body to relax and sleep.

Buckwheat was awakened by Fern telling him that many of their neighbours, having quenched their wakening thirst at the stream, were already on their way to the meeting. Although still feeling a little weary, Buckwheat roused himself and ambled outside to find Beaufort and Corntop waiting for him. The four plodded steadily down past the solitary oak. Buckwheat picked up a few small green acorns that had fallen in the wind and then, arriving at the stream, drank deeply and long. Feeling refreshed, he moved off at a quicker rate so that his fellow beings could be informed of things to come.

The plans of the Cadre were accepted without reservation by all the badgers present, the only discordance being on behalf of the infirm. Whilst some were pained at the risks involved in moving the elder members of their families, most of the badgers insisted that they should be allowed to take their ailing relatives with them on the understanding that they would not delay or hamper the progress to their eventual destination. Others with responsibilities for the safeguarding of the young ones felt that the original idea should be kept to. It was agreed that where it was obvious that a sick or old badger could not survive the rigours of travel it would be allowed to travel only the first night, irrespective of its family's good intentions. The rest would be allowed to remain part of the group, as long as they did not disrupt the progress of the others.

Eldon, having rested and by now getting a better grasp of the community's attitude to the emergency, projected himself in a much better vein that evening by qualifying all the remaining necessary explanations. Some of the badger families were eager that the journey should start that very night, but most of these did not have elderly or ailing relatives, and others wanted time to allow their sick to improve. It was Palos who stepped forward to persuade them that no one should overreact, as this would only encourage panic and disorderliness. He believed, as did everyone else he had spoken to, that they should wait for some further sign of man's impending visit.

Palos's willingness to wait had a calming effect on the congregation, and the sense of urgency that had prevailed was replaced by a more patient attitude.

Buckwheat was asked to speak by many of the badgers and he again reminded them of Bamber's plea that they go whilst they still had the chance. He believed that it would not be wise to start that night, but that final preparations should be made, particularly letting Harvey know who his charges would be and informing the badgers in the Cadre Hall of the names of the infirm who needed to be sheltered and left after the first night's journey. Many were in agreement with Buckwheat, but the others wanted to believe that Cilgwyn would never change and that Palos's suggestion should be accepted. Buckwheat realised that for the escape to succeed it would need the support of all the badgers. He eventually conceded that they would wait until such time as danger showed itself and then, as one, move to their new and promised land. They would find it because Bamber had said so and they would recognise it as soon as they were there. In the meantime preparations had to be finalised, and they should feed and rest as much as possible, as every extra bit of strength would be needed to sustain both mind and body.

Beaufort found himself strangely excited at the prospect of such an adventure and noticed, as he discussed the matter with Gruff, Fircone and his other friends, that Kronos and his usual entourage had separated, and that each one was engaged in discussion with different groups. He thought it very odd that Kronos and company should show such a desire to assist their fellow beings. Beaufort noticed, too, that none of these groups was part of the families or relatives of his own circle of friends. He decided that perhaps he was being too suspicious about something that could in fact be quite innocent. Nevertheless, he felt uneasy.

Beaufort, with Corntop, made his way to the feeding ground and they were soon caught up by his parents. Buckwheat hardly said a word but kept glancing at Beaufort, as if he were searching for something in his face and was disappointed and dismayed not to find what he was looking for.

As the evening air was slightly damp, the worms were numerous on the surface, and there was plenty, too, for everyone on the wild strawberry bushes. Beaufort enjoyed his meal, savouring everything with great relish, but as his appetite became satisfied the pangs of having to leave the only place he had ever known shunted the excitement aside and was replaced by melancholy. Buckwheat, noticing his sudden silence, asked what he thought about being required to become guardian of his fellow kind on the journey to tranquillity or oblivion. Beaufort had never considered being appointed to act in any sort of protective capacity over others, except over his own family. Buckwheat was disheartened at such a reply and explained to Beaufort that every Cilgwyn badger was a part of one big family. Could not Beaufort understand that he, Buckwheat, did not get involved in the day-to-day affairs of the community for self-satisfaction but to return in some small way his gratitude for the happiness that being part of Cilgwyn had given him?

Buckwheat wanted Beaufort to understand that the longer the journey went on, the more neighbours, friends and even relatives would be lost, and that it was possible that he, Buckwheat, would not survive the journey. Beaufort should search for a new leader ready to take his father's place at the head of the march and who could lead with dignified calm, with assurance and firmness yet understanding.

Beaufort's initial resentment at receiving another lecture slowly turned to an understanding of what his father's teaching had been in aid of. He realised lovingly that his father represented everything a leader should be. Whilst he could never possess such qualities, should the time come, he would know what to look for. The resolve in Beaufort's face made Buckwheat hope that somewhere inside his son the spark of kindred spirit was alight and that perhaps in a few moons it would start to glow and burst into flame, lighting up the paths of the next generation.

Chantar and his family were only a short distance behind Buckwheat's, on the path to their setts. Chantar barked out his recognition and Buckwheat turned to await him. Chantar's concern for the effect that Buckwheat's efforts might have on his old friend quickly vanished as he saw the look of contentment in his eyes. Chantar silently thanked Logos for letting him have the close friendship of a badger of such immense strength of character, a strength that was reflected in his own family and others. He and Buckwheat parted company from their families as they travelled on to the Cadre for the latest assessment of the situation. Eldon had arrived earlier and appeared to be arguing over matters with Palos and Molyar, who had curtailed their evening feeding so as to be at the meeting before Buckwheat and therefore not miss anything. Palos had mistimed his first bid for glory and power but he was determined not to make the same mistake again.

The council was informed by Rhea that there were eighteen badgers too ill to be transported for more than one night and that some of those would not survive even that. There were seven others who felt that they did not have the strength to travel and requested that they journey the first night only and then be hidden and left with the others. Three of the families had stated that they would be responsible for taking their ailing parents onwards and all agreed that this request be granted. They were then told that there were thirty-seven cubs under four moons, and forty-five other cubs that would come under Harvey's supervision. Eldon could not see any sense in delaying the councillors' rest further, as it was just as important to them as to the others, and terminated the meeting, moving off to his bedchamber to get as much undisturbed sleep as possible.

Buckwheat and Chantar left for their setts, deep in thought, imagining all the events that could transpire on such a perilous journey. Buckwheat bid his friend farewell as he entered the sett for what he believed would be the last time, although he still hoped in his heart that there would be many more times.

There was a calmness at Cilgwyn that morning as the rest of the community returned for their day's rest after their night's foraging, but this was shattered a few hours later by the sound of strange noises coming from the ground above. There were murmurings and rumbling sounds, accompanied by high-pitched barking, and Buckwheat knew that no badger barked like that.

Beaufort and Buckwheat sprang to their feet immediately they were aware of these unrecognisable sounds. Buckwheat edged in front of Beaufort to one of the entrances to sniff out the meaning of these odd cries. The scent that greeted him sent terror racing through his heart, as evil seemed to be wafting its way into the sett. A soft, gentle breeze, instead of helping to sweeten the air of their sett, became the purveyor of henbane. There seemed to be many different voices, each sound sending a chill of fear into Buckwheat's bones. At first, feeling as if he would give way to panic, he turned to find Beaufort so calm and unafraid that he felt guilty at having condemned his son's placid, unresponsive nature in years gone by. There were advantages sometimes in taking a calm view of life. His mind returned to the events taking place above. Were they trapped or would it be as Bamber had said, the first two days spent shutting up their entrances, then the destruction? If that was how it turned out, then tonight they would be on their way and their mission of survival would begin.

Buckwheat went to scent the air from the dawn side entrance to his sett, and as he travelled he noticed that the movement of air through his home had ceased. Thudding sounds came from the end of the passageways. Where there should have been a glimmer of light bending round the corner of the angled entrance there was complete darkness. They were all being shut in. Buckwheat quickly informed his family that all but one entrance had been sealed off and that small air inlets had been placed in the closed-up entrances. They appeared to be long and narrow as no light penetrated them, and surrounding these shafts was the scent of destruction. Buckwheat silently pleaded with Logos to be allowed to make the journey. He didn't have to finish it, as long as he could help the community to get away, to get his Beaufort and Corntop to Elysia.

The noises were no longer overhead, and when the sun had reached halfway down its falling curve, the sounds had completely disappeared and the scent lost its strength, but those voices and the sudden sharp loud bangs still lingered in Buckwheat's memory. He knew that, like his family, the rest of the community would not emerge until total darkness was upon them. Then they would gather together and prepare to leave, and then slip away.

His faith was strong; he believed that all creatures who had faith in Logos would survive. Was there not a time when a similar calamity had struck at their ancestors? Had not Logos allowed two to be spared, to have faith in themselves and become the forebears of the first arrivals at Cilgwyn, just as the badgers of Cilgwyn would now begin again, in their new-found paradise?

8

Farewell Cilgwyn

Buckwheat had gathered his family ready to depart from their sett, and they moved out as the sun bade its last farewell to the badgers at Cilgwyn. As they emerged they heard frantic squeals coming from higher up the slope. Buckwheat galloped as fast as he could to find out what it was that was causing such wails of anguish. A small group of badgers had gathered in a circle near the centre of the community. As Buckwheat came upon them, he became aware of whimpering as well as squealing. He burst through the badgers, only to halt suddenly at the sight that lay in front of him. He quickly turned to prevent Fern and Corntop, who were following up behind, from witnessing the spectacle. Buckwheat told them to find Eldon and request that he, Palos, Chantar, Molyar and ten or more other senior males come quickly, and also to tell all female badgers and cubs to keep away. Buckwheat turned back to find Beaufort, frozen as a statue, staring blankly at the mound of dead badgers that had been the cause of the wailing and fearful cries.

Buckwheat ordered all the females and the youngsters who had seen the terrible sight to leave and shelter in the Cadre

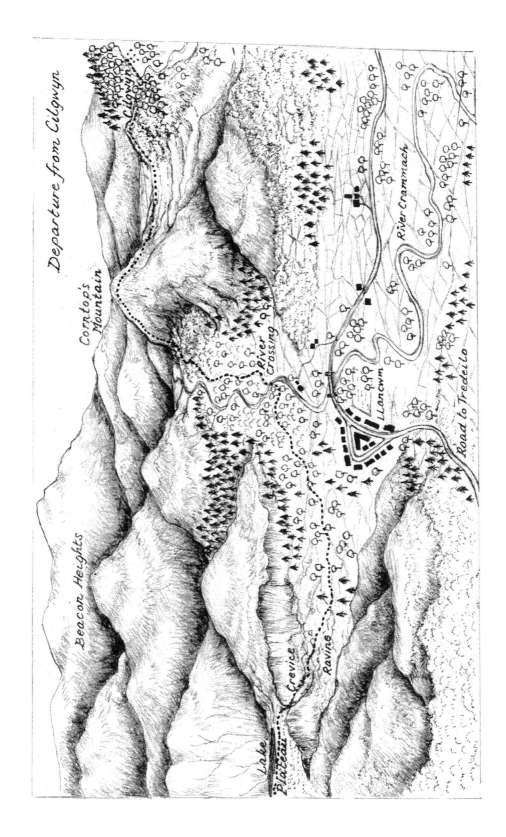

halls. He jolted Beaufort into action by telling him and the other males to separate the dead badgers in order that they might be identified and counted. There were twenty-three of his neighbours lying on that once peaceful earth, twenty-three friends who would not be joining him on the sunset journey. Twenty-three torn and mutilated bodies, of which he recognised most by name. He saw one of the males bending over one of the bodies, tenderly stroking the face and then moving to the next and the next, repeating his loving gestures. Buckwheat moved to him, to find it was Fircone. He had lost his mate of only fifteen moons and his two female cubs of just three. Buckwheat, now joined by Beaufort, moved along the other dead and recognised Honeyberry, who, despite being widowed for some years, had continued to live on her own. She was practically torn to pieces, as if she had been attacked by a hundred foxes. There was Bilberry with a hole in the side of his head; another with the same mark was Logan, who had become a father of five cubs just four moons earlier. They had never harmed anything, gentle law-abiding badgers, destroyed on their first acquaintance with man.

Eldon and the others Buckwheat had asked for arrived, and for a moment were transfixed by the scene of bloodshed and devastation that confronted them. Buckwheat then called Eldon and his council fellows to one side and explained that there was no time to lose before the journey started. There was not even time to bury the dead, they had to be left as they were, as every moment wasted brought the enemy that much nearer. Eldon and the others needed little persuasion to get away from the certainty of such a cruel and brutal death. Eldon's lingering hopes of waking to a change of plans were shattered. He was now as keen as anyone to get away and barked out that everyone was to gather as they had done for the community meeting, just below the ridge. Buckwheat turned to find that Beaufort was standing beside Fircone, and moving to Fircone's other side, consoled him as best he could as they moved down to the gathering.

There were three hundred and forty-one badgers instead of the expected three hundred and sixty-four who assembled on the gentle slope late that evening. Harvey had already organised the cubs into columns of twelve, some of their mothers at either side of the group, and Buckwheat could see that the old and infirm were being supported by their relatives. Then, with Beaufort, Palos and the other monitors, he moved into the main body of badgers, ready to encourage those whose efforts began to flag. Eldon barked, and movement rippled in an increasing line as his loyal subjects rose and prepared to follow him to their destiny to the promised land of Greyears's prophecy. How many would survive to fulfil such a dream?

Eldon's pace governed the advance of the badgers as the tight-knit mass of bobbing black-and-white symmetry crossed the stream at the far end of the valley and moved into the woods, which shredded the group wider. It was ideal, suiting young and old. Eldon had got so far out of condition with his slothful existence that his pace was casual, even though he himself believed it to be bold and vigourous.

Buckwheat noticed that a few of the old and infirm were already suffering and wished that before their struggles became impossible they would be over the first rise and out of sight of their birthplace. No matter what happened that target was the minimum they must achieve. He moved amongst the struggling little groups, seeing the concern and worry for their ailing relatives that cast deep, anxious frowns on their faces. After a short distance he trotted forward to meet up with Eldon, turning back to see if Palos, Chantar, and Molyar had seen him so that they, too, would join them. It had been prearranged that if one of the councillors came upon a difficulty affecting the whole group, he would meet up with the leader, the others joining to discuss and sort out the problem. Buckwheat explained the predicament of the struggling badgers and expressed his opinion that they should halt as soon as possible for a short rest to allow the failing badgers to recover some of their strength. Palos thought that halting them would be mad and that if they were going to stop after travelling such a short distance, there would be little chance of them clearing the ridge that night. It would mean leaving themselves exposed to the sight of man when he returned. Three hundred and more badgers would never be able to conceal themselves completely. Buckwheat was asking over three hundred badgers to put their lives in jeopardy for the sake of a pawful.

Eldon, while not really struggling, had been thinking of the first resting place soon after he had set out at the head of the column, and he expressed his opinion that stopping to rest would enable everyone to feed at the same time, thus giving renewed strength and vigour to all, and so they came to break for their first rest. Palos was clearly annoyed at the decision and turned away sharply, closely followed by Molyar. Buckwheat's eyes followed Palos as he returned to the crowd, and he also noticed that Kronos and his cronies were in quite an animated discussion. Buckwheat's concentration was broken by a slurping sound coming from behind him, and as he turned he could not help but smile at the nonchalant manner of Eldon, who was eating worms as if it were just a moonlight stroll.

Fern and Corntop were turning the undergrowth over, searching for grubs and beetles, when Buckwheat came upon them. He explained what had taken place, and the two females whickered their admiration for his forbearance towards the afflicted and gave thanks to Logos for having Buckwheat's cloak of protection over them. Buckwheat queried Deaufort's absence and was a little embarrassed at his obvious pride when told that his son was busy helping to gather food for the old ones.

Buckwheat quickly gulped down a large mouthful of grubs that Fern had uncovered and then trotted through the foraging badgers to help Beaufort. On his way he noticed one of Kronos's friends busy gesticulating and talking to a group of adolescent male badgers. Then Buckwheat saw Kronos himself also engaged in discussion but with a different group. By the time he arrived at the badgers who were being tended by Beaufort, he realised that he must have passed six or seven groups being addressed by either Kronos or one of his friends. He mentioned the matter to Beaufort, who replied that Palos had visited the sick ones and had snapped at them that they must do better and strive harder so that they would not place everyone else in peril. The depressed families of the helpless badgers were now full of remorse and guilt and Buckwheat saw defeatism in their eyes. He whispered gently to them, as anger swelled up inside him, that they shouldn't take too much notice of Palos as he was overeager to protect everyone and had allowed his own nervous tension to be exposed.

Buckwheat then tugged Beaufort after him as he went in search of Palos. He saw him addressing yet another group, but this did not deter him from calling out Palos's name in a voice that was flint-edge sharp, cutting through the air as piercingly as a blast of ice-laden wind. Palos looked startled as he heard his name being called and, seeing it was Buckwheat, responded by first running, then, remembering his equal station, ambling up to him. It was the closest Buckwheat had come to striking a badger in anger in his life. He fought hard to control himself before he eased the tension inside him by lashing Palos with his tongue, threatening such violence that Palos slowly cringed until he could look at Buckwheat no more and saw in the eyes of his fellow badgers that while Buckwheat was alive his own chances of becoming leader had gone. Kronos, hearing the disturbance, had stood behind his father while the vehement tirade rushed from Buckwheat. He now stepped forward, not to defend his father's actions, but to criticise Buckwheat for making a public issue of the matter, thereby creating fear and mistrust amongst them all when it was a show of unity that was needed if they were going to pull through. Buckwheat knew that he, too, had been wrong to let his anger get the better of him and felt ashamed that he had given such a chastisement to Palos for creating discord when he himself was now guilty of the same thing. Corntop, seeing that Beaufort was uncertain whether he should interfere, stepped forward, towards Buckwheat and Palos, and put the matter in greater perspective by asking whether the badgers believed that it should be one for all and all for one in their endeavours to escape from the slaughter that lay just behind them. The old ones must be helped and encouraged, not have their spirits lowered even further by being admonished for something that was no fault of theirs. Barks of approval broke out and Corntop scurried away to shelter in Fern's company and be soothed by her gentle ways. Eldon had now arrived on the scene and, after taking Buckwheat and Palos aside for a few moments of brief discussion, turned and informed the waiting badgers that it was time to move on.

Out of the woods they moved, converging as the trees no longer separated the rows of badgers. Buckwheat, having seen that Harvey and his assistants were coping magnificently with the young, had returned to the old ones, cajoling and encouraging them with every stride. Knowing that the mantle of Buckwheat's protection was over them, the families and friends of the old had gained in confidence and went forward with even greater determination than when they had first started out.

Meanwhile, Beaufort, carrying out the task he had been set of mingling between the rows of badgers, saw, a short distance in

front, Palos and Kronos arguing with each other. It appeared
that Kronos was getting the better of his father. He saw him
leaving Palos's side with an admonishing gesture and then join
up with his own clique, who had been moving forward a few
badger's lengths away. Kronos was full of smiles as his stride
matched his friends', who were grinning and patting his back as
if he had won a great victory. Kronos believed that he had won
and knew in his heart that his father would no longer be between him and his bid for leadership when the time for such a
move presented itself. What was equally pleasing was that he
had inflicted his first wound on Buckwheat.

Beaufort increased his pace to catch up and pass Palos. The
discomfiture of the councillor was obvious to all who glanced at
him. His head bowed, his face crestfallen, he was no longer a
prospective leader but a broken, pitiful old badger. As Beaufort
eased his pace to that of the others, it was not long before he
realised that they were going forward in a series of ten or so
paces of steady progress, then slowing down for four or five.
Going ahead to investigate this strange pattern, he discovered
the cause to be nothing more than Eldon himself. It was as if
Eldon were out on a foraging expedition without a worry in the
world. He would slow down to pick up whatever food he could
find, worms, grubs, beetles and even a mushroom or puffball.
His mouth full, he would saunter the next ten paces, swallowing
his savouries, then slow down to gather his next mouthful. At
this rate their night's mission would undoubtedly fail, and to
avoid delaying things further by asking Buckwheat to advise
Eldon to speed things up, Beaufort barked loudly his query as to
why the pace was slowing down. Eldon turned his head and,
realising his absent-mindedness, returned to the steady, continuous pace that was required, feeling somewhat abashed but
smiling to himself as his filling stomach gave him satisfaction.
They made good progress during the final hour and at last came

within barking distance of the ridge. As the land inclined more steeply, the final stretch to the top of the ridge was more arduous than anything they had previously covered.

Buckwheat had by now joined up with Eldon, turning to ascertain whether the other councillors had seen him. He was quickly joined by Chantar and Molyar, but Palos had stayed behind, dejected and lost. Buckwheat suggested that a brief stop be made so that the old ones could summon up enough strength to conquer the daunting task of the incline ahead. If they didn't rest, he felt that the efforts needed would defeat some of them, and a few would never live to scale the ridge.

Eldon, being the sort of badger never to decline such an invitation, immediately barked a halt to the journey. Molyar said nothing and turned round to walk back to join Kronos and his group, ignoring Palos, his lifelong friend.

Again Beaufort returned to assist the sick and aged. It was obvious to him that there were two badgers in particular who would need a miracle to survive the climb ahead, and even if they did, they would not be long on this earth, as such an effort would almost certainly take its toll. As Beaufort shook his head to clear away the cloud of sadness that had overtaken him, he saw his father gazing at him intently. They were seeking in each other a solution, knowing that one could not be found.

They saw, too, that while the other badgers squatted, Kronos and his friends had split up once more and were again busying themselves chatting and urging some point or another to various groups of badgers, badgers who had no family ties with either Kronos or his friends. Buckwheat and Beaufort wondered what the conniving, insufferable rogues were up to, but soon cast aside their thoughts as more urgent matters were at hand.

The signal from Eldon came soon after Buckwheat had roused him from a deep sleep. He would never understand how any badger could reach such a level of suspended animation in so short a time after what was, to him, a casual stroll. He felt sure that Eldon had complete confidence that he would return to his Utopian grandeur once the ridge ahead had been surmounted. Jason would turn in his grave if he knew of his son's lackadaisical philosophy and behaviour.

Returning quickly to join his ailing charges, he found that Fern and Corntop had joined with Beaufort in assisting the fragile seniors to triumph over their adversity. Buckwheat saw, too, that Fircone, despite his grief, was assisting a very old boar badger whose own family had been killed during the early part of that fateful day.

The struggle that ensued in the attempt to get all the badgers over that rise was to remain in the memory of Buckwheat and most of the others until they died. What Buckwheat had estimated would take only a short period of sustained effort took much longer. The badgers covered only half the distance in the time that he had estimated, and the length of the procession stretched further and further. Buckwheat suggested to Eldon, Chantar and Molyar that it would be best if Eldon made every effort to scale the remaining distance as quickly as possible while extra badgers assisted Harvey and his youngsters to maintain the same speed. Buckwheat suggested that five families of similar numbers to his own and experienced in parental care should assist Harvey. Buckwheat, with his own family and Fircone, would stay behind to help the stragglers to the top. Chantar and his relations, together with other groups of badgers, were soon attaching themselves to particular invalids as the final effort commenced.

It was not long before cries of happy voices rained down from above him, and Buckwheat realised that the main group had succeeded in reaching its target and he hoped that this would encourage something extra from his beloved dependents. They moved just a few paces at a time, but there was no point in prolonging the suffering of the stronger of the stragglers, and the healthiest of the weak badgers were urged to go ahead as quickly as they could, leaving Buckwheat, Chantar and their families to help with the back markers. Fircone could not get his old boar to go any further, as his will to survive had gone. Fircone somehow got the old one onto his back, and biting the greying hairs on the old one's paws, which were clasped round his neck, he rose and started out with his burden, which had become so endearing and companionable to him. Buckwheat looked up and saw Fircone valiantly striving to save his new friend's life.

Some of the way carrying, then pushing, prodding, nudging and lifting their old friends, it was quite some time before the last of the badgers took their final steps over the ridge. Buckwheat and all the others collapsed with sheer exhaustion from their Herculean efforts. As he lay panting he saw Fircone caressing his old companion with joy in his eyes. The old one had survived, and the achievement and rest were quickly restoring a vitality into his old limbs that belied his sixteen years.

Beaufort regained his strength quicker than Buckwheat and, checking the well-being of the last few ailing badgers, appeared crestfallen when he came to help his father to his feet. Beaufort felt cheated when he told Buckwheat that as far as two of the badgers were concerned, their efforts had been in vain. Successfully scaling the ridge, their fight to succeed had been too much, and as they rested the final and everlasting peace had overtaken them and they would journey no more, other than that final elevation to eternal life.

Eldon, who had either been feeding or resting the past hour and more, unexpectedly showed his sorrow at the loss of two adventurers, aged though they were, but at least they had died in their attempt for freedom rather than being brutally murdered in their own homes.

Buckwheat asked Eldon to convene the council and went to fetch Palos as Beaufort moved over to inform Molyar. Buckwheat found a very dejected Palos lying down alone, deserted even by his mate, Tawna. He glanced up on hearing Buckwheat's voice but refused to attend council. He no longer wanted any part of it or its members and just wanted to be left alone. Despite Buckwheat's continued pleading there was no change in Palos's attitude, and Buckwheat returned, bitterly disappointed in the badger who had changed from being an eminent figure to a pathetic one.

Buckwheat informed Eldon of Palos's response and advised that the badgers and their families seek out resting places that were well concealed for their rest in the day that would soon be dawning. As soon as this was completed the badgers should eat as much food as they could in the little time that was left before the sun broke out of its own sleep and lit the earth with its enriching warmth.

Eldon then barked the command, and the badgers moved, spreading in an enlarging circle, deep into the wild undergrowth of bramble, bracken and fern. Cleverly hidden entrances were made into the many bramble bushes, while some badgers decided they would bed in the green fern, pulling the stems down over them in such a manner that they would completely obliterate the light of the sun. After their explorations the badgers were soon feeding hungrily. No longer the selective foraging they had enjoyed at Cilgwyn but voraciously eating anything edible that crossed their path. As the lightening sky gave its first warning of the sun's imminent rise, the badgers received sharp reminders from Buckwheat and the other monitors to disperse to their new-made setts. Buckwheat could not see Eldon, but this did not bother him as he tunnelled into

thick bracken behind Beaufort, Fern and Corntop and they pulled it down over them as they sought the rest that they so desperately needed. Eldon would no doubt be slumbering in a bed of comfort prepared by Scylla, his wife. He had probably fallen asleep long before anyone else had half satisfied their hunger. Buckwheat was showing signs of great strain after his labours of the past few days and Beaufort realised that his father's age was telling on him and that he would not be able to endure such pressure for a very long period. Beaufort decided that he would try to carry out more of the physical side of things, leaving Buckwheat to concentrate on his wise counselling.

9

Kronos

The constant scurrying back and forth of a few ants on Beaufort's face irritated him enough to awaken him from a heavy sleep. He moved his tongue over his snout, picking up some ants, and shook the remainder off as his senses flooded back.

He was immediately aware of an unusual silence and, pushing his head up through his cover of bracken, he saw that the sky was now of lavender hue, touched with a fuzziness of saffron. Beaufort began to understand how much the previous night's effort must have exhausted everyone, as normally at this time of day the badgers would be preparing themselves for the night's foraging and domesticities. The stillness was only occasionally broken by the call of a settling rook.

He rose, shaking bits of bracken off his coat, and snorted his greeting to any of his comrades who were awake. Surprisingly there were quite a number, and he then realised that it was their fear that made them silent and that they were waiting for one or another to make the first move in the strange surroundings.

In a few moments practically all the badgers had freed themselves from their daytime cover. The strain had not completely left Buckwheat's face, and Beaufort became more aware of the task his father had taken upon himself. Buckwheat barked at the watching badgers to forage and eat as much as they could before they started out once more on their flight to freedom.

Buckwheat told his own family to do likewise and joined them in their search for worms, larvae grubs or anything that would help to sustain them on their trek into the unknown. The whole area became as busy as a wasp's nest, and snuffing and snorting sounds abounded as the badgers concentrated on their work. After a while Buckwheat moved quietly up to Beaufort and asked him if he had seen or heard anything of Eldon. It was only then that they both realised that he had not emerged with the others. Buckwheat immediately barked for the others to be silent, and then they could hear a rhythmic snoring coming out of a clump of bushes. Buckwheat and Beaufort went toward the sound. Quickly the others followed and then, prising the bushes apart, they looked down at the round figure lying on its back with a grin of pure contentment on its face. Yes, it was Eldon, and soon infectious guffaws were breaking out until they were all laughing. Eldon stirred, not realising how helpful he had been in easing the apprehension that had been so strong within them. Buckwheat's tensed face had eased. Well, Beaufort thought, Eldon certainly had some uses.

The lantern of the night had now reached its brightest, and the sky, with its galaxies, clusters and constellations, twinkled and sparkled, giving a beauty to the earth that held Beaufort in a spell of wonderment. He lowered his eyes to see that the main body of the badgers had gathered, awaiting instructions. Seeking guidance from Buckwheat, Beaufort's eyes roved over the badgers to try to locate him. Not seeing him, he turned and looked up at the ridge, and there, silhouetted against the sky,

were the figures of three badgers, Buckwheat, Fern and the unmistakable portly figure of Eldon.

The memories of years gone by rushed through Buckwheat's mind as he huddled close to Fern. The threesome were feasting their eyes for the last time on the moonlit panorama of their beloved Cilgwyn. This would always be their home, but Buckwheat would search for a new Cilgwyn, not for himself but for Beaufort, Corntop, Fircone and the generations to come.

The three badgers turned in unison and slowly walked down to the waiting assembly. Buckwheat turned to Eldon to offer his advice for the night's journey but held back his words as he noticed that his old compatriot's eyes were glazed with tears and he was using all his strength of will to hold them back.

Buckwheat's arrival was greeted with the news that two of the ailing badgers had taken their separate journeys to Asgard during the day's rest and that ten of the others were too weak to continue. With everyone's safety in mind, they had decided to stay until either their strength returned or they were beckoned by Logos. Fircone would remain to look after them, one of the ten being the old boar he had carried the night before. Although some of the relatives wished also to stay, they were persuaded to leave by Buckwheat, who advised them that the fewer that stayed, the better the chances were that those remaining would be undiscovered. Two other infirm badgers decided that they would journey on, but at their own pace, following the scent of the main party until they would eventually catch up with it. Fircone impressed upon Buckwheat that they should regularly use their scent glands so that, when it was time for him to bring his small group, he would have little difficulty in finding them.

Eldon appeared now to have regained his composure and was about to bark the signal to move on when Kronos intercepted, asking why everything was being organised without everyone having his say. Fircone, nervous for his elderly wards, barked in annoyance with such vehemence that Kronos immediately stopped his objections and moved so quickly behind Eldon that the journey started suddenly without Eldon's signal being required.

There appeared to be no major obstacles ahead of them that evening. The land ahead was flat, covered in scrub and bush with frequent outcrops of limestone interspersed. It seemed to Beaufort that they might be able to put a fair distance behind them that night but he worried for his friend Fircone, the splendid badger who consistently showed his devoted chivalry towards others. He quietly prayed for Logos's mantle to cover his friend and allow them to meet up again quite soon.

There was a much quicker pace to their travels and the moon still had a fair amount of its night's life left when they had covered a greater distance than the previous night. Occasionally they came across the scent of the fox and rabbit, but there were not many signs of the area being populated other than by insects, beetles, worms and birds. There wasn't a tree in sight, but their path was well hidden by gorse and bracken. There were too many of them for their tracks to be covered completely, but they hid their dung well into the bracken as there was no time to dig their usual pits.

Their progress pleased Buckwheat and he recognised many things as being the same as at home—the clumps of hawthorn partly strangled by the purple-veined vetch that climbed up its sprigs, full of summer's sap, the air now and then being perfumed by the lovely smell coming from the sweet-tasting trumpets of honeysuckle. Phalanxes of the heady foxglove swayed as the surging group of badgers brushed past, onwards, ever onwards into an abyss of paradise.

Feeling his legs growing a little weary, Buckwheat eased his pace, only then realising that it was he, closely flanked by the ever-faithful Fern and Corntop, who was leading the band of badgers that was spread out behind him. He saw Beaufort, Chantar, Gruff and other monitors helping the older ones. His face creased with a pang of worry as he could not locate Eldon and he thought for a moment that the old leader might have been left behind, searching for some titbits of food. He stopped the march and looked for Eldon's bulky figure, the badgers remaining silent as they awaited their orders. Then Buckwheat's attention was caught by the playful frolics of some of the cubs, and there was Eldon playing with them. Harvey could now share his responsibilities with his new partner. He couldn't have a better one, Buckwheat mused. Eldon would soon be regaling his young friends with tales of the past, substituting himself for the heroes in the legends of olden times.

As Buckwheat sighed with relief, the tiredness in him became stronger and, looking at his weary compatriots, he suggested that as there was not much time before the birds began to herald the new day, they had better find what food they could before discussing plans for the next night and then bed down for the day.

There seemed to be nourishment in plenty, the thick humus about the bracken full of cockchafer grubs, earthworms and moth larvae, and, tired though they were, the badgers packed their stomachs as quickly as they possibly could.

Buckwheat, Beaufort and Chantar had joined up with Eldon, who considered it a marvellous idea to stop and find such abundant food. He thought that they might regard it as suitable for their new home. The others quickly realised that Eldon would never fully understand the seriousness of their predicament and they decided it would be futile discussing ideas and plans for the pilgrimage that confronted them.

They returned to the waiting badgers to explain that they would continue with the same system the following night, first feeding, then making, hopefully, the same progress as they had achieved since leaving Fircone and the old ones behind. The badgers were by now eager to prepare their open setts for a well-earned rest, but Vulcan, one of Kronos's allies, expressed the opinion that everyone would feel happier if the council were brought up to full membership and a replacement found for Palos, who now sought no one else but himself. It would create a greater sense of security for everyone if they could see that their lives were still being safeguarded by the same rules and regulations that had protected them for generations past.

Buckwheat glanced at his son, and Beaufort, realising his father's intentions to nominate him, shook his head, forbidding him from doing so. He quickly explained that he believed membership on the council should be spread amongst different families, that this was traditional. But Buckwheat, annoyed and disappointed, moved away, shaking his head and muttering to himself.

Vulcan, finding no objections to his suggestion, quickly proposed Kronos as the new member. The listening badgers were by now more interested in settling down to slumber than in raising objections, even if they believed they should do so. There were no other proposals and Kronos found himself a badger of status, which seven months ago he would never have believed could be possible. Buckwheat's mutterings were even louder as he pulled the bracken over him. Beaufort, somewhat dazed at the speed of Kronos's election, tried to shake the shivers from his back at what he had allowed to happen, suddenly feeling he had caught a wasp by the sting.

10

Corntop Climbs a Mountain

The day had passed without incident, and the foraging period went by quickly. Eldon continued to share the fostering duties with Harvey, and Buckwheat found himself at the head of the column once again.

The terrain had now begun to change, the bushes and bracken giving way to heather, and the land ahead appeared to rise in a gentle gradient to the horizon. Buckwheat's concern was easing by the hour and he began to feel that good fortune was at last rearing its head out of the traumatic events of the past few days.

Travelling without stopping soon brought them to the horizon point that had seemed so far distant when they had started off. The ground now sloped more sharply, through heather first, then dense woodlands, primarily beech but with a few pines clustered here and there. Buckwheat was happier still when they got under the cover of the trees. He had been worrying about concealment for the next day's rest as the heather would never hide such a large number of badgers.

As they made their way through the woods the sound of

marching paws became thunderous as it reverberated under the umbrella of the frondescent roof. This resonance was broken only once, by the high-pitched death squeal of some small animal that an owl had successfully plucked from the woodland floor.

Buckwheat halted after he emerged from the woods and the trailing group faltered, then closed up on both sides. Buckwheat took a few steps forward, turned round, glancing to his left, then to his right, his relaxed mood allowing him to be amused at the sight of a line of small bands of badgers stretching across the edge of the woods, over three hundred faces peering through the gaps in the trees. They saw, as he did, that in front of them there was scrubland with plenty of bracken, but then, alarmingly, the little dell narrowed into a range of steep hills, the summits being sparsely covered.

Unhesitatingly, Buckwheat sought out Eldon, Chantar, Molyar and Kronos to offer his suggestions for the remainder of the night. It was quickly agreed that they shelter either in the woods or the scrublands. It would be too dangerous to leave themselves exposed on the hills ahead. They would satisfy their appetites, have a full rest and then they would feel strong enough to climb the hills during the following night.

Some of the pads on the paws of the younger cubs were beginning to feel tender, but Rhea, the healing badger, soon provided a soothing oil made up of balm and hissop. It was important that pad wear was dealt with as soon as it appeared, as nothing would deter progress more.

The next night darkness fell earlier due to the skies being filled with thick and heavy clouds that promised rain. Beaufort worried a little that the scent marks might be washed away by the time Fircone commenced his journey.

The rippling movement of the badgers seemed more pronounced as they moved through the scrubland that night. They huddled close together, as there was no light from the moon and only the sound of rustling as they kept mute, heading towards the foothills along unfamiliar terrain, free of the comforting scents that would normally be found on their well-worn paths at Cilgwyn.

Buckwheat took solace in the thought that as they became exposed on the higher slopes of the hill, they would at least be hidden by the dark clouds, but as he led the refugees up the foothills the first drops of rain began to fall. They proceeded steadily up the lower reaches, but the vegetation had now become scarce and it was mostly frost-worn rock that their paws gripped upon. Then the sky began emptying its ever-threatening downpour upon them and they were saturated in less time than it took a badger to eat a few worms. It was difficult to recognise one badger from another as the rain lashed into their faces. The hot air of weeks past had made the atmosphere oppressive and many trembled as the lightning forked and thunder cracked its roar at the hillside.

Their hustling pace slowed considerably as they slipped and slithered on the wet lichen and moss-covered rock beneath them. The heavy rain continued without abating and Beaufort hurried as best he could through the struggling throng to draw his father's attention to the group that was now straggling a long way back. Unfortunately the back markers found the hillside more treacherous than the leaders as they sought paw-holds on a surface that had been made more slippery due to the constant scrambling made on the surface by those ahead.

Buckwheat was surprised at the distance between himself and the rearmost badgers, and rather than allow the pace to slow even more, he told Beaufort to pass the word for the group to fan out so that their paw-holds would become easier.

Buckwheat thought that if he could find something for them to concentrate on, they would be distracted from the misery of their pain-racked discomfort. He muttered his idea to Fern and Corntop, who had steadfastly kept up with him, and it was Corntop who suggested that she should forge ahead on her own as far as she could travel, hopefully reaching the summit, where she would wait for them. The pride of the boar badgers would not allow them or their families to be shown up by a young sow. Buckwheat thought Beaufort would stop Corntop from venturing ahead into unfriendly and unknown territory, but before he could tell her of Beaufort's right to decide, Corntop had forged ahead. This was the second time that Corntop had shown her quiet but determined qualities of concern for her fellow kind. Buckwheat watched, as she disappeared into the wall of rain that was ahead, with a fondness and love no less than he had for his son. His heart warmed at her quiet courage and he knew that her ways would always be ways of pleasantness, and her heart would always follow the path of peace.

The news of Corntop's daring deed soon spread to all the badgers and it seemed as if it had had the desired effect on them, as the pace quickened, the males strenuously urging their families on. They could not leave her alone on the mountaintop for too long a time and they responded with tenacity and a new vigour. Beaufort, fearful for Corntop's safety, was now leading, his heart telling him to surge ahead to find her although Buckwheat had persuaded him that this might weaken the effect of her heroic action.

Buckwheat was now feeling his years drag on him as he strained to keep up the pace Beaufort was maintaining. This infertile, acarpous mountainside was steadily weakening the physical as well as the mental state of all of them. The line of badgers was being broken in many places, as the weakest could no longer keep up. Buckwheat felt that there was a visitation of Ahriman upon them.

On they struggled, no longer marching but crawling, sliding, stumbling, with broken claws, ruptured pads, lacerated limbs, their soft belly fur torn, their eyes stinging from the whirlblast of gale-force wind and frenzied, cascading rain.

Then, after what seemed an eternity, they came through the rain cloud that had skirted the upper reaches of this colossus of a mountain. The weather cleared and the sight that confronted Beaufort brought joy to his heart, for at the peak of this eminence was the statuesque figure of his cherished Corntop. Buckwheat could now see her, too, and for just a moment forgetting the rest of his charges, he inhaled deeply, first with relief, then with immeasurable pride. This noble female badger, his son's wife, was surely on the side of the angels. She would always be safe, for she walked humbly, her paw closely held in the paw of Logos.

As the stragglers arrived at the peak the noise of admiring grunts and growls at Corntop's brave dedication reached a crescendo, and Buckwheat, feeling the power of Logos about them, suggested that, before they commenced the descent down to their day's rest, they should give thanks to Logos by saying together the prayer that all had been taught when they were cubs.

The Badger's Prayer

To the Creator we ask and plead
Just for the simple things we need.
We thank you for life, we seek not much,
Grass and clover, herb and rush,
For peaceful nights under silent cloud
Touching paws, coats standing proud,
Little we need to keep us merry,
Worm and grub, corn and berry.
Away from man, never to be found
Slumbering safely under ground.
To roam at will, through meadow and lea,
Harming none, to wander free.
Enjoying each day, every hour,
The sun, the moon and the flower.
Part of life's joys, giving none sorrow,
Please grant a peaceful morrow.
Keep us from evil, let us be wise,
Let compassion be our eyes,
Then getting old, we shall seek rest
In your Island of the Blest.

11

The Disaster

With a renewal of their faith, the protection of their Maker and a belief that the worst was behind them, the badgers commenced the descent of the mountain with strong hearts.

It did not take long, however, before their confidence began to wane once more, their minds filling with trepidation, then panic and then horror as their gradual pace quickened. Their paw-holds gave way to slithering, tumbling, rolling, falling, their already battered bodies were torn and smashed on the froth-covered, flintlike surface of the mountain. The rains had made the sloping hill into one gigantic slide anointed by the devil himself, and it had become a network of plunging paths.

The badgers spiralled and twisted as they rolled and it became an unstoppable stampede. Some believed that they were entering Sheol, and yet, although it seemed an eternity, it was all over in a few fleeting moments, their uncontrollable onwards rush coming to a halt as their pain-racked bodies crashed into the thickening growth of heather and gorse.

Buckwheat, breathless and winded, lay where he had come to a painful stop, and as his dazed mind cleared itself, the sound of squealing, terrified badgers crashing into the vegetation echoed around him. The sounds intensified and then died away before giving way to agonised screams, wails of torment, pain and sobbing.

Buckwheat raised himself and, quickly disregarding his own aches and pains, searched about him, surveying the devastation that lay on all sides. Many of his companions were motionless and he saw some with their limbs broken and twisted, some with their heads at impossible angles, some with blood gushing out of terrible wounds. His faith in himself collapsed as a wave of guilt swept over him. It was he who had led them on this path. It was he who had brought them to this destruction. But quickly shaking his wretchedness away, the strength that was ever present in his soul again reared itself into a tower of a badger as he moved amongst the injured, his mind searching frantically for a method of restoring calm and order. His courage returned a thousandfold as he saw Beaufort, Fern and Corntop making their way towards him. They, too, had escaped serious injury and, other than a few sprains and bruises, had survived without permanent harm.

They came across Eldon, sitting up in a state of stupefaction, his mind still trying to understand what had happened. Buckwheat shook him until signs of life returned. Eldon looked pitiously at Buckwheat, utterly and hopelessly incapable of thinking straight, but his sense of responsibility to the young ones was paramount and, ambling off in search of them, he left the duties of stewardship to Buckwheat. It was with incredulity that Buckwheat and his family gazed at Eldon as he trundled away. This awkward, stumbling, portly badger had survived without so much as being winded, his appetite having assured him his safety.

Buckwheat soon organised Chantar, Kronos and Molyar into arranging small groups of their families and friends to go amongst the badgers to assess the situation and report back as quickly as possible to him, so that decisions could be made for their safe protection before the new day arrived.

Beaufort went to where the loudest of the poignant cries arose and his eyes met a sight that he would never forget. While his own family was practically unscathed, others had been far less fortunate. There seemed to be dead and dying badgers everywhere. He saw Rhea, the Healer, rise from a young cub, shaking her head. Although there wasn't a mark on it, it had broken its neck in the fall. Then Beaufort saw his friend Gruff's parents lying still, their lifeblood pumping out of the gaping wounds that were stretched across the sides of their bodies. When Beaufort had finished inspecting his charges, he found it difficult to choke back the tears. Nine of his companions had already come to the end of their travels, four more had such severe injuries they could never recover from them, and of the other thirty-odd he checked, there were at least three whose injuries would take a long, long time to heal and then only with a great deal of care.

Beaufort was the last of the badgers to return to his father. There was an air of shock, disbelief and near hopelessness about the circle of badgers that surrounded Buckwheat. When Beaufort had reported, Buckwheat announced that nineteen badgers had died, fourteen more would not see the next moon and twenty-seven would need the care of angels to restore them to normal physical health again, although there were many more who would be permanently scarred for the rest of their days.

The grim resolve in Buckwheat's voice roused his small audience from the depths of their despair. The bodies of the stricken badgers had to be moved. They could not be buried and would have to be hidden in the bushes and undergrowth, in vegetation that would conceal them the year through. The injured would also have to be placed in hiding where their wounds could be tended in the day. There would be little rest for any of them, as each walking badger was given a task, either moving the dead or gathering food or medicinal herbs and flowers.

Buckwheat realised that as they busied themselves with their work they were exposing themselves to danger. It was nearly the time of the midday sun when all the dead had been hidden away. Six more had sighed their final breaths and they, too, had been buried, and the remaining eight of the unrecoverable were hidden as best they could be in one group, surrounded by gorse and fern. The other mutilated badgers were split into their family groups, and Rhea advised each family how to make and administer the various remedies that had been with their kind since the time of the great waters.

From the more verdant vegetation lower down the slopes, many plants were brought back: wild thyme for fatigue, colt's-foot and safflower for the congested chests and coughs, yarrow or milfoil, with its aromatic lacelike leaves, easily recognised by its small white flowers tinged with pink and purple. The leaves were crushed in the badgers' jaws and were then spat into a small pile before being rubbed into the wounds of the badgers, stopping the poison entering their bodies.

There was the oil from the wormwood, its leaves deeply cut and covered in fine hair and used as a liniment to ease the aches of the sprains and bruises. Many more items from nature's med-icine store were administered, together with the tenderness of the caring badgers, and a number of the afflicted had improved considerably by the time the sun eased its threatening light over the hill above them.

Buckwheat called all the senior boars together and suggested that, as they were in no condition to travel that night, they should fill their stomachs with as much food as they could hold, and that all of the badgers should rest as much as possible, splitting the duties of nursing the sick into equal periods of time, so that each one would have done its share.

Beaufort sensed the relief amongst his colleagues, but also noticed a feeling of apathy at the idea of having to go on with their journey to find their new home. Beaufort also realised that Kronos was aware of this, and once again a shudder of foreboding ran down his back.

Before the sun returned nine more badgers had left the road to Elysia and had stepped onto the path to Asgard. Buckwheat, while feeling saddened by the loss of his brothers and sisters, felt consoled that they would no longer have to endure the agonies of their fatal wounds. Some of the less seriously injured had regained sufficient strength to become mobile, but there were three or four whose recovery was balanced on the edge of a sliver of slate. Buckwheat, dismayed by the passing of so many, knew that somehow he had to persuade the survivors to continue their journey. His thoughts returned to the previous day when his eyes had fallen upon the devastation that lay about him. Then for a moment he had felt defeated and had thought that their journey had ended in failure, but now his total commitment to find lasting peace had returned, and with strengthened confidence he strode to address his friends.

12

Buckwheat's Courage

The unofficial leadership of Buckwheat had, up until then, been accepted without any murmurs of disapproval, but as he addressed the congregation that now remained there were increasing whispers of discontent and disgruntlement. He informed them that, after resting through the day, plans would be made to continue their journey while providing for the safety of the sick and wounded. These would be decided by the council members during the first hours of darkness. Discontented cries rose from many directions, and Kronos, seizing the opportunity of leading at least some of the badgers, became the speaker for the disheartened ones. Their numbers increased as he stressed the need to make a permanent home in the lush verdure that lay a short distance down the hill, where those searching for herbs had found wooded glades abundant with food, shelter and everything else a badger could need. Some had even reported hearing the sound of running water not too far distant.

This lavish description that Kronos gave was enough to sway an ever-increasing number of badgers to his way of thinking, and soon his opinions were being cheered to the echo. Kronos stressed that their safety was more or less assured, as no other beings would believe that they had climbed and descended that torturous mountain. He said that he believed too many lives had been lost already and that he did not think that there were many of them left who could survive any more obstacles of that kind.

Although Greyears argued that they had not been given the promised sign and that there were some that would never believe Kronos whatever he said, most of the badgers gave their support to stay. Buckwheat realised that more restful and peaceful hours would have to pass before there could ever be a proper understanding of the need to move on. They must be made to see that splitting into two factions would cause greater troubles and more unhappiness.

Most were content with Buckwheat's suggestion to postpone the decision for at least another night as they believed that the beauty of the valley below would persuade anyone who reached it to stay forever.

The badgers rested most of the day, the females still adhering to their tasks of tending to the sick. The weather had remained dry, although the sky had been overcast. As most of the badgers stirred from their sleep, the air was heavy and humid. Buckwheat hoped that their short journey to the rich and fertile pastures would be undertaken free of rain, although the heavy air told him they would be lucky if the night passed before the sky once more let forth another of its downpours.

The eagerness of the badgers to settle in their new sanctuary became apparent to Buckwheat as they commenced the short walk, well before the evening closed the day. As Buckwheat entered the verdurous glades he had to admit to himself that they were indeed in an oasis of wondrous beauty. There were many shades of green surrounding him, emerald, jade, malachite, beryl, and he could see a kaleidoscope of colours emanating from the masses of wild plants that had inhabited the wood in peaceful harmony since time itself began. There was goldenrod, meadowsweet, meadow cranesbill and the yellow agrimony; there were bluebills, hartbells, bright scarlet poppies and purple-coloured campanulas. There were wild strawberries, wild raspberries and the large crimson fruit of the wild rose. There was oak, beech, alder and elder, birch, elm, horse chestnut and sweet chestnut. There appeared to be worms in the thousands, crane-flies, honey-bees, red-tailed bumble bees and more. The sounds of joy and delight coming from the badgers were mingled with the sound of the evening chorus of birds: blackbirds, thrushes, starlings, finches, yellowhammers, willow-warblers and white-throats.

Buckwheat could see that his own family was filled with enchantment, and he realised that there was no way in which he could get the bewitched and entranced badgers to discuss journeying onwards. Something drastic would have to occur before he would ever be able to persuade them to move on from this new-found paradise.

Although some of the more responsible badgers were waiting for instructions, Buckwheat could only mumble that as far as that evening was concerned, everyone could forage and settle in their nests and just enjoy themselves. The appetites of every badger, even Eldon, had been completely satisfied in a very short time, and so sated were they that many made their beds well before half the night was through. As Buckwheat settled into the soft bedding of freshly cut grass and fern, he felt the aches and sprains from his fall down the mountainside beginning to ease away. Although grateful that his companions would at least find some happiness after the recent tragedies, he could not stop the spasmodic shivers that gripped his body as a frightening sense of personal danger swept over him.

Buckwheat's uneasy sleep was brought to an end as he heard

his name being urgently grunted out. Beaufort could not believe his ears, yet that voice could belong to no other than Fircone. And it was Fircone that Beaufort could see as he emerged from his warm and snug bed. Fircone, recognising Beaufort, rushed over to him and, also finding Buckwheat there, recounted the events that had been his fate during the past days. The halcyon night ceased as Fircone told them that he was the sole survivor of the party that had been left behind. It had been only two nights after the main group had gone ahead that the enemy had descended on the temporary abode of the old ones. Fircone had heard the destroyers approaching with their dogs and had urged the badgers to separate and run as far as they could, hoping that some might escape. Fircone had taken the old one who had been in his special care since Cilgwyn with him, dragging, pushing, urging and sometimes carrying him away from the danger, eventually sheltering when they were out of earshot of the sounds of their foe. After darkness came Fircone had left him to return to search for survivors. He found all the badgers but he wished he had stayed with the old one, for they had been savaged by the dogs. None had had the strength to put up any resistance and had lain exhausted as the teeth of their brother animals, who were now guided by man, had sunk into their flesh, ripping them to pieces.

Fircone's grief was intensified when he returned to the old one to find that the strain had been too much for him, but he was thankful that at least he had died escaping the ravages of pain. He stayed to find out if he could detect the route the marauders intended taking. For two days he kept shadowing the hunters, staying at a safe enough distance but keeping just within hearing range of them. In the nights he returned to check on what they were doing. At first there appeared to be no definite plan about their searching, then the humans had set off in the direction that Buckwheat and the main group of badgers had taken. Fircone had followed them each day, sometimes picking up the scent of the Cilgwyn nomads, and had sheltered in a wood during the night of the great storm. The hunters returned the following morning and made rapid progress to the foot of the mountains, where they stayed for most of the day. They appeared to have trained a large bird, although it had no scent and looked nothing like any birds Fircone had ever seen. It made a roaring whirring sound as it moved up and down the side of the mountain. The men set up their homes at the mountain base, and when the day had finished their camp became lit up by firelight and from white lights that were suspended in the air or held in their hands. Fircone had skirted their camp, sometimes startled by the barking of dogs, but when he had got onto the heather on the hillside above the camp, the scent of his friends was much fresher and there were tracks galore. Fircone realised the hunters had discovered the path the badgers had taken, and if they continued to maintain such progress, they would soon be in striking distance of his friends. He decided it was time to warn his brothers of the impending peril. He crossed the mountain as they had, seeing immediately that there had been a disastrous accident, and now he had found them. He believed that with the help of the noisy bird it would not be more than a couple of days before the hunters were amongst them.

The cherished tranquillity of the previous evening now lay in fragments, as fear, despair and near panic once again took hold of the travellers. There were some, Kronos amongst them, who wanted to move on there and then. He was interested only in self-survival, the safety of others not concerning him. He would not agree to Buckwheat's suggestion of staying until the following night. Buckwheat tried to reason with Kronos that it would be futile to move on then, as day would shortly break, and they would easily be seen, if they travelled during the day, by the giant bird that Fircone had seen. It would be best if they all stayed together and planned the next step of the journey. It was hazardous enough as things were, and it would be catastrophic if the badgers separated and went in every direction. The small support that Kronos had diminished and then disappeared completely as the promised rain began to fall, a light drizzle at first and then a cloudburst as thunder and lightning roamed the sky.

The heavy rain did not abate for even a moment during the day, but at least there were no roaring winds. The glen, having received considerable rain during the past few days, had now become saturated and its floor was no longer a viridescent meadow but sported a chequered pattern of dripping green vegetation and splattering pools, the pools increasing in size as the rain continued to fall.

Fourteen badgers, who were far from strong enough to continue travelling, had to remain. Buckwheat allowed two of the wives to stay behind and administer to the sick, and when they achieved a return to health they could follow the trail of the setting sun. In his heart Buckwheat felt that never again would he see these badgers, yet he hoped that, should they fail, their passing into Asgard would be peaceful and without further suffering.

It was in the pessimistic belief that they were doomed to everlasting trials of endurance and tribulations that the badgers followed Buckwheat out of the glen they had believed to be paradise. The undergrowth was sodden, and they splashed through pools of water, feeling miserable and dejected long before they made any real headway. The clouds had cleared from the heavens, leaving the moon to shine clearly from a star-studded sky.

There were frogs and toads aplenty, but they ignored these as worms had come to the surface in great quantities and they foraged purely by instinct as they laboriously forged their way through the dank and sodden vegetation. The ground underfoot became more marshlike and swampy, and the trail they were leaving would be easy for others to find, man or beast, as the plants and greenery became downtrodden by the continuous pressure of the badgers' paws. They were into lands bearing different flora from that of the glen. Now they brushed through toadflax, ragweed, tansy, trefoil, bindweed and bent grass. The noise of running water, which had been heard in the peace and quietude of the glen, could be heard once more, becoming louder with their every step. It was obviously fast-running water, for its sound changed to a roar as they broke out of the vegetation. The badgers found themselves on the bank of what was normally a slow, meandering river but was now a raging torrent in full flood. It was carrying the spoilage of the heavy rains back to the sea. No land creatures could survive a single moment in that whirling vortex. Tree trunks that had once stood proudly on the banks further upriver had had their roots pulled from the earth by the velocity of the water and bobbed along the surface at an alarming speed, as leaves in a waterfall.

Buckwheat knew they had to cross the water and sent scouts to look for a safe place to cross. Beaufort went upstream with Fircone and Gruff; downstream went Zoilos, Whortleberry and Growler. The other badgers were told to rest by Buckwheat, forage if they wanted to, but to keep their distance from the river's edge. Some of the young sows were whimpering. Buckwheat understood their misgivings and asked Fern, Corntop and the stronger-willed badgers to go amongst those who cowered and trembled to help their confidence and courage to shine through. He was full of admiration for his old leader, Eldon, who with Harvey had become real stalwarts in protecting the cubs. They had gathered the cubs about them and, even at this dangerous time, were retelling stories of long ago, especially tales of courage and humour. The very young soon had most of their worries removed as they became totally hypnotised by Eldon's enactment of the stories.

Beaufort and his companions had returned to report that there was no place upriver where they could cross. If anything the flow appeared to be faster as many streams entered the river, causing dangerous currents and swirling eddies. Zoilos returned shortly after, explaining that the further downstream they went, the stronger became the scent of the animal man. They had found a flint-chipped path across the river with hedges of stone, but as they explored and investigated its suitability they saw lights suspended in the darkness a short way from the other side of the path and, remembering Fircone's description of the hunters' camp, retreated back to Buckwheat. On their return journey they noticed that some of the dislodged tree trunks had jammed and perhaps, with the utmost care, could be crossed. There was no alternative. The courage of the badgers was at such a low ebb that nothing would persuade them to go within scenting distance of the man-used river path.

They moved through the reeds and the tall rushes, passing the willow-herb, water figwort, hawkweed and burweed, their coats becoming covered in burs. Then they saw the trees and Buckwheat caught his breath as he told himself that to cross there would be a miracle. His heart told him that few would attempt to cross until they saw some badgers succeed. Buckwheat had to summon all the courage he possessed to commence the attempt at crossing. He was astonished to see that Kronos had joined him. Beaufort desperately tried to persuade his father to change places with him, but Buckwheat would have none of it. He concentrated as hard as he could on firmly gripping the trees with his long claws but soon released them as the waters bumped the tree trunks and nearly made him overbalance. He was trembling, but it was not at the danger of crossing but as if something dark and sinister were close at hand.

Beaufort and all the others watched spellbound as Buckwheat moved from one trunk to another. As the two badgers passed the middle of the river, Beaufort could see his father gesticulating at Kronos. Buckwheat seemed to be having great difficulty in balancing on a particular log, and when Kronos attempted to place his paw on the log, it had the disastrous effect of spinning it. Beaufort could not believe what happened next, and he barely recognised the sound as his own when he let out a cry of terror. He saw the log turn upside down on itself and then he saw his father hurtle into the surging, swirling waters. For a few moments the head of Buckwheat could still be glimpsed bobbing up and down as he was carried downstream in the roaring river. The noise of the river drowned out any cries for help.

Beaufort was still hoping to see his father reach shore when Kronos appeared in front of him, having returned back across the tree trunks. The alarm in Kronos's voice was not matched by the guileful cunning that was in his eyes. For an instant Beaufort wanted to bury his teeth into the throat of Kronos, extinguishing his life forever and sending him back to Sheol, where he surely belonged. He felt the restraining paw of Fircone, who then galloped away downstream to search for Buckwheat.

Beaufort followed quickly and they searched the riverside, in the reeds and rushes, amongst the tree roots that had had their supporting earth washed away, stopping often, hoping to hear Buckwheat's call above the roar of the water. Fircone went to search under the hanging boughs of a willow and his call brought joy to Beaufort's heart. But Fircone was crouched at the river's edge, the boughs of the willow partly submerged in the swollen floodwaters, and in their grasp they held Buckwheat. Beaufort rushed towards Fircone to help free his father but the spear of immeasurable grief struck into his heart as the sorrowful Fircone turned to try to stop him, but he brushed his friend aside as he would not believe his father was dead.

The paws of Beaufort dug into his father's coat and, with a single heave, pulled him out of the submerged branches onto the bank. He caressed him, rolled on him, pummelled his chest, but his grief became unbearable as he eventually realised his father would lead them no more. Beaufort turned to find his friend crying loudly to the heavens, asking why it was necessary to end the life of a badger who bore malice to no one and whose soul carried nothing but godliness. He fought hard to hold back his tears, having to choke his sobs as he saw that Fircone's eyes showed that he, too, felt the grief of Buckwheat's death, but Buckwheat had left his indelible mark on them. Though they at first thirsted for vengeance, they knew that such thoughts of revenge for their own self-satisfaction had to be set aside if Buckwheat's dream of reaching Elysia was to be realised.

They dug deeply under the drier side of the willow. The wet earth was excavated quickly and they lowered Buckwheat gently into his resting place. Beaufort scattered some yellow-headed ox-eye flowers on his father's body, the sign of reverence conferred only on the noblest of badgers, before Fircone covered the little grave with earth. Buckwheat was no lesser a badger than Bamber and merited the final resting place of chivalrous badgers. As Beaufort turned away his determination strengthened as his heart was fired by an oath to his dead father that he would get them to Elysia. He now understood what his father had sought in him and he would never stop trying to follow the example his father had set. He did not believe he would ever approach the qualities his father had borne, for Logos had surely lit a burning light of understanding in Buckwheat's heart, a light that would never go out.

13

Where Have All the Badgers Gone?

DAILY NEWS

Cilgwyn, South Wales
Friday, 10th May

A spokesman for the Ministry of Agriculture's badger extermination unit stated today that the largest colony of badgers ever recorded has been uncovered in the South Wales countryside. Whereas culls of over a hundred badgers have been achieved in other parts of the country, it appears that many more than this inhabit the remote area known as Cilgwyn.

Due to the immensity of the sett system, it has been decided that Major Robertson, director of operations, will personally supervise the extermination of the badgers at Cilgwyn.

MORNING TRIBUNE

Cilgwyn, South Wales
Saturday, 11th May

Major Robertson inspected the Cilgwyn sett system soon after his arrival today in this beautiful but lonely part of the countryside.

At a press conference called by the Major, he stated that the badgers of Cilgwyn seemed to be quite special. The intelligence required in the planning of the sett system, the intricate network of pathways and the camouflage of the natural vegetation has been admired by many members of the extermination units.

The Major confirmed that more members have been recruited for the extermination units and that the maximum of efforts will be made on Tuesday next, when the plan formulated to eradicate the badgers from Cilgwyn will be put into effect.

He stated that his team will start their work from the eastern side of the colony, systematically blocking up the tunnels, then gassing and finally using excavators to collect the dead badgers before filling in the tunnels. Some of the dead badgers will be sent to the Ministry's laboratories for an assessment of the levels of tuberculosis with which they might be infected.

DAILY CHRONICLE

Cilgwyn, South Wales
Saturday, 11th May

Seven Days of Torture

Major Robertson confirmed at today's press conference that no effort will be spared during the next few days to eradicate the badgers from Cilgwyn. He said that he and his teams are totally confident that the task will be completed by the end of next week.

There has never been a case of Bovine TB recorded in any species of animal life that has lived in this peaceful valley. Yet a large colony of one of our native animals is being put to a savage, cruel and lingering death, their nervous systems paralysed by poisonous gas. When this fact was emphasised in a question to the Major, his only reply was that as soon as the Cilgwyn operation has been completed, all the units will be concentrated on the rest of South Wales to finally eradicate the badger from the country.

DAILY NEWS

Cilgwyn, South Wales
Friday, 17th May

The controller of the government's badger extermination units, Major T. G. Robertson, called a press conference at the end of today's activities.

He stated that he and his teams were unable to say why so few badgers had been found at Cilgwyn, when the sett system clearly showed evidence of one of the largest colonies encountered since the extermination programme had begun. However, he had now been informed that the disturbance caused by the "blocking up" of the sett entrances had frightened away the badgers from their homes.

The Major added that he now believed that the badgers had scattered into the nearby woodlands but that he was confident that it would be only a matter of a few days before his trackers with their dogs would locate all the escapees and they would then be exterminated.

THE MORNING TRIBUNE

Cilgwyn, South Wales
Friday, 17th May

Temporary Reprieve for Disease Carriers at Cilgwyn Setts

DAILY CHRONICLE

Cilgwyn, South Wales
Friday, 17th May

The government's badger eradication units, which are now concentrating their efforts in the remote countryside of South and Mid Wales, received their first setback today when their plans to exterminate the population of a large colony of badgers were unsuccessful.

When the units arrived three days ago they were informed by reliable and experienced wildlife experts that the Cilgwyn setts were the largest encountered since the programme had begun. After two days' preparation, the first setts were gassed yesterday afternoon, resulting in the slaughter of twenty-three badgers. It had been anticipated that today, when the central areas of the sett system were gassed, that possibly over one hundred badgers would be exterminated. However, it was quickly realised that the carefully planned procedures were not going to produce the expected results. Usually badgers will emerge, frantically trying to escape the choking gas, but today none appeared. It was at first thought that the strength of the gas and a high pump pressure had caused the animals to die instantly, but when the sett entrances were opened, no badgers were to be found.

Eventually Major Robertson issued a statement to the press stating that this would cause only a minor delay to the programme and would not affect the planned completion date of total extermination, which was fixed for the end of June.

However, a spokesman for the conservationists present stated that the mysterious overnight disappearance of the badgers from Cilgwyn could prove to be extremely significant.

14

The Leader

It was with a new determination that Beaufort made his way back to the surviving badgers, now nearly one hundred less than the original number that had set out on the trek to safety, but his heart was heavy with grief. His friend Fircone walked silently at his side, he, too, remembering the family he had left behind at Cilgwyn, unburied but at least safe in the arms of Logos.

They emerged from the riverbank, out of the sodden frondescence to see that the badgers were grouped in a semicircle around Kronos, who was addressing them with an oration both articulate and inspiring. It was a speech that had been rehearsed for a very long time. He had already accepted that Buckwheat was dead and had assumed the position of leader without obtaining the approval of the rest of the badgers.

Kronos's nonchalant disregard for Buckwheat's sacrifice of his life proved too much for Fircone to accept in his sorrowful mind and, charging through the crowd, he would have leapt on Kronos but for Beaufort knocking his paws from under him and restraining him from any further aggression by the command in his voice. For a moment Fircone thought it was Buckwheat who had spoken.

Fircone went to comfort Fern and Corntop as Beaufort announced that his father had been buried and he hoped the badgers would make the attempt to cross the river without further delay. This is what his father would have wanted and his sacrifice should not be in vain.

As Beaufort moved through the listening badgers many felt hopelessly lost, as the one badger they believed they could depend upon had gone. Beaufort halted sharply as once more he could hear Kronos attempting to show off his qualities of command. He was encouraging the badgers to cross, advising them that by getting to the other side of the river they would be taking a giant step towards their freedom. Beaufort could not bring himself to turn and listen to the voice that with every word was becoming more intoxicated with a sense of power. There would be time enough when they reached the other side for Beaufort to look into the face of Kronos and leave him in no doubt that his treachery had scarred Beaufort, and that before the journey was over he would ensure that both justice and vengeance would be Kronos's prize.

Beaufort's fears that the persuasive tongue of Kronos would capture the support of the badgers were alleviated as he heard the crunch of badgers' paws sounding heavier and heavier behind him. The first good thing that had happened since they had set out that night had occurred in the river. More tree trunks had floated down and had become more firmly lodged, making the crossing far more secure, and not only that, the water level was no longer rising but beginning to fall. Beaufort, then Fern and Corntop, crossed safely. Fircone had stayed behind, staying close at hand to Kronos. There would be no "accident" this time.

The comparative ease with which Beaufort's family had

crossed dispelled the others' fears and they began crossing one after another until there was a continuous trail of them stretching from one side of the river to the other. Eldon and Harvey had each got an orphan cub on his back and, telling the parents of the other cubs to do likewise, brought the young badgers safely over. The night was drawing to its end and the badgers needed no instructions to hide themselves in the vegetation to rest through the forthcoming day. When Fircone, being the last badger to cross, had landed safely the badgers discovered that many of the cubs were missing but their dismay changed to laughter as from a dense patch of foliage came the distinguishable sound of Eldon snoring, and snuggled up to him were the missing cubs, exhausted just like the rest of them and already fast asleep.

Beaufort's nest was silent that morning. There was grief in each one's heart, and the importance of his father's leadership became increasingly revealed to him as he let his thoughts drift back over the journey. There was no one left that could match up to him, yet a new leader had to be found. Beaufort could think of no one but Fircone to take over the leadership. While Fircone might have some shortcomings, he had displayed many virtues that were desired in a leader: loyalty, courage and concern for his fellow badgers. With help from the council members Fircone would be the right choice to lead them, but, as sleep finally overtook him, Beaufort's heart cried out for his father.

The slumbering of the badgers had been heavy that day as the mental and physical strain from the past couple of suns had drained their energies completely. They awoke with limbs stiff from their torpid sleep and at first they were like sloths as they began to forage in the riverine woodland.

The ever-alert Fircone so mistrusted Kronos that he had awakened earlier than the others and had kept watch on the malevolent badger. He had seen Kronos rise and, with the company of his confidants, circulate amongst the other badgers. They seemed to be encouraging them and patting them with their paws. Fircone's spine chilled as he pondered over the evil deeds that were being concocted in that villainous mind.

Beaufort, comforting Fern and Corntop as they foraged with little appetite, had been assessing the situation and wondering where to go and what to do when the foraging was over. His thoughts were sharply disrupted by Eldon calling for the badgers to assemble. At Eldon's side was Kronos, who avoided Beaufort's searching eyes as the bereaved badger ambled forward to listen to what Eldon had to say.

Eldon, for all his shortcomings, showed the dignity of his breeding when he asked his audience to remember with humble thanksgiving their old friend Buckwheat. He had undertaken the leadership when it had needed the strongest of badgers and had carried out his task with dedication. Buckwheat's firmness had been a major factor in getting the community as far as that riverside, and finally he had given his life for them in trying to find the path to safety. His name would be part of badger lore for centuries to come.

Chantar, Buckwheat's closest friend for many years, started to add his own tribute but could not finish as he was overcome by the sorrow in his aching heart. The duplicity of Kronos knew no bounds as he, too, joined the list of badgers rendering tributes to Buckwheat. After finishing his hypocritical words of praise, Kronos stated that, from his conversations with many of the senior and respected badgers, it was imperative that a new leader be appointed immediately and, as tradition dictated, an existing member of the council must be elected. As he was a member, he offered himself as a candidate. He believed the leadership now required a youthful vigourous badger, and, needless to say, the first priority would be the welfare of the community. There were shouts of approval from his cronies and also from the groups of young boars that had a member of Kronos's clique amongst them. When the sporadic shouts of support had finished, Kronos suggested that Eldon should temporarily take over the leadership and take charge of the election procedure.

It was apparent to Beaufort that Eldon appreciated that if ever there was a moment of crisis, this was it. His face looking stern, his voice stentorian, he accepted the task with the dignity and poise his father had possessed when he had been the leader. He accepted Kronos's nomination of himself and, asking for a seconder, was immediately answered by Zoilos. When he asked Chantar and Molyar whether they wished to be considered, both answered negatively, explaining that while they felt up to the demands of being members of the council and helping the leader in the formulations of policies and assisting him with other tasks, they did not feel that they were capable enough to accept the mantle of leadership. Chantar, who might have considered acceptance at one time, now missed the strength and wisdom of Buckwheat, and his mind and heart would be heavy with sorrow when he should have a clear head to assume such demanding responsibility.

Beaufort couldn't believe his ears and his jaws gaped open in astonishment. His muscles relaxed as he saw Corntop shaking her head vigourously as she pleaded with her eyes to stop this threat of despotic leadership from becoming true. His reticence and avoidance of being in the limelight seemed to leave Beaufort forever as he asked Eldon's permission to speak. He asked if it was possible for a council member to be elected to replace Buckwheat before the election for leadership took place. He was immediately interrupted by Kronos, irritated and angered by the attempt to delay his investiture. Kronos stated that the council members had already decided to deal with the issue of leadership first, and it was imperative that there should be no further hindrance in order that firm directions could be given to the badgers to enable them to continue their journey and assure their safety. More roars of approval were rendered by his cronies.

This did not deter Beaufort from continuing with his request for a ruling on the matter. He now stood below the raised mound of earth on which Kronos, Eldon, Chantar and Molyar were standing, his eyes burning into those of Eldon and Chantar, begging them to understand what was happening. His pleas were reinforced by the voice of Fircone stating that traditions would always be important but that the circumstances were very different from those at Cilgwyn and he saw no reason why Kronos should object. There was nothing that could transpire that would jeopardise the well-being of the badgers. Others, including Greyears, Harvey and Growler, now voiced their support.

For quite a few moments disorder reigned until the barking of Eldon began to be heard above the cacophony of sound. He stated, with a clear and firm tone, that as the new leader, especially one that was inexperienced in council affairs, would require all the assistance possible, it perhaps would be best if the points put forward by Beaufort were discussed by the council members and voted upon.

Beaufort became fearful, as now out of earshot of the small council group that had moved away for privacy, he could only watch as Kronos appeared to be using all the power he possessed to persuade the others to accept his point of view. The meeting was soon in discord and snatches of conversation could be heard on the wind. This led to some of Kronos's allies starting to encroach upon the council meeting. The excitement was now mounting and a fierce argument between Eldon and Kronos was developing as the badgers once more encircled the four badgers of government.

The arguments for and against raged back and forth between Eldon and Kronos. Eldon's determination lifted Beaufort out of his nervous pessimism, and it was the experience of the older leader that eventually won the day. It was decided that as their "debate" was leading them nowhere, there should be a vote. Kronos, believing that Molyar would certainly vote for him, and that perhaps Chantar would not bother to vote due to his mind being full of grief, was confident he would be elected. At first it would be a tie and that would be enough to continue the argument until either Eldon's insatiable appetite betrayed him or he became fatigued. The badgers waited with stilled breath as the vote was taken. It was a tie. No matter how depressed Chantar was, he could never bring himself to support Kronos even if Chantar had been certain Kronos was right, and he unhesitatingly cast his vote in Eldon's favour.

Kronos accepted the result with reluctance and suggested the meeting break up for some foraging and reconvene later when the matter would be discussed further. His face twisted with rage as Eldon raised himself, turned and, facing Beaufort, announced that there was no need for any postponement as he would exercise his right as leader and use his casting vote, which he now did in favour of Beaufort's proposition. There was absolute chaos as grunts and cries of approval rang through the air. Kronos's friends were screaming their nonacceptance of the result and scuffling broke out as they tried to subdue some of the cheering elderly boars.

Fircone and Gruff leapt to assist the victims of this aggression and, snapping vigourously at the attackers, soon had the ugly situation under control.

Eldon, speaking once more, declared that he had never felt so ashamed of his comrades as he did then. Did they realise how ashamed Buckwheat and all the others that had been lost would have been if they could see them now, behaving like demented and rabid creatures? To continue in this fashion would lead to self-destruction. The threat of man would become meaningless as the badgers would destroy themselves. They had survived centuries by living under the guidance of a freely elected Cadre and there was no chance of survival if they were now to stray from that pattern of life.

Buckwheat would have been proud of his old friend, thought Beaufort, and his admiration and reverence for Eldon grew by leaps and bounds. He would nominate Fircone for council membership, with Eldon again taking up his duties as leader. Fircone's sometimes fiery temperament would be kept in check and his complete devotion to the badger commune would be a great asset to the Cadre. He, too, was a tower amongst badgers, just as his father had been, and now as Eldon was proving to be.

Grunting Fircone's name to Eldon as a nominee, Beaufort was astonished to find Fircone refusing the nomination and remonstrating with him profusely. Fircone asked Eldon if he could address the badgers and, not waiting for anyone's consent, began speaking in his gruff and curt manner. He had had no experience of public speaking and had none of the niceties of oratory, but he began extolling the virtues of the only badger that he believed was wise enough to take the empty Cadre chair. A badger who had the respect of the community at large. A badger who placed the survival of the other badgers before his own. A badger who had learned from the greatest of leaders. This badger was the paragon of badgers, this badger should feel duty-bound to accept this responsibility: This badger was Beaufort.

Pandemonium broke loose as Fircone's words stirred the hearts of the attentive badgers, and their grunts of approval joined in unison as Beaufort's name rang out time and time again. Beaufort, standing alone, away from the others, felt a nudge in his back. He glanced around to see who was behind him, but there was no one there. He moved towards the rostrum, nodding acceptance of the nomination, and there was Eldon welcoming him with a twinkle in his eyes. Eldon announced that it was obviously not necessary to vote, and he proclaimed Beaufort as the new Cadre member, which was received by most of the badgers with jubilation.

The Cadre went into further session, but first Eldon ordered the spectators to carry on feeding and said that when there was further news for them they would be called back. As the Cadre convened Eldon asked the others to squat facing him and without ado stated that priority should be given to leadership. Beaufort expressed his belief that all the badgers would be delighted if Eldon once more assumed command, as his leadership and the manner in which he had controlled the vitriolic situation earlier spoke for themselves. He was firmly supported by Kronos, who much preferred Eldon to Chantar as leader. Kronos had conceded that this council would never accept him as leader but there was always the chance that Eldon would return to his forgetful lackadaisical ways, giving a real opportunity for Kronos to assume command.

Eldon, expressing his gratitude at their confidence, staggered everyone present by saying that he believed that although there were times when perhaps he was suitable to be the one to manage the affairs of the community, there were too many occasions when he knew in his heart that he could find neither the strength nor the wisdom that was his father's or Buckwheat's. And for any leader to succeed, particularly at this time of adversity, it required a badger blessed with these qualities in abundance to carry them through. There would be no point in discussing his being reappointed as he was adamant that he could not and would not accept the leadership again. He felt it only fair that all the adult badgers should have their say in this matter. As tradition dictated that the leader would be elected from one of the council members and he believed that the badgers had already shown they were prepared to accept Beaufort as their custodian, it was his intention to propose Beaufort as their new leader.

Kronos, seething with rage at Eldon's words, spat unintelligible words of venom. His face was contorted and twisted into deep hatred for Beaufort, and in his fit of wrath he swore to himself that not many full moons would pass before he would kill Beaufort.

As Beaufort grasped the relevance of Eldon's intentions, his immediate intention was to object and to continue to persuade Eldon to change his mind, but as he rose he felt the pressure from a restraining paw on his shoulder and, understanding the significance of the gentle touch, acknowledged his acceptance of the leadership. As Eldon walked back to the foraging badgers, the others trailed behind. Beaufort lingered awhile and looked back to the patch of wild barley that had been the meeting place. For a moment that was quicker than lightning there was a glow enveloping a youthful-looking badger smiling with joyous pride, its face that of his father as he had looked when Beaufort was a cub. Beaufort knew that his oath to his father before he was buried was being controlled by a medium too great and too powerful to deny, and his faith in the successful outcome of his task became complete.

The badgers had once more gathered around Eldon, who had only the company of Chantar until Beaufort rejoined them on the mound. Kronos and Molyar had disappeared into the gathering throng. When Eldon announced the Cadre's decision and requested that they do him the honour of accepting his nomination of Beaufort as the new leader, the grunts of overwhelming approval crescendoed into an almighty roar. Beaufort, now standing proudly between Fern and Corntop, found his breath being crushed out of him as he was hugged by Fircone, and then felt his back pounded by the other badgers.

This euphoric state of affairs suddenly ended when the raucous voice of Kronos could be heard barking that he was not accepting the situation. He said that the badgers were fools to place themselves in the custody of Beaufort's stewardship. Had not there been many lives lost under the control of Beaufort's father? Beaufort would be no less reckless than Buckwheat had been.

Suppressing his own anger and restraining Fircone once again, Beaufort calmly asked Kronos what his intentions were. Kronos announced that there were others who were not prepared to place their hopes of survival in Beaufort's care and that they preferred him rather than Beaufort as their leader. They would separate themselves from the rest and seek a new home under Kronos's paw. They would be leaving immediately and would forge ahead to find a new haven. Any badger over eighteen full moons would be welcome to join him, boar or sow, but no cubs or badgers of eight cold times or more.

There were no further additions to Kronos's party, which numbered forty-seven. Kronos further announced that any badger conforming to the requirements could join him at any time he wished, and he would show them all that he, Kronos, was the rightful leader by finding Elysia first. He would prepare Elysia for them, and then the badgers that now preferred to support Beaufort would change their minds and beg him to become the leader of the Cadre.

Whilst Beaufort was glad to see Kronos depart, relieving the rest of the community of his evil and Ahrimanic ways, he felt the unhappiness of the parents who were losing a son or daughter to the maniacal usurper settle as a cloud over them, and he knew that this would not be the last he would see of Kronos.

There were two enemies now, the animal man and the animal badger—Kronos.

Beaufort's first act of leadership was to emphasise that with

the faith he had in the badgers' courage, and helped by the guiding hand of Logos, he would without doubt help them to succeed. He kept telling them of his imagined Elysia, even sweeter than the land of dreams. He asked them to remember with respect the lives lost already in the search for a valley free of threatening shadows. He spoke for those silent lips when he reminded the badgers that they would be constantly under their gaze from Asgard. He told them that they would remain for just one more day's rest before moving on towards the setting sun.

He had to keep their confidence high. He would make arrangements for a new full Cadre and he would organise a team of younger males to keep encouraging the others. He would not let them lose hope for he knew that hope deferred would make their hearts sick, and sickened hearts would lead to their oblivion. With trust and hopes kept high they would succeed. Yet he knew that he had to remember that their happiness would sometimes be tested by the most labourious and perilous of tasks and that he must never lose the substance by grasping at the shadows.

15

P.A.W.S.

THE SUNDAY TRIBUNE

South Wales
Sunday, 19th May

The badger extermination unit under the direction of Major T. G. Robertson met with further success today when they tracked down some of the badgers that had deserted their Cilgwyn setts.

Ten mature badgers were trapped in an area of fern and brush only three miles from their homeland. Tracker dogs raised their quarry and marksmen swiftly disposed of the creatures.

The Major issued a press release reaffirming his confidence in his trackers and congratulating them on their swift location of the escapee badgers. Although these represented only a small number of those that had fled from Cilgwyn, those still free would soon be discovered and gassed.

The Major confirmed that helicopters would now be used to assist in the operation.

DAILY CHRONICLE

Cilgwyn, South Wales
Monday, 20th May

Major Robertson and his badger extermination units were once more thwarted in their cold-blooded endeavours to wipe out one of Britain's natural animals.

Ten aged badgers, weak from their efforts to escape the Cilgwyn slaughterers, were trapped by over thirty tracker dogs. The animals were eventually shot and killed, but not before the dogs had severely mauled them.

Even press reporters representing journals in favour of the government programme were sickened by the brutality of the badgers' final moments.

On a more hopeful note, it has been reported that tracks of a large number of badgers have been sighted, indicating that they now realise that they must flee and find a refuge where they will be free of man's threat of total extinction.

DAILY CHRONICLE

South Wales
Thursday, 23rd May

Four days have passed since the slaughter of the ten aged badgers, and although some badgers were discovered in lone sett systems and killed, the Ministry's extermination teams have failed to trace the fleeing Cilgwyn badgers.

While any badger's death is to be regretted, these killings are tempered by the success of the fleeing badgers in eluding their persecutors. A fleet of helicopters is covering the area in a concentrated search for the animals, whose fate is increasingly capturing the public's sympathy.

The results of the autopsies carried out on the forty-two badgers from the South Wales area confirm that there are no traces of tuberculosis.

The conservationists and Badger Protection League members, heartened by this information and sensing a swing in public opinion, have formed a special unit to save the Cilgwyn badgers. The unit will come under the banner of "Protests Against Wanton Slaying" with the apt abbreviation of "P.A.W.S."

DAILY NEWS

South Wales
Friday, 24th May

The admirable efforts of Major Robertson and his badger exterminators were rewarded today when their persistent chase resulted in the death of nearly thirty badgers. Their bodies were found at the foot of Beacon Heights a few miles from the village of Llancwm. Most of the animals had died after falling down a steep cliff and crashing onto rocks and stones. Some surviving badgers attempted to escape but were quickly dispatched by the marksmen. Nearly sixty badgers from the Cilgwyn setts have now been destroyed and the extermination unit is confident that those still at large will soon be found and eradicated.

DAILY NEWS

Llancwm, South Wales
Monday, 27th May

Stop Press

Cilgwyn badgers have met their fate. Tracks of large numbers of badgers found at river edge in Welsh countryside indicate that all have drowned.

Television news, 9.00 P.M., *Monday, 27th May*

Although it was reported earlier today that a large group of badgers had drowned in South Wales, it now appears that they have in fact successfully crossed the river Crammach. Numerous tracks have been sighted supporting this view.

P.A.W.S. supporters are delighted by this discovery and report that an increasing number of people are contacting their headquarters offering their support to the campaign to save tho bad gers. A spokesman for P.A.W.S. is convinced that the latest attempts by the badgers to escape from death will encourage many more members of the public to join in the campaign to stop the government's extermination plans.

16

Sheol's Disciple

For the first time in his life, the comforting paw, the encouraging words, the fostering guidance, the security of a cloak of wisdom were no longer with him, and Beaufort understood the torment of loneliness. The awesome task bestowed upon him made him cry out in his dreams for the return of that paternal mantle of protection.

Yet within Beaufort stirred the seeds of greatness and the hairs on his body stiffened as the awareness of a Grey Eminence guiding him surged through his veins, and his mind struggled to accept the belief of the potential within him. He awoke with his thoughts still distorted by the figments of his dreams. He had entered the past world, the haunt of the mentors and chivalrous ones of his own existence. He had awakened the echoes of his ancestral homes and he went amongst his charges inspired, no longer just the willing worker and badger of Samaritan thought, but a true leader who would have to prove to be exceptional in this critical time.

The first task to fall on Beaufort's shoulders was to form the Cadre. There were only two survivors from the one that had governed at Cilgwyn, Chantar and Eldon. It had lost the valiant Buckwheat, the weak and disloyal Palos, and now Molyar had deserted under the influence of Kronos. At least Beaufort could ensure that their replacements were unanimous in their purpose of vigilance and safekeeping. The new Cadre would have to become a close-knit fraternity in as short a time as possible.

Beaufort thought long and hard over what recommendations he would give to his badgers. He realised that confidence in himself as leader must be held by his charges for there to be any chance of safe deliverance. He could never show his doubts or fears. He had to be decisive, firm yet benevolent, tenacious yet tolerant, forceful yet caring. He would need a strong Cadre to help him carry out his mission. They would all have to believe as one, nursing with patience when the going was difficult and encouraging when the badgers' faith fragmented like a sun-scorched earth.

There was a tremor of excited silence as Beaufort gathered his followers about him. He remembered the qualities of character he had to show, though he could not help feeling slightly nervous as he recognised badgers of greater years than himself. Yet they, too, showed their eagerness for Beaufort to succeed, and respect and approval glowed in their faces. He announced that Eldon and Chantar would remain as Cadre members. Their experience and the wisdom of their years would be invaluable, but he would also need the vigour and drive of younger badgers, as this combination would supply the essentials for the broader spectrum of planning and guidance necessary for success. Beaufort explained that this would only be an interim Cadre. The new members would be by appointment and not by election, and the permanent Cadre would be elected when they had found their new home. He did not want there to be any refusal or argument from either the two new members or any other badger. He then called forward Fircone and Gruff, and was delighted that his choice met with rapturous approval from all around.

The embarrassment in Fircone's face amused the others, and as he felt the skin underneath his face hair become hot, he was glad that he had such a profuse face covering, as he was sure he would have looked like a solitary poppy in a large green field.

The arms of Beaufort went round the shoulders of his two friends, and their mutual respect and pride relieved them of any inhibitions that might have lingered. The new Cadre sat in purposeful discussion for nearly half the night. The air was warm and the sky, with its nesting moon, was heavy with high cloud. As the five council members withdrew from their labours of planning, Beaufort could feel an increased contentment amongst the other badgers. They had foraged well; worms, grubs, beetles and larvae were found easily and in great quantities on this virgin patch. The badgers were grooming in pairs or in family units, and their calmness added strength to Beaufort's resolve. As he began to forage for himself he passed a large hollow and saw that Eldon was reassuring the cubs before he, too, sought to diminish the worm population. Harvey was teaching the younger cubs the method of grooming, but his instructions were falling on deaf ears for the young ones had lost their concentration and had turned with adoration to look at Eldon. They really loved him and looked forward to his epic tales of badger heroism. Eldon and Harvey, too, had captured the hearts of the cubs, who easily put aside their fears and worries. Eldon's mind, being such that it needed only to absorb the necessities and simple things of life, was really that of a young cub and it was this that had enabled him to get the youthful badgers to have complete faith in his words and deeds. What Beaufort had feared might be the most difficult aspect of his assignment had become the easiest, and although still having Buckwheat's loss about him, he felt a surge of well-being engulf him. He quietly gave thanks to Logos for the innocence of the young ones and for the forest that would not wither away as long as there were flowers in the fields.

Having eaten, Beaufort barked and commanded the badgers to pay attention to his words. He began to explain to them the plan that had been put together at the Cadre earlier. Their journey would continue the following night. They would forage for a short time at the start and end of each night, travelling onwards during the periods in between. Every fourth night they would rest to allow the weakest to regain their strength. In order that they would not waste time searching at the end of each night's travel for a safe place to rest, scouting parties consisting of the fittest badgers, male and female, would go ahead in fours each night, two reporting back every quarter journey of the moon, their instincts telling them the time to return should the night light become masked by cloud.

Progress would be steady, the same rate being maintained from start to finish on each night's journey. They were to cover their tracks as best they could, trying not to walk in mud or soft earth, no scratching of paws on bark of trees, all dung to be concealed under foliage, and no grubbing or digging up of earth in search of food. Whilst there were too many of them for the signs of their nightly repasts to be completely obliterated, those following would still have the problem of taking the right path each day.

The fourth night, the rest night, would be spent grooming, teaching the young about the edible and poisonous trees and plants, and where to look for various foods. Some aspects of the cubs' instruction would have to be postponed until they arrived at Elysia. These included digging and earth removal, tunnelling, sett building, bedding collection, cleaning of bedding, climbing trees for insects, claw cleaning or any other badger requirement that might betray their steps to freedom.

As soon as the sunlight dimmed the following evening, the badgers were energetically foraging and preparing to continue their journey. It was soon time for the scouts to set off, and although Fircone suggested he should take charge of them, Beaufort gently reminded him that his presence would be of greater importance to the main group as the elders responded more quickly and with greater effort when Fircone was there to encourage them.

So it was that Growler, Whortle, Buckmast, Kingcup, Canda, Bumble, Dandelion and Buckthorn set off to prepare a scented trail for the group to follow. The journey took them through warrens, thickets, little dales of fern and flowers, the scouts reporting back on schedule until the final two were waiting for them at a place suitable for the day's rest. Everything had passed as Beaufort had hoped, and the next night went by as uneventfully as the first, except that the area selected to bed down for the day was thick with bilberry bushes with their light green leaves still sporting some pink flowers, but more important, carrying masses of blue-black berries. Eldon, with so many types of food in abundance, and delighting in the company of the cubs, who were now beginning to understand the reasons for their quest, was enjoying himself as he had never done before. His tongue soon became the colour of the bilberry juice as it wrapped itself around cluster after cluster of deliciously sweet berries. The other badgers satisfied their hunger on other things as well, but Eldon's appetite for the bilberries seemed to be insatiable. Though his craving for them remained undiminished, he eventually had to stop as the gasses from the fermenting juices in his stomach caused severe flatulence and soon ripples of laughter were coming from the other badgers as they saw Eldon, sprawled back into his bilberry shrubs, unable to control his burping, his stomach distended to the maximum and his eyes half closed.

The third night after Beaufort's elevation to leadership commenced as planned; the early part was spent feeding, then they
continued with their travels once more. There was an eagerness
about the badgers that enabled them to make good progress
through well-covered grasslands. They had been travelling
through what seemed an endless valley ever since they had left
the riverbank. There were hills on either side of them but quite
some distance apart. They passed by many a copse and thicket.
There were trees in small clusters, the wild service trees, oaks,
wych, elm, holly and blackthorn, and the rest of the ground was
covered in rye grasses or plants such as saxifrage, buttercup,
ribwort and yarrow.

The first two scouts returned earlier than expected, informing Beaufort that they had come across the tracks of Kronos and
the other deserters but that they had not actually caught sight
of them. The scent had been fresh and was of the same night.
The tracks were rather obvious and Beaufort and his badgers
would have to reduce the distance travelled, as time would now
be wasted covering up the tracks of the irresponsible Kronos
badgers.

When the second pair of scouts returned, they, too, confirmed that Kronos was taking a meandering pathway and that
it had frequently crossed the route being searched and prepared by the scouts. Beaufort was not happy with the knowledge that Kronos was in such close proximity to his group of
badgers and knew that he could never relax for a moment when
that fiend of a badger was close by. He felt sure that whilst
Kronos might be leading his defectors, the mind of Kronos
worked in such a way that he would surely be concentrating on
plans for a mishap to occur to Beaufort himself or the main
group of badgers. Kronos would try to lower their spirits to such
an extent that more badgers would defect until the majority
supported him.

Whortle and Canda, the third pair of scouts, returned with similar information, and when the blackness of night began to luminesce and the first twittering of the birds was heard, the group finally arrived at their new resting place, where Growler and Bumble were awaiting them. Growler explained that they had in fact gone further ahead than the rest area to ascertain the whereabouts of Kronos but had failed to find tracks or scent of other badgers and, therefore, they believed that the area they proposed as a resting place was safe and secure.

The badgers had made tremendous progress during the previous three nights, and it would be well worth a night's stay in their new abode if it meant that they would make as much progress during the next three nights they planned to travel. Beaufort discussed with his council members the possible intrusion of Kronos and decided that guards should be posted a short distance away from their camp during the following day and night and that they should be changed at regular intervals.

The rest night was enjoyed by all the badgers. Those weakened by the experience of the mountain were now fully recovered and Beaufort hoped that those left behind to heal their wounds would be allowed to settle and live out their days in peace. He knew he would next see them in Asgard; he would not see them on this earth again. Even if they tried to follow, they were too frail to cross the river. He had to believe that they would not suffer anymore.

During the night the cubs returned to their families, the orphans remaining with Eldon and Harvey, and for the first time since they left Cilgwyn practices that had been forgotten returned to them. The parents were keen to impart their knowledge and the cubs were eager to learn. One of the most important lessons was about berries that would cause harm. There were some poisonous shrubs and plants in the vicinity, the woody nightshade with its bright red berries that, if eaten, would cause severe sickness, sometimes resulting in death. There was nightshade with its berries still green, although they would soon become black. These berries would cause severe pain and quite often would be fatal if consumed. Berries seemed to have an almost hypnotic effect on young badgers. Some were delicious, like the wild strawberries and raspberries, the bilberry and the blackberry, which they had not yet tasted. There was bramble in abundance but the berries had only just started to redden and, as Eldon pointed out to his listeners, they would soon fill out and blacken and then they would taste exquisitely delicious. He showed them that there were one or two blackberries more advanced in their development than others and already filled with sweet juices. He thought it would be unfair for only two or three of the cubs to be favoured by being given a taste of them and drooled with the thought of the pleasures to come as he took them into his own mouth and swallowed the nectar.

The following three nights went by peacefully with excellent progress being made. Every one of the badgers looked forward to the journey, believing that the more often they travelled, the sooner they would arrive at their final destination. They had passed many horizons, they felt well and their spirits were high as they marched during that third night. Beaufort was less apprehensive at the continuous encounters with Kronos's tracks. They always seemed half a nighttime ahead by the strength of their scent. He was pleased at the pace they were maintaining as, although they had young and old to support, they seemed to have covered as much ground as Kronos's party had done.

He became more anxious when only one of the third party of scouts returned to him. It was Buckmast who reported that the scent of Kronos had become much stronger and that his partner, who had accompanied the last pair in their forward scouting, would report a little later. This decision was taken after one of the scouts, Dandelion, thought she heard movement close by them as they skirted a dense copse. The scouts had investigated, and the familiar scent of Cilgwyn badgers was nosed. It was a very recent scent, but they had caught sight of nothing.

Beaufort, at the front of his troop, with Fern and Corntop just one step behind, forged ahead. Soon he picked up the fresh scent of both badger and fox on the slight breeze that came towards him. It strengthened and suddenly Beaufort's head lifted high as the scent was no longer just that of a fox or badger but of the blood of a badger. He increased his pace, calling for Fircone and Gruff to join him, telling Corntop to hold back the others. They approached the base of a raised mound of sandstone and there they found Dandelion. She had had patches of her coat torn from her, her ears had been ripped in shreds, her face was a mask of blood and her throat gaped open with the warm blood still trickling away, though she had died awhile earlier. Beaufort stood aghast at the awesome spectacle and his coat stiffened as the thought of Kronos flashed into his mind. He searched for answers to the many questions that now flooded his brain. Could Kronos be so mad? Surely no other badger would kill his own kind just for the sake of killing? Why had they killed Dandelion? Just then Beaufort saw Fircone's head appear behind a clump of some tall grasses and on going over to him saw that he was looking down on the body of a she-fox. The vixen was in a similar state to Dandelion and looked as if she had died in her struggles to get to an opening in the sandstone. Gruff entered the small crevice in the rocks where the scent of fox had been powerful and inside he found the mutilated bodies of three fox cubs, one partly eaten.

Beaufort could not understand it at all. He knew that a she-fox with cubs would attack a lone badger if it trespassed near her earth. This had happened when an adolescent boar badger had roamed too far from Cilgwyn, but he had not known a fox to kill a badger before. Dandelion, feeling hungry, must, for some inexplicable reason, have decided to kill and eat the fox cubs when she came across them as she searched for the scent of Kronos. Beaufort found it difficult to accept this theory as he knew that badgers would take carrion or even kill young rabbits when food was scarce, but the supply of more favoured foods was plentiful.

His attention was drawn to Fircone, who was examining Dandelion more closely, prodding the wounds with his paws, turning her body over to look at the marks on her other side. Fircone was silent as he moved away from her, over to the fox, repeating the examination process on its body. Then he stood back and declared, with rising anger in his deep-toned voice, that Dandelion had not killed the fox, but more important, the fox had not killed Dandelion. The bite marks on the fox were indeed those of a badger, not of one badger but of at least three or four. It was the same teeth marks on Dandelion that had caused the wrath in Fircone. The two corpses lay there as a result of being attacked by a group of badgers. The scent was not unfamiliar and it could only mean that Dandelion had been slain by badgers who only a short time ago had been her companions.

Beaufort was now convinced that he and his own group were dealing with a badger who was not only jealous and cruel but also one whose craving for power was so great, he had become quite insane. His maniacal influences were taking hold of his followers and he had persuaded them that there were worms in the sky and frogs in the trees.

The three badgers dragged the bodies of badger and fox into the fox's lair. They would, with the fox cubs, be soon united in Asgard, where peace was eternal for all animals as had once been so on earth, for in the beginning the calf had lain down with the lion.

They covered the signs of disturbance as best they could by brushing their tails over the telltale tracks on the soil. Then they quickly returned to the others and, without explanation, moved on. Beaufort increased the pace as he was now concerned for the safety of the two scouts ahead, Buckthorn and Kingcup.

The march continued past the time when they should have halted for the day's rest. There were already streaks of light in the east when Beaufort called a halt to their travels. The badgers would have to shelter where they were. The scouts would not have travelled further on and indeed Beaufort had expected to find them some considerable distance back.

Calling Fircone and Gruff to him, Beaufort quietly told them to keep the knowledge of Dandelion to themselves for the time being as he did not want to alarm the others. He ordered that the guard be doubled that day, keeping a sharp lookout for the returning scouts. Kingcup and Buckthorn, two of the most loyal badgers he could wish for, would never accede to Kronos's wishes. Beaufort, knowing the strength of character his two scouts possessed, trembled at the thought of what fate would be dealt them by Kronos's paws.

17

Escape and a Threat

The scouts had still not returned when Beaufort and his pioneering band set off on their journey once more. They had now been missing for four nights, and their scent had been lost, with that of Kronos and his deserter companions, three nights earlier, and Beaufort feared greatly for them. He had told Fircone and Gruff to keep their worries to themselves and, rather than cause uncertainty in the minds of the other badgers, had told them that the three scouts, including Dandelion, must have decided to shadow Kronos in order that they could be forewarned of any deviousness that Kronos might conceive.

They were now coming to the end of the valley. It had stretched through many woods and meadows but the terrain had changed and there were many rocky outcrops occurring. The hills that had been their distant companions, funnelling them ever onwards, were converging, and Beaufort could see that before the night was finished they would reach the end of the kindly vale.

As they reached the foothills Beaufort, hoping to find a pass between the tors at the end of the valley's taper, decided that they would skirt the hills, but his hopes began to diminish as the faces of the hills became steeper and less vegetated. The steep slopes became even more precipitous, and soon Beaufort realised that they were in a ravine as the cliffs reared up on both sides of them, cliffs as polished as marble from the earth's up-heaval of a millennium of moons past.

There was no animal of hoof, pad or claw that could hold fast on that glassy surface, and even the lightest of breezes would dislodge a fly. The floor of the ravine was now covered in boulders, which would never allow seed to take hold. Its craggy, hard surface could not retain water, and as the end of the ravine came into sight, Beaufort realised that their forward march would be halted, and there was no way out. Although crevices reached upward where the two ranges of hills finally met, they were of such a steepness that they were impossible to climb. Beaufort ordered the badgers to turn about. He told them they would have to seek a path over the hill and, remembering the events of the last mountain climb, they would shelter until the following night, when they would tackle the climb with energies refreshed. They would postpone the ascent if the weather threatened to turn to rain. There had to be a pathway somewhere. To go back through the valley would surely bring them into the clutches of their pursuers.

The badgers were feeding in the twilight of the following day, Beaufort having ordered an early start. The badgers had noticed that buzzards and kites were circling in the sky over the basin of the ravine that had curtailed their previous night's travels. This puzzled Beaufort, as the floor of the ravine had been devoid of any living or dead matter, but circling birds of prey usually meant decaying flesh or a life form that would soon succumb to its final sleep.

Beaufort, leaving Gruff with the main party of badgers, accompanied a score or more of the others, including Fircone, to investigate the cause of the birds' behaviour. As the small group retraced their steps of yesternight, they could just make out in the fading light some unfamiliar shapes at the very base of the cliff. As they tentatively approached they became aware that they were looking at apparently lifeless animals. They approached slowly, and when they were sure that the spirit of Ahriman had left the bodies, they moved forward briskly, only to stop abruptly as they realised that the strange shapes were of their kin. As they rushed to inspect the bodies, Beaufort and his colleagues became aware that above the scent of death there was the familiar scent of Cilgwyn badgers. Beaufort's face became anguished as he recognised the markings on the crumpled bodies. There lay the earthly remains of five of the original Cilgwyn nomads, amongst them the two scouts Kingcup and Buckthorn. The other three were a young boar and two young female badgers who had defected with Kronos. Fircone was peering up the cliff face searching for the place from where this horror had occurred. He lowered his inquiring gaze to look at Beaufort, unable to comprehend this chapter of misadventure. He saw that Beaufort was staring at the bodies, his mind in total concentration, his eyes hard and full of seething anger. Beaufort uttered the name of Kronos and then he explained his undoubted convictions that the paw of Kronos had once more dealt its blow of iniquity. There could be no other explanation for what he knew Kronos would term as an accident. Why should it have happened to both of the scouts? The other three must have disagreed with Kronos's murderous plans and they, too, had had to be sacrificed to assist his ambitions. Beaufort now believed that only by destroying Kronos would the badgers be freed of the threat of harm coming to them from one who had once been their brother.

The small search party dragged the bodies over the rocky surface into the bramble and bracken where they did their best to conceal them. Beaufort did not want the winged carrion-eaters to deface the badgers and he did not want the attention of the man hunters to be drawn to their present camping ground.

Beaufort's firm and direct commands were met with instant obedience, and Fircone commented to Beaufort that he must surely now understand why they had chosen him as leader. Fircone assured him that evil always met its doom. Kronos, he explained, was weak as the seed clock of dandelion that the wind drives away and, anyway, he knew that Beaufort walked with Logos, just as his father Buckwheat had done. Fircone's intention of reassuring Beaufort did not succeed, for Beaufort's mind was fraught with worry as to how the other badgers would take the news.

The eyes of Beaufort's merry troop, which had shone with happiness over the past eleven moon-filled nights, lost their sparkle after hearing of the badgers who had met their death in the ravine, though the badgers' faith in Beaufort remained as steadfast as their belief in Logos. The scouting system was abandoned altogether as Beaufort would not risk placing any more of his badgers in peril of Kronos's wickedness.

They had to veer away from the setting sun, towards where the coldest of winds blew from when the time of the snows was with them. They kept close to the fringe of the hill's sheer cliffs, and when the moon was full and bright above them, they heard the trickling sounds of water. Beaufort realised that the sounds were too subdued for the water to be falling free from a great height and that it must be following a gentle slope down the hillside. There had to be a cleft in the rocky eminence, and soon they saw the moon light up a silvery, glistening path through what had seemed an impenetrable wall. There were shrill cries of delight from many of them, and Beaufort's relief was immense. The worry of going back and cancelling out their hard-won gains was over.

When they reached the bottom of the gentle waterfall, Beaufort discovered that Kronos had also taken this route, but on being able to see the water shimmer in the moonlight as far as the hills became a gentle slope, he assessed that should Kronos appear on that path he would be seen in time to take evasive action. Beaufort gave the command to advance. The footholds were safe and the climb was easy. It would have been quite different if the heavy rains that had saturated them on their last climb had been following them. That night, however, the result of that force having occurred time after time during centuries past enabled the badgers to succeed in their ascent of the hill. The crushing power had forged a safe path in their journey of escape, and far more quickly than any of them had envisaged, they were safe and sound on top of the cliffs, on a plateau of fertile soil that bordered a fairly large expanse of water. This was the collecting point of the streams that ran down the slopes ahead. They relaxed in the soft night winds that carried the scent of heather towards them. The nervous tension left them and the badgers reclined in the shrubbery. It felt so good, as if they were laying up in lavender.

It was soon time to gird up their loins and continue the journey, which had already lasted the full life of a moon. They edged around the dry land that hemmed in the reservoir of water and were soon amongst the heather that covered the gentle gradient above them. On the lower slopes the heather was sporadic in its growth and the rest of the ground was covered in mountain or alpine grasses. Their nostrils were soon filled with an unfamiliar scent, which was not the smell of herb or tree but warm-blooded, although not the smell of man. They slowed down warily. The moonlight kept creating flickering white patches in between the clumps of heather, and then they realised that these white clusters were waving. They seemed to float above the ground, ponder for a moment, then float on again. It was Fircone who courageously decided to take a closer look at the ghostlike figures. He discovered that they were animals that he had not seen before and not phantoms at all. Their bodies were similar in shape to the badgers, but their legs, which were black, as were their faces, were thinner. The crunching sound was caused by the strange ones eating grass, and he quietly watched them as they consumed anything that grew above the height of a flea. He felt quite safe for it was a known fact in the animal world that grass eaters never ate the flesh of any other animal and would seldom resort to violence except when protecting their young.

As Fircone made his presence known to the animals, they let out cries of alarm and scattered in all directions. Then, seeing they weren't being pursued, they resumed feeding, though occasionally lifting their heads to get a better glimpse of Fircone. Having seen the strange animals scatter at the sight of Fircone, and hearing the plaintive bleating of fear, Beaufort encouraged his band to move up. While Beaufort had not seen these animals before, he tried to remember the teachings he had been given when a cub, but it was Harvey who brought his memory to the fore by saying they were special peaceful animals. They were sheep and belonged to Logos. They did not even fear man and lived peaceably amongst them. Beaufort could not understand why man should have chosen to persecute the badger when the lamb of Logos could live by man's side. He was not to know that they not only provided man with their outer covering for warmth but also were daily taken as food by man as the badger took the worm. Beaufort felt only Logos understood the mysterious intricacies of the living earth.

They followed paths that had been worn on the hillside by the grazing sheep. The sheep scattered whenever the badgers came too close to them, but their wariness waned as they began to accept that these were kindred spirits and soon they no longer interrupted their feeding to make way for the badgers now walking amongst them. Indeed, some of the youngest of the sheep were leaping and running at the cubs, who joined in the youthful fun by dancing around their new playmates. They were soon leaving their new acquaintances behind, and Beaufort, glancing back at them, saw a small group of young sheep disappointedly watching their departure.

From the top of the plateau they could see the valley stretching out of sight behind them, and as they encircled the hill the pastures that had been their home for the past twenty-odd days disappeared from view. It became apparent to Beaufort that Logos had opened the gates of mercy to them and was swiftly ushering them on their way to their new settlement. There was no need to continue marching upwards for they had reached the other side of the hills without having to scale the peaks that had towered above them. They descended through the heather, then bramble, gorse and bracken into a curved arc of birch trees and oak, emerging out of the woodlands to find another arc awaiting them. Beaufort halted his companions sharply, as the arc facing them was constructed of badgers with Kronos standing ahead of them. His eyes, full of guile and cunning, were ablaze with his new sense of power.

There was a flurry of movement behind Beaufort and then a thud and he turned to see that Gruff had brought Fircone down by tripping him. Beaufort commanded Fircone to restrain himself from doing anything violent. Beaufort quietly explained that he would deal with Kronos in his own way, without creating a spectacle or giving an opportunity for there to be a bloodbath.

Kronos welcomed Beaufort with a voice that oozed as the sap from the pines, asking whether they had travelled safely. This

only made the hairs of Beaufort and Fircone stiffen further. Kronos then inquired whether three young ones who had missed their families and had freely left Kronos's forward party had made their way back to their families, who were with Beaufort. Not waiting for Beaufort's reply, Kronos continued to extol the success he had achieved with his group, and upon reflection he felt that it was right and proper that the final and total success of their venture should be of the highest priority. He had discussed this with his own followers, and they were in full agreement with him and his suggestions that the two groups should merge but Kronos would continue to lead his group to prepare a safe path ahead, allowing them all to make greater progress. At the end of each night he would sit as joint leader with Beaufort to plan the next night's travels. They would have alternate meeting places: The first night he would come to Beaufort's group, the second Beaufort would come to Kronos, and using this method he felt sure that their new home would be found within the life of the next moon. His supporters barked and grunted their support, and once again, before Beaufort could utter a word, Kronos continued. He suggested that his second-in-command, Zoilos, and Fircone should also be accepted as deputy leaders, adding their strength to the initiative and intelligence of the new joint leadership, and then, when the final success was achieved, the badgers would return to the pattern of Cilgwyn. If Beaufort was still their choice as leader, then it would be accepted by all.

There seemed to be some support for Kronos's reasoning amongst Beaufort's group, but Beaufort understood that many were ignorant of the wickedness that lay behind Kronos's thinking. Their minds were too innocent to accept the possibility of there being such an ogre of a badger who felt nothing for them and was only disguising his evil intentions.

Beaufort walked with purposeful gait towards Kronos, commanding both Gruff and Fircone to hold the others back. Then, staring at Kronos, he was about to declare his contempt for him when the voice of Eldon boomed out from behind him.

The clarity and resolute tone of Eldon's voice silenced all as he stated that Cilgwyn had successfully survived storm and tempest, plague and pestilence, fever and famine and all other crises when a single leader had been in command and this would always be so. There could be only one leader. He could be advised, but sole leadership was paramount. If there was more than one leader, the badgers would become just like ants on a branch floating down the river, each one thinking he was guiding, but the branch would really be going with the flow.

Eldon was prevented from continuing by derisory interruptions from Kronos's followers, but a thunderous yet sharp bark from Beaufort restored the audience to silence. Again showing his contempt for Kronos and what he represented, he declared that while any or all of Kronos's supporters would be welcomed back into the fold and their selfishness instantly forgotten and forgiven, Kronos would never again be allowed to be part of the Cilgwyn badgers. The fox had carried too many different teethmarks, and the marks on Dandelion were not those of the fox. Kronos had lifted the veil from himself, exposing nothing but evil, and for his deeds he would forever wear the badge of infamy.

As his own group became fully aware not only that Dandelion was dead but also that she had been murdered by her own kith and kin, there were cries for vengeance. Beaufort had his suspicions confirmed that there were some of Kronos's supporters innocent of the horrendous fate that had befallen Dandelion, as some prepared to leave the arc that supported Kronos, but the fanatics in Kronos's band attempted to prevent them from doing so. Upon seeing this, Beaufort, knowing that his group heavily outnumbered Kronos, ordered that those wishing to rejoin him be allowed to do so. Failure to obey this order would result in immediate retaliation and fearful vengeance would be brought upon Kronos and any other badger who prevented the badgers who wished to return from rejoining him. Even the crazed Kronos believed Beaufort would carry out his threat of retribution and nodded his agreement to release those wishing to leave him. Eight of the younger badgers, only two or three moons into their adolescence, came back to their families, heads bowed in shame at their earlier act of disloyalty, but their families who had missed them welcomed them with all the love they possessed.

Kronos moved back into the close proximity of his gang, his jaundiced eyes simmering like hot sulphur lakes, and then he moved away, his group, now reduced to thirty-six badgers, trailed behind him. There were pleading shouts for others to return, but Beaufort knew that evil, when allowed to grow, developed into the grip of a hypnotic spell, and those still with Kronos were now completely under his influence.

The stentorian voice of Beaufort barked his final warning to Kronos that if he came within sight of Beaufort again, he would order that vengeance, which was held by all to be the sole right of Logos, would be borrowed and brought down upon the head of Kronos.

A few moments after Kronos had disappeared Beaufort declared that they should rest for the remainder of the night and the following day in the glade where they had encountered Kronos. He was too tired to do any foraging, his thoughts were awhirl, his body still quivering from the anger that was within him and he wanted to believe that he would never set his eyes on Kronos again. He told himself that he had tried to believe this before, his burning brain kept erupting with constant promptings that there would never be release from the threat of Kronos until the charlatan was buried in the depths of Sheol. He hoped that his decision to allow Kronos to seek refuge in exile would not prove to be the undoing of their determined fight to live free.

Corntop appreciated the immensity of the task that had fallen on her loved one's shoulders and realised that Beaufort was totally unaware of the stature and prowess of leadership that exuded from him. She comforted him and explained that all his charges loved him with such intensity that they would abide by every word he uttered. They were devoted to him and there was happiness amongst them, particularly within the parents of the prodigal badgers that had returned. Badger parents always worried about their offspring, no matter how old they were, for the young of badgers are cubs until the parents die.

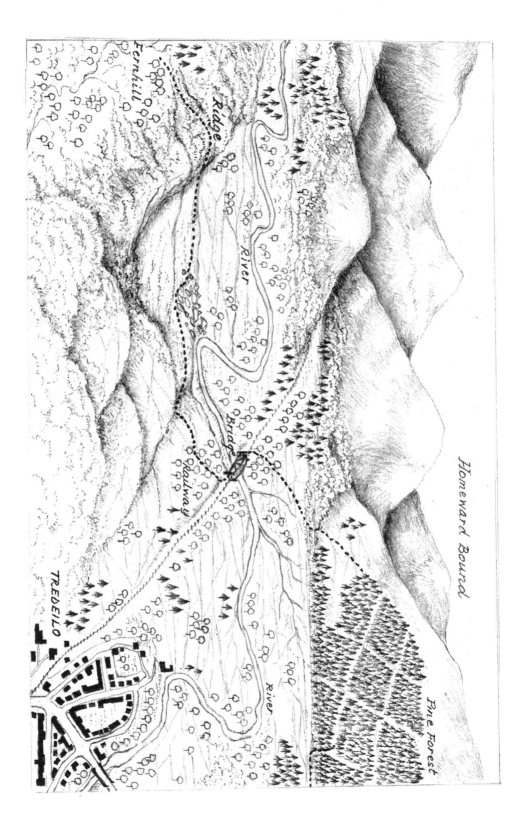

18

Fox-Fire

DAILY CHRONICLE

Thursday, 11th July

At a press conference called by the Ministry of Agriculture's Special Committee (Badger Eradication), a spokesman for the department stated that the following directives had been issued to Major T. G. Robertson, controller of badger extermination units.

1. The extermination programme must be successfully completed by 31st July.
2. Further military personnel would be sent to South Wales to ensure total success of the extermination unit by the amended completion date.
3. Six more helicopters would be made available for air search, bringing the total up to twelve.

4. The department, while appreciating the public's increasing concern for the animals, insists that the extermination programme must continue until there is no further risk of infection.

DAILY CHRONICLE

Llancwm, South Wales
Friday, 12th July

The saga of the escaping Cilgwyn badgers continued early this morning as this quiet country village was awakened by the sound of heavy lorries roaring through its main street towards the extermination unit camp based less than a mile away in a meadowed valley.

There were more than twenty trucks carrying army personnel and over thirty vehicles, some with trailers, carrying stores and equipment.

Later in the day I managed to get an interview with Major Robertson, who is confident that with the increase in manpower and other resources, the remaining area of Mid Wales still to be cleared of badgers will be covered with days, perhaps a week, to spare.

He added that the extermination programme had now passed the original completion date because of the wildness of the heavily forested area, and progress had been slowed down as the unit had to ensure that none of the escaping badgers backtracked, creating further problems.

When asked if he was aware of the public's changing attitude to the operation, the Major refused to comment.

It was later learned that the reinforced extermination unit would tomorrow carry out a full-scale drive through the valley, which stretches for just over six miles and ends at the foot of precipitous cliffs. As it seems certain that the group of surviving Cilgwyn badgers is somewhere in this area, the conservationists' reaction to this scheme was anger and dismay.

DAILY NEWS

Llancwm, South Wales
Friday, 12th July

Reinforced Extermination Units Have Trapped Cilgwyn Badgers

Tomorrow will probably bring the news that the strengthened extermination teams have finally caught and destroyed the elusive disease-carrying badgers of Cilgwyn.

They are trapped between the unit's camp and the ravine at the foot of the valley. Once these animals have been destroyed, the remaining area of Mid Wales still not cleared of badgers should be quickly covered. This newspaper, together with the *Morning Tribune*, has continuously supported the plan to exterminate the badgers and now looks forward to congratulating the government's extermination unit on the success of this operation.

Television news, 5:45 P.M.,
Saturday, 13th July

Less than an hour ago reports from Llancwm in South Wales suggest that once again the badgers of Cilgwyn have eluded the extermination units.

Over three hundred armed personnel as well as trackers believed that the badgers were fleeing ahead of them as they carried out a systematic search while advancing towards the cliffs at the end of the Llancwm valley. However, it appears that when the troops arrived at the rock-strewn area at the foot of the ravine the badgers' tracks vanished. The director of the extermination units was not available to give his views on these latest reports.

Television news, 9:00 P.M.,
Saturday, 13th July

Further news has just come in from Llancwm, where it was earlier reported that yet again the Cilgwyn badgers had avoided capture and shooting. A spokesman for the conservationist group 'P.A.W.S.,' accompanying the extermination units, has confirmed that proof had been found that badgers had recently roamed the area at the end of the Llancwm valley. He stated that one of his colleagues had found the bodies of three partly buried badgers. Although it was late evening and the area had been in complete darkness, the bodies had been discovered by their emission of a soft, incandescent light, which had aroused the curiosity of the conservationist. Upon investigation he discovered that the phosphoric light, which had no heat and occurred in decaying matter, was the light known as fox-fire. There can be little doubt that this latest escape by the badgers will add to the growing concern by the public for the badgers' survival. A representative of the farming industry, when asked to give his views on the latest development, stated that he could think of no reason why the badgers should continue to evade capture other than that it was due to some unknown but powerful intervention.

19

The Pines

As Eldon awoke from his restless slumber he became aware of a strange silence that was on the earth. He slowly turned his head from one side to the other, noticing that what badgers he could see in the undergrowth were still asleep and, although he could not locate the sun, there was still some time before darkness would begin to fall. The badgers had been travelling now for many moons; the warm-time days had long since passed and they were well into the time of the falling leaves. He usually enjoyed and fully appreciated every moment of the resting hours, but his previous night's unsatisfactory foraging had had its effect upon him and the day's rest had created a gigantic vacuum that would be even more difficult to fill if the frost had already taken its grip on the ground.

Eldon sniffed the air and felt much happier when he found the evening to be a little warmer than of late. However, it was still cold enough for his warm breath and the air rising from the sleeping bodies to change into spiralling vapours as the warmth encountered the cold barrier above them. He held his breath and let his ears seek out the evening adieus of the feathered world, but there were no caws from the rook, no quacks or cackles from the wild duck or goose, no chirps from the thrush or cheeps from the robin. There was a complete absence of the birds' usual salute to the oncoming night. Eldon's sense of hearing was acute, as was that of most badgers, and this highly developed sense told him that all was not silent as he could discern a faint, soft, gentle rustling. Rising and pushing his head through the covering bracken, he saw that the flakes of the first winter snows were falling and that the sky was heavy with its hoard of many flakes to come. He was grateful that the air was warm enough to keep the frost away, but he knew that whilst foraging would be easier with the worms being more available, as they did not have to bury themselves away from the burning frost, this advantage would soon be lost should the promise of more snow fulfil itself, and he decided it was time to rouse Beaufort and the others from their rest.

Beaufort had silently thanked Logos many times for the clemency he had shown in the weather. But he had known that sooner or later it would change for the worse. He understood that the needs of plant and soil required the days and nights of rime and even snow in order that the parasites could be controlled, allowing the earth to be bounteous in the next warm time. He wasn't at all surprised when Eldon informed him that the snows had arrived.

Although the pelage of the badgers gave considerable protection from the cold, it had always been their custom to seek shelter under the earth's surface, particularly during the time of the long, cold nights. The amount of winter feeding would not be sufficient to provide them with energy, stamina and warmth. The arrival of the snow now meant that their day routine of travel and resting would have to be changed, and Beaufort, having felt the chill of the winds become icier, had already decided that when the snows arrived, the travelling time would be reduced by half each night, and if the snowfall was heavy and laid thick on the ground, then they would only travel every other night.

It was the first time that any of the cubs had seen snow. The younger of them were more inclined to roll and play on the fresh white covering but were soon brought to order by Eldon and Harvey and urged to concentrate their energies on foraging as their lives might well depend on the energy they could store for the times ahead. The badgers were finding worm and beetle larvae in greater numbers that evening and, having longer to satisfy their appetites, were quite ready to move on when the time came for their journey to continue.

The snow was falling thickly, and their scratch marks in the soil for worms were covered completely before they left their latest abode. Beaufort had instructed that while they were marching over the cold white hillock they should keep close to each other. The night was silent but for the crunching of the badgers' paws in the snow. Instinct led Beaufort in the direction of the setting sun as he could not see very far in front of him, the new moon being obliterated by low, heavy cloud that unceasingly released its delicate, fragile contents.

Beaufort was glad that the snow was softly spiralling down and not being driven against them by the high winds that were another element of the cold time. He turned to see that many of his followers had patches of snow sticking to their hairs, which with the badgers' body heat or the movement of the marching feet occasionally slipped off. Beaufort decided that as the snow seemed likely to continue to fall through the night they would seek shelter in a pine grove or woods as soon as they could find one.

The pads of their paws were hard enough to withstand the constant cold that touched them each time they pressed into the snow as they strode onwards. Although the badgers were quite capable of surviving the cold and the snow, it was the blizzards that took their toll, especially when followed by heavy and sustained frost. When this weather came it soon developed into the silent killer of the animal kingdom, especially of the animals that had homes above the ground and the birds, which fell to the earth, having frozen to death on their roosting perches in the trees.

Beaufort knew that this unkind weather would eventually arrive. If it lasted many nights they might be forced to seek more permanent shelter to enable them to survive. In the cold times past he had always been comfortable during those heavy frosts because there had always been the sett, where he could snuggle up to Fern or Corntop.

The badgers' march became more laboured with each stride, and Beaufort informed them that when they came to the first clump of pines he would call a halt to the night's journey as their energies were wasted on the little progress that was being made. There was no species of life that would be abroad in this weather, not even the upright animal man.

Beaufort's acute sense of smell picked up the faint odour of pinewood and, slightly altering course, he led his tired companions into the shelter of spruce and fir. The trees, Sitka and Norway spruce, Douglas and Grand firs, Lodgepole and Scots pine, were tightly knit and provided a secure and welcome bastion against the adverse weather that prevailed above and outside those sturdy trunks. The forest floor was thick with the discarded refuse from the trees, cones, bark, twigs, needles and weather-broken branches. The exhausted badgers pressed their bodies into the woodland floor, huddling close together for warmth, with no intention of moving until the end of the following day.

Beaufort's head was fraught with worry as he struggled to think of a way of defeating the snow. The pursuers who had been given domination over all other creatures were, he felt sure, relentlessly on their trail and somehow they must continue with their journey or find somewhere to hide until the cold time was past. He wished hard for the touch of a vanished paw and the sound of the voice that was still.

20

Blizzards and Despair

For the next three days the snow clouds released their contents on the countryside below, then the heavens cleared, leaving a mackerel sky above the pine grove. The scent of the pinewoods, unrelenting in its pungency, became a main factor in Beaufort's decision to leave the shelter that had been their haven during those days. The badgers were becoming irritable. Everything had the same smell, they could taste it even on the grubs and larvae of the wood-boring beetle and saw-fly that they found in the bark or under the pine needles. The badgers awoke and went to sleep with the overwhelming aroma filling their nostrils, their own scent glands proving ineffective against the concentration of pine fragrance. Even their coats had absorbed the odour of pine.

Beaufort, Fircone and Eldon sat under the outermost firs looking out at a snow-covered landscape. Visibility was good but the contours of the land were difficult to perceive, as everything seemed to merge into a wall of sheer brilliance, a vivid whiteness that took their breath away. The panorama's horizon seemed to engulf them, the distant skyline sweeping around them on both sides. The sun glowed defiantly to the left of them, and although it would soon set, its rays were still strong enough to gild the skyline to their right, while the dark blue sky seemed to settle on a layer of musk mallow pink, which faded into the whiteness of the snow below.

Beaufort, although marvelling at the beauty of the land, knew that a clear sky at nightfall in the cold times, especially when the earth was covered in a blanket of snow, usually meant that the frost would take a vicious grip on them. The birds returning to the shelter of trees would have had difficulties in finding food with so much snow on the ground and had left it later than usual to return to their roosting places among the branches of the firs and pines. He saw that they were in groups of two or three, except for the solitary woodcock. He recognised this familiar feathered creature as a few had frequented the skies and bushes at Cilgwyn. This gentle bird, with plumage the colour of the oaks' fallen leaves and the pale hues of dead holly leaves, normally sheltered in the thick cover of bush or scrub, but the snows would deny it its usual abode that night. Most animals had a degree of nervous watchfulness in them, but the woodcock trusted nothing. When it had young in its nest it needed only the slightest of noises to alarm it and it would fly off with its fledglings tucked into its thighs.

The three badgers, after surveying the white countryside, rose up and barked in unison the command to the other badgers to gather for their journey across the snowlands, and as was the custom, Fern and Corntop walked immediately behind Beaufort as he led them towards the vanishing sun.

The perpetual crunching of paws on the frost-touched snow was the only sound the badgers heard in the early part of that moonless night. Beaufort, during the early stages of the night's journey, had arranged for the majority of the strongest badgers to walk at the head of the column, allowing the weaker ones to march over the compressed path made for them by those ahead.

They were soon out in the open countryside. Now and again they passed small clumps of snow-covered bushes, and by the time that Beaufort had planned to search for cover for the day's rest, he was concerned that there were no signs or scent of suitable protection. He had noticed the night air getting slightly warmer and the hoariness left his coat. The stars had also disappeared and he hoped that their screen of cloud was high in the heavens. There was no alternative but to march on, but his fears for his charges, who were following him faithfully in a serpentine trail, increased rapidly as a flurry of snowflakes began falling. For a while the flakes were hardly noticeable, the odd one or two gently touching his eyes. But the crunching sound of the badgers' paws was now being drowned by their murmurings, and Beaufort understood their anguish as a place of shelter was what they sought but as yet could not find.

There was soon another sound added to the night as the stillness of the night air was broken by a light wind, which had already started to make the thinly falling snow begin to swirl. They had travelled only a short distance further when the wind began picking up and the fall of snow intensified. Soon the wind was howling with savage ferocity and the snow whipped into their faces. The badgers were in the midst of a blizzard. In times past they would have rushed back to the shelter and warmth of their setts, but that night they were left to the mercies of the elements, blinded by the snow and buffeted by the strong winds. Beaufort felt that the cords of Sheol were tightening around them.

It was useless going on. They would have to rest where they were, and the badgers lay down, surrendering themselves to whatever fate awaited them. Closely grouped for warmth, they would occasionally, one or another, rise and shake the snow off their bodies.

The maelstrom of white made many of the badgers believe it would be their last vision on earth, and the longer it continued, fewer and fewer badgers rose to throw off their new cloaks until eventually all of them just lay still, and the blanket over them thickened as the snow relentlessly fell.

The light of day filtered through the white mantle to Beaufort's anguished eyes and he pushed up through the snow, hoping the light would help to reveal some means of shelter nearby, but as he brushed the snow from his eyes, he realised that the snowstorm prevented him seeing much more than he had been able to see before. He did notice, however, that the wind was whipping some of the snow off the ground and depositing it in huge drifts against the shrubs and bushes that were scattered around them, and he realised that the wind could possibly be their friend as it might prevent them from becoming smothered under a great depth of snow.

Many were the silent calls to Logos for help during that day, and it was only when the filtered light began to dim that their pleas were answered. Beaufort, emerging out of his shell of snow, saw the last rays of the sun streaking the sky ahead and a clear sky above him. The stars had begun their faint twinkling, which would soon brighten in the darkening sky. The desire for food was great in every one of them, but their safety was of paramount importance and every badger knew that no more time should be lost before they attempted to move on to find a place of safety. As Beaufort once more led them through the snow, which brushed the chest and flanks of the leading group, he decided that when they found shelter, there they would stay until the snow had melted and the terrain was recognisable as countryside again. The warm air that brought the snows and that had given way to the biting winds had changed once more, and it became colder with every stride.

The efforts of the leading badgers soon began to place a tremendous strain on them, and Beaufort instructed that the front marchers should be changed frequently so that their slow but steady walk could be maintained. They recognised very little, as grotesque and threatening shapes of mounds of snow loomed towards them. There were sprigs of ragged thorn peeping through the snow and trees that appeared to have no trunks but only bare branches growing out of mounds of snow. Many of the badgers were now nearing a state of collapse, and the pace of their travels was not much quicker than a snail's. Some moved forward only because they were pushed from behind, while others found momentum purely out of their knowledge that shelter had to be found if they were to survive.

The snaking column was becoming separated in many places and Beaufort frequently had to call back to Fircone, Eldon, Chantar and Gruff to urge everyone to keep close together. It was no longer a march but a series of lurches and stumbles, then slithering and sliding as their path widened into a gentle slope entering a wooded valley. There were patches of ground where small clumps of trees had prevented the snow from covering it with any great thickness, and Beaufort desperately prayed that they would find a shelter of pines, but his faith was close to breaking point as the trees receded and in front of him rose a snow-covered hill.

The column halted as one as Beaufort sat back, despairing and close to defeat. He felt Corntop and Fern brush past him and bravely enter a thicket that lay directly in front of them. Although it was mostly covered with snow, Beaufort could see that the thicket was comprised of thorn, holly, bramble and wild rose, which had taken root at the base of the hill. Corntop and Fern were slowly parting the strands and loops of bramble and then they vanished into the thick undergrowth. A moment or two later the group, to a badger, all but disposed of their coats when the bark of Corntop boomed at them from out of the briar and thorn. The badgers were momentarily paralysed with terror, as they believed that some terrible misfortune had befallen the two sow badgers.

Then, through the shrubbery, the happy face of Fern appeared barking excitedly and she beckoned with her paw. Beaufort panted with relief and dashed towards Fern, who then led him through the briar, thorn and holly, and Beaufort saw that the thicket had hidden the entrance to a large cavern that went deep into the hillside. He could now also see Corntop looming towards him from out of the darkness. He quivered for a moment as his nostrils picked up a very faint scent of the destructive creature man, but so faint was the scent that Beaufort relaxed as he realised that it was from many times past, and with the shrubbery that shielded the cavern from easy discovery, he believed that they had found a sanctuary that would be their home until the snow had gone.

The badgers needed little persuasion to enter the cave, their exhausted bodies yearning for a peaceful resting place. Nothing would have made them travel a step further. They were tired, wet and frozen, their resistance to further perils and dangers at an end. They would have to recover from their ordeal quite considerably before they would even contemplate taking another stride.

The duties of leadership, which Beaufort had promised would be of the highest priority, could not stop him from joining the others and falling into a deep sleep. His breathing became slower and more restful, becoming uniform with his companions', and soon the cavern was filled with the resonance of grateful slumber. These walls had witnessed slumbers of this depth in ages past when the bear had frequented the areas and had taken refuge for its hibernation.

21

Fircone and the Cave

The brushwood screen that hid the cavern from the outside world was being pierced by sunbeams when the first of the badgers opened their eyes after a very deep sleep. Their stirrings were not the only sounds that roused Beaufort from the last few moments of his slumber. He could also hear quite a number of badgers coughing.

He felt uncomfortably warm, and when he got to his feet he could see that the body heat of the badgers was causing considerable steam to rise from their snow-sodden coats and condense on the roof of the cave. This had been happening for some time, for the condensation on the cold ceiling was causing large droplets of water to drip back onto the badgers' coats.

Beaufort understood that the steam-laden atmosphere could be nothing but unhealthy and asked Fircone and Gruff to take some of their brothers and remove part of the screen so that the warm, stale, damp air could escape, allowing better access to the fresh air outside. He had not experienced these sorts of conditions before, but instinct told him that only harm would come if they remained in that thick, lung-congesting atmosphere.

The circulation of air improved greatly as the cave opening was exposed to the refreshing cold breeze that had been barred from the cave for such a long time. The badgers, stimulated by the heady tonic of clean, pure air after recovering from their exhausting exploits, realised that they were hungry, and Beaufort, seeing the urgency of their needs in their eyes, authorised them to venture out to forage but not to roam too far from the cave.

Beaufort had asked Fircone to stay behind to check over the cave with him. He thought of asking Eldon, too, but knowing Eldon's appetite, he could not bring himself to inflict such an act of cruelty on the old stalwart and protector of the young. They ventured slowly along the tunnel, which was very wide and very high to them. They knew of no animal that could burrow and produce a sett of that size. It had been made by some creature, of that they were sure, for the sides, the floor and the roof were jagged, and would have been smooth if it had been made by ice or water.

Though the tunnel had curved and shut away the lighted entrance, they were accustomed to living in darkness and could see quite easily in the murky gloom. The walls and the floor had little moisture and the air was stale and dank. Now and then the faint scent of the upright one was just discernible, but this was as stale as the air itself. There were some loose objects, strange to the two badgers, lying here and there, most of them with the feared scent about them, but they were as old as the mists of time. Some still had the strong smell of trees on them, one or two smelling exactly like the oak, some identical to the beech, but they were not trees. There was no bark, no twigs, no leaf or acorn or mast, and they were smooth and flat. There were things that were similar in shape to birds' nests or very large acorn tops but they were of some sort of smooth stone. The tunnel started to slope away and the badgers lifted their snouts to scent out ahead of them, finding nothing to cause them concern, and agreeing that they had come far enough, they turned back, feeling satisfied that this large and ancient sett would be quite suitable to shelter all of them from the snow and wind and even their pursuers, at least until the weather improved enough for them to carry on with their quest for a peaceful existence.

On returning, Beaufort and Fircone were surprised to find that some of the foraging badgers had already returned to the cave and were huddled together. They could not have found enough food in such a short time to have even begun to fill their empty stomachs, and as Beaufort approached them he could hear that some were wheezing, some were coughing and all of them had eyes that were inflamed and watery. As he bent over them to inquire what was ailing them, he could feel the heat from their bodies. They were burning with fever and he realised that their fatigue had weakened them enough to be smitten by the disease that had sometimes afflicted the old ones in the cold times at Cilgwyn. But only one of the seven stricken badgers was old. There were two of the last birth times and the remainder were only a little older. The fever had triumphed over their starvation and had made them weak. Beaufort, having told Fircone to forage for a spell and then report back to him with the other council members, went out of the cave to look for Fern and Corntop. He found them under some leafless oaks digging the snow away from the ground and searching for acorns. They would find very few worms with so much snow on the frost-gripped ground. The other badgers were also digging, not only for acorn or beechmast or even chestnut, but also seeking out the corms of the arum, the roots of comfrey and dandelion. Beaufort informed his mother and Corntop that sickness had struck some of them and he suggested that the two of them, with Rhea, the healing badger, should organise the tending of the sick and comfort them while he would arrange for food and any remedial plants that he could find to be sent in to them in the cave.

He then sought out Eldon and discovered him barking, grunting and gesticulating to some young cubs. He had quite a pile of arum corms in front of him and was explaining to the young ones that they could eat only the corms themselves and under no circumstances eat the shoots that were on the corms. The shoots had to be bitten off and spat out, as they were poisonous and if eaten would make the cubs suffer great agonies, even death.

When Beaufort told him that the badgers must stop eating the corms, Eldon looked crestfallen, not because he was particularly partial to roots or corms of any kind, but they were better than nothing and they were all he had been able to find since he left the cave to forage.

His disappointment faded as soon as Beaufort said that they were needed for some badgers who had fallen sick with fever and who were now lying in the cave too weak to fend for themselves. Eldon once again affirmed his inherited qualities of compassion and concern for his fellow badgers, though he had let them become dormant during the latter part of his leadership at Cilgwyn, by telling his young charges to each gather a few corms in their mouths and follow him back to the cave.

The hunger within Beaufort reminded him that he must find some food for himself, as he must not allow himself to weaken and fail in his duty. He was fortunate enough to find some dung from a deer beneath a tree that had had its bark eaten, most probably by the same deer. Turning the dung over, he found quite a number of dor beetles. Though they were dead, they were still quite acceptable. Soon he dug up some pignut and then found the body of a rook that had succumbed to the cold weather and had fallen from its perch to the ground. He was never very keen on carrion but it had to suffice in times of scarcity. He decided that he had eaten enough to return to the cave and see how the care and nursing of the sick was developing. Fircone, Gruff, Chantar and Eldon were awaiting him at the entrance, as they had been instructed, but their faces were grave and Beaufort soon understood the reason. He was told that there were now over thirty badgers who had succumbed to the disease-bearing phantom from the land of hoar and rime.

The care and treatment of the sick was well in hand and the female badgers had been organised into nursing groups that would forage for a time then return to relieve the group that had been assisting Rhea, Fern and Corntop in the care of the suffering. Beaufort was reassured by Corntop that they were taking some food for themselves in order that they could maintain the strength needed for the supervision of the afflicted. Rhea explained that some of the patients were quite critical and that it was not just a chill but far more serious. The lungs of the diseased were congested and filling with a fluid that could suffocate them or cause their hearts to stop beating, and it was imperative that they find the roots of the marshmallow. This was a very dependable remedy for clearing the lungs, and it would be far better if more badgers concentrated their efforts on finding this healing herb rather than gathering roots and carrion for the sick, as they would not need food until they began to recover and the fever had been overcome.

Beaufort organised ten groups of badgers, each of them being six in number, to spread out and search for the sickly, sweet-flavoured root of the marshmallow, greyish-white outside and white as milk inside, which could be found only near ditches, streams or any other type of watercourse.

When Beaufort had examined the cave with Fircone, he had

felt that he would be able to relax as the badgers could rest and forage at will until their strength was restored but he was now extremely worried that, with the lack of food and unexpected exertions of the tasks newly thrust upon them, they would have to spend a far longer time in the cave than he had visualised. This could put them in even greater peril, for each sun they spent in that cave, the nearer their persecutors would be to them. They could not move on and leave the sick behind. He knew that both Fern and Corntop would refuse to go whatever he said, as they had had to leave too many to the mercy of the chasing killers as it was. Beaufort decided at that moment that there would be no more of it. It had to be all for one and one for all from now on.

It seemed to Beaufort that Logos must have been very displeased with the breakdown of the pattern of Cilgwyn and was setting a path full of soul-destroying obstacles in their search for a new life. They would have to prove they were worthy of another chance even though Bamber and Buckwheat had sacrificed themselves to appease Him. How many more trials and tribulations lay ahead, Beaufort wondered? He had taken such a long time to understand what Buckwheat had been at great pains to ensure was lovingly and religiously maintained at Cilgwyn. Beaufort now fully realised that every luxury had to be earned and everything was a luxury, starting with the earth, but sometimes, he had to admit, he had difficulty in finding an answer for the searching eyes of his companions, wondering why so many misadventures came their way, and now this pestilence. He turned his eyes skywards and kept asking, in silent thought, why the world that seemed so near was so hard to get hold of?

He shook the entanglements of his thoughts out of his mind as three of the mallow-seeking groups returned successfully. They took the curative plants back into the cave and placed them in

Rhea's welcoming paws, but Beaufort, who had followed them, was staggered to find that many more had become victims of the dreaded illness. His worries increased a hundredfold when he saw that amongst the huddled mass of the confined was his friend, the bravest and strongest badger of them all, his beloved Fircone.

Corntop told of how Fircone had refused to rest and take succour, and had continued fetching and carrying foodstuffs for those who were comforting the sick. He had carried on when others would have collapsed from the tremendous effort he had been giving. But Fircone had pushed himself too far, and when returning with some beechmast his legs had given way beneath him and he had fallen unconscious at the entrance to the cave. It had taken five of the badgers to lift him and carry him inside the cave, into the tender care of Rhea, but his total lack of concern for himself had placed Fircone in the jaws of death, and Rhea said that even if she managed to squeeze some of the sweet and sickly marshmallow root juice down Fircone's throat, it would be a miracle if he survived and that it was now only the will of Logos that could save him.

Beaufort left the cave quietly and, finding a place of solitude, lay prostrate on the snow, beseeching the Creator to spare Fircone. The big badger was needed by all of them if they were to succeed, and his friend's kindness of heart, his devotion to the weak and infirm, his unswerving loyalty and unselfishness deserved all the help he could get.

Fircone's unexpected collapse pushed Beaufort to the precipice of defeat, his belief in their eventual success severely shaken, his strength of mind and purpose weakened to the point of capitulation. Yet the stout heart of this badger remained steadfast, and this, together with the calmness and determination that radiated from Corntop, was sufficient to rekindle the resolve and conviction that whatever penance they were given, whatever adversity came their way, they would overcome such challenges. All the distance that they had travelled, all the steps to come would be worth that moment of true happiness that they would one day experience.

As the next few days passed by more and more of the badgers were struck down by the dreaded disease. Their laboured breathing caused Beaufort great distress and he feared that some of them would never again enjoy the delights of roaming and foraging under a moonlit sky. There were very few badgers who rested their weary bodies during that time in the cave and the nights went by as if they were clouds in a storm-blown sky. There were less than fifty of the badgers capable of standing, though the fever had left most of those who had been the first to become infected. Beaufort would never understand why he had escaped the disease, as had Corntop, Fern, Rhea, Bramble, Greyears, Eldon and forty-two of the cubs, and their valiant efforts in supplying medicinal roots, food and loving care to the inflicted convinced him that they could move mountains.

The snow had kept away but it clung to the earth's surface as the frost very rarely left them. Even in those adverse conditions, Rhea's knowledge of the likely location of the beneficial roots enabled Eldon and his young army to maintain a steady and sufficient supply. They also managed to deliver quantities of beetle, worm and grub for those who were showing signs of recovery, but this task became increasingly difficult as the numbers of improving badgers grew.

The frosty nights were taking their toll of the feathered world and never a morning went by when the badgers didn't discover the frozen rigid corpses of wood-pigeon, sparrow and starling at the foot of the trees. Eldon was relentless as a taskmaster, but he never once had to scold or threaten his infant helpers, even though they were all of tender age. The urgency and necessity of the demands put upon them were accepted with courage and an undaunted spirit that belied their age. The knowledge of flora that had been passed down through generation after generation to Rhea and the expertise of Eldon in applying his unique talent for discovering such a varied range of food were the essential factors in restoring the afflicted to good health.

Soon more than half of the sick ones had overcome the infection but were still too weak to forage for themselves. It usually took three days of succour before they became strong enough to venture outside and seek sustenance enough for their own needs. A stroke of good fortune arrived one morning when Eldon, returning to forage with his cubs after taking a short rest, saw, as he came out of the cave at daybreak, some birds circling in the sun-tipped sky. This usually meant that another animal had become prey to its hunter or some other misfortune had befallen it. The birds were hoping to get some pickings or, if it was not dead yet, descend upon it as soon as its life departed.

Eldon gathered his group together and advanced, keeping in view the birds that hovered effortlessly in the sky. He had known these birds to attack young cubs, especially when the weather prevented them from catching their usual prey, such as small rodents, which sheltered longer in their dreys or nests. The birds had, on more than one occasion, plunged down from the sky with fantastic speed, digging their talons deep into the flesh of nestlings, weakling badgers whose days were less than a life of a moon, lifting the cubs and soaring away to their nests, where they would swiftly bring to an end the young badgers' lives.

There were four pairs of buzzards, and though they were larger than most of the birds that inhabited Cilgwyn, they were of a cowardly nature and more often than not flew away when chased by the crow or rook.

These large, short-necked, broad-winged birds of prey were brown in feather with strong talons and beaks that were curved to tear into the flesh of their victims. Eldon also noticed that there was another bird amongst them, similar to the buzzards but of a different colouring, its head feathers paler and its chest and leg feathers more a rusty red than brown. Its tail was deeply forked, the buzzard's being straight and short. This was the red kite, which was seen only on very rare occasions at Cilgwyn.

Eldon took the young cubs around a small spinney and the snow-covered ground fell away to a stream, and there lay the animal that was the focus of the birds' attentions. As they drew nearer to the partly submerged body, Eldon saw that it was a female deer that had seemingly misjudged its leap across the stream and had slipped on the frozen banks, falling heavily onto a jagged rock that rose above the water. The creature's back had taken the brunt of the blow and had broken, leaving the poor creature defenceless and in agony. It would lie there, perhaps for a night and a day before its final moment of life left its body. The birds, if forced by hunger, might attack before that time arrived, tearing at its skin and pecking at its eyes whilst it still breathed. The deer would endure the savage beaks and talons until its life blood drained away.

These thoughts and visions persuaded Eldon that the creature had to be put out of its misery. Although the ailing badgers would normally disregard this meat, as there was little else to be found, they would gratefully accept it now. The difficulty was not only in the transportation of the carcass back to the cave but also in the actual slaughter of the creature. Eldon knew that he could not bring himself to sink his teeth into the deer's throat and keep his jaws locked until the animal breathed no more. The thought of doing this was repugnant. What if the animal moved as he tried to choke it, would the warm blood gush into his mouth? He shuddered as he thought about it and decided he would have to go back for Beaufort. He explained to the cubs that as a leader he had never been called upon to carry out such a sordid deed and, as there was no one else to call upon, it would be necessary to fetch Beaufort.

Eldon recoiled with horror as Titan, the strongest and most venturesome of the cubs, leapt down on the deer, catching its windpipe in his jaws, attempting to shake its head as if fighting a fox. Eldon was transfixed and felt admiration for his young hero cub, tinged with regret as the death-rattle came from the fine, noble and elegant creature.

Titan stood back and looked to Eldon for his approval, which was readily given. Eldon made a mental note that on the next occasion that he showed the cubs the methods of acquiring sweet and savoury foods, he would include Titan in his demonstrations. In fact, he would ask Titan to sample the food before he tasted it himself.

They waited a short while until Eldon was sure that the spasmodic nerve-twitching of the deer was finally ended and its soul had departed to Asgard, where it would have eternal safety and could even lie beside the lion. The badgers gripped the deer's legs in their mouths and began the task of pulling it back to the cave. The kite and the buzzards swooped down on them when they realised they had been deprived of their meal, but there were too many badgers for the birds to contemplate making serious attempts to retrieve their lost prey.

Some of the cubs were sent back to the cave to tell Beaufort of the "find" and that there would be some delay before Eldon, his cubs and the sizeable load of food would arrive back. The toiling cubs had to exert all their strength to drag the corpse through the undergrowth, although it was made a little easier by sliding it on the hard-packed snow. They were practically exhausted when they got to the cave, and it needed Beaufort's assistance to eventually get the meat inside the cavern, where the ravenous badgers soon devoured a considerable amount of the still slightly warm flesh.

The following night had been the crisis point in Fircone's fight to survive. Beaufort had stayed by his friend's side, cooling his face with lumps of hard-packed snow. Fircone's breathing seemed to stop at times, his stillness giving way to periodic gasps, and his body burnt with a fever of such intensity that Rhea warned Beaufort to expect the worst as she had not known a badger to survive a fever of such dimensions before. Beaufort caressed his big friend in his paws and his love and respect for Eldon grew even more as he saw that on the other side of Fircone, Eldon was patting and soothing the big one's shoulder, sometimes closing his eyes and mouthing silent words.

The night was nearly through when Beaufort began to feel the fever leave Fircone's body, and when he saw Eldon rise to take charge of the cubs once more, he knew Fircone would survive and he bent his head down on Fircone's chest and wept unashamedly. He took some marshmallow roots and, after crunching them in his mouth, tried to squirt the juice into Fircone's mouth. At first very little appeared to get past Fircone's teeth, but eventually the big one's tongue slowly appeared and unconsciously licked the first sustenance he had received for many days. Moments later his eyes flickered, then opened, and although very debilitated, those eyes acknowledged Beaufort with everlasting gratefulness and an oath of affinity until the end of time.

Seven more suns came and went before there was total recovery amongst the badgers, and it was only then that Beaufort, Corntop, Fern, Rhea, Eldon and the cubs could take their well-earned rest. Fircone's strength had quickly returned and he was now back to his old self again. He insisted that Beaufort and the others who had worked continuously through the many days of hardship and suffering should rest their tired bodies and that he would take charge of things while they rested. Fircone ordered all the other badgers out of the cave to forage and instructed them that they were not to return there until he permitted it, to allow the valiant to have their peace.

There were no dreams or visions in the sleep of those resolute badgers who had unstintingly and tenaciously fought so long to free the infirm from their bond of illness. They slept as if in a trance through the day and through the night. Their efforts to awaken were sluggish as they labouriously stretched their limbs and stiffly yawned their appreciation at such a fortifying sleep. They were surprised to see the sunlight pouring in through the opening of the cave and could not understand where the rest of the badgers were, for they, too, should be resting during the day after a night's foraging. Eldon sat up, quickly followed by the others, and cut short his query to Beaufort as to the whereabouts of the others. He thought he was dreaming, for on the floor of the cave around them were piles of different foods. There were worms in abundance, some crawling away, trying to find a hiding place in the stony floor, and pupae, larvae, beetles, haws and carrion. Directly in front of Eldon was the largest mound of earthworms and slow worms he had ever seen. Eldon tested his dream by tentatively catching a worm in his mouth. The taste was too real for it to be one of his feastful fantasies, and he was positive that the dream that had regularly occurred over a long, long time had at last come true. The sound of the other badgers accepting the foods of Asgard shook the lethargy from Eldon, who was soon munching, crunching, biting, swallowing and slurping one mouthful after another. He continued eating well after the others had had their fill, determined that no food should be wasted, yet even he had to struggle over the last few morsels.

The excited voices and sounds of appetite being vigourously satisfied finally died away and it was then that Fircone allowed the other badgers to follow him into the cave. The sight that greeted them was that of totally contented badgers, fully re-

stored and fully fed. They were trying to hold back their laughter, but ripples of merriment kept breaking out as they looked at Eldon, who was sitting down with his back against the wall, his legs out in front of him and his paws lying on his stomach, so full of food that the skin could be seen stretching taut between his soft underfur. The joy on the faces of those few badgers was sufficient reward for Fircone and the recovered, who had spent the night collecting and preparing this sumptuous feast.

Their joy was made complete when the first drops of rain began to fall outside. It meant that the frost had gone and soon the snow would melt and be washed away. They would be ready to move on as soon as nightfall came. Eldon, although thankful for the shelter that the cave had provided during such troubled times, was glad to get away, for though he had enjoyed the farewell feast, his memory of that place would forever be the petrified eyes of that deer, its flaring nostrils as it gasped and panted in such rapid breaths, and its quivering body. He was thankful that those signs of overwhelming fear were removed by the prompt and thoughtful action of Titan, and had been glad when he saw those large and beautiful soft eyes of one of the earth's gentlest creatures close in everlasting peace.

22

Fishing and the Owl

Though the illness in the cave had left its mark on many of them, the badgers continued on their relentless journey to freedom. The snows had kept away, but the weather had still been unkind. Most nights they had sheltered under brushwood or under pines, protecting themselves as best they could from either the cold biting winds or heavy frosts. Beaufort had limited their marching to every other night as he realised that the badgers did not have the strength that they had before the snows had come.

The distance that they now covered during a night's march was considerably less than that which they had achieved before they arrived at the cave, but they had ranged over moorlands, through valleys and rounded many hills without losing further life. Their consumption of food had also fallen, as it became less and less available, and it was a welcome relief to discover one evening, as they settled under some spruce pines, that they were close to a river that had many pools containing considerable numbers of trout.

Eldon's uncanny knack of finding sources of food had come to the fore again. His scent-twitching snout had led him to the riverside, and after gazing for a few moments at the placid surfaces of the river-fed pools, he realised that his long since used skill at catching fish would be needed once more. Although there was the nuisance of bones, the delicious pink white meat far outweighed such a trivial hindrance. He returned to inform Beaufort of his find, suggesting that the badgers spread themselves out along the river inlets and pools. He would take six of the cubs under his personal supervision so that he could show them how fish should be caught. Beaufort was pleased with this idea as it would not only help to feed them but would also divert their thoughts from the drudgery of constant journeying.

The cubs, one of them being Titan, followed closely behind Eldon, who led them to a pool where he had seen the silvered fish create ripples in the shining waters, shining under the moonbeams that lit up the tranquil countryside, on a night that was the first for some time to be free of frost or wind. Eldon knew that the majority of the badgers had not gone fishing before. A large number of them hadn't ever tasted fish, and many of them showed their ignorance by leaping into the shallow pools and frightening the fish away. If this approach to catching was allowed to continue, very few of the badgers would taste the succulent gifts that were on offer. Beaufort wasn't too confident himself, and seeing the concern on Eldon's face at the thought of such a wasted opportunity, ordered the badgers to stop their useless attempts and to gather on the riverbank to learn how fish should be caught from Eldon, the master of all skills connected with food.

Telling his audience to keep quite still and silent, and adding a warning that what fish he caught were for the use of his own cubs and himself, Eldon gently waded into the cold water of the pool, his thick, grey coat giving considerable protection from the water's chilliness. He stood on a rocky platform that was barely submerged by the water, his right forepaw raised and his eyes staring intently into the water, which was close to his other front paw. Suddenly he made a bearlike sweep with his raised paw and deftly flipped a trout out of the water onto the bank behind him and, turning, softly grunted to Titan that he should cuff the fish on its head and, when it was quite still, gather it up and guard it along with any others that he would toss to them. With unbelievable regularity Eldon continued his successful flipping out of fish, and when he had caught ten he slowly withdrew from the waters and told Titan to take his place. Titan copied Eldon's stealthy approach and slowly walked into the water. He stopped momentarily as the coldness of the water surprised him, but stifling his gasps, he continued until he stood on the same spot where Eldon had patiently gazed into the black glistening pond. Titan could see the fish moving in the water that reflected his own shadow, and watched one slowly move towards his feet by just a quick movement of its tail. He dashed his paw into the pool but nothing came out. Trying to hide his cubbish disappointment at his failure, Titan turned to Eldon, seeking his help. He was quickly told that he must not attempt to catch fish that were moving. Titan prepared himself once more, his right paw raised, and checked himself more than once when he was unsure if a fish was resting. He would not fail in front of his audience again, and with tremendous concentration he leaned over the pool, poised as an adder that was about to dart at some unsuspecting prey. Then, without further hesitation, Titan moved like lightning, catching the biggest fish so far and flipping it on to the riverbank, right at Eldon's paws. Eldon's belief in his protégé's abilities were affirmed. This strong boar cub, already as big as some born three years earlier, possessed qualities that would make him something special in time to come.

Titan rejoined Eldon on the bank, although he had wished to carry on displaying his new-found prowess. He saw the admiration in the other cubs' eyes and his elation was matched only by his love and reverence for his adoptive father and mentor, his dear beloved Eldon.

The other badgers soon dispersed to the other pools, endeavouring to follow Eldon's instructions and catch for themselves their own suppers. Eldon, meanwhile, was showing his young companions how a fish should be eaten. He had taken the largest one between his paws to enable the cubs to see more clearly what he was doing, and slowly his teeth prised away the flesh from the bone, and he smacked his lips with each mouthful until only the head, tail and skeletal frame was left. He wanted to make sure that the cubs fully understood the procedure by going over it again on another fish, but he realised there was little sense in doing this for Titan and the others were already enjoying their first taste of this new source of food. The cubs were now very quick at learning and Eldon quickly grabbed another fish.

Although many of the badgers failed to catch anything for themselves, enough fish were caught for all to have a taste. To satisfy their appetites they searched for worms, larvae and the beetles that were hidden underneath the bark of the spruce trees.

The following night in the period of foraging before their travels commenced, Eldon and his cubs were to be found again catching and devouring fish. So successful were Eldon and Titan, they had no need to look for worms. The river turned sharply to the left of their intended route, and as they ventured further the journey took them once more in the direction of the setting sun. The badgers seemed to be in a more contented frame of mind that night. They would have a lot to be thankful to Eldon for when they reached the day of glory. They broke out of the cover of trees and thicket halfway through the night, and the terrain they had traversed was a primrose path compared to what now confronted them. Ahead lay a range of mountains, which they would have to climb, for domineering peaks surrounded them. Yet again a test of their worthiness of Logos's protection was set before them, and although disheartened, Beaufort understood that to eat the nut one had first to crack the shell.

It had become necessary once more to adjust the schedule of travelling time, the effort of climbing and descending the mountains being so demanding that it sapped the strength of even the strongest badgers. Fortunately it had not been necessary to climb to the summits of the mountains, which were bare of vegetation. They had managed to keep within the limits of the heather-covered slopes and this had saved them considerable time and effort. A new moon had come and gone before they left that mountain range, and as they descended into another strange valley they could see on the horizon a steep, stone-crested crag, which did not appear to be part of another mountain range. They could not see any other summits beyond it, and Beaufort hoped that their path would become easier once they had surmounted the formidable barrier that lay before them.

The comfort of the softer grass, instead of stone and heather, was readily appreciated by all of the badgers, and Beaufort decided that they would stay in this peaceful glen for five suns in order to regain their fitness. Food would be more varied and plentiful in the fertile basin. Some of the badgers were distraught from hunger and were soon consuming tufts of winter grasses. But Beaufort's heart jumped with joy as he saw snowdrops displaying their white blooms, the first signs of the rebirth of plants, buds and the promise of kinder weather.

The tiredness of marching deserted the weary travellers and

their walk became rather jaunty as the first sign of the country-side's awakening became apparent to them all. They were soon amongst bracken and small clumps of firs as well as beech, ash, lime and crabapple. The spinneys had clusters of hawthorn, dogwood, wild privet and spindle. They could safely rest in the little haven before they made their attempt on the awesome heights that towered over them.

Beaufort's happiness at having found such a peaceful and relaxing resting place changed abruptly as the screech-owl told them it was annoyed at them for having disturbed its hunting grounds with their unwelcome presence. Beaufort looked at the consternation on the badgers' faces. The older ones knew that the cry of the screech-owl quite often foretold death, and Beaufort also knew that he would have difficulty freeing himself of foreboding thoughts during the stay in what they had first thought was such a beautiful glen. He hoped the screech-owl's warning was just part of badger lore and would prove to be empty.

23

Out of the Mouths

A chequered pattern of rivulets criss-crossed the floor of the valley and the water from the melted snows that had mantled the peaks of the inhospitable mountain range they had recently climbed now filled the time-worn furrows of the channels. There brook and burn, rill and runnel merged into a single, meandering stream that widened as it travelled through the valley, meeting up with other streams, a lattice of shimmering silver forming the embryo of a river that took the water back to the sea.

Beaufort gathered the badgers together, instructing some of the young adult boars to act as marshals, flanking the main body as they moved through what was left of the valley before they encountered the foothills and ventured up the barren wind-swept tract that loomed threateningly ahead of them.

The weather was in their favour, as the night air was surprisingly warm and the moon was casting a gentle pearly lustre upon the earth around them, enhancing the beauty of the valley they were about to leave. The soft light helped Beaufort as his eyes searched the upland scene to find the least hazardous pathway through the low foothills and scarps and up the towering rugged crest that challenged, with cruel defiance, their attempt to advance. Then, thankfully, Beaufort saw, to the right of the slab-sided cliffs, a rock-strewn slope of scree and boulders, and though hard on their pads, their paw-holds would be more secure. However, his gratitude was short-lived, as the sense of foreboding that had been with him during his restless slumbers of the day returned, even stronger than before.

The badgers started their night's march without their customary enthusiasm, for they sensed the trepidation and caution that emanated from Beaufort as he tentatively led them through the final stretch of the valley. They ambled through hawthorn and elderbushes that were bare of leaf, the moonlight sufficient to expose the long since deserted nests of a number of birds. Beaufort thought of the warm times when the heavy-leafed shrubbery hid the frenzied activity of infant bird life, when the goldfinches and hedge-sparrows stretched their wrinkled necks from their small nests, the thrush and blackbird from their larger nests. He could see the brittle platforms of the doves and wood-pigeons in the bare branches of the trees, brittle and flimsy, yet so cleverly built that not even the storm winds could dislodge them.

The night was a time for predators, yet other than the sound of the shuffling of the badgers, all was silent. The atmosphere was eerie, and the badgers were taut and tense as they moved through the nervous air. Beaufort was always happier when the badgers were hidden by shrubbery and trees but this was one night when he would be glad to escape from the furtive and ghostlike shadows being cast by the bright and clear moon. The stillness of sound was sharply broken by a fearful squeal not far ahead of them. Beaufort recognised the noise of a frightened rabbit, and then he jumped nervously as through the undergrowth directly in front of him a stoat broke its cover, an adult cony, now lifeless, draped on either side of the stoat's firmly clenched jaws. Although the stoat, like the weasel, polecat, and pinemarten, was a distant cousin of the badger family, the suddenness of its appearance left the badgers frozen. The stoat, being in its homelands, turned aside and with bounding gait the slender animal raced away, still carrying its prey. Beaufort had only once before seen a stoat in the cold times. They were usually reddish-brown with white underneath, but now this one was mostly white, as white as snow except for the black at the end of its tail.

The heart-thumping experience of the stoat's appearance was soon left behind as the badgers continued on their journey. Beaufort's pace increased as they came into the outer fringes of the woodland, his suspicious mind relaxing with every step as the foothills came into sight. A short series of gentle terraced drops through the narrow rivulets and they would be at the base of the foothills, free of the ghostly and haunted vegetation.

Beaufort slowly ambled down the damp, stepped woodside, having to dig his paws deep into the soft ground to prevent himself from slithering into the shallow waters of the brook. His progress was made even more difficult by having to climb over the roots of a clump of alder trees, roots that twisted and wound into the slow-moving water. Beaufort lifted his paw over the last of the roots and, as he was about to take his first step into the water, he shook with terror. A long, drawn-out moan came from within the darkness of the half-submerged roots, followed by a hissing sound and then a high-pitched chatter. Beaufort's body snapped backwards with fright and, falling and slipping, he withdrew quickly from the tangled roots to the comparative safety of the wet, sloping ground. A sleek and streamlined body emerged from the alder roots. Its flattish head had small ears and a whiskered muzzle, and it stood on its hind legs for just a moment, showing a beautiful, short, close-fitting, dark brown coat before diving into a pool that lay a short distance down the bank. Beaufort stared in stupefaction as the creature broke the surface of the water. It began to emit a shrill whistle, which was quickly answered by a similar sound coming from the dense undergrowth the badgers had left behind. The other badgers, seeing Beaufort's look of amazement, began chuckling, as not being so close to the unexpected activity as Beaufort and therefore less alarmed, they realised he had stumbled across the holt of an otter. Beaufort relaxed a little on hearing the increasing sounds of laughter. He turned around and became conscious of his embarrassment, which only made his companions' mirth increase, until even Beaufort himself joined in as he understood that the fears of the unknown were becoming magnified in the minds of not only the badgers but also himself. Yet what was frightening them was nothing more than the normal and natural life-forms of the nocturnal woodlands. He was glad that the mood of foreboding that veiled the badgers' minds had been lifted as they crossed the bottom level of the valley and on to the foothills. The badgers were chatting to each other, ready to attempt to scale the immense and lofty uplands in better heart.

Beaufort led the column of friends around the foothills until they came to the boulder-strewn base of the scree-covered pathway that led up the mountain slopes. The loose and jagged scree was spread much more widely than Beaufort had estimated when he had first seen it from the woodland cover. While this did not increase his worries, he was disconcerted by the height the path reached. It was far, far higher than he had envisaged, its lofty terminus only just within range of his vision, and then above that a crest of sandstone, stiff and erect, prominently displaying its stubborn resistance to the ravages of the changing elements and to the animals who wished to cross over the savage crags to fertile lands beyond.

The badgers began the ascent, knowing that it would take a

stupendous effort if they were to succeed in scaling the summit before the sun began to brush the sky with its pale, honeyed glow. This would leave them exposed on the mountaintop and place them in the most vulnerable position that they had been in since they had left Cilgwyn. Beaufort knew there was no alternative, and because conditions would never be better, they could not delay the ascent a moment longer.

The badgers experienced tremendous difficulty clambering over the sharp-edged talus rock. Some of the stones were as small as cubs' paws others larger than a full-grown badger. These rocks had once been part of the massif itself but had been split by the action of frost through the ages. The moon had left the sky and the night was the darkest that Beaufort could re-member. The terrain, savage and forsaken by Logos, was now a series of monstrous blurred shapes that loomed menacingly at them. As soon as they scrambled over some of the large stones, there appeared another row of boulders to overcome. Though the sight of the badgers was not sharp, and though it could not compare with the hawk's by day, they did possess the power of night vision, being nocturnal by nature, and the density of the darkness did not unduly worry Beaufort. What did concern him was the increasing realisation that they would be far short of the summit after the night was over.

Beaufort was surprised at the tenacity of some plants that fought to survive on the unyielding ground. Now and then, between the smaller pieces of scree, there were glimpses of the three-leafed rush, tufted fescue, gentian, the purple saxifrage and the peppery-tasting stonecrop. He compared the plight of these gentle forms of life with that of himself and his companions, all fighting to survive against an ever-threatening enemy. For the badgers it was man, for the plants it was the continual bombardment of rock fall as each year's frost cracked the surface of the stone-clad summit.

He found new strength and inspiration from the example being shown by the plants in their determination to survive. Beaufort encouraged his companions with every stride, cajoling, urging, pleading, reassuring, rallying and sometimes shouting his demands for greater effort. Although the badgers' paws had been hardened by the prolonged travel, many were the lacerations on their pads and many claws snapped off, but they had become used to such minor inconveniences. Up they went, Fircone and Gruff making sure there were no stragglers and keeping the tail-end of the column as close to the leaders as was possible.

The day dawned with the badgers closer to the peaks than Beaufort had thought possible only a short time ago, and when the sun had revealed its total form, the last of the badgers eased their tired bodies onto the topmost reaches of the scree. They were nestled against the final steep ridge and accepted without argument Beaufort's statement that they could not stay there for long. They would have to climb the wall even though it would be during the sunlight, for if they stayed on the ridge, they would be taking an even greater risk of being seen by their foe.

Beaufort searched the faces of Eldon, Fircone, Chantar and Gruff, hoping to find a helpful expression, a spark of a suggestion in their eyes, anything that would help formulate a method to get over the crag. The faces of his council colleagues were no different from those of the other badgers; there was no alarm or uncertainty. They were undoubting, full of expectancy for Beaufort's directions. Their cublike faith in him tore at his heart and his body trembled at the magnitude of his responsibilities. Yet behind these faithful eyes shone the greater power of love, of their love for him, which would always give him renewed confidence in himself.

He told his loved ones to rest for a few moments and then he would explain how they would tackle the wall. Beaufort turned to face the formidable pale brown rock face, which was cracked in many places. There were small protrusions where the rock above had fallen away to the path below. Whilst some of the badgers might succeed in clawing themselves up the rock, many more would meet the same fate as the scaling rock, falling away to the scree path below, breaking their bodies to pieces on the jagged edges of stone.

The longer Beaufort searched for a solution, the more impossible the task seemed to be. It was not a matter of choice—there was none. The problem seemed insoluble, the obstacle insurmountable. He turned again to face the badgers, trying desperately to hide his look of consternation and racking his brain for an answer. He let his gaze drop to the ground as he turned back towards the unrelenting barrier. He drooped despondently and sighed as he began to imagine the disappointment his charges would feel when he told them that they could not go on. His heart was breaking, and disconsolate and dismayed, he began to prepare his words for them when suddenly he felt a paw scratching at one of his front legs. Beaufort glanced to his side and saw that it was one of the youngest cubs, an infant who perhaps could barely remember Cilgwyn. A cub who had spent most of his life travelling, a cub whose chances of growing up now seemed to be more remote than ever. The cub's name was Rowley. He was a member of Eldon's small band of orphans and he felt a strong brotherly love for Titan. It was Titan who had brought the shy, nervous youngster up to Beaufort's side. Beaufort smiled at Rowley, believing that the young one, understanding his dilemma, had come to encourage him. His eyes began to brim with the slow-burning tears of defeat when he felt the scratching on his leg once more. Beaufort again turned to Rowley, who shyly lowered his eyes. Beaufort then noticed Titan on the other side of Rowley, and saw that he was nudging his young friend.

Rowley lifted his head to speak to Beaufort, but other than a few squeaks and splutterings, his attempt to say something proved futile. Beaufort put his paw gently on Rowley's neck and encouraged him to whisper the words he felt he needed to say. Titan now nudged his young friend quite vigourously, but this only made Rowley more nervous and Beaufort found himself gently persuading Titan to restrain his enthusiasm. With a look of exasperation and muttering words at Rowley, Titan withdrew from the odd couple, the leader and the most junior of the badgers—one of the most magnificently proportioned badgers

there had ever been and the most diminutive nine-moons badger that ever came from Cilgwyn stock. Beaufort looked into
Rowley's eyes and saw that this was no coward, as Titan had
been muttering, perhaps a pipsqueak of a badger but with a
heart as big as any. Beaufort felt that whatever the circumstances may have been, he would never have found the courage
to speak to a senior badger, let alone the leader, when he had
been a cub. Yet of all the badgers present, it was this small round
ball of a badger who had sensed Beaufort's predicament.
Beaufort, understanding Rowley's timidness, assured him that
his company was appreciated more than he would ever know.
He comforted him, consoled him and encouraged him with soft
and gentle persuasion to confide in him as a friend and to treat
him as a father, for that is what he had now become, the father
of them all. The staring, frightened, small black eyes of Rowley
began to melt into adoring worship as Beaufort further explained how proud he was that Rowley had shown such courage
and how full his heart was with love for all his companions but
now particularly for his new little friend.

Rowley relaxed more and more, no longer frozen in awe but
warmed by the loving sincerity that was in his leader's voice. He
suddenly blurted out a jumble of sounds, some of which were
understood by Beaufort, but he still couldn't quite understand
what Rowley meant, for Beaufort thought Rowley had said
something about climbing or making a tree.

For a moment Beaufort was at a loss for words and smiled at
his young friend as if to convey his appreciation for the assistance given, but he could see that the young cub was very
serious. Though the situation was now desperate, Beaufort
could not bring himself to dismiss young Rowley's cubbish and
playful wishes, and he turned to the rock face once more,
searching for some inspiration.

As his eyes became fixed on the unyielding rock, he became conscious that Rowley was again speaking to him. He tried to concentrate upon his close inspection of the summit but his searching gaze kept being broken by the odd word from Rowley disturbing his thoughts. Cubs, strongest, smallest, trees, climbing—the ramblings of the young cub were now beginning to irritate him.

There appeared to be no alternative. They would have to return down the rock-strewn path and shelter in the woodlands that had been their home just a day ago but now seemed so far away in time. They would send out a search party to find a way around the mountain. Beaufort turned to issue the new orders to the badgers, knowing how downhearted and disappointed they would be. He cleared his throat and the badgers fell silent awaiting instruction, except for the little cub, who was still rambling on about things being possible in trees. As Beaufort turned to Rowley to tell him to be silent, his clouded mind cleared as if lit by lightning, revealing a dawn of understanding. This was no cubbish prattle coming from Rowley but instead his words were creating a possibility, a distinct possibility that there was a way to scale the craggy barrier.

Beaufort huddled closer to Rowley, now urging him to speak slowly and clearly about the ideas he had to get them over the mountain. Rowley looked in amazement at his leader. He had already explained so many times. He would never understand the behaviour of adult badgers. They expected the cubs to understand more quickly than adults could, for Eldon had told the cubs quite often that he was only going to tell them once, but here was the leader wanting to be told for the umpteenth time how to climb the wall.

Rowley once more explained his idea. First, two strong adults would brace themselves against the rock face, their backs to the wall, then two more strong badgers on all four legs would become supports by the two upright badgers holding them tightly. Then another two badgers would climb on the backs of those that were being held and they would brace themselves on the two badgers leaning back against the wall. Two more would then climb up on to the shoulders of the last two and would brace themselves against the rock face, then the smallest and lightest of the badgers could climb up this framework of badgers and over the edge to freedom.

Absolutely amazed, Beaufort sat back on his tail. When all had seemed lost, from the least expected source, from the meekest of badgers, from the last of the Cilgwyn dynasty, had come a gleam of hope that could possibly light the way to their new home. This scrap of innocence, who a pig's whisker ago had seen life only through its mother's eyes, had now given Beaufort the final conviction that though the hidden paw might seem not to hold the badger in its protective grasp for many of the days, it would never let them go. Whilst there was stock such as Titan and Rowley, the future of the Cilgwyn hierarchy was assured, these nutshells would truly become hearts of oak, each minaret a colossus amongst towers.

The innocence of Rowley's naivete brought tears that filled his eyes as he realised that the cub was completely unaware of the importance of his idea. Feeling confused by Beaufort's reaction, Rowley timidly asked if he had done wrong, thinking for a moment that he was about to be scolded. He cowered as Beaufort leapt towards him, expecting a severe buffeting about the ears, only to find his breath being crushed from him as his leader hugged him closely. He felt his paternal protector tremble as the gentle paw of Beaufort stroked his head time and time again. Beaufort's body had a warmth that Rowley had nearly forgotten, having last experienced it in his mother's protecting caress at Cilgwyn.

It did not take long before the badger-made stairway was formed, a few moments of paw and body adjustment and all was ready for the first ascent. Rowley, being the smallest, was the first to go, and seeming more like a giant squirrel than a badger, he swiftly clambered over the badger-formed steps and soon was looking down at the badgers, shouting that there were trees as far as the eye could see, more trees than there were stars in the clearest of night skies. Titan quickly followed Rowley, then it became a procession, stopping only to change the badgers that formed the stepping-stones. It was when Beaufort, Fircone and the badgers who formed the wall were the only ones left to climb that Beaufort realised the difficulty that those remaining would face in climbing the wall. He was working out a method of hauling them up from above when Titan's, Rowley's and the other cubs' faces peered over the edge of the cliff, shouting to them to stand clear. The badgers who had formed the steps quickly joined Beaufort and Fircone as they stood aside. Then a fallen tree with quite a number of its branches still intact slid down from the cliff top, creating a means of escape for them, and soon they were all on top of the cliff. Beaufort's amazement at the wisdom of the cubs increased further as they pushed the tree away from the surface so that it fell crashing on the scree to the valley below. They even understood the necessity to hide their means of escape. They understood, really understood, that the journey was being undertaken to survive.

24

Lost in the Swamp

The sun and the moon had been companions in the sky for nearly half the day. The moon was now at its zenith, but the sun was already setting. The badgers, having been on the move through night and day, were now very tired and night was again returning. Beaufort, surrounded by the badgers, surveyed the panorama that stretched far ahead, the next skyline appearing faintly in the far distance. He saw that trees, mostly in varying shades of green, stretched out of sight along the valley's sides. The valley itself, the longest they had encountered, was a mosaic of contrasting greens, browns and yellows, interspersed now and then by the twinkling reflections from brooks and streams. It seemed ideal for giving cover and the fertile fields below would provide ample food, particularly worms.

Though the snows had stayed away since the time in the cave, and the frost and cold winds had not been their companions for quite some time, Beaufort reminded himself that the cold time was a treacherous and misleading period. It quite often clearly told animals and the earth of its vicious nature, then lulled everything into false comfort before it returned with its cruel sting. He shivered, too, as the elation of climbing the mountain left him and the sense of foreboding returned, niggling at the back of his mind.

As everyone was so tired, he decided that there was not much point in attempting to journey any further that night. They would make for the nearest cover and rest until the following night. Beaufort felt confident that rapid progress would be made in that long valley and that this time everything would be in their favour, but his spine chilled again with the unexplainable feeling of ill fortune that constantly clouded his thoughts.

The badgers proceeded down the gentle slope of the mountain. While the hillside they had conquered was savage and bare, the side they were now descending was kinder in every way as the bare summit top gave way to heather. There were no pathways, the earth being completely covered in a thick matted carpet of the evergreen shrub. As they walked over the springy surface the odd cluck arose from a bird sheltering in the protective warmth of the close-knit growth.

The terrain levelled out into a moorland plateau before it fell again to thickly growing evergreen trees. The badgers were eager to get to their resting place and, although tired, found sufficient energy to maintain more than a steady pace, which increased as they came onto the bleak expanse of moorland. As the soil became wetter the heather gave way to sedges and grasses, and the remnants of the purple-fruited bilberry, cowberry and crowberry. The grasses became more spongy as the peat became more boggy.

Although Beaufort had never experienced such dark, damp, oozing soil, he had heard of these acid and sour-smelling moorlands. There had been one in the valley that fell behind the rising sun at Cilgwyn. It certainly would not suit badgers as, while damp soils produced worms, this black peat devoured the history of the earth's surface and yielded nothing. They were marching over ground that was covered in deer sedge, mat grass, purple moor grass and heath rush. These plants supported birds such as golden plovers, curlews, dunlins, meadow pipits and ring ouzels at various times of the year, the same terrain sometimes providing for the needs of merlins, hen harriers and buzzards, birds that had paid only rare visits to Cilgwyn. A short-tailed vole scuttled over a dry patch of sedge, disturbed and amazed by the invasion of so many unknown large animals furred in twilight colours.

The soil had become waterlogged, water covering as much of the land's surface as did the mosses or the sporadic growth of insect-eating sundew, bog bean, butterwort, bog myrtle and march cinquefoil. The progress of the badgers was impeded as they crossed further into the bog land, the sphagnum moss squelching as each paw went deeper with every step. They were grateful for the occasional hummock that arose out of the doomed growth. The peat, lacking elements essential for decomposing dead plants, preserved such plants for generations until such time as the bog dried out. Most of these bogs spanned many centuries and Beaufort wondered whether any of his ancestors had walked the original crust that lay beneath the foul acidity that had engulfed the plateau they were now halfway across.

The ground quaked with their steps before the skin of moss separated as the badgers' claws pierced into the black, oozing sludge. They had found it necessary to spread out across the bog, it having become impossible to follow in line as the pathways being made by the pawmarks went deeper and deeper into the peat, to such an extent that their stomachs brushed against the clinging, sucking mire. The travellers increased their efforts to get to the trees and pressed on through the ever-wetter soils. As they weaved around the pools of stagnant, dark brown water, their journey was taking much longer than

Beaufort had anticipated. It seemed to him that they were all in a race to get to the safety of the pines. The sound of squelching and squashing paws on that soggy ground were the only sounds of the night until a scream came from one of the badgers who had become trapped in the slough.

Every badger stopped as if turned to stone. Beaufort quickly looked toward the sound of thrashing paws and saw that one of his friends was buried up to his neck. Two others were attempting to reach the trapped one and were getting into difficulties themselves. Beaufort barked to Fircone to make his way slowly to the struggling badgers and carefully prod the ground in front of him to ensure that his paws fell on secure ground. Beaufort asked for four badgers to stay behind and instructed Eldon and Gruff to lead the others across the remaining stretch of bog. Their pace would have to slow down to a crawl as each step would have to be tested for safety.

All of a sudden the night air had taken on a distinct chill. The weather had decided to turn colder and Beaufort was filled with an icy dread. He tentatively made his way with his small party of rescuers to the scene of frenzied struggling. Fircone was attempting to grasp the paw of the outermost victim but Beaufort could see that as Fircone leaned forward, he was becoming more deeply immersed in the black mud. He shouted for Fircone to withdraw and made up his mind that the badgers with him would link limbs and form a tendril. They would inch their way over the surface of the sucking bog and then pull the writhing, squirming victims to safety. As he sought the best possible lie Beaufort saw that there were not three badgers trapped in the quagmire but four. The one he had missed was so small it could hardly be seen. Beaufort let out a stifled cry of anguish as he recognised the features of his new-found friend, the little face of Rowley, barely visible above the mud. Rowley could no longer lift his submerged front legs above the surface.

His eyes were calm, glazed to a lifeless expectation, his body very slowly slipping, hair by hair, into the depths of the clinging, swallowing morass, into an inescapable grave.

There were five badgers stretched out in a line in front of Beaufort and Fircone, who positioned themselves ready to pull them back as soon as they had one of their trapped friends in their grasp. Beaufort recollected that he had asked four badgers to stay, yet there were five forming the spiralling stem that crawled across the sphagnum fabric. The rearmost four were the ones who had been ordered to stay, while in front of them another young badger fought with frenzied determination to save the smothering badgers. It was Titan who had seen young Rowley in difficulty when that cry of terror had sliced through the chilling air. He had become part of Rowley, and Rowley, small as he was, had captured a large part of Titan's heart.

Titan squirmed across the soggy mire until his claws were touching Rowley's head, and grasping the hairs, he barked to Beaufort, Fircone and his supporting links to pull. But the grip of the soggy peat proved too strong and Rowley screamed with pain as the hair was torn from his skin. He began to sob as he realised what a desperate situation he was in. Titan was not deterred and, edging nearer to Rowley, he slowly and methodically began to dig away lumps of the retentive gluey bog. One of Rowley's front legs was soon freed, then the other, and they quickly locked into Titan's hooked paws. The trailing body of badgers began heaving back, with Beaufort and Fircone pulling on the limbs of the back marker.

For a few moments there appeared to be stalemate, as Beaufort and the badgers would not relax their Herculean heaving, nor would the bog relent in its grasp on poor Rowley. Then came a long, drawn-out sucking sound as at last Rowley became free. Titan told him to scramble across the backs of the others to Beaufort and safety. Rowley galloped across the bad-

gers' backs and leapt into Beaufort's arms. Only then did he feel safe and it seemed ages before Beaufort could prise the small mud-ball away from him.

Beaufort set Rowley down and resumed the attempt to save the other three sufferers. They managed to carry out the same rescue procedure for one of the others, but the first badger who Beaufort had seen trapped had nearly disappeared. His ears were already under the surface, only his snout was visible above the oozy sludge, while the other struggling badger was in a state of panic as he thrashed vigourously with his paws to get a firm grip on the surface. Beaufort's barks to remain still fell on deaf ears as the frightened badger frantically struggled for life. The area surrounding the two trapped badgers could not bear the weight of Titan as he strove to get nearer to them, and he soon found himself getting stuck in the cloying, grasping marshy peat. Beaufort and Fircone saw that any further attempts by Titan would seriously jeopardise his own safety and ordered the creeping interlocked badgers to withdraw. There was nothing else they could do. The small group huddled together as they watched the two poor badgers go slowly to their deaths. One of them had completely disappeared, whilst the other, who had only a few moments ago been whirling his front legs in a frenzied final attempt to survive, had now become quite still. Beaufort was glad he could not see the doomed badger's face as the back of his head slowly sank, the white-tipped ears seeming to float on the top of the bog. As Beaufort watched in anguish, there was one final movement and then they were gone. There

were a few gurgling sounds, a few bubbles and the surface of
the bog returned to its deceiving tranquillity, entombing two
animals who had fought for so long to find a safe place to live,
only to meet a terrible fate.

Though there had been many obstacles to overcome,
Beaufort and the badgers had tried to meet everything with
heartwarming confidence. Here, when everything seemed to
be easier, they had once again been reminded of the cruelties
that life thrust upon them. So often they had been shown that
danger and delight grew on the same stalk.

The badgers, saddened by the tragedy of the bog, no longer
zestfully walked to their day's resting place. It was an undigni-
fied, disconsolate group that ambled from the plateau, down the
slope studded with loose boulders, to the forest that would soon
be their restful haven. Some of the boulders were large and
Beaufort thought there was an air of mystery about them. They
were known as tilting rocks or Logan stones, finely balanced,
yet not even storm winds had been able to dislodge them,
although it appeared to Beaufort that it would be quite simple
for just a single badger to push one over. Incredibly these pre-
cariously placed stones must have been there since the ice had
gouged through the mountains creating the valley down below.

The ground was covered with thick bracken and bramble;
gorse, too, had found its home and, with other shrubs and
bushes, formed a natural enclosure to the shelter of the forest.
Beaufort could see that one side was bare and decided to find
out why this was so. He pulled up short as he neared the area
void of plants. He realised that there would never be any plants
here, as the ground fell away steeply, vanishing into the gloom
of increasing blackness far below him. Beaufort retreated carefully, and sternly gave strict instructions that no matter what
the reason, the badgers were not to venture near the cliff edge.
He needed no more tragic accidents. He held himself responsi-

ble for everything unpleasant that occurred to them and the vision of those white-tipped ears disappearing into the bog would be with him for many moons.

The badgers foraged for worms, moth and butterfly larvae. Although miserable, they were hungry and needed to satisfy their appetites before they settled down to a long comfortable rest. Beaufort was foraging well away from the cliff edge but nearer to it than any other badger. He could not bring himself to trust the obedience of the badgers, not until that night was over anyway. He intended to restrict the hand of fate as best he could. At the edge of the forest grew a small clump of birch, covering the ground between the firs and the precipice. They were bare of foliage and Beaufort could see the distinct outline of mountains through the branches. He carried on unenthusiastically seeking food for quite a while but his heart was too full of sadness and he was eating from habit, not from desire. It was getting closer to the time when the sun would push the hills apart. His thick coat did not prevent him from feeling the frosty air, and as he glanced through the branches of the birch he saw that the sky had changed and had become full of dense, heavy cloud, hanging low over the countryside. As Beaufort wandered down through the bracken to find warm shelter, the skies warned him that the cold time was about to expose its sting and flakes of snow spiralled slowly down. As he felt Corntop snuggle closely to him, he became aware of how much he missed their constant companionship at Cilgwyn. They had drifted apart, but he knew that as soon as Elysia was found, their lives would resume the loveliness it once held. She had been his morning star since he had been a yearling cub and she would be the last star to fade when he took his final walk to Logos under a golden night sky.

The ground was soon covered in snow. It was clinging to the branches of the pines and Beaufort hoped the cold time would not stay long, although he understood the different seasons were necessary for life of any sort to survive. The year was now aged, but it would eventually yield its vicious grip to the rebirth of species, to the time when every leaf was green. As the snow continued to fall Beaufort was glad they were already in their shelter. He held Corntop closely, as strange thoughts of the snow-covered countryside stirred in his mind. He knew how miserable and depressed badgers became when the earth was covered by snow and food became scarcer, yet how odd it was that it made the land appear as if everything was in total unity. He found comfort in Corntop's touch and in the words his father had said to him when they had been snowbound in their sett at Cilgwyn: No cold time lasts forever, no birth time misses its turn. He fell asleep, seeking Elysia in his dreams.

25

Nature's Plan

DAILY CHRONICLE

Saturday, 26th October

It would appear that the Ministry of Agriculture is beginning to heed public opinion. After a meeting of members of the committee dealing with badger extermination, the following news release was issued:

1. The numbers of military personnel involved will now be reduced.
2. Due to the extremely difficult conditions encountered by Major Robertson a new date for the completion of extermination will not now be given. The extermination unit will be allowed further time in order that the programme can be carried out successfully.
3. Due to the partial extermination of badgers, there have been no new cases of tuberculosis infection in cattle for over two months.

The *Chronicle* believes that the decision to reduce the number of armed forces has been made to appease members of the public who are increasingly concerned about the continuing persecution of the badgers. Although the strength of the extermination units is to be reduced, it is nevertheless being allowed to continue, and unless the government can be persuaded to listen to public opinion and bring to an end the folly of this barbarous act, there can be little doubt that eventually there will be no badgers living free in this country.

DAILY NEWS

Thursday, 31st October

Should Badger Extermination Programme Be Reviewed?

It would seem that as no new cases of bovine tuberculosis have been noted during the past twelve weeks, the termination of the badger extermination programme should be seriously considered.

This newspaper, along with others, originally supported the programme, which has been largely successful. It is believed that every attempt should be made to capture some of the elusive Cilgwyn badgers but not to kill them. The captured animals should be tested for tuberculosis and if these tests prove negative, then the government should end the badger extermination scheme and should consider the creation of a National Reserve in the Llancwm area in South Wales.

DAILY CHRONICLE

Monday, 4th November

The centre of London was brought to a near standstill yesterday when a massive demonstration was held in support of the Cilgwyn badgers.

The protest march started at 9.00 A.M. and many spectators joined the long procession to add their support.

In Hyde Park, later in the day, one of the leaders of the P.A.W.S. organisation, after pleading for the government to stop their programme immediately, quoted the words of a letter written in 1855 by the Indian Chief Seathl to Franklin Pierce, President of the United States:

What is man without beasts? If all the beasts were gone, men would die from great loneliness, for whatever happens to the beasts, happens to man.

The P.A.W.S. organisation is making arrangements for petitions to be circulated. It is understood that some government opposition M.P.'s are preparing a bill to end the unwarranted continuation of the slaughter of the badgers.

DAILY CHRONICLE

Tuesday, 19th November

Yesterday evening the P.A.W.S. organisation, together with the *Daily Chronicle,* held a prize-giving ceremony for the winner of the competition arranged during the demonstration in London to promote the understanding of animals and the need to protect this country's natural heritage.

The poem, "Nature's Plan of Living," by fifteen-year-old Caroline Allyson from Plymouth, won her not only a certificate but also an award of two hundred pounds. Caroline promptly returned the cheque to the P.A.W.S. organisation in support of the cause.

The panel of judges had awarded the prize to Caroline as it felt she had captured the essence of nature's plan of co-existence, accepted by every animal except man.

Nature's Plan of Living

The swallow takes the may-fly,
The bat will take a moth,
The shrike will spear a sparrow
But none are killed in wrath.
Worms consumed by badgers, moles
Owls seek out a mouse or voles.
Eagles soar and hunt for prey
They eat to live another day.
The fox kills not for pleasure
It leaves in carrion store
Its many kills provides its needs
To live through rime and hoar.
The lion hunts the zebra
Others will share its feast
All creatures become victims
Yet hate lies not in beast.
It's nature's plan of living
It's her eternal troth
That beasts may kill in hunger
But never once in wrath.

Television news, 5:45 P.M.,
Sunday, 24th November

Uproar has arisen as a result of reports from
Beacon Heights, the mountains that surround

the Llancwm valley, that government trackers have found tracks of the Cilgwyn badgers.

A spokesman for the extermination unit stated that it was Major Robertson's intention to strike camp early tomorrow in order to pursue the badgers and complete the eradication programme.

The Meteorological Office has issued a warning that further heavy snow can be expected over South Wales by tomorrow evening, which could make it extremely difficult to follow the badgers' tracks.

DAILY CHRONICLE

Beacon Heights, South Wales
Tuesday, 26th November

Heavy snow has been falling in this area since yesterday afternoon and drifts of up to five or six feet now block most of the country roads. Emergency action has now been taken to air lift the trackers and all other personnel in the area.

With little promise of an improvement in the weather during the next few days, a conservationist spokesman stated that although the snow had prevented further persecution of the badgers, he was extremely anxious about their ability to survive in the cold weather.

Television News, 9:00 P.M.,
Tuesday, 26th November

Due to the continuing heavy snowfalls over the Beacon Heights, the Badger extermination unit has had to abandon its plans to pursue the Cilgwyn badgers. We have just heard that a bill to stop the eradication programme will be put before Parliament immediately after the Christmas recess.

It is very probable that no further badger extermination will take place. The P.A.W.S. organisation, while appreciating that Parliament has reconsidered its extermination plans, has expressed fears that the severe weather could destroy the Cilgwyn badgers.

26

Furrows in the Sand

The badgers, though weary and pawsore, spent a restless day in the thick, auburned bracken. Its crispness had gone and dead ferns had become limp and soggy under a thickening cover of snow. As the day went by the grey-coated animals became less enchanted with the enclosure that had promised so much refreshing comfort. Quite early they started to drift from the undergrowth into the shelter of the trees, first in twos and threes, then, as the snow became thicker, they left in scores. Well before the time of the overhead sun, all of them had deserted the open field and tried to settle into the bed of pine needles and cones that smothered the forest floor.

It had not been very long since their previous experience of living under pines. They had got to detest the nostril-filling pungency of the pinewoods air, and they remembered how glad, the last time, they had been to leave. The badgers lay dejected at the prospect of spending the next few days in that atmosphere. The older badgers were even more despondent, as their highly developed instincts told them that the days of snow would be many and that before they were over the full moon would fade away, rest and return to a new fullness before the snows would leave them. This strange power was felt more strongly in some of them, but it was built into them through heredity and most were unable to ignore or resist it. Even the man animal was sometimes under its influence, but through the ages had lost the awareness of it just as he had lost other senses.

Beaufort had seen that many of the badgers were becoming increasingly distressed. Some of them stood on all four legs, swaying their heads to and fro. He knew that whenever the badgers behaved in this manner, they were subjecting themselves to anxieties caused by fear of the unknown, becoming more convinced as time passed that they were about to face unavoidable disaster. There had been a few occasions at Cilgwyn when similar demonstrations of trancelike movements had taken place. Beaufort faintly remembered the first occasion he had witnessed such strange behaviour during the birth time after his own when Cilgwyn had been subjected to prolonged and torrential rains, which had lasted many days. The lower valleys had filled with floodwater, and the lower setts, where cubs of only a few days' life were lying in nest chambers, had become threatened. He shook away these memories and, hearing the cries of the cubs, realised that Eldon had also been overcome by this hypnotic trance. Beaufort saw that Eldon was struggling to retain normality; one moment he was swaying back and forth, then he was stumbling, and he seemed to be attempting to tell the cubs something.

Beaufort hurried over to his revered friend and managed to get Eldon to remain coherent long enough for him to give an explanation for his odd behaviour. It slowly dawned on Beaufort that the badgers held in the trance were being governed by phenomena of unexplainable forces which could be broken only by the removal of the fear that engulfed them. Beaufort, having been told by Eldon of the instinctive and ominous warning of snowstorms and his uncertainty that the cubs could survive exposure to such a long period of freezing temperatures, understood that he would have to take drastic action, not only to maintain his credibility as leader but also, more important, to convince the badgers that they would survive, whatever the danger, and find everlasting joy in the tranquil land of Elysia.

It seemed to Beaufort that he was meant to be the eternal warrior, continually fighting adversities that seemed to have been stirred up by the whole world pulling at the devil Ahriman's tail. His stubborn unflagging refusal to concede defeat against overwhelming odds more than surprised him, as it was a characteristic that had not shown itself when his father had been alive. The resolute qualities of his leadership came to the fore as he barked out his very firm demand that the badgers form a circle around him. Not even Fern or Corntop recognised the voice thundering from underneath the pine branches as this order was given. Each word, clear and precise, cracked powerfully against the snow-clad slopes. The badgers were startled by the mighty sovereignty that ascended over them, and those who had been seized by the compelling demand to sway in the throes of their depression were jerked out of their trance. Beaufort's words rang with clarity, inspiring awesome wonder amongst the audience as the badgers, understanding the message that they were being given, gained new heart.

Beaufort realised that the badgers needed more than this to boost their morale. Their fading hopes had become even more forlorn as they feared for their chances of surviving a long period of snow. They had become increasingly wrapped up in melancholia, were homesick and they needed the shelter of their chambers in the setts at Cilgwyn. As Beaufort's words boomed out, repeating his instructions, many of the badgers, not quite sure if what they heard the first time was true, began to understand. The squeaks, chuckles, paw-thudding, back-slapping, squealing, dancing, jumping and barks of joy led to a bedlam of delight. They were to rest, not just for a night or so, but until the cold time was over. They were to dig out setts, homes they knew and loved, warm and friendly, snug and protective. They were returning to the ways Mother Earth had intended for them. They knew that it was only temporary, they knew that it was not their Elysia, they knew that when the time came for the buds to come out of the sheaths they would move on. But this did not detract from the sheer pleasure of appreciating that for a little time at least they would once again have a real home.

There wouldn't be sufficient time to construct a colony of interjoining setts, but only to build a series of small groups of setts, each with four or five sleeping chambers capable of housing about twenty badgers in each. Beaufort's sett would be situated in the centre. The setts would be excavated in the softer earth that surrounded the hedgerow of the enclosure, but none were to be built on the side adjacent to the cliff top due to the possibility of accidents. In any case, as Beaufort explained, the hard rock would prevent any worthwhile digging.

If the badgers had been left to their own endeavours, such was the eagerness to dig setts that the whole area would have become dotted with holes. They were promptly stopped by Beaufort, who, with the help of Fircone, Eldon, Chantar, and Gruff, co-ordinated the others into digging parties. Beaufort, with his council colleagues, marked out the main entrance to each sett, all entrances being equidistant from each other. Beaufort, not wanting to dampen the badgers' enthusiasm, explained that while the sooner everyone was housed the better it would be, no matter how hard they worked, it would take more than three nights' work before the setts could possibly be completed.

Eldon insisted that he occupy the sett in the top corner of the enclosure where there was an opening in the hedgerow that would allow the cubs easier access to a play area. Beaufort smiled at Eldon's air of innocence, for he had forgotten to mention that it also afforded the quickest access to the best feeding grounds. As families became families again the state of happiness that prevailed was similar to the hubbub of activity of birth times, when excited fathers, grandfathers and grandmothers rushed between the homes of other relatives conveying the news that cubs had been born.

Although the cubs had little or no experience of digging setts, they soon got the hang of it and, under the excellent supervision of Eldon, were soon making greater progress than the other badgers. Working in two teams of five, one would be doing the actual digging while another would scrape the soil back over the lip of the entrance, where it would then be spread around over the entrance area. As the badgers went deeper into the side of the hill, it became necessary for a third badger to enter the tunnel. The second badger would scoop the loose earth onto the stomach of the third one, who would be lying on his back. He would clutch at the earth and a fourth badger would catch him by the hind legs and drag him out of the tunnel to discharge his load. The front badger would keep clawing away, even winkling out fairly large stones, and then, arching his back, would bring his hind legs forward, place his hind paws against the stone and, in a series of jerks, eventually get the stone out of the tunnel.

There were very few periods when the snow didn't fall during the night. It was a constant source of trouble as far as the digging was concerned. The areas surrounding the sett entrances became muddier and muddier, necessitating frequent visits to the pine trees so that the badgers could scratch the bark with their claws to remove the sticky mud.

Beaufort saw that things were working out well. Gone were

the fears of the unknown, and though the snow was causing problems, it did have the beneficial effect of covering up the scarred earth. When the digging was finished the snow would have removed all but the smallest trace of earth excavation. He moved among the badgers and was rather dismayed to note that each time he approached one, the badger stood back in great reverence. He didn't like the feeling of isolation this gave him. He had always been one of them, but he was not to know that the story of his leadership that day, coupled with the description of his voice, which through the myths and legends of future times would be said to have travelled across the world, had separated him forever from his own kind. The badgers' adoration for their leader came from their total confidence that Beaufort was indeed the acolyte of Logos's protection.

He noticed that he was not the only one to feel excluded, as he saw that while Fircone was assisting here and there, none of the family groups had invited him to join them. Beaufort was about to ask Fircone to be part of his sett when the opportunity to do so was taken from him. The instinctive perception that was so strong in Rowley's character showed itself again. The young cub rushed past Beaufort, stopping for a moment to bow his head to him, then, catching Fircone by the leg, he began to tug him in the direction of the cubs' sett. Fircone started chatting to Rowley, and for a moment Beaufort thought Rowley had said something disrespectful to Fircone, as the big badger lifted his paw as if to cuff the youngster. His fears were groundless, as Fircone lifted the little one onto his back and the two were chuckling and laughing as Fircone jauntily carried his little friend to the home being built for them to share with Eldon and the other cubs. Beaufort forgot his loneliness as he admired the comradeship of the biggest badger he had known now carrying his comrade, who wasn't much larger than Fircone's tail.

It was at the end of the second night after the commencement of the sett digging when the sense of foreboding that left Beaufort for only short periods of time at last revealed its cause. As the badgers dug deeper into the hillside progress seemed slow, though the badgers were working just as hard as when they had started. It was taking longer to get the earth out, but some of the setts already had side chambers, and some of the badgers were collecting bedding. Unfortunately, the bedding was of poor quality and at best a little damp, but tucking it under their chins, they carried it into the setts.

It was the intention of Titan and Rowley to be the first ones to sleep in the setts and they worked feverishly to complete four good-sized nests, one for Eldon and Titan, one for Fircone and Rowley, and the remaining two for the rest of the cubs. For some reason Beaufort's feelings of solitude had been replaced by an irksome agitation, which increased just as the snow increased its covering of the land. The squeal of Rowley and the growing roar of Fircone made Beaufort jerk round to seek the reasons for such cries of alarm. Peering through the large flakes of snow, Beaufort could first make out Fircone, with Rowley sheltered behind him, standing to one side of the enclosure's access, while on the other side stood Eldon, with Titan in front of him. Both pairs of badgers were facing the corner, where Beaufort could faintly see the dim, whitened shaped of snow-encrusted badgers. Beaufort wondered whether the visitors were from another community that inhabited the area and had come seeking an explanation for the trespassing of the Cilgwyn badgers. Beaufort quickly put this out of his mind as they had not discovered any scent markers put down by foreign badgers. As the ghostlike figures approached him, Beaufort, suddenly recognising them, could not prevent himself from hissing his feelings of distrust and anger. The badger at the head of the visitors was none other than Kronos. This most wicked of badgers, Sheol's disciple, had once again returned amongst them.

It appeared to Beaufort that Kronos and his friends had been travelling for some considerable distance. He couldn't really distinguish the line of black-and-white patterns on their faces, but their scent was unmistakable as the scent of Cilgwyn badgers. Kronos's eyes looked long and hard at Beaufort and at first seemed to plead for understanding. Beaufort, whose coat had remained fluffed up, a normal reaction when badgers became angry or defensive, softened as he began to think that Kronos and his breakaway group were seeking help and wanted to return to the fold. If this was what Kronos and his allies really wanted, and if they were sincere in their remorse for their misdemeanours and really wanted to become brothers again, who was he to stop them? Nothing would make Beaufort happier than to be able to lead all the surviving Cilgwyn badgers into Elysia. The lack of caring females, the hollowness of their existence bereft of the sounds of young cubs, the desolation of leading a nomadic life apart from their kin, the prospect of a life devoid of love and dependence had brought these unfortunate badgers to their senses. They, too, had the instinctive knowledge that snow time would be hard and long-suffering. They wanted to be part of them again, they wanted to come home.

Perhaps these anarchistic creatures had come to their senses and were seeking acceptance to be part of Cilgwyn's great family again, having realised that to forget one's forefathers is to be like a river without its streams, a stream without its spring. The homecoming would be remembered as a day of joy and the rebellious badgers would be accepted with love and affection. There would be no chastisement, but they would be welcomed with genuine heartfelt gratitude for returning to their families.

As Beaufort was about to greet Kronos he saw that the look in the badger's eyes, the badger he had promised to destroy if he ever saw him again, was not pleading but hid a disguised evil malevolence. Beaufort's kindly gaze turned to one of stone as he barked quick-temperedly, demanding to know what Kronos wanted. The other badgers had seen the paternalism in Beaufort's eyes and were surprised at his sudden change of attitude. Realising the distrust and anxiety that was in Beaufort's voice, Fircone moved quickly through the friends of Kronos, brushing them aside as he strode towards his leader's side.

Kronos addressed Beaufort in a voice loud enough for everyone present to hear. His kind and condescending manner irritated Beaufort. Kronos expressed the deep concern that he and his followers felt for the safety of their old friends from Cilgwyn. The oncoming snows had finally persuaded them to do their duty and to come to the assistance of the stranded badgers. There was no need to dig their setts, as he and his friends had already prepared a substantial number lower down the valley on the other side of the forest, where food was plentiful and where the flora was even more varied and beautiful than Cilgwyn. He described how there were oaks and beech trees, streams with fish, ponds that would carry frogs and toads, soft green-covered earth that was bountiful in its supply of worms. There were wild strawberries, wild raspberries, crab-apples, all of which would become available in their harvesting times. If ever the hunters of Cilgwyn came upon them, they could easily escape into the cover of the forest.

Kronos and his friends were prepared to share the control of the new community with Fircone, Eldon and the other elders under the guidance of Beaufort. There was no need for any of the badgers to punish themselves with the unnecessary labours of preparing homes in the bleak hillside. They could make permanent homes in the valley, where cubs could be born again. The young females looking forward to the joys of giving birth for the first time could, if they moved to the new homes built by Kronos, now look forward to rearing their own cubs when the

earth began to give new warmth and growth to life everywhere.

There were stirrings of excitement coming from some of the
young sow badgers. Beaufort understood that their desire to
become mothers was only natural but they had to understand
that the journey was far from over. They had yet to find Elysia,
and Beaufort did not want the births of cubs to become a dis-
traction in their search for these tranquil pastures. He had told
them that mating was forbidden until they were safe and secure, safe not just for a night, not for a few moons, not even an
age of birth times, but for eternity, when man and beast would
become united in everlasting harmony.

Beaufort, now fully aware of Kronos's true intentions, understood that the devious brain of this evil one had not changed.
Kronos had spoken of lasting friendships, but his understanding
of love and loyalty was nothing more than furrows in the sand.
Beaufort could not be deceived, he knew that this scourge of a
badger, this black-hearted parasite, this tentacle of Sheol, was
once again attempting to usurp him and place the other badgers under Kronos's own rule of tyranny. The voices of Titan
and Rowley came from the rear of Kronos's badgers. They
shouted for Kronos to go away, they didn't want him or his
friends near them. The uninvited guests parted, letting Kronos
see who it was that had dared to speak against him. Kronos,
annoyed and angered that cubs so young as these should speak
to him in that manner, turned to Beaufort and asked what had
become of the rules and regulations of Cilgwyn. What weak and
pathetic leadership allowed pip-squeaks to be so disrespectful of
their elders? What sort of future could the badgers have if they
had to depend on a badger whose weaknesses would destroy
them, a leader who couldn't even control these young upstarts,
young cubs who were nothing more than wrens believing they
could dominate an eagle? He then marched up to Rowley, and

to accentuate the difference in size, Kronos stood on his claws and stared, his eyes full of hate. Rowley shrank back, only to find the protective paws of Eldon and Titan about him.

Situated at the rear of his own badgers, Kronos, having already lost control of himself and having forgotten the need for him to gain Beaufort's confidence and trust, turned on the wise badger and issued a threatening challenge. He warned Beaufort that he was not prepared to wait any longer to see his friends from Cilgwyn go to their inescapable destruction under the feeble and spineless leadership that now existed. He would return before the snows ended, when the weather had begun to take its toll and when the misguided followers of Beaufort had discovered that their strength was deserting them. He would return with his badgers, fit and healthy, and rescue them all except for Beaufort and his council of friends, who would feel his vengeance and who would be finally destroyed.

The intruders vanished into the thickening flakes of snow, disappearing as quickly as they had arrived. They had come and gone without discovering that every badger who had heard him, except his own, held Beaufort in such reverence that no one and nothing on earth would persuade them to desert him. Their leader had the blood of Logos in his veins and was indestructible.

Beaufort knew that Kronos was mad enough to attempt to carry out his threats. He spoke gently to his attentive audience, announcing that though the weather was bad, sentries would have to be posted around their encampment to provide warnings of any attack that would come. Then, concluding that nothing would ever change Kronos from his evil ways, Beaufort pronounced sentence on him. If Kronos was seen again, he was to be captured and put to death. Though it seemed barbaric and alien to Beaufort's teachings of love, loyalty, faith and peace, there was no alternative to the course of action he had taken if

Kronos were to be prevented from tyrannising and frightening the badgers with his constant threats and hostility.

The badgers were soon back at their tasks of digging out and preparing their setts, no longer taking Kronos's wild promises seriously but absolutely confident that Beaufort could guarantee their survival. Beaufort, however, noticed that a number of the young sows were not concentrating on their work but discussing their longing for cubs of their own. He knew that if an attempt was made on his badgers, the young females would be the most vulnerable. For even if Kronos accepted the fact that he could never replace Beaufort or the existing council, he would need the females in order that his own group could multiply and form a separate community.

Beaufort arranged with Fircone and Gruff that they would be responsible for organising and supervising guard duties, changing them frequently so that they would not have to endure the cruelties of the weather for too long at one time. He yawned with the weariness that the demands of leadership had brought upon him. He kept telling himself that he was no different from the rest of them, he wanted cubs of his own too. He wanted to enjoy the sanctity of parenthood with his beloved Corntop. He hadn't asked for this leadership. He had done his best to avoid such responsibilities and had sought a quiet homely life. It seemed to Beaufort that his fate was not in his own hands but that he was under an influence of some mighty power, far too powerful for him to understand.

On his way back to the cover of the pinewoods where he would seek a place to rest, Beaufort was interrupted by Corntop calling him from the entrance of the sett being prepared for them and Fern. He had wanted to share it with other badgers, but they would have none of it. This sett was special and would house the Great One and his family and no one else. He ambled slowly over to his bride of the last birth time and embraced her

lovingly. He wasn't even allowed to devote his loving attentions to her for more than a few moments a day. Corntop told him there would be no need to shelter under the pines anymore as the sett was ready for them. They shook their bodies vigourously, throwing off the snow and wetness from their coats, and Corntop led Beaufort into the mouth of the sett, along the tunnel into a large nesting chamber. The floor was covered with a thick layer of dead grasses, bracken and heather. How it was dry he could not fathom, and to collect it some of the badgers must have travelled far up the hillside. He sank into the welcoming bed, mumbling that he could not understand how they had managed to make it so comfortable. He thought he heard Corntop say that the badgers hoped he wouldn't object to them taking the opportunity to repay a little towards his care and guidance of them. Beaufort opened his eyes and found even more comfort in the darkness of the sett, dark as a wolf's mouth. He glanced at his mother, Fern, who was also settling down for her rest, and saw that she was deep in thought. He knew that she was remembering the last time that they had slept in a sett, when their beloved Buckwheat had been with them.

Beaufort also remembered the sight of carnage that had greeted him when he had emerged from his last night's rest at Cilgwyn. He thought of the journey they had come on, the trials of fortitude, the sacrifices of life, the necessity of their travels, and even this was not enough hardship. They had found that they also had to face the threat of harm from one of their own kind. He closed his eyes, but before they shut the door of consciousness Beaufort could still see Kronos standing on the toes of his paws, screaming out his promise to destroy him and his close friends, sowing dragon's teeth amongst the badgers. He saw Rowley retreating from Kronos's threatening pose until he found safety in Eldon's and Titan's touch. Together the badgers would surely survive, but separated and unable to conform to the traditions of the past, they would destroy themselves. Such destruction was Kronos's inevitable fate. Beaufort fell asleep, reminding himself that those that stood on tiptoe didn't stand firm.

27

Eldon

The sun failed to show itself for four days, but this did not prevent the badgers from completing the excavation of the setts. Two were situated on the lower part of the enclosure where the ground was flatter and took much longer than the others to complete. The soil was more clayey than that further up and the badgers found difficulty shoving the scrabbled earth out of the tunnels. The badgers designated to do the actual digging found that their claws became quite useless after a short time, becoming clogged with the stiff, clinging mud. It became necessary to shape the clay into round balls, which became larger as they were rolled out of the sett between the badgers' forepaws.

The snowfalls lessened during the fifth night and by the morning the snow clouds had broken apart, allowing the sun to shine down on the cold white countryside. This slight break in the weather enabled the badgers to spend the day carrying out some long-needed grooming. They would normally have sat in shallow bowls in the earth to undertake this task but this was not possible due to the snow except for the area under the pine trees which they so disliked. The grooming operation began with the badgers carrying out the cleaning of their own coats, twisting and contorting in every way possible to get at every part of their bodies. They would scratch, nibble and lick their coats, but they would never clean their faces with their own claws. This was done later when the badgers huddled together in small groups and mutual grooming took place. Beaufort took heart from the fact that the badgers were enjoying a routine task that they hadn't been able to carry out for such a long time. He removed a lot of dead hair from his own coat and it began to look quite respectable again. When he finished he settled down with Corntop and Fern and they began to clean each other's faces by nibbling at the knots that had occurred and then licking the hairs clean. Beaufort saw some of the sow badgers cleaning their cubs as if they were only a few moons old. They held their offspring down with their front paws and then methodically inspected every hair on the cubs' bodies. He couldn't help laughing when he saw that both Eldon and Harvey had developed the same maternal instincts and were carrying out identical methods of grooming on the orphans. Beaufort continued to watch the old patriarch teaching and caring for his new family of cubs. Eldon had never mentioned a word about Scylla, his wife, who had perished when so many had met their deaths on the mountainside. He had joined with her only because it had been expected of them, but it had never been a close relationship, and Beaufort believed that Eldon felt guilty about his treatment of Scylla, regretting that he had not tried to make their unification a happier one. Eldon seemed to realise how much happier life could have been if he had devoted more time to building a strong family life. He had seemed to suffer from a crushing inferiority complex arising from his fear of falling far short of his father's demanding standards.

Now, freed from the responsibilities of leadership, Eldon had become the happy, jovial, caring badger that he had wanted to be all his life. Beaufort could see that Eldon had found contentment and had discovered true happiness. Eldon really had his own family now and he intended to be a father to orphan cubs until the day he died. He loved his young friends and thrived on their infantile dependence. Eldon had soon finished cleaning the cubs and sat upright on his haunches. His face was being licked by Titan, and his tail, which he had been unable to groom properly because the size of his stomach prevented him from twisting round, was being nibbled at by Rowley. The tail was acting as a support, enabling Eldon to lean backwards, and the ecstasy on his face told its own story as he scratched his belly with slow, deliberate actions of his front paws.

It had been a day to remember, and the weather, though quite frosty, had failed to dampen the spirits of the badgers. They were at the highest state of happiness since they had left Cilgwyn. They found plenty of worms in the excavated soil, supplemented by carrion, birds that had failed to survive their scheduled life spans, as the low, heavy, grey clouds covered the sky and the snow began falling again. Though preferring to forage during the dark hours, the badgers, having satisfied their appetites earlier than usual, had cherished the thoughts of being able to sleep underground and had been keen to return to the setts and enjoy a quality of rest that they had desperately missed.

Beaufort had appreciated the long spells of rest he had been able to have in his sett but perhaps he had had too much, for that night he became quite restless and imagined hearing strange sounds coming from outside. He once rose up to investigate and, poking his snout out of the entrance, discovered that the snow was falling thicker than ever and that the sounds must have come from the branches of the trees as they strained and creaked under the weight of snow.

The night hadn't finished when he was awakened by cries of

anguish coming from some of the other badgers. He quickly blinked the sleepiness from his eyes and went out of the sett to seek the cause of these shouts of panic. He found some of the sow badgers wailing and was thunderstruck when he learned that a number of the young sows were missing. They must have been abducted, as they would never have gone off on their own. But there also must have been a certain amount of consent on their part, as they could easily have given warning of their predicament. Beaufort realised that the majority of Kronos's group was formed of suitable young boars, and the young females who had gone had failed to find the strength of will to restrain themselves from obeying the natural desire to set up their own homes. Beaufort felt betrayed by the frailty of the weak-willed sows. Not only had they let themselves down but, through their act of stupidity and selfishness, they had shattered the community's recently achieved peaceful contentment.

There was no doubt that the sows had been aided and abetted in their elopement. The scent marks of Kronos's gang were found close to some of the setts and the scent of Kronos himself had been detected only a fox's step away from the enclosure's opening. The demon had already started to put his evil plans into effect and Beaufort knew such plans and ideas could be terminated only with Kronos's annihilation. Beaufort considered sending a search party to trace the whereabouts of Kronos's colony but did not feel that this would be of any benefit with the weather the way it was. If they found it, he would have to dispatch many of his most able boars to have any hopes of reclaiming the young sows. This could place the badgers remaining behind in an extremely vulnerable position and Beaufort was not prepared to jeopardise the community's well-being in order to assist those who had so easily been led astray. He assured the families of the lost ones that when the snow had gone and before they continued with their journey, they would descend on Kronos in force and retrieve those who had lost their way.

The next few days passed without incident and the families that had lost their daughters endured as best they could the sadness of their missing loved ones. The majority of the badgers had returned to their daily routines quite affably. They cleaned their bedding, they covered over their dung pits and prepared new ones, they dug ventilation holes into their sett systems. Although at Cilgwyn these necessary chores had never been popular, here everyone was glad of the chance to get back to the old customs and were disappointed if they had no work to do. As each day passed they appreciated more and more the serenity and paradisaical existence that had been theirs at Cilgwyn.

The thick snow lying on the ground restricted the range of activities that would have normally been part of the cubs' training. There was so much time on their paws that Eldon had tremendous difficulty in keeping them occupied. It was Titan who discovered the joy of sliding on the snow. He had ventured outside the compound and had climbed a little way up the hill, keeping well within sight of the sentry badgers. Feeling a little bored, he had decided to satisfy his cubbish inquisitiveness and had walked up the steep hill to find out what the curious white shapes were that mysteriously stood out against the skyline. He was halfway up the hill when he realised that they were the tilting stones, now nearly twice their size as they formed barriers against the drifting snow.

He sat down on the deep snow and surveyed the landscape below him. He found it hard to identify most of what he could see, as nearly all of the regular features of the forest and valley had taken on grotesque and bizarre outlines, and had become more misleading by the world seeming to consist of only two colours, black and white. Titan, then turning his attention to the sett area, couldn't instantly identify many of the figures. They seemed so much smaller at that distance, but he could still make out the portly figure of Eldon, the massive frame of Fircone and the majestic Beaufort. He had been sitting there for quite a little while when he began to feel the cold begin to penetrate the fur on his haunches and realised that his body heat had begun to thaw the snow. As he tried to rise his feet slipped from under him, and before he had time to catch his breath, he was sliding on his back at breakneck speed down the hill towards the huge pile of snow that had drifted against the hedgerow that separated the compound from the hillside. He hurtled down at an incredible speed, his body sometimes soaring in the air, then thudding back on the snow, and then, abruptly, his uncontrollable descent was over as he crashed into the deep drifts of snow.

Eldon and Fircone had seen the cub come streaking down the icy slope and plummet into the pile of snow. They and others who had also seen the accident rushed to help him and stood aghast as a pillar of snow emerged. It began to shake and lumps of snow were scattered everywhere. As the embedded white crushed flakes came away, the badgers recognised the unmistakable features of Titan. He was grinning broadly and, not realising that the onlookers had been frightened for his safety, told them he had never enjoyed anything as much as that fantastic ride, it had been so exciting and exhilarating. His eyes twinkled with merriment and his innocent delight proved too much for Eldon and the others, who were soon laughing, not only with relief, but at the vision they still had of their first sight of that comic creature, the impish Titan coming out of the tomb of snow.

Titan was highly excited and couldn't climb the hill quickly enough in order to slide down again. He urged the other cubs to join him on this marvellous adventure, telling them that they would experience travelling at a speed faster than the swoop of the falcon, faster even than the flash of lightning. But Eldon insisted that Titan didn't go as far up the hill as he had done the first time and he would allow the other cubs to join in only on the understanding that, as they were smaller than Titan, they could slide only from shorter distances.

The other spectators returned to their daily tasks, leaving just Eldon, Fircone and the cubs. The two adults watched the cubs enjoy the uninhibited pleasures that arose from their playful activity. Fircone went to fetch Beaufort, as he thought it would be a wonderful tonic for him to witness such youthful delight. As Fircone and Beaufort returned they heard the whickerings and squeals of the cubs change to shrieks of mirth. They could hardly believe what they saw as they came through the gap in the corner of the compound. The pair of towering badgers were soon holding their sides, chortling with uncontrollable laughter. It was not at the cubs who had just slid down the icy slope, but at Eldon, not sliding on his back like the cubs had done, but on his belly. He came down at an alarming rate, spinning round and round, the roundness of his portly stomach acting like a pivot. As he was about to crash into the snow barrier, the speed at which Eldon had revolved turned him into a blurred grey cloud. The silly old badger had not taken into account that his weight would cause him to go much faster than the cubs, and as he hit the small rise made by the cubs digging in their feet to stop themselves from becoming buried, he was propelled into the air over the first mound of snow, over the hedge, landing flat on his back on one of the dung heaps still in use in the enclosure. As soon as Beaufort, Fircone and the cubs could stop their convulsive laughter, they rushed round to make sure that he wasn't hurt. To their surprise they ran into him gambolling back, telling them that nothing was going to stop him having another turn. He stopped just long enough to explain seriously that he believed it essential that he experience the sliding activity himself. As he couldn't quite see how the cubs were enjoying it so much, he wanted to ascertain the amount of risk involved and to assure himself it was quite safe.

Beaufort and Fircone remained for some time, watching Eldon and the cubs slide over and over again down the hillside, which echoed with the sound of their merry cries. The two big badgers had never laughed so much in their lives, astounded at the inventiveness of the cubs as they thought up new ways of descending. As the pair left the scene of play, they shook their heads in disbelief at the latest method of sliding. There was Rowley, sitting on Eldon's cushioning paunch, and with the cub held tightly in the old one's limbs, the two of them slid down the bank of snow together.

Beaufort had cheered up considerably and had gone around the setts checking that the badgers were reasonably content and giving a few encouraging words to every one of them. When he had finished he thought it was time to call a halt to the cubs' long period of play. He couldn't quite see Eldon bringing an end to the sliding, not until they had completely worn away the snow. He returned to the foot of the slide paths and saw that his old friend had had to concede that he was no longer a cub and regretfully had stopped taking part himself. Beaufort, joining Eldon, suggested that they all return to the confines of the compound. Eldon barked to the cubs that they could have one final slide each and, if they behaved themselves, they could return and continue with their fun and games the next day.

As each cub finished its slide it took up a position close to Eldon and Beaufort, who had moved to the access corner. The group grew as the cubs joined them until only Titan was left to take his turn. He began to climb the hill, but when he had taken only a few steps, a loud cracking sound came from the higher reaches of the hill. The badgers looked up to find out where the noise had come from and froze in terror as they saw that one of the tilting stones had become dislodged and was careering down towards them. Beaufort had the wits to shout a warning to the badgers in the enclosure as he realised that the boulder would tear through the hedgerow into the forest below. He saw that Titan was mesmerised as the falling stone gained momentum and was standing in its path. Beaufort barked a thunderous roar for Titan to jump and then he saw Eldon rushing headlong towards the cub. As the stone was about to smash into Titan's frozen body, Eldon dived, pushing Titan out of the way, unharmed. Beaufort heard a sickening crunch as the impetus of the falling stone was checked and, rolling gently into the hedgerow, came to rest.

As the thumping of Beaufort's heart eased, he heard a stifled groan coming from the snow-covered spot where Titan had been standing. Beaufort cried out at the sight of Eldon lying facedown. He dashed to his side, kneeling down to comfort his dear friend, and saw that Eldon had taken the full force of the huge chunk of rock. Eldon's poor body had been smashed, its life all but crushed out. It seemed that there wasn't a bone left unbroken and blood poured out of countless wounds, staining the white snow crimson-red. Beaufort heard Fircone dragging cubs back, telling the other badgers to take care of them. The commotion made Eldon flutter his eyelids, and as he managed to hold Beaufort's paw, he murmured a few sounds, then coughed as his throat rattled, his head falling to one side, the blood running from the corner of his mouth.

Beaufort continued to kneel at Eldon's side, desperate to wake up from this nightmare. He kept talking and talking to the still, silent form of a truly great badger. He gradually became aware that his heartfelt grief was not part of a dreadful dream but reality. Beaufort fought hard not to open his eyes, determined not to accept the truth. He needed Eldon's constant, reassuring loyalty and dependability for him to ever think of reaching Elysia. It seemed such a cruel fate, that those who were prepared to devote their lives to the love and care of their fellow beings were destined not to see the promised land.

His heart full of sorrow and his mind incapable of sound reasoning, Beaufort found, on opening his eyes, that he could not see, his vision blurred by the tears welling up in his eyes. It was then that Titan broke free of Fircone and rushed to Eldon, flinging himself upon the lifeless figure that had been the only father he had really known. Titan was no longer the brave and hefty cub. He was now a nestling crying and wailing for its food, for warmth, for love, for protection, for its reason to want to live. This poor, unhappy cub had had its heart torn out of its body twice in such a short time. His life had been saved for him to suffer the agonies of losing his loved one all over again.

The trembling paws of Fircone struggled to pull Titan off Eldon's body, but the cub fought hard to hold on to the badger whose heart had been big enough to share with all the cubs. Titan did not wish to return to his young cub friends, not even to Beaufort or Fircone. He knew that Eldon could not return, and that his beloved friend would soon be taking his final journey to a land where sorrow and unhappiness did not occur, and Titan wanted to go with him.

It needed six of the badgers to prise open the tight, clasping paws of Titan, and as they pulled him free the young cub flung his front paws around Fircone's neck, burying his head against the big badger's shoulder, sobbing and sighing. Fircone took him back, together with the other young cubs, to their newly occupied sett. There he and Harvey would stay awake, consoling and nursing the cubs. The young ones had become frightened as they realised that the joys they had just begun to experience had gone, replaced by an unhappiness that hung over all of them. They, too, began to weep, and Fircone was glad to find Corntop and Fern coming to assist in consoling them.

Meanwhile, Beaufort had told Gruff to get some of the other boars to help him carry Eldon's body back to Beaufort's sett, where he would stay until the following night, when they would bury him. Shortly after Eldon's body had been placed inside his sett, Beaufort instructed Gruff to stay guarding the entrance. He then asked Chantar to arrange with some of the older sow badgers for them to give further help in the cubs' sett, replacing Fircone as he had need of him.

Fircone was soon at Beaufort's side, and after a few words had passed between them, they began to climb the hill. They followed the track that the boulder had carved through the snow and earth. They walked slowly up that hill, leaving the noises of the enclosure behind them, until there was just the sound of silence, broken by the slow soft crunch of their paws stepping in the snow. As they climbed over a slight ridge, they could see where the stone had once stood, its tracks ending within a frog's leap of the ridge. It was not the only track they could see, for surrounding the small pieces of rock that had for ages past held the great stone from falling were the prints of badgers' paws.

Fircone bayed in anger, the bloodcurdling sound ringing round the mountain. Its chilling tone made Beaufort shiver, for he knew that Fircone was uttering a terrible oath, swearing an unretractable promise to the heavens that he would take vengeance. Fircone, if necessary, would give his life to revenge the death of the old badger whom he had come to respect and cherish with all his heart. Fircone then called the name of Kronos three times, promising he would have no mercy for the most villainous of badgers that had ever been born.

Fircone wanted Beaufort to give his approval for a group of sixty or seventy of the boars to search out Kronos and his band of assassins and destroy them once and for all. Beaufort was sorely tempted to agree but he believed that it would probably be when these badgers were absent that such another tragic event would occur. He knew, too, that by placing the sentries on the ridge, yet still within sight of the compound, they would be sure of sighting Kronos if he made any further attempt at causing harm to them.

Beaufort knew that Kronos did not have the patience to withstand a lengthy period of waiting to inflict further discomfort on the badgers. He was certain that sooner or later Kronos would decide to make a final and determined effort to take over the leadership and that it would come from an all-out attack planned with exceptional cunning and guile by the master of doom and destruction. It would be necessary for Beaufort, Fircone and Gruff to keep the badgers at peak alertness, the sentries being checked and double-checked throughout the night and day. They would be ready for Kronos and his rabble. They hoped it would be soon, for they thirsted for revenge, but Beaufort sighed deeply as he told himself vengeance never was sweet. It could not bring his old friend or his father, or any of the others that had perished, back to them.

Beaufort spent the following day making fastidious arrangements for the burial of Eldon. He decided that his old colleague should have his final resting place on earth in the sett that had been excavated for himself, Corntop and Fern. The sorrowful halo that surrounded the compound contributed to the feeling of utter dejection being experienced by every one of the badgers, but particularly by Beaufort and the cubs. Titan stayed in his sett all day, shutting himself away from the rest of the world. The grief-stricken cub did not sleep, but kept his eyes shut, no longer wanting any part of a life that could give such joy and love and then, in one single stroke, destroy forever everything that was meaningful. Titan, the lively, high-spirited cub, irrepressibly jovial and frolicsome, the young one who was the substance on which the continuity of the Cilgwyn badgers was based, had become so dispirited that the wish of death was fast approaching. Beaufort had never known a badger to change its attitude once the death-wish had taken possession of its mind. It gave up its will to live, and though such a badger might be in first-class health, it would soon die, not from weakness or starvation, but from pain unable to be borne, the pain of unrelenting grief. Fircone sought out Beaufort for his advice on how to awaken Titan from the chrysalis of death. Titan reminded Beaufort of Fircone when he was a cub, strong and boisterous, daring, always ready for a challenge yet loyal, dependable and hiding a heart that could love with a burning intensity. Beaufort decided that he and Fircone should take immediate action if they were to save Titan from inevitable death. The two boars went into the cubs' sett and, catching hold of Titan, shook him violently and then dragged him outside. The rough handling brought the cub out of his netherworld, and with Fircone and Beaufort looking down at him, the cub began to whimper pitiful and mournful cries. Beaufort's heart went out to him, his sympathy equalled only by his own feelings of grief at the loss of his benign friend.

Beaufort repeatedly told Titan how desperately he was needed and that Eldon needed him too. The cub sat upright on hearing that Eldon wanted him, not understanding how this could be so. Beaufort went on to explain that Eldon could not be reborn in Asgard unless a member of his family said the prayer at his burial. Beaufort said he was surprised and disappointed that Titan was prepared to let Eldon down when he was needed most. How could Titan say he loved the old badger when he turned his back on him? He was sentencing Eldon to roam the in-between world of Gehenna, a place above the clouds, buffeted by eternal winds, which continually changed its form and where departed souls waited forever, barred from entering Asgard or Sheol.

Beaufort's condemnation of Titan produced the desired effect. Titan leapt at Beaufort, hurt and angry at what he believed was an injustice to his undying love for Eldon, and then the tears ran down his face. He would never desert Eldon, how could anyone think such a thing, of course he would say the prayer. His pent-up emotions were finally relieved as his tearful fury subsided and he nestled his head on Beaufort's shoulder, beginning to find comfort in Beaufort's soothing and encouraging words.

The burial sett had been completely cleaned out, and all traces of Beaufort and his family's occupation removed. The tunnel floors and walls had been scraped clean, leaving fresh clean earth, and the floors of the sett covered by the dark green glabrous leaves of ivy. Eldon's body now lay on a dais of juniper twigs covered in ivy leaves. The sunset was cold and the sky glacial green and the lip of the horizon ember red as the badgers walked past the peaceful body, each one bending over the still form, gently nuzzling the face, then walking on. At the corners of the square-shaped platform stood an honour guard, Beaufort, Gruff, Fircone and Chantar. It was laid down that the lying-in of a deceased leader should be honoured by the remaining council members as the guardians and also the pall-bearers. After each badger had passed the body, they acknowledged Titan, nodding their heads as a sign of their condolence. The badgers then formed a corridor leading up to the burial tomb. The four pall-bearers gently lifted Eldon's body and slowly carried it into the ivy-covered tomb, laying it softly down on the dark green leaves. The four badgers then withdrew, and as they stood in silence, Fern, Corntop and four other senior females gently laid coronal clusters of holly, glossy green with berries red as blood, leaving the face of Eldon exposed. The sow badgers scattered the yellow-green ruffled flowers of aconite over the holly and then they, too, withdrew and joined the sombre mourners. Beaufort escorted Titan into the sepulchre and the two badgers stood for a moment, looking lovingly for the last time at Eldon's face. Beaufort then covered the old one's face with a layer of holly leaves and bent over the leafy embalmment to place small leaf-wrapped parcels of worms, beetle and larvae at his side. Beaufort heard the soft patter of teardrops fall on the holly leaves as Titan bent his head over the body and, placing his paw on the young one's shoulder, ushered him outside, his throat hoarse and dry as he gulped back the tears.

Four other male badgers, led by Gruff, then began filling the burial sett with earth, compacting it with their paws, and as it was about to be sealed, Titan, standing proudly, said the eulogy:

Guide him safely from this earth
This badger bold, of noble birth.
Grant him his peace, this worthy one
As he rises on the rays of sun.
Take him gently, ease his way
As he goes to you this day.
Our hearts cry out as we all sing

Our sad farewell to our beloved King.
Lead him to the land of dreams
Flower-covered with honey streams.
This lord of badgers, we honour today
Take him gently, ease his way.

As Titan finished speaking his head drooped and Beaufort saw the tears glisten between the cub's tightly shut eyelids, but the young courage had returned and the cub did not want the others to see him cry any more. Beaufort gazed up as the sun fell below the skyline, thinking of Eldon as the old leader started his final journey, up to Capricorn, the southern gate of the sun, over the rainbow bridge, through the halls of Gladshelm and Valhalla to live again.

Before the badgers dispersed, Beaufort carried out the final task a leader had to fulfil before the final ceremony ended. It was traditional that the eldest living son of the deceased was given the blessing of the seven gifts of Asgard. There were no cubs by Eldon but Beaufort unhesitatingly called Titan to him and, placing his paw on the young one's head, pleaded that Eldon, upon reaching Asgard, would ask that his adopted son be granted the seven gifts: wisdom, understanding, counsel, fortitude, knowledge, righteousness and love of the Lord Logos.

The silent badgers left the assembly in twos and threes. They went to their setts to reminisce about Eldon and Cilgwyn. Beaufort saw Fircone talking to Titan, the big one with his paws on the cub's shoulders, looking deeply and lovingly into the brave little face of the cub. Beaufort could not hear clearly what was being said but he managed to catch Titan's plea to Fircone for the big badger not to get old and he understood what they were talking about. The need for Titan to know he was loved was obvious, and for the first time since Eldon's tragic death, the glimmer of a smile appeared on the cub's lips. As the two badgers walked close together back to their sett, Beaufort knew that Titan once again had a father.

Beaufort was now left alone in the compound, and looking up to the star-filled sky, he let his own tears flow. He saw in the darkness of the night the large, kindly face of his dear, loving friend. He turned in the direction of the cubs' sett, which for a few days would be his temporary home, and slowly walking towards it, he began to understand the fullness of sorrow. It brought memories not of sadness but of joy, those moments of happiness that couldn't come again but would be with him always.

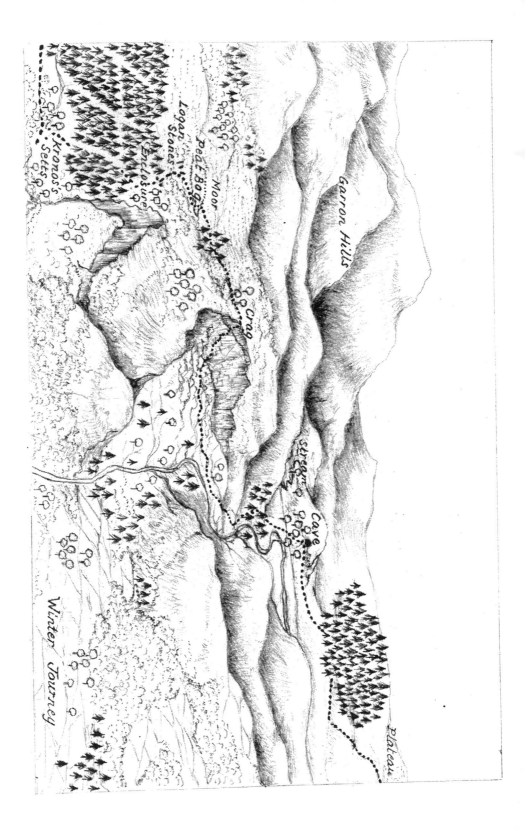

28

To the Death

There had been many periods of snowfall during the few days following Eldon's departure and at times Beaufort wished that the badgers had the ability to achieve a state of torpidity long enough to see them through this cold time. He had risen from a troubled sleep, his body longing for rest, but his mind, too disturbed for him to relax, had seemed to awaken him within a few moments each time he had fallen asleep. As he emerged from the sett he was grateful that the snow had stopped falling. The compound looked as if it had been seen only by the sun, moon and stars, its new thick covering of white brilliance completely concealing the presence of life of any sort. The blizzard conditions that had prevailed around the countryside had their advantages, as they hid the badgers from their pursuers, but did restrict the amount of food they could find. Beaufort wistfully wondered what it must be like to awaken after such a long sleep, becoming alive again as the earth began its promise of fulfilment.

The chilling air was most uninviting and Beaufort was a little envious of the squirrels in their dreys, the smooth snake curled up tightly beneath a shelter of thick heather, the hedgehog snoring away at the bottom of a hedgerow or the natterjack toad inert under a stone or in a little hole it had found beneath the ground. He shrugged away such idle thoughts as he appreciated that every day was worth living, and each moment that he was awake reminded him that happiness was always attainable, no matter the misfortunes of the past, the present, or those hardships yet to come. He shivered as the air filled with the sounds of the cawing of the lich fowls, the dim shapes of these creatures of the air faint in the overcast sky as they, too, searched for food, earlier than usual, for the sun had not quite begun to lighten the darkness of the night. They were taking the opportunity to search for those unfortunate enough to have succumbed to the cold moons' claws of death. Beaufort looked at the inhabitants of the sky, soaring, then wheeling round and round before gliding in a slow descending spiral. Swooping to sight their prey, they would soar upwards and start their search all over again. This unrelenting quest for some dead or dying flesh into which they could sink their curved beaks would not be very fruitful around that area, for Beaufort knew that whatever carrion there had been had already been rapaciously consumed by the hungry badgers. The souls of the squirrel, a rabbit, a few voles and a wood-pigeon would have their journeys to Asgard delayed until it was time for their predators to ascend the rays to the everlasting existence.

Though the sky was overcast, the cloud cover was higher than it had been and Beaufort knew that the badgers would be able to spend more time out of the setts than had been possible during the previous few days. He found that he was becoming more unsettled, especially since he remembered that Buckwheat had never liked the presence of lich fowls over Cilgwyn, his father having always believed their visit to be an omen of ill fortune. This memory made Beaufort shiver and the ever-present threat that Kronos would show his paw once more clouded his hopes of finding relaxation. Every waking moment he was conscious of his responsibilities, and the constant irritation that came from Kronos's threat to destroy his friends, as well as himself, made Beaufort feel even more burdened. This irritation would soon reduce him to the size of Rowley, just as the continuous dripping of water would make a grain of sand from a boulder. The demon that Kronos had become would hasten his attempt to usurp Beaufort and his rule of wisdom, tolerance and love. The fire of hate that burned in the evil one's heart would become fiercer and then burst into flame. Beaufort barked to free himself from the thoughts of despondency and terror that were beginning to engulf him. The snow-covered scenery gave such a peaceful and silent air to his surroundings, but his private world was racked with torment and apprehension.

His barking brought a quick response and Fircone, Titan and most of the other boars were soon at his side in the pine-screened reservation. They were following the instructions of Beaufort, that whenever one of the badgers barked, all the boars had to swiftly surround the inside of the perimeter of the enclosure. The most senior of them, together with Beaufort and his council, would form a circular core within the boundary, ready to repel any raiders that succeeded in breaching the outer fortification. Beaufort felt a little shamefaced at unnecessarily causing alarm amongst his fellow badgers, but swiftly assumed control of the situation by informing his friends that he was testing them to check if they were on their guard as Kronos could strike at any time. Kronos had failed to hide his cloven foot and the badgers had to be in a state of readiness that would prevent Kronos from achieving his evil and wicked desires.

Beaufort had also ordered that when the alarm was raised, all females and cubs were to remain in their setts, and he was surprised to discover that the cubs had disobeyed his orders.

They had gathered around Titan, the most prominent of them being Rowley. He had adopted a fighting stance, with his hair fluffed up, his teeth showing under curled lips and uttering staccato whinnyings of defiance. Rowley's posture was sufficient to stop Beaufort from severely admonishing the cubs. Beaufort had glanced at Fircone, who, behind eyes filled with gentle mirth, was having great difficulty in preventing himself from bursting into laughter.

The qualities of character that were so apparent in the young cubs again delighted Beaufort. He was surprised by their sense of justice and integrity, their understanding of the difficulties they faced, their sterling endeavours to lighten the tasks of others rather than be burdens on their society. By their unselfish and unstinting efforts they earned the admiration and respect of their elders by making such a tremendous contribution to the welfare of all of the badgers. Above all, the quality that pleased Beaufort most was their unquestioning loyalty to the community as a whole. They had, undoubtedly through Eldon's influence, never given a thought to deserting Beaufort for the life of luxury so promised by Kronos. They seemed to have the special instinct, felt by the very young, that wickedness, real wickedness, could lead only to the permanent darkness of evil. Beaufort felt reassured by his belief that he had little to worry about when the future of his badgers lay in the youthful wisdom being displayed by the cubs. The voice of his conscience told him that the voice of righteousness was the fountain of love and that violence covered the mouth of the wicked.

Beaufort felt quite uplifted by the comradely spirit of the other boars and he sauntered over to Corntop and Fern, enjoying the feeling of contentment that the cubs had given him. The tingling on the back of his neck made him tremble with excitement as he visualised the end of the snows, the melting snows, the vanishing snows, cleaning the earth and revealing its rejuvenation. Above all he looked forward to the rebirth of their little nation in land not too far afield. He couldn't explain why he should all of a sudden know their new permanent home was not so far away. His confidence at the outcome of Kronos's intended assault grew by leaps and bounds. He could never have visualised such a rebirth unless Kronos was to be defeated. Corntop could see the look of contentment on Beaufort's face, as if he hadn't a care in the world, and she asked him to explain why he appeared so pleased with life, but he found himself unable to give a simple answer to the question. He told Corntop of the pride he felt at belonging to such a noble band of badgers and of the inestimable pleasure he received from just being in their company. He related the morning's events, of his solitude, his embarrassment, Rowley's gestures of defiance, and the love and reverence he could see and feel in the other badgers. He still couldn't understand the warmth that came from the other badgers' eyes, a look of confidence and expectation, which gave him so much assurance. They made him have no doubts that they would follow him every part of the way to Elysia. He couldn't understand why such devotion and loyalty could be for him when he had been their leader for such a short time. Corntop knew that he would never understand and that his greatness would always be visible to all but himself. The badgers had needed a leader who could rise above their depths of despair and display a simplicity of soul, caring compassion and sincerity, and give them an unshakeable faith that he would take them home. The others understood that Logos had been at work when Eldon had nominated the reticent young boar as their leader. Beaufort's name had been carried down through the skies on the voices of their forefathers in Asgard, for they knew that true leadership must be for the followers not for the enrichment of leaders.

Beaufort could vaguely hear Corntop's words of love and

affection as he dozed off for a short nap. His mood of relaxation had all but dimmed his eyes when sharp barks of alarm rang out from the hillside. Beaufort lost his drowsiness as if he had been plunged into icy waters and he dashed out of the sett. Before he had a moment to assess the situation, Kronos and his band were attacking them and he found himself the target of three of the strongest assailants. The shortage of food seemed to have had a greater effect on the badgers than Beaufort had estimated, for they were being flung to one side as the fitter and stronger badgers of Kronos charged at them.

It was obvious that Kronos's plan was for Beaufort and the other council members to be slain first, and then being leaderless, the followers of Beaufort would surrender and Kronos would swiftly assume the vacant leadership. Beaufort grimaced with pain as the claws of a challenger gouged his flanks. He tried to grip another by its throat but found it impossible as the strength of his three opponents was proving too much for him. He found himself being thrown to the ground, and he wriggled and squirmed to avoid the teeth of another badger sinking into his neck. He fought valiantly, knowing he would never submit, and as he found his strength waning he could hear the faint voices of the females in the background. But these were not voices of terror but of anger. The sows had emerged to assist their boars.

Beaufort felt two of his foes being pulled away from him and he managed to regain his paws. His foe, whom he recognised as Windross, began to circle around him, searching for the chance to leap at him and get a grip on him with his teeth. Beaufort could see the brainwashed eyes crazed with fear, as Windross now realised he was on his own and was frightened of Beaufort's strength and power but equally he dreaded being humiliated in Kronos's eyes and then having to suffer the consequences. Beaufort stared hard and long at Windross and, boldly stepping forward, contemptuously brushed the young boar aside. He saw that many of his own boars were wounded and carried deep scars from the bites, clawing and scratching of the enemy. The battle began to subside as the added strength of the sows' tenacious fighting began to take effect, as they fought with the ferocity that they usually showed only when defending their cubs.

The snarling and hissing now came from one quarter only and Beaufort could see that Fircone was involved in a bitter struggle with two burly badgers, one of them Oatos and the other Zoilos, the brother of Kronos. Zoilos was of similar build to Fircone, perhaps a trifle shorter, and there was no doubting his determination to kill Fircone. Oatos, trying to assist Zoilos in bringing Fircone down, was being hampered by the heroic efforts of Titan and Rowley. Titan had taken a grip on Oatos just above his tail, while little Rowley was clinging to one of Oatos's legs. Oatos kept trying to shake the little cub off by flinging his leg in the air, then bringing it forcibly down, dashing the small cub constantly against the ground. Beaufort and Gruff leapt forward, and sinking their teeth deep into Oatos's hide, made him squeal, letting go his hold on Fircone's back. Oatos was pulled away from the struggle of the giants, and seeing the figures of Beaufort and Gruff towering over him, he immediately submitted. Titan had relaxed his hold, too, and stood guard over the defeated badger. Beaufort then found that young Rowley was still holding fast and it was with some difficulty that he prised the cub's jaws apart. Rowley, seeing that his opponent was defeated, then stood up but could not resist giving a final nip at Oatos's leg.

Beaufort knew that any intervention in the fight between Fircone and Zoilos would not be welcomed by his friend and he decided he would help only if Fircone faced defeat. At that moment honours appeared even: They were running and fighting, darting in and out at each other, seeking an opening where one could deal a telling blow. Screaming and snarling, Zoilos leapt at his foe, claws raised to drag over Fircone's eyes. Fircone, silent in his endeavours, dodged beneath the plunging claws and raked across the breast of Zoilos with a sudden deft slash of his claws. The two stood at bay for a moment, swinging their faces close to the ground, now rushing, now backing off, then Zoilos rushed in swiftly, bit hard and then pulled away. Fircone dashed at Zoilos but missed in his attempt to charge Zoilos to the ground, and Zoilos countered by quickly wheeling and, seizing Fircone by his thigh, hurling him high and wide. Fircone was on his paws in an instant and closed again on Zoilos. They feinted at each other, and Fircone had begun to growl deep and slow. Beaufort could see the black anger smouldering in his friend's eyes and he knew that this was a fight to the death. Their breathing was slow and deliberate, their coarse grey hairs standing stiffly out as if they were gigantic hedgehogs, their backs steeply arched as they circled and snapped. Fircone appeared to stumble and Zoilos sprang forward, but Fircone had been waiting for this. He swung his head underneath the diving body of Zoilos and locked his jaws as his teeth drove through the fur on Zoilos's neck into his throat. Fircone turned Zoilos onto his back, still firmly gripping his windpipe in the death grip. Fircone would never relax that hold, not even in death, until he felt that life had drained completely away from his victim. There was nothing that Beaufort could do but witness with all the others the killing of Zoilos, who continued to thrash the air with his powerful legs. This vain attempt to survive began to slow and the badgers heard the bones of Zoilos's throat crunch as Fircone tightened his hold. Zoilos struggled feebly and then a rattling sound came from his gaping mouth. His limbs seemed to straighten and quiver before they folded and became limp. Fircone relaxed his grip, rose and stared down at the face of a cruel and bullying badger, still showing its hatred, its death-mask frozen, with lips curled, mouth wide open, revealing its vicious teeth.

As Fircone turned away from the lifeless form, blood dripped from his own wounds, leaving a thin, red line over the snow. He looked at Beaufort and, without uttering a word, his eyes tried to explain the necessity for taking Zoilos's life. He lowered his gaze as he saw that his friend and leader understood. Fircone, turning to face the silent spectators of his battle, saw the cringing figure of Kronos alone and whimpering. The hateful slave of evil crouched and grovelled on the snow-covered expanse that was open to the cliff. Fircone began to walk towards Kronos, intent on dragging him before Beaufort. As he marched towards the cowardly badger, he heard Kronos pleading forgiveness for his mistakes and his innocent, though confused, actions. Fircone growled to Kronos to stop the ingratiations, he didn't want to hear any more lies and falsehoods. Fircone's voice grew louder as he began to thunder out the names of those who had

been murdered by this villain of villains—Buckwheat, Dandelion, Whortle, Dewberry, Eldon, and the names rang out their
own sentence of death. Kronos started to back away, screaming
and sobbing, his fear of Fircone increased, and with every stride
that the big badger took, his backward crawl became a scramble. Then suddenly there was a long and interminable wail as
Kronos found the ground behind him had disappeared and he
fell to his end into the gloom of the depths below the cliff.

29

Fresh Green Leaves

Though being an attendant to a killing of a badger was abhorrent to Beaufort, the demise of Kronos made him feel his shoulders were at last free of the burden that had weighed heavily on him ever since he had become leader. Logos had cursed the earth because of man's disobedience. Previously the earth had borne only plants pleasant to the sight and good for food, but after the curse it also bore thorns and thistles and sometimes creatures like Kronos. Beaufort peered over the edge of the cliff but could not see the ground below, it was so dark, a bottomless pit, one of the entrances to Sheol. It was a gangrenous, mould-ridden sett of everlasting ages, where in the deepest part Ahriman awaits, blowing at the seed-heads of black dandelions, letting them scatter about the earth, awaiting their return. One of these seeds, which had grown to spread its poison, had now festered and died, returning to its pod of blight.

Beaufort, hearing a commotion behind him, had to stand aside as a party of captive badgers dragged the body of Zoilos across the snow to the cliff edge. They were under the supervision of Fircone, who kept urging them to pull harder and harder. They jumped at every command he made and cowered with humiliating shame, for they weren't sure what Fircone's intentions were. Some were frightened at the thought of being pushed over the cliff; others, who could not believe that Fircone would enact such punishment upon them, were fearful of being bitten by Fircone with every step they made. He did not allow them a moment's relief from their fears and he made them go quicker and quicker until they had practically reached the edge. The disreputable badgers, who by their own irresponsibilities and ignominious behaviour had brought dishonour to themselves and their families, began to whimper and cry for mercy. They were only a step or two away from falling over the cliff when they stopped of their own accord and fell prostrate on the snow, begging forgiveness. Beaufort did not intervene. Fircone had carried out the punishment admirably and he knew the big fellow had no intention of sending them to their doom. Fircone then thundered at them to stand and look at him: The first one to disobey would be the first one to be thrown over the cliff. At every command Fircone gave them, they seemed as if they were being struck by forks of lightning. Fircone made them push Zoilos's body to the very edge and roared at them to push it over, to join Kronos. The brothers would be perfect companions on their way to Sheol, and Fircone sharply demanded whether any of the petrified badgers still believed that Kronos should have been their leader. The shamefaced badgers meekly squeaked their replies in a unanimous disavowal of the alien. Fircone said he could not hear them and repeated the question once more, this time demanding they speak louder. He repeated the question six or seven times, each time roaring at them to bark their answer louder and louder. He then snapped at them to return to their companions, who were being kept under guard in the centre of the compound.

Beaufort saw that the other captives hung their heads in

disgrace, the whole lot of them in abject misery and no more than beggarly outcasts. Their feeling of guilt was overwhelming and they flinched as the younger cubs, led by Rowley, strutted around them, cubfully taunting and rebuking them for their dishonourable deeds. Beaufort had remained silent ever since Kronos had vanished into the depths below and he saw no reason to break his silence as Fircone continued to inflict more and more humiliation upon the scoundrels' heads.

Fircone advised them that they were to stand trial in front of Beaufort and the members of the council, witnessed by every badger who had remained loyal and true. This would have been the way of things at Cilgwyn, but their actions were far more serious than any of the misdemeanours that had sometimes occurred when they had inhabited that beautiful and peaceful valley. They could expect no mercy, only the severest of punishments. Murder had been committed, damage to life and limb had been carried out by them, and such crimes warranted the sentence of death.

At this suggestion the prisoners began to tremble, not so much at the thought of dying, but of dying dishonourably. They would be spurned by Bragira, the one who welcomes slain heroes to Asgard, and sent to Sheol. It was then that Gnos asked permission of the council to speak. The council members looked at Beaufort for his decision and, still remaining silent, he nodded his approval. Gnos then stood in front of the four lines of captives, each row consisting of eight badgers. The prisoners were surrounded by their victors, and a gap as wide as the lowest branch of an oak tree was long separated them on all sides.

Gnos, looking at Beaufort's face but unable to shed his shame and look into his eyes, began to relate the sorry tale of life under Kronos's rule. They had realised their folly and misguided impetuousness not many days after they had deserted their honourable council and families. They had lived with increasing guilt as they were forced to endure the rule of tyranny and dictatorship that Kronos had imposed on them. They had often considered making a bid for freedom but, having been witness to the cruelty of Kronos's vengeance at the slightest hint of revolt or disloyalty, they had become prisoners of fear. Those who could no longer live in such a miserable existence and had attempted to escape were dealt swift and horrific punishments. Zoilos would attack them and disable them by breaking their limbs in his powerful jaws before inflicting deep gashes on their flanks and face with his long, curled claws. He would tear chunks out of their pain-racked bodies and then they were left to die slowly, screaming and moaning with pain until the loss of blood eventually brought them their final peace.

Kronos had seemed to have a mystical hold over Zoilos's mind, so much so that he had convinced him that he would one day be recognised as a god. Zoilos had become totally infatuated by the thought that one day he, too, would become a mighty badger of power, and as the brother of a god, everyone else would be forced to carry out his biddings. Whenever Kronos left their sett area with a party of badgers, he was accompanied by Zoilos, leaving some badgers behind under the watchful eye of Vulcan. Vulcan, another badger who had cruelty emblazoned on his heart, was perhaps even more cunning than Kronos but seemed to have been biding his time until Zoilos could be disposed of. Vulcan, when left in control in Kronos's absence, was always given strict instructions to kill without delay any badger who misbehaved or showed any sign of defection. Vulcan had taken every chance he had to goad and criticise the inferior intelligence of Zoilos, but a few days earlier, when he had been sent on a scouting mission with Zoilos, he had failed to return and it seemed that he had met his fate by Zoilos's paw. The whole existence of the badgers under Kronos had been one of terror, and there wasn't one of the guilty badgers who hadn't wished for time to be turned back so that they could start again. They now genuinely wanted to be part of the life that Beaufort and his followers were seeking and longed to become part of the community again. They had thrown away a real chance of everlasting happiness for a few moments of madness.

Gnos assured the council that none of the badgers would be more devout in its following than the captives. Their hearts had not been in the fight and that was why they had so quickly surrendered. If it was necessary for the severest of punishment to be given for their misdeeds, was it necessary that all his companions should be executed? He begged the council to find compassion in their hearts, and if they needed to make an example of one badger, he was prepared to become the recipient of the death sentence, but he begged that the others be allowed to return to the fold and be given penances so that they could be seen to pay for their guilt.

Beaufort rose from sitting on his haunches and moved forward into the group of prisoners. He stopped in front of each one of them, looking every one of them in the eyes. His face was solemn and grave and not a word was said by him to any of them. When he had finished his inspection he returned to his council colleagues, then he slowly turned to face the badgers. For a few moments there was utter silence. Beaufort, his head bent forward, appeared deep in thought. He then inhaled deeply; the onlookers waited expectantly. Their leader, a badger of such awesome majesty, was about to pass judgement. Beaufort said he appreciated that the guilty badgers felt remorse for their actions and was grateful that one of them had found sufficient courage to give account of their guilt. He had no doubt that their souls, tarnished by Kronos, were redeemable. They were not as the souls of Kronos and Zoilos, which had been possessed by the spirits of Sheol from the time of their birth. Their guilt was undeniable, the suffering and anguish they had brought upon their friends was immeasurable, and the wounds that they had inflicted on them would show the scars for many, many moons. Gnos had asked the council to find compassion. Could they not understand that wise rules and regulations, proved and adhered to throughout the ages, had to be not only strictly enforced but also seen to be enforced? Such rules were the basis of justice, but justice could be done only when it was tempered with compassion. Compassion meant that each badger would feel tenderness and concern for the others and, surprisingly, the greatest example that Beaufort had ever been privileged to witness had taken place that day. It was not the assistance the sows had felt compelled to give the boars, it was not the involvement of the cubs, who had found such marvellous courage to protect the Cilgwyn heritage, it had been displayed by one of those who stood in front of them, ashamed at his and his friends' inexcusable conduct. The words that Gnos had spoken had come from his heart. Whatever his experience under Kronos, he had learned the true understanding of unselfish caring and compassion for others. Gnos sought forgiveness for others at the expense of his own life, and such a badger was worthy of a place amongst them. This badger and the other wretched ones would indeed find forgiveness but it would be some time before their misdeeds would be forgotten. Badgers who had the integrity of heart that Gnos had clearly displayed were to the procreation of the Cilgwyn dynasty as acorns were to the giant oak. Beaufort told them that he had searched the eyes of every one of the prodigals and had found, without exception, that all of them earnestly desired the chance to prove their worthiness of being respectful members of the community.

The dishonoured badgers would, for the duration of the life of the present moon, assemble together every morning and evening so that their shame could be seen by the others and the scars of their guilt would become deeply embedded in their hearts. They would find food for the elders before they could forage for themselves, and they would be responsible for the cleaning and preparation of the dung pits and also provide all the bedding that was needed by the other badgers. Under no circumstances were they to be helped with their tasks or this would cancel out the lesson they had to learn. When the new moon arrived they would once more become equal members of the community, but until then they would have to live with the ignominy and disgrace they had brought upon themselves. Beaufort then looked at his followers, slowly and deliberately moving his head from one side to the other so that every badger became aware that he was addressing each one personally. He emphasised that the sentence given was sufficient and that he did not expect any individual recriminatory action. They were not to defame, defile or ostracise the culprits. The guilty would be ignored during the specified period of time, but then they were to be given every opportunity to become proud and dignified members of the community once more. They were to return to their family setts, where they would surely find the first signs of forgiveness.

As Beaufort turned to leave the assembled badgers, Gnos stepped forward and asked permission to speak once more. Beaufort, not wanting to prolong the ceremony into an occasion of mitigating, tearful and self-pitying speeches, was reluctant to allow Gnos to continue. Gnos's voice was no longer despondent but eager and keen, and it was this new-found enthusiasm that at first puzzled Beaufort and eventually persuaded him to listen to what Gnos seemed to believe was urgent and important enough to say. Gnos said while it was not perhaps the opportune time to make helpful suggestions, he begged the council's forbearance and patience, but he believed he would be doing a disservice if he did not advise them to visit the sett area that had been under Kronos's control. It was surrounded by a much better supply of food, completely sheltered from the cold winds of the hillside and many setts had already been excavated, it having been Kronos's intention to use this fact in his attempt to persuade the badgers to desert Beaufort. Furthermore, the young sows who had been too weak-willed to spurn their selfish desire in a moment of stupidity were already residing there and desperately wanted to be reunited with their families.

As a result of Beaufort's decision to make an immediate inspection of the site, the badgers found themselves leaving the compound and moving to their new home in the valley below. Gnos had understated the benefits of their new abode; it was more in keeping with Cilgwyn. Though covered by deep snow, there were streams where food could be more easily found. The snow on the banks was constantly being thawed by the cold running waters and revealed slugs, snails, beetles and worms in far greater numbers than had been found around the compound. There were the rotting trunks of dead pines, hiding a multitude of bugs, beetles and larvae of the black and yellow saw-fly. Some of the trees had been hollowed out by the green-and-red woodpeckers seeking worm and caterpillar by pecking through the wood to get at them. Beaufort was glad they had moved from that enclosure of death and destruction but he would always remember it, not for the curtailment of Kronos's evil transgressions but as the resting place of Eldon, his elderly friend whose shadow would forever be with him.

There was quite a bit of organising to do before the badgers began to relax in their new homes, and Beaufort, feeling exhausted by the day's events, decided that Chantar and Gruff should undertake the arranging of the families into their setts. He saw a beetle scuttle under the cover of a hollow log and instinctively swooped upon it. Looking into the log, he saw that butterflies were hibernating there, fast in their cold-time sleep, clinging to the inside roof of the log. There were peacocks, tortoiseshells, and painted ladies, each one displaying forgotten colours of the warm time. He had also noticed the first shoots of the primrose and cowslip by the banks of the stream. There didn't seem to be any omens of misfortune in this peaceful dell, just the simple reminders that life was about to start again. He hoped that now they were free of Kronos, they would find the urgently needed rest that was essential if each badger's dream of discovering Elysia was to come true. Beaufort did not want to think about any more adversities. They had escaped from man, they had defeated the harbinger of evil, they had survived the elements. Surely they now had only to wait for the snows to disappear? The cold moons did not last forever, the fresh green leaves never missed their turn.

30

Termination

THE MORNING TRIBUNE

Friday, 27th December

Tribune/News Badger Rescue Plan

The *Morning Tribune* and the *Daily News* have decided that immediate action should now be taken to try to save the Cilgwyn badgers. The continuing blizzards are creating considerable public concern for the badgers and we are receiving hundreds of anxious phone calls and letters each day.

Together with the *Daily News,* we are pleased to announce that we have prepared and will sponsor a rescue plan.

We have hired helicopters, air observance specialists and, in addition, we have acquired the services of Dr. Hans Lindstrum, Scandinavia's leading authority on wildlife and an expert in animal behaviour in Arctic conditions.

Immediately there is an improvement in the weather, the plans will be put into effect.

An air search will be carried out from Llancwm to Tredeilo covering an area of approximately three hundred square miles. As soon as the badgers have been located, bedding, food and other requirements will be dropped.

DAILY CHRONICLE

Saturday, 28th December

Conservationists Denounce Tribune/News Badger Rescue Attempt

The conservationist organisation P.A.W.S. is to apply to the courts for an injunction to stop the attempts of the *Morning Tribune* and the *Daily News* to rescue the badgers. A spokesman for P.A.W.S. stated that its committee was unanimous in its condemnation of this scheme, which could prove disastrous to any surviving badgers.

Television news, 12:30 P.M.,
Friday, 3rd January

The editor of the *Morning Tribune* newspaper has confirmed that the plan to rescue the Cilgwyn badgers is now in operation.

Television news, 5:45 P.M.,
Friday, 3rd January

Our reporter from Tredeilo, South Wales, has just phoned in with the news that Dr. Hans Lindstrum, co-ordinator of the *Tribune/Daily News* badger rescue operation, has located recently excavated setts on heathland in the forest on the slopes of the Garron Mountains.

However, Dr. Lindstrum considers that they have not been inhabited for between seven to ten days. Any signs indicating the path the badgers have taken have been obliterated by the covering of thick snow.

THE MORNING TRIBUNE

Tredeilo, South Wales
Saturday, 4th January

Cilgwyn Badgers Survive

Our attempts to rescue the badgers brought welcome relief during these cold winter days. There can be little doubt that the large clusters of setts discovered by our rescue team, led by Dr. Hans Lindstrum, belonged to the nomadic badgers of Cilgwyn. The setts were discovered in an L-shaped clearing close to a pine forest on the lower slopes of the Garron Mountains, only three miles from the market town of Tredeilo. Darkness prevented the rescue team from continuing with the search, but at daylight, if weather permits, the rescue attempts will continue.

DAILY CHRONICLE

Monday, 6th January

Stop This Persecution

Members of the Badger Protection League go to court this morning where their application for an injunction will be heard in an attempt to prevent the *Daily News* and *Morning Tribune* newspapers from continuing with their rescue plan.

The League is also applying for an order to stop any other organisations or individuals from interfering with, searching for, or killing badgers until the proposed new protection bill becomes law.

Television news, 12:30 P.M., *Monday, 6th January*

In the high court this morning, the Badger Protection League successfully obtained an injunction preventing any person or organisation other than the P.A.W.S. organisation from attempting to make any contact with the badgers in South Wales.

The objections to the injunction were withdrawn by both the *Daily News* and the *Morning Tribune* when it was learned that Dr. Hans Lindstrum was now prepared to give evidence in support of the Badger League's application.

Television news flash, 11:15 A.M., *Wednesday, 8th January*

It has just been confirmed that a small unit of the government's extermination team left the town of Tredeilo, South Wales, early this morning in search of the badgers from Cilgwyn, believed to be now living near the Garron Mountains. The unit, headed by Major Robertson, included the senior tracker as well as four marksmen. A spokesman for the Ministry stated that he could not comment on the matter until further information had been received.

Television news, 5:45 P.M., *Wednesday, 8th January*

The Ministry of Agriculture announced a few minutes ago that Major T. G. Robertson and a small number of men, part of the original government badger extermination programme, have located a large sett system less than a mile from where Dr. Hans Lindstrum discovered a group of abandoned setts.

The Ministry stresses that no specific orders had been issued to Major Robertson to continue with the programme and regrets that eight badgers were shot and killed at the Garron Mountains setts late this afternoon as they tried to escape from the setts after gas had been used. Other tracks in the vicinity clearly indicated that a considerable number of badgers had left the sett area only a day or so earlier.

DAILY CHRONICLE

Tredeilo, South Wales
Thursday, 9th January

This small market town in South Wales was besieged today not only by television units and pressmen but also by many visitors outraged by the continuing killing of the badgers despite the new Badger Protection Act due to become law within two weeks.

Major Robertson met some members of the press in the Public Hall early this morning and stated that although he had now received orders to cancel the extermination programme they had not been received until that morning. He confirmed that all members of the extermination team would now be dismissed and that they would return to their bases. As Major Robertson left the hall he was confronted by angry protestors and had to have police protection in order to get to his official car.

The leader of the P.A.W.S. organisation expressed his dismay at the latest senseless slaughter but took some encouragement from the news that a large number of Cilgwyn badgers still survived.

31

The Three-Eyed Bird

Beaufort emerged from his sett and, looking at the tranquil snow-covered scene, thought how idyllic the area was. Kronos had, without doubt, chosen as perfect a place as one could find, situated at the head of the valley and sheltered by the forest and the hills sweeping around behind them. Beaufort felt he would not be surprised if the promised signs manifested themselves there. When the rains came and the weather began to warm, the snow would clear to reveal a sparkling fresh countryside, eager to start again, its colours no longer tinged by the ravages of time, but full and vibrant. Then would come the return of warm-time birds, first the wheatear, bobbing and chasing after the flies. This small, thrushlike bird, with its conspicuous white rump, black wings and tail, its head covered in a grey crown, white eye-stripe and black cheeks on its face, would announce to the countryside that the warm times were on the way, its squeaky little warble and its grating "chack chack" calls being amongst the most welcome of sounds to the rural inhabitants. As the days became warmer the numbers of different species of birds arriving after their cold-time absence would increase: the nightingales, the wood-warblers, the swallows and martins, the cuckoo and then the swifts, the last of the visitors to arrive.

The eerie silence of the snows was occasionally broken by the hoot of an owl, a late caw of a rook or the groaning of the snow-laden branches of the firs. It was an evening of sighs, and the cerulean sky was clear of even a whisper of cloud, the lichen on the trees gilded by the molten sun, which would soon be hidden by the hills. Beaufort had treasured the deep and contented sleep he had had that day, and the later emergence of the other badgers told him that they, too, were relishing the comforts of their new home. He thought he could hear faint sounds of snoring coming from the setts. Nothing stirred and even the cubs were asleep. There seemed little likelihood of Beaufort having company for quite a while and it seemed to him, as he became accustomed to the stillness of the evening air, that the badgers' snores were becoming louder and longer. It was only when the soft but heavy droning became continuous that Beaufort realised that it was not the sound of the badgers sleeping that he could hear, but a strange moaning purr that came from the sky. The deep, heavy hum began to fill the air and Beaufort could not recall a bird that would reveal its presence with such overpowering tones. As the sound became louder Beaufort began to think it must be an extremely large flock of some sort of water-bird going to or coming from distant lands. The noise now roared across the valley and became so loud that it awoke the badgers. They came out of their setts to investigate what had shattered the silence of the peaceful countryside. They searched the sky, trying to pinpoint the source of the sound, when all of a sudden a gigantic bird roared over the woods of pine. The badgers cowered as the monster whirred above the forest with tremendous power. But it was neither the size nor the sound of this giant of eagles that terrorised them, it was the fact that it had three eyes staring down, searching for them. It had a white eye, a red eye and a green eye that flashed in anger as it whirled around and around, determined to find them. As the mighty bird disappeared back over the trees, Beaufort could hear that some of the badgers had begun to whimper and squeal as they became gripped by the overwhelming fear of the three-eyed leviathan. The sounds of fear were interrupted by the bark of Fircone telling them it was a bird that carried man, and that it was the same bird he had seen when he had been on his own, after the massacre of the old ones, shortly after they had left Cilgwyn. The badgers began to panic, fast becoming convinced that their long journey had all been in vain. They were about to become victims of savages who had little respect for anything that could not hurt them. Beaufort gave one short, sharp bark and the badgers stopped their cries of anguish to listen intently. The leader of the badgers, in a slow, deliberate voice, rebuked them for panicking so easily, telling them they had become void of courage. He would show them there was nothing to fear. He and Fircone would enter the trees and go in the direction of the sound, which could be faintly heard coming from the other side of the forest. The badgers were aghast at the bravery shown by two of their leaders and whispered that they were truly Nephilims.

Beaufort and Fircone quickly went on their way, keeping the faint whirring sound directly ahead of them. They knew they were safe under the trees as the bird was too huge to come through the branches. They heard the sound become louder with every step, and as they came into the twilight in the trees on the outer limits of the forest, they scented man. Fircone checked his stride but Beaufort furtively moved from tree to tree and peered out from behind a broad pine, looking at the enclosure from where they had moved only a few moons ago. Fircone hid behind another pine, also looking at the site of the deserted setts. The two badgers allowed their snouts to direct their eyes to where the scent of man came from. A shadowy figure became the focus of their attention. It was walking slowly by the sett entrances, prodding, searching, then standing back and waving its white paws to the sky. At this showing of paws the large bird began to descend, its green light flashing around the darkened scene. The two badgers became transfixed as they saw the bird push out its long, thin, snakelike tongue, which then seemed to twist itself around the man, lifting the upright one back into its mouth. The badgers decided they had seen enough. Beaufort was certain of one thing, the man had been looking for badgers, and as the man was searching their old home, it was obvious the badgers hadn't been seen in the valley below. Telling Fircone of his beliefs, he also made him promise not to say anything about the gigantic bird's awesome powers.

There wasn't a badger who had moved from the spot they had been standing on when Beaufort and Fircone had left in search of the sound, but when the two badgers emerged from the pines on their return, the badgers surged forward, eagerly awaiting the news. Beaufort stopped on the bank above the setts, rose to his full height and told them that the man animal had been searching around their old homes. At this news the badgers started their cries of woe but were immediately stopped as Beaufort growled his annoyance. Beaufort had positioned himself as high above the others as he could, as he wanted his words to be full of significance and to leave the badgers in no doubt that he believed in what he was saying. He went on to tell them that they would have to move on, as they couldn't take the risk of being found. There were too many tracks that would lead the man from the old setts to the new, but they had always managed to elude their pursuers before and they would do so again. Though it might have seemed a good idea at the time, the decision to dig setts to shelter them through the snows had only delayed the discovery of Elysia, and that was the only place they could be sure of living free, free forever of shadows other than their own.

The badgers were soon assembling behind Beaufort, who was ready to lead them away from the home that had lost its enchantment. The leader looked around to check that everyone was ready for the journey, and seeing that there were a few groups murmuring amongst themselves, he impatiently barked for them to close up with the others so that they could start their journey. Some of the badgers reluctantly obeyed, pleading with some young females to join them. Beaufort felt he had enough on his mind without having to contend with the ditherings of these young sows. Gnos, seeing Beaufort's displeasure, bounded forward and explained that ten of the young sows were too afraid to go on, as they didn't want to have their cubs born out in the snows. Beaufort couldn't believe what he had just heard and thought that fear had unbalanced their minds. What cubs could they be talking about? Then the truth slowly dawned on him. They had mated with some of the boars that had supported Kronos. Beaufort's eyes met those of Gnos, and Gnos knew that his leader had realised the truth, for there was little but contempt in his eyes. Beaufort, who a short time ago had felt so refreshingly alive, now was weary and disheartened. He ponderously walked over to the pregnant sows and tried to convince them that they would reach Elysia before the cubs were born. He argued that if they were to delay implantation, the birth of their cubs could be postponed for quite a long time, through the moons of buds and shoots, through the suns of flowers and warmth, even to the next time that the leaves would fall. This special gift to the badgers from Logos had been given so that when times were difficult and food was short, the sow could wait until the time was more suitable for the cubs to be born. The sows said they knew this but that the journey had already taken longer than any one of them had imagined and still there weren't any signs. It could be just as long again before they found the promised home. These were going to be their first cubs and they would rather take their chances by staying in the warm setts, where, if Logos willed, the cubs would be born. Beaufort could have forced the sows to follow, but this could jeopardise the lives of the others as progress would be slow. But he did not want to be cruel or unjust as he cared deeply for all of them. When he gave his permission for them to stay behind, he saw that the happiness and joy that shone from their eyes could not be greater than if they had arrived at Elysia. Gnos told Beaufort that as he was responsible for taking one of the sows as his mate, he would also like to stay on and protect them. He gave his oath that when the cubs had been born and were strong enough to travel, he would follow Beaufort and the others to Elysia. He would take the trail of the setting sun, and one day he would find them. Some of the young boars also wished to stay behind with their newly betrothed, but Beaufort was adamant that all but Gnos would accompany the main party. They would be needed to assist the older ones through the journey, especially through the early days to come, for the snow was still very deep and Beaufort's instinct had told him there was more to come. He had decided that Gnos could stay only because he would be needed to lead the females and cubs when that time came and the boars should know that it was very rare for a sow to tolerate the presence of her mate when the time of birth became near as she could become extremely aggressive.

The travellers eventually moved away. The snow was too deep to disguise their trail, and by the time the last of the column had journeyed through, the furrow that Beaufort could see being cut in the snow by the front marchers became a wide flat-based ditch. He had made up his mind to follow the course of the valley for as long as they could, as too much time would be lost if they tried to climb the hillside in such deep snow.

Though the shallow streams were bitterly cold, Beaufort led them into the waters and marched in them for quite a long distance before once again climbing out back into the snow. The sky, with its myriad of twinkling stars, appeared to be blacker than Beaufort had ever seen before, and his eyes hurt a little as the whiteness of the snow began to make his vision blur. Sometimes he fell into hollows that had been hidden by the snow; quite often he had to be pulled out of drifts that more than covered him. They would have to seek the cover of the forest before sunrise, as the stark contrast of their colours would stand out against the snow. Beaufort, for some reason, believed that as long as they kept marching, they would not be found by their pursuers. He did not question his faith for one single moment, but was afraid that some of the others would begin to despair. His intuitive mind had convinced him that when the earth awakened they would find their very own pastures. It couldn't be much more than the life span of the next moon before they arrived there.

Beaufort had never been one to daydream in his younger days, but he was now finding himself frequently drifting into moments of wishful thoughts. It was one way to stop himself from being too preoccupied by the tedium of constant upheavals and travel. The heavy responsibilities of leadership were not the cause of his weariness. Neither was it his total commitment to the safety of his friends; it was this that gave him such determined strength to carry on. He felt tired trying to find excuses and reasons for why the journey was taking so long, particularly when his companions were beginning to lose hope and he was unable to provide satisfactory evidence that they would soon be home.

The badgers had climbed up the lower slope of the valley into the cover of the pines. Though they disliked the strongly scented shelter, they were glad to get out of the cold wetness of the snow. They ate what food they could find, but worms were scarce and there was only sufficient carrion for the cubs. They slept in fits and starts during the day, not really regaining the strength they had lost during the previous night's march, but they were far from weak due to the restful time they had had in the setts. The following night differed little from the previous one, except that when dawn broke the sky became overcast and the wind began to blow the snow into clouds of whirling vapour. The badgers had moved well into the forest and could scarcely see the glint of light through the trees. They had barely settled when they heard the whinnying and whickering of a badger coming from the edge of the forest. Beaufort recognised the identifying call as that of a Cilgwyn badger, and he and Fircone rose and advanced towards the cry. They had taken only a few steps when they recognised Gnos and two of the sows that they had left behind. The three unexpected arrivals tottered forward, appearing exhausted and near collapse. Gnos explained that he and his companions had covered in one night the distance that Beaufort and the others had travelled in two. Beaufort was amazed at this effort, and although he was glad that the sows had changed their minds, he began to express his annoyance with Gnos for not sticking together with the rest of the females when the sadness of the boar told him that none of the other young sows would be coming.

Gnos was visibly shaking as he told Beaufort that early the previous day he and the young sows had been awakened by the sound of men's voices. Gnos had stayed close to his mate in their sett, and the other young sow had stayed in hers. The men had remained throughout the day and they could hear the sound of a dog and sharp echoing cracks followed by squeals from some of the other sows. The men had left the setts shortly before darkness, and when Gnos thought it was safe to emerge, he discovered that only he, his mate and the other sow had survived. He had found two of the sows lying lifeless a short run away from their sett entrances, both with holes in their heads, while the others lay dead, either on top of earth dug out of their sett tunnels or in their setts. There were no marks or signs of blood on these, but they had bulging eyes. Gnos could not enter the setts where the bodies remained, for the air inside made him choke and gasp for breath. The three, who had survived only because their setts were on the opposite side to where the men had commenced their fiendish work, had known that they must leave immediately and had followed Beaufort's trail as swiftly as their legs would carry them.

The quiet moans from those of little hope began to rise amongst the branches of the evergreen trees. Beaufort did not want this lack of faith to spread and was quick to bark his disapproval at such weakness of spirit. He again declared his conviction that if they marched each night, they would not be caught, and when the new moon, which would reveal its hair-thin crescent the next night, had finished its cycle they would, he felt sure, be nearing Elysia. Being concerned that the men might try to follow their trail with the help of the three-eyed bird, he summoned Fircone to walk with him to the outskirts of the trees. Its roving falcon eye would surely be able to see the tracks leading into the woods. For days Beaufort had wanted the snow to thaw and disappear, but the sight of it lazily floating down from the sky gave him great joy. He wished for the snow-fall to become thicker and his heart filled with increased hope. The snow began reeling down, swirling in the rising wind. The harder the wind blew, the quicker the tracks would be filled with drifting snow. They couldn't always depend on such kind responses to their wishes, but Beaufort wanted it to snow only long enough to cover their tracks, hoping the snow would cease falling before night arrived. He had told his companions that they would be safe if they kept travelling, knowing that he would never be able to convince them that it was safe to stay because it had snowed. Beaufort began to think of the young sows who could no longer fulfil their lives by raising cubs they had so dearly wanted. Over a hundred badgers had perished in their efforts to obtain a place of freedom, a small secluded piece of earth which would be of very little consequence to man, but a nation to the badgers.

They had rested so deeply inside the forest that they were oblivious of the perpetual settling of the snow. The winds disturbed the tops of the pines, but they were so densely situated that the badgers underneath were completely sheltered from the blizzard's rage. Beaufort delayed the start of the night's journey as many badgers slept late, still weary from their previous travels and not having been able to rest until well after dawn due to Gnos's arrival. When Beaufort had gone to the forest edge to view the countryside in order that he could plan their route of escape, he found that it was impossible to see more than a few steps in front of him. It had snowed throughout the day and the winds must have been strong for much of the snow had drifted into gigantic bizarre shapes. The wind had now died down but the snow continued to fall with calm insidiousness. He knew there was no possibility of the badgers walking through such thick snow, so deep that in some areas it would tower above them, and if a badger stumbled into a ditch or trench, it would be buried alive. Beaufort then remembered the view they had had when they had successfully scaled the rocky summit. He remembered that the forest seemed to stretch out of sight and he could have bitten himself for not realising it before. There was nothing to prevent them from travelling through the sheltered pines where he had seen narrow pathways every now and then bisect the trees, and though they might be thickly covered in snow, they shouldn't prove to be too much of an obstacle. They would certainly be able to travel further than they had in the snow. Beaufort knew the woodland stretch wouldn't go on forever, but until they arrived at its end they would make use of its protection.

The ease with which the badgers journeyed through the trees seemed to urge them to quicken their stride. Beaufort found it necessary at times to curb the speed of their marching. It seemed as if they were pushing themselves to the maximum because each step taken would get them more quickly to Elysia. They were loath to accept Beaufort's advice that they were capable of doing only so much in a day. He explained that they should know that if they galloped, they would tire more quickly than if they walked, although he was glad that those of little faith had become invigorated by the feeling of enthusiasm. The crossing of the pathways was far less difficult than he had imagined, and there were areas of the path, particularly where a tree was close to the edge, where the snow had drifted up to the tree's lower branches. Where the snow had been swept up by the wind, there was only a thin layer on the ground. The badgers covered a greater distance that night than any other night they had travelled since leaving Cilgwyn. Their pleasure was short-lived, for as the dawning rays of the sun began to shine through the trees ahead of them, they came to the end of the forest. It was not one of the forest pathways that Beaufort had at first hoped it might be, but the opening to a bright white world that now lay before them. The long valley had also come to its end, as now the terrain was a series of low hills, and the hilltops furthest away, which were now being tinted a rich orange and yellow, looked like a clump of sulphur tufts.

Beaufort looked up at the sky. It was no longer burdened with the dense low-lying clouds that had hidden its infinite blueness, and though the wastes of snow stretched to the horizon, the air was no longer cold and icy. His instincts told him that the snows were over, but looking above the distant hills there were high wisps of clouds, filaments of curling grey hair, moving fast towards them, and he knew that the snows would be replaced by squalls and storms.

The snow lay thicker than any of the badgers had ever seen, making it impossible for them to continue on their travels. Such was the depth of the white frozen covering, nothing would venture far from home, man or beast. Those who dared would be lucky to survive to see their homes again. The badgers had no other choice but to stay in the shelter of the trees. Beaufort hoped the snows would clear as quickly as possible, for the supply of food for over two hundred badgers would be short and would not sustain them for more than two days. They might find a few beetles, the odd worm, some pine weevils buried in the dead pine needles and perhaps some fungi bracket on the trees, but their ravenous appetites after travelling for so long would be far from satisfied during the next few days.

Having told the badgers they would rest until the snow had thawed sufficiently for them to go on, Beaufort ushered his companions further back into the forest just as the wind began to howl and the first patter of raindrops was heard.

32

Red Eyes in Its Tail

Three days and nights were spent under the creaking, swishing branches of the pines. The storm had lasted for two of those days, the winds screeching through the branches of the trees, and the heavy rains thawing the snow that had lain thickly on the exposed upper branches so that the water poured through onto the badgers huddled below. They were soaked to their skins, dejected and wretched in their abject discomfort. Though the floor was covered by a considerable thickness of pine needles and cones that had fallen over many years, pools began to collect on the forest floor. Every time a badger moved it was greeted by the squelch of the saturated ground.

Beaufort ventured to the edge of the trees and was amazed at the transformation that had taken place since he had last looked out towards the far-off hills. The snows had all but disappeared, although there were a few snow bones hanging on in sheltered corners. Elsewhere the countryside had become alive with its colours of varied greens. The time of the cold moons was over. The nimbus sky was now covered with low cloud that brought continuous rain, but it had already spent its force in the storms and was now giving only a persistent soft drizzle.

The unpleasantness of the weather had little effect on Beaufort's plan, as he had come to the firm conclusion that whatever the conditions, as soon as twilight came they would move out from the trees. He knew that he must allow the badgers to forage for quite a while before they could resume their travels. He had hoped that they could have gone down into the valley, but the fields below were completely covered by the waters that had overflowed from the river. The river path could no longer be seen, its banks fully submerged beneath the floodwaters, and Beaufort realised that it would take quite a few rain-free days before the waters receded.

The whole countryside glistened and sparkled with the movement of water. The white-capped domes were now low hills, covered in green and brown vegetation, but the heavy rain coupled with the melting snow had created a multi-formed pattern of shining streams as the surplus water surged down through every nook and cranny, forging runnels and channels in the undisturbed soil. Beaufort could see that the badgers would have to skirt the hillside, and he realised their progress would be slow as they would be forced to choose their pathway carefully to avoid being pitched and tossed by the foaming torrents that seemed to rush out of the earth from bursting springs.

The steady drizzle continued to fall as the cloud-covered sky darkened with nightfall. The badgers, though drenched, were keen to get out into the open to search for whatever tasty morsels they could find. They turned their snouts up at nothing. Whatever grub, insect or beetle came their way was gratefully taken.

The badger's foraging took them on a downward path as food in quantity and variety became more plentiful the lower they went. It was when half the night was over that they at last began to feel replenished. By coincidence the rains stopped at about the same time and the cloud broke long enough for the rising moon to cast its magic over the land. As the moonbeams dipped into the valley, Beaufort stood back amazed and enthralled by the magnificent spectacle that spread out before him. The valley floor had become a plain of rippling silver, the streams and rivulets a gossamer web of sparkling lustrous streaks of scintillating light. It was such a wondrous sight that Beaufort could only believe that this was perhaps the first of the signs that Elysia was not far away. He looked at Greyears, the wise old badger who, though now bent with age, had managed to survive the journey. The old prophet's eyes were those of a young cub, eager in their anticipation of life to come. There was no need for Beaufort to ask the old one whether he, too, felt as Beaufort did. He knew that they were both of the same mind.

It did not matter that the gorse and bracken were wet as the badgers began to shelter for the day ahead. They had not travelled very far from the forest, which lay only a short distance on the upper slopes behind them. As the day dawned Beaufort saw that the newly formed lake, which was once the valley floor, was now the resting place of a large number of different waterbirds. There were the dabblers, who fed on the water-plants. Then Beaufort saw the rare visiting saw-billed merganser duck and the white-throated goosander. Some of these birds were residents, others were resting during their long-distance journeys. But to both the flooded land promised a haven, full of plant life that had had its roots disturbed by the force of raging waters. Then, as the sun began its daily travel, a kingfisher, the bird born at the end of the rainbow, flew past. It reminded Beaufort that these were not the great waters he had been told about when he was a cub, but the countryside, which for the moment was covered with floodwaters, that would leave vast deposits of richly endowing silt upon the greenery beneath.

The following two nights were spent by the badgers making slow but gradual progress toward the cluster of low hills that had been on the horizon since they had sheltered in the forest. The sun and moon had been hidden by clouds, but other than a shower or two, very little rain had fallen since the moon had lit up the valley with such a fantastic display of shimmering splendour. Now there was no longer a large lake and the watery sheen was punctuated by large patches of land. The waters were fast receding as the rivers rushed away to the seas. Beaufort had been told by the elders that they could never remember there being a time when the earth had remained under the shadow of such dismal skies as long as it had done during the current spell. The badgers' body heat had dried out most of their soft undercoats but their paws had remained wet for many, many days. There was little chance of them becoming dry as each step seemed only to bring them into further saturating contact with the oozing terrain.

Shortly after they had reached the halfway mark between the forest and the hills, Beaufort became aware of a strange sound that could be occasionally heard coming from the furthest reaches of the valley. It occurred three or four times during the day and twice more in the early hours of darkness. Then there was a lapse before it recommenced shortly after dawn. It was a noise that neither Beaufort nor any of the others could identify. The roaring, clattering sound grew louder each time they heard it. Their nightly travels brought them nearer and nearer to the source of the sound. Beaufort listened intently as soon as he heard the first faint murmurs of the mysterious noise. He had, when he had first heard it, thought it might be from another of those giant three-eyed birds, but the sound was not the same.

The whispering murmurs increased at a furious pace to a roar and then just as rapidly, subsided into silence again.

The badgers, having to backtrack as water barriers appeared before them, had found it necessary to take quite a meandering pathway to reach the furthest part of the valley, thus avoiding pools and streams and criss-crossing rivulets. Though the distance from the forest to their present position was not long, the journey had been an extremely tiring one. Beaufort had now become quite accustomed to the regular roars, which seemed to start at the foot of the hills then continue through a stretch of woodland that eventually disappeared from sight, taking the sound with it.

The night was nearly over. It had been warm and humid and then suddenly the heavens opened and the lashing rain fell with ferocity. The badgers scuttled to find shelter in the nearest brushwood and whatever protection they could find. Lightning flashed and thunder clapped. It was something that Beaufort had been expecting as he had felt that a storm was needed to drive the heavy clouds from the sky. It was over quickly, and Beaufort found that he had been right. The sky cleared and the sun's piercing rays rose above the hills. When the glow of dawn reached them and their surroundings, the badgers seemed to take a new lease on life. The earth sparkled, enticing and enchanting, a living, inviting world. Joy of living surged through the badgers, the snows and rains already forgotten.

Beaufort emerged from the cover of the sodden gorse and shook the droplets of water from his coat. He inhaled the breath of freshness that arose from the sun-kissed countryside. Invigorated with such zest for life, it would not be difficult for the badgers to be persuaded to attempt to cross the low hills that were now close to them. They only had to go through the woodland that was just ahead of them and they would take their first steps on the gentle slopes. Beaufort trembled with excitement, and not even the first of the day's roaring sounds, which seemed so close as it came and went through the trees, could cloud his euphoria. As he nestled into the shrubbery, which was steaming away its wetness under the warming sun, his mind filled with the ever-repeating message to get over the hills, over the hills.

The badgers had enjoyed their sleep, bathed in sunshine that was warm and comforting rather than hot and stifling. The brightness of the later part of the day caused most of them to awake earlier than they had done on the previous few days. They were unable to linger on in half-sleep, as their nearly closed eyes still allowed the brightness to penetrate, and when darkness fell nearly all of them had foraged enough to satisfy their appetites. Beaufort led them through the final stretch of meadow grass and shrub into the woodlands. The trees were mixed, some conifer as well as elder, beech, aspen and willow. There were already the first signs of buds on the trees. Two of the badgers broke off and tried to reach one of the branches of the aspen tree, for they knew that the buds housed the larvae of the hawkmoth, but they were out of reach and the straying couple quickly rejoined the group.

Beaufort grunted for the badgers to halt as he emerged from the woodland to discover a strange pathway cut between the trees. Beaufort, puzzled, saw that short, square tree trunks had been placed one after another, stretching in both directions as far as the eye could see. On top of these pieces of wood there were two continuous shiny bands. The gaps between the tree trunks were filled with pieces of limestone, and most of the path was covered in a greasy substance. The smell was not familiar to him but there was an acidity to it which told him that it was not for consumption.

There was another surprise awaiting Beaufort, for as he peered through the thin lines of trees on the other side of the strange path, he saw a river. It was not in flood but still flowed at too fast a rate for them to consider crossing it. The waters from the rains and snows were still being carried away by the over-flowing springs that lay deep within the hills. They had no choice but to follow the shining bands that edged the path. They travelled for some time, the river always on the other side of the line of silver birches, but Beaufort began to worry as their journey continued. Now and then he thought he detected the faint scent of man, disguised by the acrid fumes that came from the limestone rocks as he disturbed them with his paws. He was just about to tell his companions to go back to the woods when they at last saw the pathway cross the river. It was a piece of magic: The path went across the wide river without anything holding it up. The sides of the path were protected by huge grey arches made of the same substance as the shining bands, but they looked harder than any wood or stone he had ever seen. Beaufort was surprised to hear fearful wails coming from his companions. They were afraid to cross over the river, yet Beaufort knew such fears had to be overcome for there was no other way to go.

Beaufort summoned Fircone to him and explained that they would have to set an example for the others. The two of them marched across the path with confident and resolute gait, and upon reaching the other side promptly turned round and marched back again. The other badgers were now more at ease and Beaufort told them to follow Fircone and himself. Some of the young ones were still a little nervous and it was left to Chantar and his family, together with Harvey, Titan and Rowley, to escort the cubs behind the other badgers.

As Beaufort and Fircone reached the other side of the river for the second time, they heard the murmurings that heralded the roaring sounds that they had heard in the days gone by but the badgers continued to cross the river. They did not fear the sound, as there had been no cries of alarm from the animals and birds that lived in the woodlands. When half the badgers had reached the other side, fear began to spread amongst them, for as the noises became louder, the path began to shudder. The roaring clattering sound was closing up behind them, louder and louder it became, and the path started shaking and trembling alarmingly. The badgers turned to see what was causing such a terrifying sound and saw a gigantic serpent bearing down upon them, its head with three bright yellowish eyes, the centre one large, with smaller ones on either side. Beaufort and those safely across screamed at the others to run for their lives. The badgers stampeded over the river crossing, but before all of them could scramble down the bank to the safety of the grassland below, the serpent tore into the badgers at the rear of the escaping column. Beaufort cried in horror as he saw his old friend Chantar hurled into the sky and other badgers thrown up in the air as the serpent ploughed through them. A screaming whistle of triumph came from the long, winding, snakelike giant, its sides streaked with bright yellow light, and Beaufort heard its squeals of delight as fiery sparks came from its circular legs.

The badgers trembled in fear as they rushed towards the shelter of the woodlands lying at the foot of the hills. Beaufort and Fircone told Gruff to assemble all the badgers as safely as he could in the shelter of the trees. He would remain with Fircone to see if they could help the injured badgers lying groaning close to the serpent, which had now stopped. Beaufort stood aghast as he witnessed the incredible sight of humans stepping out in large numbers from the opening gills in the side of the monster. First there had been the three-eyed giant of the sky, now it was the three-eyed monster serpent that could streak across the ground at tremendous speed.

The two watching badgers heard some of the humans shouting and then saw them bending closely over the huddled bodies of the dead and injured badgers. A short time later, when the humans climbed back into the monster, he saw that two of them each carried a small body. He hoped that they were already dead so that they would not feel the pain as the monster devoured them. The serpent once more let out its piercing whistle and with a long hiss began to move away from the river crossing. It was soon roaring and clattering, the sounds beginning to diminish as it disappeared from sight.

Beaufort and Fircone were dry-mouthed as they stared at each other in disbelief. It was some moments before either could find any words. Beaufort was glad that it was Fircone who had stayed with him, for the big boar didn't even flinch when it was suggested that the two of them go back onto the path to investigate the results of the serpent's attack. They found Chantar's mutilated body at the front of the embankment and a few steps further up lay his lifeless wife, Nepra, only barely recognisable, her face crushed by the ferocity of the serpent. As Beaufort and Fircone climbed up on the pathway, they could see alongside the shining bands of the path the crumpled bodies of four more badgers, two of them the son and daughter of Chantar, Goliad and Beetleberry, the other two being Harvey and Migola. Two more bodies lay against the arch of the river crossing, and as Fircone turned them over to see who they were, Beaufort gasped as he recognised two of the young cubs, Pickle and Deva. Beaufort was deeply saddened by the loss of so many when they were so near to their promised land. With Chantar's death, Beaufort was aware that none of the members of the old council of Cilgwyn had lived to find their dreams come true.

The two badgers, having failed to find any other bodies in the area surrounding the site of the vicious attack, returned to the woodland where the other badgers were waiting. Gnos came up to Beaufort to inform him that ten of the badgers could not be accounted for. Beaufort called out the names of those they had identified as dead. As each name passed his lips cries of woe and despair came from the listening crowd, then sorrowful wails from the parents of the two dead cubs. When Beaufort had finished calling out the names, he began to issue instructions for the others to check who else was missing. For the peace of mind of the other badgers, the two bodies taken by the serpent had to be identified. Before he could finish his request, he was interrupted by Gnos, who whispered that there were only two names missing, those of Titan and Rowley. As Beaufort's head dropped in despair, Fircone could no longer retain his composure. The big badger fell on the floor, prostrate with grief, crying to Logos that he be allowed to change places with Titan. He no longer sought the sanctity of Elysia and vowed he would never jeopardise any other badgers by offering his friendship, for every badger he had shared his life with had come to harm.

Beaufort knew that to comfort his friend at that moment might result in more harm than good. He went in a daze to console his dear Corntop, and though tears glistened in the corners of her eyes, she controlled her sorrow magnificently. She realised that her Beaufort needed all the support he could get for him to hold the confidence of the dejected badgers. She would have to save her grief for calmer days. Beaufort found it too difficult to comprehend how the sign of reflecting moonbeams could have been an omen of such misery and sadness when he had believed with all his heart that it was the beginning of the entrance to paradise. His heart ached for the two cubs who had been taken away from them. They were so very, very special and he had always felt so confident and contented when they had been near him. He had come to understand how blessed the Cilgwyn badgers were to have had two such innocents among them, two cubs who had brought something of heaven into their rough earthly existence.

33

Affinity

Television news, 9:00 P.M.,
Wednesday, 29th January

It now seems that the Cilgwyn badgers cannot escape misfortune. News is coming in from Tredeilo in Mid Wales that the 6:30 Shrewsbury to west Wales train had ploughed into a large group of badgers on a railway bridge just after the train emerged from a tunnel under the Garron Mountains.

First reports indicate that eight of the badgers have been killed and at least two critically injured. The other badgers stampeded down the rail embankment into the countryside.

Apparently Major T. G. Robertson, who was in charge of the extermination unit, was on the train.

Television news, 10:00 P.M.,
Wednesday, 29th January

It has now been confirmed that eight badgers were killed by a train on the Mid Wales line earlier this evening. No passengers were injured in the incident. It has also been confirmed that Major Robertson, the leader of the disbanded extermination programme, was on the train, and has arranged for two young male badgers seriously injured in the accident to be taken to a veterinary surgery in Tredeilo.

Television news, 5:45 P.M.,
Thursday, 30th January

Members of the conservationist organisation P.A.W.S. did not find any more dead or injured badgers when they carried out a search of the area around the scene of yesterday's train accident.

DAILY CHRONICLE

Tredeilo, South Wales
Friday, 31st January

Sinner Turns Saint

In a remarkable turn of events, the previous scourge of the Cilgwyn badgers has now become their saviour. Major T. G. Robertson has stayed constantly with two injured badgers since he took them for treatment after the train crash on Wednesday evening. The veterinary surgeon said that if it had not been for Major Robertson's prompt action, they would have had to put the animals to sleep. Nevertheless, they were still pessimistic about the animals' chances of survival.

DAILY CHRONICLE

Tredeilo, South Wales
Saturday, 1st February

Badgers Going Home

After a month of intensive care, the two badgers named Romulus and Remus by their benefactor, Major T. G. Robertson, have left the veterinary surgery in Tredeilo today well on the road to recovery.

Remus, the smaller of the two badgers, has become devoted to the Major and allows him to feed him by hand, relishing his diet of grapes, sultanas and earthworms, which are supplied daily by local residents. But his favourite food is bread dipped in honey. Romulus, a large yearling badger, still limps but has fully recovered from all his other injuries. He takes his food easily, but will not allow humans to touch him.

Major Robertson, now retired from the army, has rented a smallholding for a few months where he hopes that, with affectionate care and attention, he can help Romulus and Remus to recover sufficiently so that they can be set free.

Mr. B. Stephens, the well-known conservationist, stated that the badgers of Cilgwyn, who apparently have taken up residence not too far away from Tredeilo, appear miraculously to have survived man's persecution.

34

The Rainbow Ridge

The badgers, dejected and despondent since the tragic turn of events at the river crossing, had practically given up all hope of ever discovering Elysia. They had followed Beaufort into the hills, far from convinced that their leader had taken the right path. They understood that it was imperative to get away from the place where the serpent had sprung on them, but Beaufort had remained silent over the past three nights, his face a mask of tormented misery. The leader's closest friend, Fircone, appeared to have relinquished all his responsibilities and ambled along behind the badgers, no longer seeming to care about what was happening and keeping to himself. His spirits were at their lowest ebb and he seemed to be one of the strange animals that in badger lore were simply known as the walking dead.

Beaufort's previous doubts had returned. He had felt so confident about matters only a few days earlier and had convinced himself that the days of torment and misfortune were over. He had allowed the tension that had been his constant companion since he had been appointed leader to ease, leaving him so relaxed that he was totally unprepared for the disaster that had struck them on the river crossing. He couldn't come to terms with nature's determination to provide so many calamities in their quest for a small patch of Logos's earth, where they would be immune from the cruelties of man.

Though Beaufort had accepted that hardship was the foundation of success and that laughter was enjoyed more fully after tears, he was failing to shrug aside this mood of depression as quickly as he had been able to do before when misfortune had struck. He had given little thought to planning each night's journey and had by habit followed a line to where the sun had set. It was no more than a nightly ritual and he would rise at the end of the day, forage for a time, then curtly grunt at his companions of his intentions to journey on. There was no real bitterness in his heart; he just felt that he would never understand the reasoning of Logos. He had believed that the journey was necessary for the perpetuation of the Cilgwyn badgers, but had asked Logos the same question many times since the evening of the roaring serpent. Why had Logos allowed the badgers to believe in a final glory to their travels, the reason for which was to find a sanctuary for the next generations, and then taken the foundation of the next generation away from them? The news of Titan's and Rowley's deaths had all but destroyed his faith in carrying on. As Beaufort led the badgers he rarely lifted his head high enough to see more than a few steps ahead of him. His eyes were blurred by the vision of the faces of the two cubs for he could see them as clearly as the day they showed him how to climb the rocky spur on the mountain.

Beaufort hoped that the badgers would ask him to step down as leader and appoint another to take his place. There had been no cries of condemnation or any signs of disapproval. The badgers continued to follow him blindly for Beaufort did not understand that he was now their only hope and that without him the badgers would be lost. He had led them through the gorse-covered hillock until at last the panorama began to widen. They were descending the slopes of the last hill of the range, the land ahead sweeping gently upwards as far as the eye could see, yet the highest point did not seem as high as a lofty pine. They were coming into the moraine of an ancient glacier, the boulders and rock deposits now covered by centuries of soil accumulation. Beaufort glanced towards the ridge that would hide the sun at the end of that coming day. Since the slaughter at the river they had settled for the day's rest well before the break of dawn but he had kept travelling longer than usual that night.

His attention was attracted to the ridge time and time again, and he stopped and stared at it intently, barking at the others to make their beds for the day's rest. Beaufort felt the burden of sorrow begin to leave him and now kept searching his mind for the reason that the ridge was of so much interest to him. The outline became clearer as the sun rose in the sky. The grasses and leafy plants about him were covered with the morning dew, and then Beaufort saw the faint colours of not one but two rainbows appear above the ridge, their ends falling on the land beyond, and he remembered the words that his grandfather, Adala, had taught him when he was a cub:

> *To remind us of our loved ones departed from our setts,*
> *The sparkling dew on flowers will not let us forget,*
> *Those angel drops enrich us with their glistening soft*
> *   embrace,*
> *They fell as wisps of glory from Rainbow's heavenly grace.*

The pent-up grief that Beaufort had contained within his heart for the past few days was finally released. He walked a few steps until he was screened from the others by a thick covering of yellow-blossomed gorse and, falling to the floor, at last wept bitterly, but although he had not wanted the others to see him, he was not ashamed, he loved them all so dearly. His grief and sorrow spent, he began to rise, only to find that both Corntop and Fircone were standing close by. Corntop smiled at Beaufort, glad that he had allowed his inner feelings to express themselves in the release of tears. She placed her paw on his shoulder and explained that while no one would ever understand the mysterious ways of Logos, she knew that Beaufort had been given the fortitude to accept whatever disaster came his way. She and all the other badgers believed that Beaufort had been caressed by the caring paws of Logos and that there would soon come a time when such faith would be confirmed. Fircone, seeing that his trusted friend was recovered, returned to the other badgers, still refusing to come out of his silent world. Beaufort was glad that Fircone had continued to show concern for their eternal affinity, for it told him that something would happen that would help his friend regain the joys of living.

The little verse he had remembered earlier kept going through his mind. He looked again at the dew-covered foliage and it reminded him of Buckwheat and Eldon and Titan and Rowley and Bamber, the strange visitor from the days that now seemed so long ago. It reminded Beaufort of the beginning of their journey after so many had been killed at the Cilgwyn setts. Cilgwyn, the name he had cherished but that had become a part of badger history when it had faded behind them as the badgers climbed over the ridge so many moons ago. For a moment he just stared into space. Then his body began to tingle with excitement and he began to shiver with a hallowed awareness. He understood why he had kept looking at the ridge that lay ahead of him. It was nearly identical to the ridge that was the sun-setting horizon at Cilgwyn! This was without doubt the first of the promised signs! He so desperately wanted to tell the others, but he had to be sure. He could not risk raising their hopes only to find them shattered once again. Corntop could see that Beaufort was undergoing some sort of transformation. His eyes brimmed once again with tears, but this time they were not of sorrow but of joy and she clasped him firmly to her. Beaufort saw that Corntop knew that they were just a night away from sighting Elysia. There was no need for words and she kept nodding and smiling at him. The two of them sat staring at the ridge until well into morning. They were so blissfully happy that they wanted to share these marvellous moments with the others, but they knew they would need other signs to convince them that they had arrived at their new and wonderful home. Both Beaufort and Corntop were unconcerned that their nest should be hidden for the day's rest and they lay together on the thick fresh grass, always in sight of the ridge. When the tiredness of the previous night's journey eventually overcame Beaufort's excitement, he placed his head on his paws, and as he began to drift towards slumber, he heard his Corntop speak some words that seemed to waft down to him on the gentle winds from heaven.

As Corntop stroked Beaufort's head with her paw, she whispered words that she had composed and held in her heart since her dearest love had become leader of the badgers:

> *The day will shortly come, when in a sheltered bower*
> *A leaf will unfurl to reveal a splendoured flower.*
> *There gentle hills that part will form a shell*
> *Round pleasant fields and wooded dell.*
> *A sylvan scene, free of threat and fear,*
> *The promised land, our home, Elysia.*

Beaufort was awake well before the golden yellow of the sun had lost its brightness and was eager to get on with the journey. He needed all his patience to prevent him from waking the other badgers who were sleeping so deeply. For a long time he paced to and fro between the badgers' resting places and the spot from where he could see the ridge, making his legs ache and his paws sore. He would never have been able to restrain himself from barking loud and often to awaken the badgers but for Corntop's subduing influence. Beaufort found it impossible to keep calm and roused Corntop from her sleep. She understood Beaufort's impatience but had to constantly remind him of the necessity to resist the temptation of waking the badgers to tell them of his conviction that they were at the gateway of Elysia. When the badgers eventually began to stir from their slumbers, Corntop's pacifying words had had their effect on Beaufort for he had become quite composed.

The badgers were quite surprised when they heard Beaufort barking that it was time for them to proceed on their travels. They had barely started foraging for their evening meal, but their leader sounded so commanding and confident, and his apathetic attitude since the night of the river tragedy had obviously gone. This was once again the badger they respected and revered, but they could not understand why he had so suddenly returned to the indomitable and resolute leader they knew him to be. Beaufort barked that he would be going ahead of the others and informed them that it was his intention to reach the horizon by the time the sun appeared. He did not expect them to keep up with him, but they should follow his path, feeding as they travelled. He would be waiting for them on the ridge and he would expect to see them shortly after dawn. The other badgers looked at each other in bewilderment. Why was their leader behaving in such a strange manner? They were at a loss to understand why Beaufort should find it necessary to journey into the unknown without them.

His impatience soon forgotten, Beaufort moved over the soft, yielding herbage. The gorse bushes and bramble that sometimes confronted him proved to be only minor hindrances as he skipped around them. He maintained a steady jog for quite some time, but though the gradient was hardly discernible, it was enough to eventually force him to slow down. He was still managing to walk with resolute strides when half the night had gone, his eyes set firmly on the stars that shone with crystal clarity in the blackness of the sky ahead of him.

Beaufort marched on through the sprouting curled fronds of the birth-time fern, and he was now able to see the ridge in the starlit gloom. He would reach it in time to watch the sun light up the land beyond it. The night air was quite warm, yet it had been cool enough for dew to form on the ground around him. He found that he could no longer see the stars and it was then that Beaufort stumbled, for as he scanned the sky he saw a shooting star. Pausing for a few moments, he searched the sky for confirmation of his sighting and was doubly rewarded as a stellar stream burst through the heavens. He trembled as the second sign that Elysia would soon be revealed manifested itself in the sky. The rim of the ridge became pale as the first hint of sunrise touched it gently. Beaufort increased his pace to a canter over the remaining stretch of slope that finally took him to the ridge. Then he sat back on his haunches, awaiting the fullness of dawn.

It was going to be a warm, hazy day. There were just a few specks of clouds in the paling blue sky and the touch of the ridge-top zephyrs helped to cool him after his rapid ascent. Finding that he was sitting on some limestone outcrop, he moved to a more comfortable spot and sat back into the lush-ness of clover and timothy grass. There hadn't been time for him to absorb the beauty of the expanse of the valley that opened out in front of him, but before long he began to feel a great surge of emotion and joy flow through him. The hairs on his withers tingled, as he was filled with supreme bliss, realising that this was one of the most treasured moments in his life.

This feeling of pure joy had come quietly and lingered with him for a few moments before, without warning, it slowly dissolved into the fragrant air. The scented air caused Beaufort to return to a new awareness of the countryside. It had been many days since he had last smelled the fragrance that came from the green-flowered moschatel, a plant that would scent the air only as long as the dew was still on its leaves. The clouds in the sky changed to wisps of vapour, then vanished as they released their showers of rain. As the rain fell into the valley the sun's rays reflected through the glistening drops and Beaufort saw the complete arch of a rainbow straddle the valley below. There was no need to hold back from the other badgers anymore. Here was the third sign, and looking back over the ridge, he saw that his brave and loyal companions would soon join him and see for themselves the promised land.

35

Elysia

As the badgers approached Beaufort they could sense the aura of majesty surrounding him. That Beaufort was standing at a point above them helped to enhance this image of him, not just as their leader, but as a badger mighty and powerful, towering in size and strength, august and noble, a badger whose destiny could lie only in triumph. The badgers faltered in their stride as they became aware of the joy and delight radiating from their leader. The momentary pause in their scrambling to the ridge top provided the silence Beaufort needed to tell them the news. He held his paw up, and then, sweeping round in noble gesture, pointed to the valley below them and uttered the name Elysia. The badgers' silence lasted for several moments, their mouths agape, their eyes incredulous, and then they erupted into a mass of crying, cheering, squealing, barking and roaring badgers. Two hundred and sixty grey-coated terrestrial members of the universe stood in a line on top of the ridge, looking down at the sylvan-cloistered, stream-crossed meadowland that was to be their home. The younger badgers fidgeted excitedly, eager to explore the nooks and crannies hidden in the sequestered groves. The older badgers showed mixed emotions, some re-laxed by the knowledge that the journey was over, others, al-though happy at the prospect of peace and the real possibility of living in a customary manner, were weeping. For no matter what the wonders and delights of their new abode were, noth-ing on earth would ever replace their heartfelt longing for Cilgwyn. Beaufort understood the nostalgia of those who had reached the years of senescence in their old home, but he was wise enough to know that as the days passed in their new sur-roundings, the reawakening to the pleasures of tranquil en-chantment would persuade them that life itself was what really mattered and every single moment could be a lifetime of joy.

Beaufort barked his encouragement to the others to follow and called to Corntop and Fern to walk beside him. As Corntop joined him he saw that her eyes were full of rapture. Beaufort saw a tear trickle slowly down Fern's face and understood that it was not for thoughts of the halcyon glades or for the memories of Cilgwyn; it was for the moment of loneliness that was hers as she remembered Buckwheat. And Beaufort allowed himself to imagine that his happiness might be even greater if at least Rowley and Titan might be with them.

The badgers were soon thronging into the wonderland that must surely have been the home of elves and pixies, a fairyland full of grace and beauty, alive with the colours that fanfared the time of warm, sunny days.

There were larch trees, hanging their dark green tassels, the white-flowered gean, the white-blossomed hawthorn, the fringed white petals of the chestnut tinged with crimson. There were shrubs and bushes that would provide them with a deli-cious harvest in times to come, the red cloudberry, cranberry and strawberry, and the blue-black berries from bramble and elder. Beaufort marvelled at the loveliness that was the touch of Logos where even the grasses in all their different shades of green sparkled with emerald intensity, the meadow fescue, the sweetgrass, cat's-tail grass, cock's foot, rye grass, tar grass, reed grass, and the tufted hair. He saw round-leaved willows near the sparkling stream, trees that bore great golden catkins and were loved by the butterflies.

The fragile butterflies were everywhere, the peacock, brimstone, copper, orange tip, grayling and fritillary. The birds with their multitude of songs, the pied and spotted fly-catchers, the pink-chested turtle-dove, the orange-breasted redstart with its black throat, constantly flicking its tail up and down. There were red- and pink-breasted finches, orange-striped goldcrest crowns, yellow wagtails, and, less colourful, swallows, thrushes, larks and blackbirds.

The beauty of the valley was completed by the dazzling brilliance of a myriad of blooms, their delicate and fragile petals stretching towards the sun: the pale and dark blue violets, the five-petalled white periwinkle and four-petalled blue, bright yellow marsh marigolds, golden yellow daffodils, the radiating sunshine yellows of buttercup and primrose, the white clustered saxifrage, the wild green-winged orchids, the purest of white stitchwort, purple anemones, lilies of the valley and the many pools of bluebells that grew in the shade of the trees. The swaying green ferns seemed to be beckoning the badgers towards them, inviting the travellers to rest for eternity. Beaufort was enthralled by such splendour, believing that it could be equalled only by entering the gateway to heaven.

He looked at his astonished companions, who realised that even Cilgwyn could not be compared with this lovely valley for its remarkable beauty. The badgers were spellbound by the wonders of the Elysian fields, finding it difficult to accept that they were to make their home in what had to be the most beautiful place on earth.

Beaufort could see that they were waiting for his reassurance that this was indeed their home. Although he reminded them of the signs, there were still many badgers who couldn't bring themselves to accept this good fortune. They had come so near to happiness before, only to have it snatched away from them by some unforeseen turn of events. Beaufort realised how desperately they sought some indisputable evidence that this was Elysia. He was trying to think of something that would convince them when the most incredible thing happened. There wasn't a cloud in the sky and there was still some time before the sun would reach its zenith, yet darkness seemed to be looming and the birds began to roost. Beaufort glanced at the sun, and to his amazement saw it was becoming a moon, a curved shadow already having covered part of the left arc, and it was slowly and steadily shutting the light and warmth from the earth. He had never before experienced such a phenomenon, but for some inexplicable reason he did not feel afraid. The singing of the birds faded away, and all that could be heard was the gurgling of the stream. There was total darkness and the sky was blacker than any night that Beaufort had lived through. The badgers began to whisper and small whimpering cries of fear could be heard. They were frightened that once again they would find disillusionment in a fool's paradise. Beaufort knew that they had to be wrong, his faith leaving him in no doubt that they had discovered Elysia. He began to bark his annoyance at them when the darkness of the sky was broken by a ring of fire and distant minute flames burst outwards from the fiery circle. Then, miraculously, after a few short moments of night, light pierced the darkness that had engulfed them. The shadows of the sky were parting, the sky was giving birth to a fresh new sun. The birds began singing, the bees began buzzing, the crickets chirped as the radiant rays of the sun brought them comfort and pleasure. The puzzled badgers looked at Beaufort for his explanation, and he silently thanked Logos for providing him

with unequivocal proof that this was the dawning of Elysia. He gently admonished the badgers for not understanding the meaning of Logos's sign. Could they not see that this was a very special day? The first day of their life at Elysia was the first day of the infant sun and they had reached the plains of paradise. Beaufort encouraged them to go out and explore the delights of their new-found haven. He would, with the help of his council colleagues, assess the best place for the location of the setts. They would be constructed on the same basis as they had been at Cilgwyn, and he wished everyone to understand that from that moment in time the rules and regulations that had had to be waived during their travels were reinstated and had to be obeyed. The Adamus, the scrolls of law and procedure, were to be strictly followed, and failure to do so would lead only to the collapse of Elysia.

For the next forty days the peace of the glen was disturbed by the hectic activity of the badgers. There was rest for no one, only digging, excavating and cleaning until eventually the building of setts was over. They had marked out their pathways, scented the boundaries of different crops and completed with devotion the construction of the new halls of the Cadre. As promised by Beaufort, the badgers were allowed to relax and enjoy themselves as soon as construction was finished. They had finished their foraging in a very short space of time, food was so abundant. Beaufort had retired to his comfortable resting chamber early in the night, but having become accustomed to only a short span of sleep, he had awakened with the dawn. When he came out of his sett he discovered that most of his companions had also emerged. They were grooming themselves or basking in the morning sun, enjoying themselves in the peaceful balmy day of the warm time. Beaufort surveyed the tranquil scene and felt a glow of satisfaction warm his heart. He stared at the ridge, which held a special fascination for him as it was from there that he had first seen the lovely land of Elysia. He became startled as he thought he detected something moving in the thick leafy vegetation that shrouded the ridge's crest. He stopped and strained to see clearly two strange creatures who appeared over the ridge. They came a short distance down the grassy slopes towards the badgers, then they stopped and looked at the woodland home of the badgers. Beaufort shuddered, as the intruders were of the shape that was unmistakably man. The two upright ones did not come any nearer and returned over the ridge. As Beaufort worried over this unexpected appearance, his fears intensified as he saw the two figures again. This time they were carrying a very large object, walking awkwardly on either side of it. They stopped at the same point as before, placing their burden on the ground. The two creatures then walked away back over the ridge. Beaufort was puzzled by the behaviour of the humans and in particular was perplexed by the object they had left behind. He wondered whether it was yet another example of the humans' power to wreak destruction. His thoughts were pushed aside by the reappearance of the humans. They were carrying another object, similar to the first, and they followed the same procedure as before.

By this time all the badgers had become aware of the humans' presence on the hill and they hid themselves either by going into their setts or hiding behind the shrubs, peering at the drama that was taking place on the slopes. The two humans appeared to be doing something to the objects that they had carried, and then they stood back as two smaller forms emerged from them. The two figures began to bound down the slope before stopping abruptly. The larger of the two small creatures ran back up the hill to one of the humans and stayed there for a moment before rushing back to join his waiting companion. The two animals then seemed to be running at a furious pace towards Beaufort and his hidden companions. Beaufort moved out to the shrubbery preparing to meet these strangers head-on. He would defend his companions and would fight to the death if necessary. As he moved forward he saw that the leaping, tumbling creatures were not unfamiliar and was further comforted when he recognised that he would have Fircone as an ally in any ensuing fight as he heard the pawsteps of his friend behind him. Beaufort fluffed out his coat as he prepared for the assault when, to his astonishment, Fircone charged past him, bellowing and roaring. Beaufort fell back in amazement as he saw Fircone dive at the oncoming creatures. Roars and squeals came from the furore of the entangled bodies, but as he rose up to go and help his friend, he realised the cries were not of pain and anguish but of uncontrollable delight. As Beaufort increased his pace he had to stop for a moment, his brain numbed and unable to accept the miracle that was happening. For there was Fircone, tightly clasping to him the bodies of the two creatures. They weren't just creatures—they were badgers; they weren't just badgers—they were Titan and Rowley. Fircone was sobbing, and tears flowed freely from the tender-hearted badger.

As Titan and Rowley tried to explain what had happened to them after they had been nearly killed by the river serpent, the other badgers began to reveal themselves. Soon Titan, Rowley and the still-embracing Fircone were surrounded by all of the badgers who resided in Elysia. Beaufort began to understand how Titan and Rowley had been rescued from the jaws of death and that, with the help of man, they had been returned to them. He gazed up at the ridge and saw the humans disappear over its crest. Beaufort's heart sang as the meaning of such a miracle dawned on him. It was yet another dawning of the times, the time when man had finally accepted that every creature had the right to a share of the beautiful, beautiful earth.

36

Echoes of the Past

It was the time when leaves began to take on their masquerade of gold. It was not the auburn days in the year when they had arrived at Elysia, but the time after that, when every one of the badgers was instructed to attend a meeting of the Cadre. The meeting had been called in observance of the ancient laws of the Adamus. It had been decided that the ceremony of naming the cubs should be restored, and Beaufort and Fircone, who had taken a new wife named Meadowsweet, and all the other parents of cubs, the firstborn of Elysia, waited with pride for the names of their offspring to be called out and entered in the scrolls. Beaufort was surprised and a little disappointed when the proceedings were delayed by Greyears requesting that he be heard. It was the wish of all the badgers, except the members of the council who had not been brought into the matter, that a special entry be made in the Scrolls of Legend and Heroic Deeds. The request could not be denied by the council as it was supported by the wishes of all the other badgers. The crowded halls became silent as Greyears rose to address his audience with a eulogy that he had composed as a tribute from himself and the other badgers that had been his companions on the historic journey.

Bamber, the unknown, the stranger from a distant sett,
Saved them with the warning before his death he met.
Buckwheat, son of Adala, determined and so brave,
Led them from their homeland before his life he gave.
Eldon, son of Jason, brought joy with every breath,
The guardian of the young ones, before treachery brought
*   him death.*
Fircone, son of Brymar, fearless, bold and strong,
Whose heart was full of kindness, a victor over wrong.
Titan, son of Dagmar, a cub from heaven on earth,
Destined for immortal fame, since the moment of his birth.
Beaufort, son of Buckwheat, the greatest badger of them all,
Whose chivalrous and honoured name will echo Cadre's
wall.
These names shall be remembered until the end of time,
These Towers of the Cadre that to Asgard surely climb.
Whenever badger speaks to badger, be it cub or be it old,
These valiant names shall be words of honour, or breath
*   forever hold.*

The badgers rose as one to acclaim the gallantry and wisdom of those who had led them to Elysia, their now beloved home. Beaufort saw that both Fircone and Titan, though embarrassed by the kind and honourable sentiments, held their heads high with pride and dignity. There was such a marvellous feeling of respectful affinity and devotion amongst all the badgers, and Beaufort, on behalf of his colleagues and those sadly missed, thanked them for the honour bestowed upon them.

He then called the meeting to order and sat back to enjoy the ceremony, where every badger born earlier in the year, and who was now half a year in age, would walk forward to receive his or her official name from Greyears. When all the cubs had been named, Beaufort rose again and asked his audience to agree with one final request that he wished to make. He explained to them that they could not continue to call their new home Elysia, as it was a name that really belonged to the pastures of Asgard, and it was a name that meant heavenly paradise. While he appreciated that their new homeland was as close to a heavenly paradise as any place could be, he believed it to be only right and proper that it should be given a more earthly name and he could think of nothing more appropriate than Fernhill, for indelibly etched on their minds was their first view of the little hill with its swaying ferns. The badgers rose once again to give their approval and they kept roaring and calling out the new name of their home, the hill of ferns, Fernhill.

Beaufort found it difficult to bring the proceedings to a close, as the badgers continued to enjoy their state of euphoria, but eventually they returned either to their setts or to wander through the wooded glades drenched in the warm glow of the evening sun. Beaufort saw his own cub sauntering off alone, towards a seldom-used pathway that led upwards through the gorse, to where the sound of running waters could always be heard.

Beaufort had never felt happier as he followed the path his son had taken. Though he still fondly remembered Cilgwyn, it was not so much the place but the faces of the badgers he had loved that made him cherish such sweet memories. Beaufort believed that there wasn't a lovelier place on earth than Fernhill and had no doubts at all that this was where he would enjoy every moment that he had left of his earthly existence. There wasn't a day when he did not feel that Fernhill was embraced by the protective caress of venerable badgers, the ancient and not so ancient partriarchs of noble grace.

Beaufort trembled with joy as he stood by the pink-tipped willow-herb that surrounded the pool that lay at the bottom of the waterfall. He lifted his eyes to see if he could locate his son on the path leading upward towards the spring, but his concentration was broken by slurping sounds coming from the other side of the willow-herb. Beaufort stealthily parted the stalks with his paw and had great difficulty in restraining himself from bursting with laughter. There was the plumpest of badgers, once the tiniest cub, completely relaxed, gorging himself on a rich juicy crop of bilberries. The face of the portly badger broke into a grin and Beaufort smiled back at Rowley, his thoughts drifting back to another badger of similar proportions. So many of the badgers displayed the characteristics of those who had perished on the journey. Those who had taken the path of Logos had left behind an inheritance of grace and glory, of love and laughter, and Rowley was a part of that endowment, a gift that was the quintessence of the badgers of the Cadre.

Beaufort's young son had passed the shrubbery and gorse bushes on the side of the hill and, upon hearing the bubbling

sounds of water, had continued to climb until he came across a crystal spring. As he sipped the cool and fresh sparkling water, he became aware that he was not alone and, on turning round, discovered that he was being watched by a female cub.

He couldn't understand why he had never noticed her before, as she was the most beautiful badger he had ever seen. He felt embarrassed at his shyness as she smiled at him. The soft gentle voice of this loveliest of badgers told him that she had noticed him at the naming ceremony that they had earlier attended. She said that she was the daughter of Fircone and had been given the name of Dainty. Stuttering and stammering, he replied that he thought she had a lovely name and that he had been called Bamber.

Elysia

When strolling along a country road
Stop awhile should twilight bode
Cross ditch and hedge and pleasant field
Through lofty pines, a glen concealed.
There lies a world, free from strife,
Abounding with the joys of life.
Willow, chestnut, oak and elm,
The most tranquil scene in all the realm.
Partridge, pheasant, rook and kite,
Then owls in darkness of the night.
Squirrel and fox, rabbit and fawn,
Romp and play in the summer's dawn.
Butterflies flit in sunshine beam,
Otters splash in the gentle stream.
Sweetness shrilling from finch and thrush,
Croaks of frogs come from sedge and rush,
Shrew and vole and the prying rat,
Moths escaping a darting bat.
Hare a-leaping, getting madder,
Basking lizard, zig-zagged adder,
Heron, kingfisher over pond
Surrounded by the swaying frond,
Honeysuckle with fragrant smell
Drifting over secluded dell.
There, perchance the sight you'll see
Is badgers playing, living free.